The Puzzle in the Pumpkin Patch

A Cozy Mystery

L.L. Gray

Heroic Rose Publishing

Contents

Your FREE novella is waiting

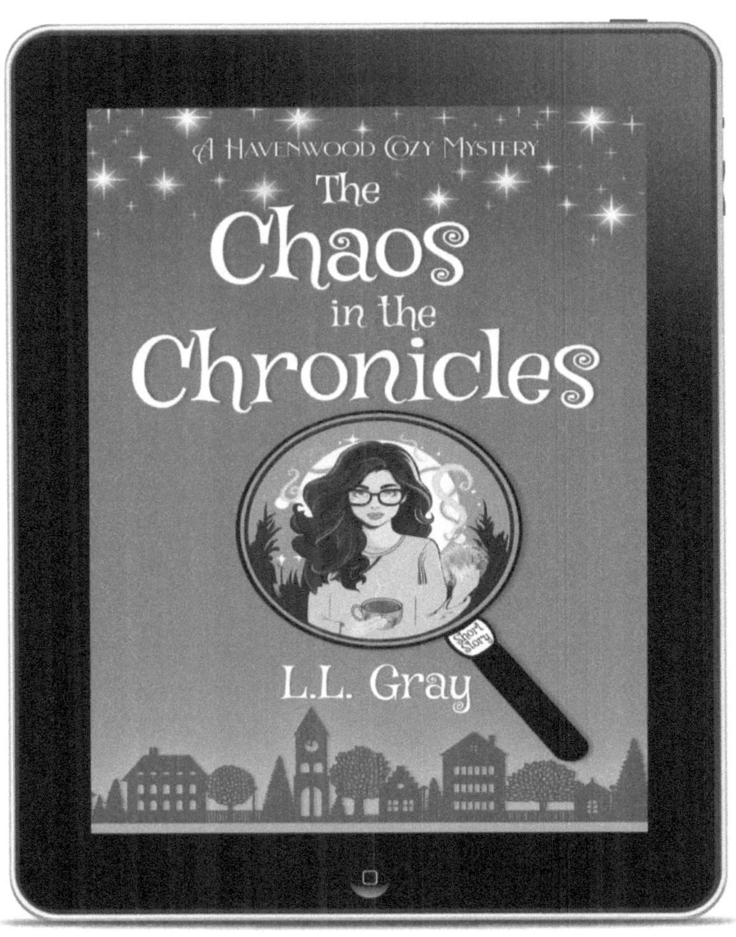

Want a free book?

Of course you do, what madness could possess someone to **not** want free books?
There's no catch - you do sign-up for my mailing list but you can unsubscribe at any time.
There's also no spam.
Ever.
Sign up here to get your free book!
https://www.subscribepage.io/havenwood

The Law of Pancakes

SOMETHING BRUSHED MY CHEEK in the darkness. I bit back a yelp but couldn't quite stop the involuntary jump and skitter to the side. I flapped my hands through the shadows, batting at my unseen assailant. My fingers flailed uncontested through the dark. Was it a ghost? A wraith? A poltergeist? Maybe it was a hex from the coven who ran the antique shop down on Black Cat Lane. What was worse? A hex or a ghost?

These were questions I'd never even contemplated before moving to Havenwood.

I stumbled backwards towards the doorway and the square of light from my apartment, looking down at my hands, expecting to see the worst. Except it wasn't anything like I'd imagined. I closed my eyes and dropped my head.

Great. I was jumping at cobwebs.

My dad would've roared with laughter if he'd seen me. Scared of a wispy fragment of forgotten web. By contrast, nothing scared my dad. Which meant, in his mind, nothing should intimidate me either. Before Master Sergeant Edward Sullivan sent his only daughter out into the world, he made sure I knew how to change a tire, fix a leaky sink, and measure twice before cutting anything. He might use his magic to do such things, but my gifts lay elsewhere, so I had to learn the mundane method.

If he knew I'd screamed at a cobweb, I wouldn't hear the end of it. Not for weeks.

"Radish ruckus, Harper! What's the hold up?" an irritated voice sounded behind me.

I looked over my shoulder to see a pair of beady eyes peering into the attic storeroom. Luna's pink nose twitched rapidly, sending her whiskers flying. Her long ears swiveled like aural periscopes, searching for the problem. Luna was my great-grandmother's familiar. Most witches picked cats, frogs, or ravens to be their constant companions, but not Granny Bea. She'd selected the cutest little white rabbit with the sharpest tongue this side of Elizabeth Bennet. When I'd inherited Granny's bookshop, Luna came with it as far as I was concerned. Not that my good intentions saved me from rampant leporine ire.

"Sorry! I didn't think it be this dusty back here. Or this large," I said, pulling my phone out of my back pocket and flipping on the flashlight to examine the jam-packed storage space.

"What kind of magical bookshop would Spellbooks be if there weren't a hidden room or two?" Luna asked from her perch on top of the narrow staircase leading to the attic.

"This isn't a room. It's more like an entire cave network," I said as the thin beam from my flashlight app illuminated a veritable labyrinth of boxes, statues, chests, and books. If I didn't know better, I'd say the attic was larger than the shop two floors below me. I sneezed as some dust tickled at my nose, and the sound seemed to echo in the cavernous space.

"*This* is what surprises you? Not the talking building, but the size of your attic?" Luna grumbled.

She was right. It had taken a while for me to get used to the fact that Spellbooks could hear me, communicate in a rudimentary manner, and even magically write on the chalkboards I had in both my apartment and the shop underneath it. However, there were definite perks to the shop being housed inside a sentient building. Such as help finding the Halloween decorations just in time to really deck the place out for the town's upcoming celebrations.

I shifted a heavy box to the side, scanning it with my flashlight as I continued my conversation with the rabbit. "I'll admit, the communication thing *was* unexpected. The issue isn't the magic. It's that this room goes on and on."

"So, your shop has great storage. Most people look on that as a good thing. What's your problem?"

I sighed, and ran a hand through my hair, finding the remains of the spiderweb that had attacked me. "Well, physics for one. Doesn't having a room this big mess with the space time continuum or something?"

"You really don't get it do you?" Luna sniffed. "Spellbooks is a *magical* bookshop. It's supposed to ignore the laws of physics, time, space, sound, light, pancakes, the list goes on. Why, the only law Spellbooks consistently adheres to is that of gravity, but I wouldn't be surprised if it was out of courtesy, so it didn't jostle the neighboring buildings."

I glanced over my shoulder. "Wait. You're telling me there are laws of *pancakes*?"

Luna's whiskers twitched. "Fluff and furballs, is that all you heard?" I grinned and swung the light back towards the crowded dusty storage space. "Pretty much. Hey, how about you hop up here and help me find these boxes?"

Luna snorted. "I didn't know Spellbooks made your morning coffee."

"What? It didn't. Wait. Can it?"

"Doubtful, but there must be some incredibly strange magic at work if you think, even for a second, that I'm coming up there."

"Why not?"

"One, I just had my fur brushed. There is no way I'm getting grime all over my coat by hopping through all that dust."

I rolled my eyes, safely out of Luna's sight, and leaned my shoulder into another box to shift it to the side. "What's the second thing?" I grunted.

"Halloween's not my favorite holiday," Luna said with a sniff.

"You must be more of an Easter fan?"

"Why? Because I'm a *rabbit*?"

That's exactly where my mind had gone, but the dangerous edge in her voice was all the warning I needed.

I backpedaled quickly while continuing my search. "No, not at all. I only meant...well, I knew you were partial to chocolate and mysteries. Hunting down all those eggs must be right up your alley." I flicked my light over the labels on the boxes. Costumes. Huh. I'd have to raid them later for the Pumpkin Parade, but my focus now was on decorations. I kept moving.

"Well, you aren't wrong there. Chocolates and mysteries make any day more delectable. But it's Christmas all the way for me," Luna said, her tone slightly mollified.

I couldn't help myself. "You're a snow bunny?" I asked.

"Now, what's that supposed to mean?" Luna's voice sharpened once again.

I chuckled softly to myself. It was probably a good thing Luna refused to come into the storage space or there was a high possibility of reenacting a certain famous scene from Monty Python with an irate rabbit. My light caught the bold label on the next box, and I shouted over my shoulder to her. "Nothing. Look! I've found the Halloween decorations. It looks like there are a couple boxes. Plenty of stuff to deck out the shop."

"Which you should've done ages ago," Luna complained as her head disappeared from sight. I heard a soft thump a moment later as she jumped off the steep stairs to my apartment below.

She wasn't wrong. Even a relative newcomer like me was aware of the scope and scale of the town's attractions for tourists. The annual Harvest Festival was one of the biggest events. It lasted over a week, culminating in a huge pumpkin parade, trick-or-treating, a costume party, and the crowning of the pumpkin king on Halloween night. The residents and shop owners worked hard to make sure it was a magical experience for everyone. However, what the tourists who flocked to Havenwood every year didn't realize was that the "magic" wasn't just good feelings and fun. It was actual *magic*.

Havenwood was a sanctuary for fantastical creatures. Most of the population consisted of what are known as mundane magic users. People who have low-level magic, but didn't want to go off on epic, life-threatening quests. A dwarf with a talent for mechanics ran the auto repair shop. A magically attuned empath was the counselor at the local high school. I even heard that the vet could talk to animals, but I hadn't personally met her.

I fell into the magical mundane category as well, and not just because I lived in a sentient bookshop or was neighbors with the nymph who inhabited the oak tree in my backyard. Just like my granny, I was a witch. However, my power, yes singular, leaned towards metal. No, I wasn't a walking human magnet, nor could I lift entire cars above my head, but if your bike spokes bent or your umbrella broke in a gust of wind, I was your girl. Okay, I've also *occasionally* used my magic to manipulate the tumblers in a lock, but it was all for a good cause, I swear! It was also a skill I never advertised, especially around my dad. He wouldn't care that I was an adult and the proud new owner of Sullivan's Spellbooks. I'd be grounded for the next eighty years. Eighty-two with good behavior. Yes, I know that makes no sense, but if you ever met the Master Sergeant, you'd understand.

Anyway, Luna was right. I'd put out a couple of plastic pumpkins and gourds, but nothing as elaborate as the other businesses on Arcadia Avenue. Even the tattoo parlor next door had a spookier display than my bookshop.

Finnegan Oakheart, the owner of Wildwood Ink, was a druid and very attuned to the natural world. I don't know how he did it, but his shop looked incredible. Vines draped in hues of midnight green and moonlit silver twisted around the doorframe, adorned with tiny, flickering fairy lights that danced like fireflies at dusk. Carved pumpkins illuminated by electric candles sat in the windows, each bearing a different rune or ancient symbol, casting dancing shadows that seemed to whisper secrets of forgotten realms.

Realms that might be fascinating to explore with a certain handsome druid.

My thoughts wandered to Finn himself. We'd only shared occasional coffees or a casual pizza dinner so far—nothing serious. Moving to town had been a whirlwind, and I knew I should focus on Spellbooks, but the idea of getting to know the charismatic druid better was tempting. I wondered...

I had to shake myself to keep my focus on the Halloween ambiance instead of my situationship with the oh so charming Finnegan Oakheart. There were things to do and spiderwebs to avoid. I mean, to drape over bookshelves. Still, it would be nice to have the help of a certain tall, red-headed neighbor—

No. Focus, Harper!

Taking a deep breath, I turned my attention back to the matter at hand. Sure, upgrading the decorations in Spellbooks was overdue, but I had been juggling a whirlwind of challenges and successes lately. After sorting out the tricky inheritance situation, tracking down the culprits behind the book thefts, and confirming the local lore about long-lost pirate treasure, even if finding it seemed like a lost cause, I dove headfirst into launching my new business.

The soft opening had gone well, but the official opening was chaotic, to say the least. Since then, I'd been focused on restocking shelves with both familiar and new titles to meet demand. Online business courses had become my lifeline, helping me navigate everything from inventory management to customer relations. Granny never really incorporated modern tech into the shop. I had a feeling it was because she didn't want technology to interfere with her connection to Spellbooks, but I was determined to update and streamline the shop's systems while still building my working partnership with Spellbooks, even if it meant facing a few integration quirks along the way.

Meeting with Granny's old accountant had been enlightening too. Learning the financial ropes of the business was essential for ensuring sustainable growth. I was starting to see the bookshop not just as a beloved legacy, but as a thriving business that could withstand challenges and evolve with the times. I tried to balance these practicalities with Spellbooks' unique magical aspects and its strong opinions about restocking. Even though it sometimes felt like I was blindfolded and balancing on a tightrope stretched between the magical and mundane, I knew by laying this solid groundwork I would ensure that the shop continued to flourish. It was more than just a point of pride. I wanted it to be not only my present but also my long-term future. Applying my questionable decorating skills to my new business had been pushed to the very back of my mind. To be honest, I'd nearly forgotten about it completely until Vivienne Silverthorne stopped by yesterday evening.

Perhaps the middle-aged matron with a terrifyingly severe stare shouldn't intimidate me, but everyone in Havenwood knew better than to mess with the Silverthornes, Vivienne most of all. The family founded Havenwood generations ago. They were a powerful mage family who had wanted to settle down far away from the sword swingers and fire breathers of the world. It was the Silverthornes who originally developed the protective spells surrounding Havenwood and refreshed them regularly, even to this day.

When the tourists encountered something fantastical, the Silverthornes' charms magnified their disbelief in magic. The magic eased their surprise just enough that they assumed all the locals were *really* into cosplay or, for example, the moving gargoyle above my shop's door was clever robotics rather that a magical creature who came to life when the sun went down. After all, gargoyles didn't really exist, right? Everyone knew that. The talking, moving gargoyle had to be animatronic with the latest microchip update, didn't he? Gideon, my gargoyle, knew how to play his part so the tourists didn't get too suspicious. Just like the rest of us did in Havenwood to uphold the grand secret.

Never, *ever* let them know that magic was real.

However, when Vivienne recently marched past my shop after threatening to shut me down for an accidental, but entirely over-the-top use of magic during my grand re-opening, looked down her aristocratic, aquiline nose at my lack of appropriate Harvest Festival decor, sniffed, and shot me a pointed glare through the front window, I knew I had to act. Vivienne Silverthorne was one of those rare people who didn't need something as commonplace as words to communicate her complete and utter disdain.

Which led me back to the mysteriously large attic. Carefully, I navigated the steep stairs with the final box of decorations. I dusted off my hands and surveyed the damage. Dust and cobwebs covered the boxes, my jeans, and the floor of my apartment. I sighed. Clean up would have to wait. Today's Harvest Festival event, the pumpkin carving competition, started at four. If I wanted to meet my best friend, Bella, in time to participate, I needed to hurry.

"Come on, Luna. Let's get to work," I said, hefting a box and heading towards the stairs leading to the shop below.

"My decorating days are long past. Besides, no thumbs, remember?" Luna said, wiggling her paws at me. "Happy to supervise though."

"Great," I grunted, carefully navigating the stairs without dropping the large box. It took all my knowledge of geometry and pivots to get the large box down into the shop. I set it down next to the counter with a sigh. "One down. Four to go." A sudden idea occurred to me. "Hey Spellbooks, any way you could give me a helping hand?" I asked hopefully.

The building gave a strange rumble and shake, which gave the impression of an old man scrubbing a finger into his ear so he could hear a young whippersnapper better. Then, the staircase behind me morphed into a ramp and, one by one, the boxes from my apartment gently slid into the shop. Another rumble later, and the stairs that connected the shop and apartment appeared once more.

Magic was so cool.

I laid a hand on the wall. "Thanks, Spellbooks, that was awesome," I murmured. I felt a faint vibration and warmth under my fingertips, which I took to mean Spellbooks was pleased with the praise.

"Well, that's one way to do it, I suppose," Luna sniffed from the top of the newly restored stairs. "Although if anyone walking by had seen it I don't know how you'd explain away the mighty morphin' staircase."

"Good planning and an excellent sense of whimsical fun," I said lightly. Luna rolled her eyes. Loudly.

"And was that a Power Rangers reference I just heard from the incredibly sophisticated Luna?"

"I have no idea what you're talking about," Luna said. It might have been my imagination, but it seemed like her whiskers twitched faster than usual. Do rabbits smile with whisker speed?

I decided not to press the point, gesturing instead toward the early morning sun fighting valiantly to break through the gloomy gray clouds outside. "That's why we started at the break of dawn today. No one comes shopping for books before they've had their morning coffee."

"Except the wisest ones who know coffee and books make the best pairing," Luna said with a sniff, hopping downstairs and settling on the front counter.

"No arguments there, but I'm grateful for the quiet morning. I want the shop fully decked out before I meet Bella this afternoon."

"If that's your plan, you'd better hurry like a hare," Luna said, waving her paws like a furry conductor, gesturing at the still packed boxes.

I grinned briefly at her, then turned my attention to the large, dusty boxes that awaited me. I knew Luna wouldn't be much help; she'd likely blame her lack of thumbs, though in truth, organizing was more her forte than physical labor. I rolled up my sleeves. Spellbooks' supernatural assistance only extended so far. It was time for me to get to work so I could go to the ball. I mean, the pumpkin patch. Cinderella probably wouldn't be caught dead in a pumpkin patch with her glass slippers, although there was that thing with her carriage, so...

Luna sprang up on the nearest box, landing with a thump and startling me back to the present. "What are you doing? Daydreaming isn't decorating, and I wouldn't leave Spellbooks to its own devices if I were in your shoes. Not after that incident at your grand re-opening that nearly got you kicked out of not only Spellbooks but Havenwood completely."

"Thanks for that happy reminder," I said dryly.

"You only learn from your mistakes if you remember them," Luna said with a sniff. "Now, hop to it!"

I opened one box and got to work because when a talking rabbit tells you to hop, you *hop*.

Unexpected Showers

THE DOOR OF THE shop swung open as I was arranging the final touches on the front counter. I looked up to see my best friend, Bella, sweep into the shop. I grinned as she set a large white box between the bowl of polished red apples and the cauldron with artistically placed plastic spiders.

"Trick or treat, heavy on the treat! Mama sends her love and a loaf of her pumpkin spice bread," Bella announced with a warm smile. Bella's parents owned one of the local bed and breakfasts, and her mom was one of the fairy folk. A brownie, to be precise. Honey had a gift for baking and was always generous with her creations, for which I was eternally grateful.

Bella put her hands on her hips and looked around the shop in admiration. "This place looks great! It's nice to see you finally and fully embrace the Halloween spirit."

I shrugged, kneading the tension from my right shoulder as I looked at the shop as if through her eyes. Cotton spiderwebs draped the shelves. I'd hidden ornate goblets, fake dismembered hands, glowing eyeballs, and other trinkets throughout the store. The décor was designed to surprise the patrons into the spooky season without being too scary for the kiddos. I'd even managed to convince the shop cat, an orange tabby Maine Coon named Mr. Wigglesworth, to share the front window with a few painted pumpkins which grinned out at the passersby on Arcadia Avenue. The plastic knickknacks I'd originally used to decorate were now regulated to sprucing up the sale shelf.

I took a long drink from my water glass and nodded as I refilled it from the pitcher on the counter. "It looks okay, doesn't it? Although, it's all thanks to Granny. I didn't even get through all the boxes of her decorations." I waved at the two half full boxes next to the counter. "Can you believe she had all this stuff in her attic? Speaking of, that place is huge! I bet I could find even more Halloween stuff up there if I had the time to sort through the equivalent of a museum storehouse."

"She must've packed up some real treasures," Bella said, peeking inside the nearest box.

"Definitely. I think I even saw a couple of boxes of costumes. We should go through them before the pumpkin parade."

Bella's eyes lit up. "Ooh, that sounds awesome! Your granny always had the best outfits at town events."

I ran a hand over the polished wooden counter fondly. "She loved Havenwood and Spellbooks. I just hope I can live up to her legacy." I scooped up the bowl of apples, positioning it on a small table near the door next to a beautifully illustrated copy of *Snow White*.

Bella waggled a finger at me. "I know what she'd tell you. She'd say to make your own legacy. But perhaps without the spiderwebs in your hair," she joked, reaching across and pulling a long, drifting strand of cotton from my wavy locks.

I batted at my hair, finding another few pieces that shouldn't be there. For a split second, a shiver ran down my spine at the thought of real spiderwebs forever entangled in my wavy hair, but upon closer inspection, they were just harmless bits of cotton. Still, the thought lingered, and I felt compelled to ensure my locks were free of any unwelcome surprises. Glancing down at myself, I noted the dust and debris from decorating had taken its toll. Before heading out, I definitely needed to change.

"I'm a mess. Let me run upstairs and change out of these clothes. I'll be back in a sec! Make yourself at home and keep an eye on any customers who wander in?" I said, waving at the shop.

Bella raised a hand in acknowledgement, already browsing through the shelves to see what sort of tricks or treats I'd hidden for unsuspecting browsers. I scooped up the loaf of pumpkin bread, delicious spices wafting up from the box, and hurried upstairs. It took longer than I'd expected to make myself presentable. However, when I peered into the mirror in my bedroom, I was pleased with the results. I wore a clean pair of jeans, a cozy purple sweater that complimented my complexion, and my favorite soft brown boots. I'd looped a cream scarf over one arm and grabbed my jacket in case it got cold during the jack-o'-lantern carving.

As I headed back downstairs, feeling considerably more presentable, I noticed Bella sheepishly mopping up a small spill on the counter.

"Whoops," Bella chuckled nervously, "I was trying to be helpful and unpack the box of figurines, but I didn't see the glass of water there and knocked it over. At least it wasn't the pitcher."

"Are you okay?" I asked, concern in my voice as I surveyed the scene and the shards of broken glass sparkling on the counter and floor.

"I'm fine. Just a little embarrassed. Sorry for causing such a mess," Bella said, wrapping the largest pieces in a wad of paper towels.

"Don't worry about it. I'm just glad you're not hurt. Let me get the vacuum, and we'll clean this up in no time," I said quickly switched into bustling efficiency mode, hurrying to the store closet, and sweeping the entire area twice to ensure no one would get cut by an errant shard as Bella mopped up the remaining water. With disaster averted, I finally had a moment to examine the intricately painted statues she'd lined up on the counter.

"These look awesome. And a little creepy," I said, examining the detailed stone creations. One was a grinning skull with red cracks that seemed to glow from the inside. Another was a black unicorn with a frozen lightning bolt sparkling on his horn. Next to the unicorn was a bat with disturbingly human-like features which reminded me of a vampire ready to shift. The final one was a wicked-looking wizard in the middle of casting a spell.

"Aren't they perfect? I found them in the boxes and thought you could use them around the shop. There's even more in here." Bella reached into the cardboard box that now had a slight water stain, holding up another small figurine for me to see. "Ooh, look at him! He's so cute, isn't he?"

I looked over to see the most adorable little purple dragon statue curled up in her palm. His wings were tucked back against his scaled back. Under two curved little horns, his eyes were closed as if he were peacefully sleeping, and he had his nose tucked under his tail like the cutest scaly puppy you ever saw.

"He's adorable!" I exclaimed.

"He definitely needs to be on display," Bella said, looking around for the perfect place to put the dragon statuette. "How about right here? Next to the register?" She settled him prominently on the counter and clapped her hands excitedly. "Just look at him! He loves his new home!"

"He does look very cute there. Maybe I can even get some gold wrapped candies to place around him. You know, as his horde? I bet the kids would love it," I said, my excitement growing. My best friend's enthusiasm was contagious.

She grabbed my arm eagerly. "You know what we should do? Hide the other statues around the shop and make a treasure hunt for the customers. Wouldn't that be fun? Create riddles and pass out little sheets so people could see if they find the statues all around the shop. If they do, they get a prize? Those that don't could always try to steal from the dragon. Once you buy the candy for him of course," she said, running a finger along the ridged spines on the statuette's back.

"Good idea! How about we hide the rest of them now, and I work on the treasure hunt tomorrow?" We hurriedly gathered up the four statues and tucked them onto shelves at random but left the cute dragon by the register. Bella was right. He really was adorable and would brighten up my day, if nothing else.

I dusted off my hands after I got the statues sorted and glanced at the clock behind the counter. "We should get going, shouldn't we? Martha told me the best pumpkins go fast, and I don't want a substandard pumpkin for my first Halloween in Havenwood."

"We can't have that, can we?" Bella said, linking her arm through mine and dragging me towards the door.

"Luna?" I called over my shoulder. Two long white ears poked out from behind a shelf, followed by Luna's quivering little whiskers. "We're heading out. Gideon will wake up when the sun sets, but until then you're in charge. There's food for Mr. Wigglesworth and some extra veggies for you. No fighting while I'm gone, you hear me?"

Luna tipped her head and thumped a back foot in a rapid staccato. "What if that mangy cat gets uppity?"

I rolled my eyes at Bella, but discretely enough that Luna couldn't see. "The only thing Mr. Wigglesworth is getting is fat if he doesn't start cutting back on the treats. Leave him alone. He'll probably sleep the entire time we're gone."

"I'd better find my headband just in case. That fetid feline stands no chance against the silent attack of a ninja rabbit."

"No! No attacks. No ninjas!" I pressed my palms together in supplication. "We don't need a repeat of the great pizza disaster. How about you go into the sunroom and watch that TV show from the 80s you're enjoying? The one with Miss Marple?"

Luna huffed out a breath. "It's always better to be prepared. I'll get my headband and *then* watch Miss Marple." She hopped away before I could protest further.

I sighed and let my chin drop to my chest in defeat. Bella chuckled at my melodramatic reaction and headed outside, wrapping her scarf a little more securely around her throat as a chilly autumn breeze gusted down Arcadia Avenue.

While her back was turned, I pressed a hand to the wooden doorframe. "Keep an eye on them, will you, Spellbooks? Just until Gideon wakes up?" I whispered. The little stone gargoyle above the door was not only a striking part of the shop, but he was my nighttime security guard. Between him and the magic of the sentient bookshop, I was confident the store would still be standing when I returned. Well, fairly confident. The wood warmed under my palm, and I felt tiny vibrations eerily similar to chuckles ripple across my hand as if Spellbooks could read my mind. I didn't think it could, but as Luna pointed out, I was still getting to know my bookshop.

"Come on, they'll be fine," Bella said, tugging on my arm, oblivious to my communication with my shop. In Havenwood, magic was a well-guarded secret, but the fact that Spellbooks was sentient was an even bigger one. As far as I knew, only a handful of people in the entire world knew about the unique properties of my bookstore, and I was pretty sure I was supposed to keep it that way. I hadn't told a single soul about Spellbooks since I moved to Havenwood. Not even Bella.

"Okay, okay, but I want it on the record that tonight is all about treats, no tricks. Got it?" I said, pretending to look stern. I grabbed the sign I'd made earlier to say Spellbooks was closed early for the town pumpkin event and taped it prominently in the window.

"No promises!" Luna shouted from somewhere in the depths of the shop.

"You heard her!" Bella said with a laugh as she dragged me out the door. I barely locked it before Bella's enthusiasm for the Harvest Festival swept us both away.

Sensei of the Pumpkin

BELLA DROVE US OUT to the Moonshadow Pumpkin Farm, taking the back roads to avoid the swarms of families and tourists that flocked to Havenwood during the Harvest Festival. She finally eased the car into a parking spot in the crowded lot, and we headed toward the long rows of orange pumpkins set up behind the pretty white farmhouse with a large, wraparound porch. Cheerful music poured from a set of speakers on the porch, and a small stand with refreshments did a brisk business in hot apple cider as the evening chill set in.

The music faded as a woman with long braids wearing a plaid jacket and jeans stepped up to a microphone. "Welcome to the annual Havenwood pumpkin carving here at Moonshadow Farm!" Excited cheers met her words. The crowd drifted closer, listening attentively.

"I'm Lara Moonshadow, and this is my husband, Clark." She indicated a tall man wearing a matching plaid jacket who smiled warmly and waved to the crowd. Polite applause greeted the introductions.

Bella leaned over and whispered in my ear. "She's a witch like you, but her gifts tend towards herbology. She's the real secret behind the success of this place, but Clark has a completely mundane gift for making corn mazes. At least, I think it's mundane. It would be a strong contender for the 'most-random-magic' if it's actually his power."

I nodded silently in acknowledgement as Lara continued. "We've been running this farm for over fifteen years and will be around if you need anything at all, but first, a few housekeeping things. If you need the restrooms, they're in that building, between the goats and the corn maze. Most of you have already found the refreshment stand here, but if you haven't, I highly recommend the hot apple cider direct from Bert's Apple Orchard. Make sure you say hi to Bert behind the counter there and go down to see him at the orchard for some more fall fun." She pointed to a man with large ears and a wide smile who waved cheerfully in between pouring cups of steaming cider.

Lara continued. "Now, to the main event. The pumpkins are all set up right behind me as you can see. Feel free to select the one that calls to you and get to carving. The farm helpers are all wearing pumpkin badges and can help you with getting carving tools, payment, pencils, or anything else you may need. All entries for the jack-o'-lantern contest need to be on the table here by the porch by six o'clock sharp. Late entries are disqualified. I'm looking at you, Mason." She pointed two fingers towards her eyes and swiveled them towards a short man I recognized as the owner of the auto repair shop in town.

"Now, if I remember right, I had it here by six," Mason shouted from the crowd, a thick Scottish burr coloring his words.

Lara put her hands on her hips in obviously well-rehearsed faux irritation. "Six pm. Not six, November. Wrong month, entirely!"

"I still think that disqualification was bogus! You should've been more specific!" Mason shouted back over the good-natured chuckles from the crowd.

Lara grinned and flung a hand forward. "Mason Forham, everyone! Calendars may not be his forte, but a finer mechanic has never graced this green earth."

"And because I like Lara so much, despite her silly rules, ten percent off to anyone who can show me a carved pumpkin until Halloween!" Mason called out. Cheers and laughter rose in response to his offer.

Lara spread her arms wide. "Well then, I'd best stop talking! May the spirit of Halloween inspire you!" She stepped away from the microphone and her husband enveloped her in a warm embrace, both of them wearing proud smiles as they gazed out at the crowd. The farm hummed with excitement, the decorations and atmosphere a testament to their joy at hosting this beloved town event. People mingled, laughter and chatter filling the air as everyone wandered toward the glowing pumpkins.

"Let's get to it," Bella said, rubbing her hands together eagerly. "What are you going to carve?"

I followed her out to the rows of pumpkins set up in front of the corn field. "I don't know. I've never done it before."

Bella stopped in her tracks and grabbed my arm. "Wait. Really? I thought you were joking! How have you gotten this far in life and never carved a pumpkin?"

I shrugged. "There weren't a lot of pumpkins on the bases my dad was assigned. Besides, he was always more into the family or historic holidays. The man throws a mean Labor Day brunch. His stuffed burgers are legendary."

Bella rolled her eyes. "I'm sure, but still. *Halloween*? Seriously? You've never made a jack-o'-lantern? You poor, deprived child," she furrowed her brow and shook her head sadly at me.

"There's still time to fix the problem," I said with a grin at her antics.

"Absolutely!" Bella grabbed my arm, heading towards the back row where the biggest pumpkins sat on the ground. She started rattling off all the important aspects to look for in a good carving pumpkin, but the handsome man walking in our direction drew my attention away from the pumpkins. My heart gave a little flutter as our eyes met and a smile turned up the corners of his new goatee. I thought it suited him and somehow made the charming, handsome druid even more attractive. Finn owned the tattoo shop next to Spellbooks, which had partially prompted my decorating frenzy this morning. When we first met, I'd erroneously suspected him of a crime he didn't commit. After the real culprits were exposed, I'd wrestled with guilt for a while. Now, instead of guilt, I found myself intrigued by the possibility of a future with Finn. What would that look like? Was I even certain I wanted to start something serious with the guy next door? Couldn't that lead to complications if things ended badly? But what if they didn't? What if I was rationalizing myself out of the start of something amazing?

"Harper? Are you even paying attention?" Bella asked.

"Hmm what? Oh, sorry. I got distracted."

Bella looked up from the row of pumpkins and grinned as she clocked Finn heading our way. "I'd get distracted too if I were in your shoes. How's it going with the attractive druid next door?"

A small smile I couldn't control danced over my lips, and I blushed. "Finn's a nice guy. I'm just...er...taking things slowly at the minute. I'm new to town and besides, I have Spellbooks. I've signed up for those business courses, you know. Learning the ropes of running the shop is taking up a lot of my time."

Bella arched an eyebrow. "Well, just remember that there are ways to have fun other than burying your nose in a book."

"You're right. There're always audiobooks," I said with a wink.

"You're incorrigible," Bella muttered. "Books won't keep you warm at night, that's all I'm saying."

"Good evening, ladies," Finn called before I could answer, finally working his way through the crowd toward us. "Have you picked your victims for tonight?"

Bella struck a mock indignant pose. "Can you believe Harper has never carved a pumpkin before?"

Finn placed his hand to his heart. "A travesty! But don't say that too loudly in this town. The Silverthornes might throw you out on principle. Here, let me help you find the perfect pumpkin for your first time," he said, crouching down to examine the orange orbs in the dirt.

"Can they really do that?" I asked Bella under my breath.

"For not having carved a pumpkin?"

"No, I mean, throw someone out. For...whatever reason," I murmured, my palms going sweaty at the thought of losing Spellbooks.

Bella shook her head. "Vivienne might think she can, but no. The town wouldn't stand for it. Although the Silverthornes own much of the town, so they could make life here pretty difficult if they put their minds to it. Which means you should carve one as quickly as possible. Just to be safe. Perhaps with the help of a certain handsome druid?" She nudged me with her elbow.

"Here we go," Finn said, hefting a pair of medium-sized pumpkins by the stem and cutting me off before I could formulate an appropriately snarky response. I shot Bella a *look* before turning on my smile to full wattage.

"They look great, thanks Finn," I said.

"Where are you two setting up your carving station?" Finn asked.

Bella pointed to a plastic table on the fringe of the general chaos of happy tourists and excited kids. "How about over there?" she asked.

"Perfect," Finn said, heading that way, pumpkins in hand.

"Mind if I join you?" an unfamiliar voice asked from behind me. I turned to see a young man about our age with dark skin and a bright smile walking towards us. He carried a pumpkin casually tucked under one arm.

"Alex!" Bella exclaimed, rushing by me and flinging her arms around the newcomer. He grinned and squeezed her to his side with his free arm.

"Good to see you, Bells. How's it going?" Alex asked.

Bella fought free of the embrace and squinted up at him. "Why didn't you tell me you were coming back?"

Alex shrugged. "I wanted to surprise you. Besides, I knew you'd never miss a pumpkin carving." He winked at her and then stuck his free hand out towards me. "I'm Alex Johnson, an old friend of Bella's."

"Harper Sullivan. A new friend of Bella's. Kind of," I said, shaking the offered hand. Alex raised an eyebrow, and I gave a little shrug. "It's a long story."

"Well, we'll have plenty of time while we carve," Alex said. I noticed Bella hadn't left his side yet.

"Alex! My man! When did you get back to town?" Finn exclaimed as he rejoined us after depositing the pumpkins. He grasped Alex's hand and jostled his shoulder in a friendly manner.

"Yesterday. The Italians are great, but they can't hold a jack-o'-lantern to Havenwood at Halloween," Alex joked, his face lighting with good humor.

"I hear that. Look, we're just over there," Finn said, pointing. "Care to join us or do you have someone you're here with?"

"No, I'm here on my own," Alex said. I didn't miss the small, pleased smile that flitted across Bella's face.

"Great! Let me get my soon-to-be masterpiece, and I'll meet you over there," Finn said. Alex nodded. He and Bella headed off towards the table Finn had commandeered. I hung behind, waiting for Finn to select his vegetable victim for the night.

"What's his story?" I asked, tipping my head towards where Alex and Bella were laughing. She touched his arm familiarly and tossed her hair back in a way that had me thinking they were more than just old friends getting reacquainted.

Finn glanced up and grinned. "Who? Alex? He's a good guy. He and Bella were an item in high school, from what I heard, but that was before my time here. Rumor has it she went off to college and he went to culinary school. They called it quits because of the long-distance thing. When they both moved back to town, it seemed like the fates had aligned to bring the two of them back together. That's when I met him. But then, he was offered this amazing opportunity to study under master chefs in Europe. It was too good to pass up. So, he went. Bella wouldn't say it, because she's a good egg and a better friend, but I think she was pretty broken up over him leaving."

"And now he's back. Is he just visiting or back for good? Where does that leave the two of them?" I asked, studying the pair.

"Only time will tell, I guess," Finn said as we strolled towards the table. "Any idea what you are going to carve?"

I chuckled ruefully. "Anything that doesn't bring dishonor upon me, the table, or Spellbooks."

"You can never go wrong with tradition. A grinning, toothy face isn't too hard to carve," Finn said, plopping his pumpkin next to mine.

"Sold. Teach me your ways, oh sensei of the pumpkin," I joked.

"Awesome title. Did you level up since I was last here?" Alex asked Finn.

"Only time, and Lara Moonshadow, have the answer to that," Finn returned with a grin.

"Well, a friendly wager then. Whoever's pumpkin ranks higher in the jack-o'-lantern contest buys pizza on Friday for the four of us," Alex said, offering Finn his hand across the table.

Finn laughed and gripped his hand. "I'll happily buy if I lose, but if I win, you're making those pies. No way I'm passing up a chance at a personalized pizza by a real *I-tal-ian* chef," he said, drawing out the word in a horrendous Southern accent.

Alex chuckled and pumped their hands up and down. "I'm not Italian, but I'd be happy to make the pizzas. *If* I lose that is. Which won't happen."

I leaned over towards Bella, cupping a hand around the wrong side of my mouth and loudly stage-whispered, "Did we just get free pizza for doing nothing?"

Bella waggled her carving knife at me. "They get the pleasure of our company. Twice. More than pays for a pizza in my mind. Am I right, guys?"

Finn started busily organizing the knives for cutting, while Alex grabbed a pencil and started drawing on his pumpkin. "How about that carving, eh?" he said a little too loudly. Bella and I shared a chuckle at their antics.

Finn showed me how to core and empty the pumpkin before outlining my pattern so the carved space would show the light from a candle placed inside to the best advantage. He wrapped my hand around the carving knife, pressing it firmly against the hard outer shell of the pumpkin.

"Now, don't be shy. You're really going to have to go for it," he said, stepping back to allow me space to make the first cut.

I drew in a deep breath, aligned the knife against the line I'd drawn to represent the face's eye and...the pumpkin moved. I froze, blinking in surprise. Maybe Alex or Bella had knocked the table, causing my pumpkin to roll? I glanced up at them, but the pair were engaged with their own carving. I looked back at my pumpkin and tried to reach out to grasp it by the stem.

It rolled away from me of its own accord.

I yelped and jumped back. It wasn't my imagination. The thing *had* moved! Seemingly of its own volition!

As if sensing my fear, the pumpkin swiveled to face me, the eyebrows I'd sketched on waggling mischievously as its drawn-on mouth moved in a silent, taunting giggle. Then it jumped off the table and rolled away across the field.

I clapped a hand to my mouth to keep from shouting out in surprise, and my heart thundered in my chest. This wasn't normal. Pumpkins didn't move, and they surely didn't make faces at you. Did they? Was this a Havenwood thing, or was this some kind of Halloween trick they were playing on the new girl?

Jumping Jack-o'-lanterns!

I grabbed Finn's arm. "Did you see that?" I rasped, pointing with my carving knife after the runaway pumpkin.

"See what?" Finn asked, looking up from his own pumpkin.

"My pumpkin! When I tried to carve it, the thing shimmied out of the way!"

Bella looked up at me and then at the pumpkin. She gasped in surprise as she saw it continue to roll away. "Is this some kind of a prank?"

I held up my hands, protesting my innocence. "No trick! It moved, then it laughed at me and rolled away! Look!" I pointed again, but this time I noticed several other pumpkins had joined mine near the farmhouse. Babble from the crowd crescendoed as carvers from nearby tables noticed the runaway pumpkins. I overheard some snippets of conversation.

"...jumped off my table!"

"I swear, the thing moved of its own accord!"

"It just rolled away!"

"I thought I heard it giggle. But that's ridiculous! Who ever heard of a giggling pumpkin?"

A moment later, Lara Moonshadow stepped back up to the microphone. "It appears we have our very own Halloween prankster in the house tonight. Or should I say, in the field?" Nervous chuckles met her words. She smiled reassuringly out at the crowd. "My husband found several spools of fishing line attached to certain pumpkins. It was a clever trick, making it look like the pumpkins were moving on their own, but I can assure you, that's the end of tonight's tricks. On to the treats! My staff will be around with some free samples of salted caramel pumpkin bars made by our own Honey DeLuca who owns the Enchanted Oasis Bed and Breakfast. One taste and I'm sure you'll agree with me, these bars really are magical!" She snagged one from a passing helper and bit into it, moaning dramatically in pleasure. "Make sure you grab one before supplies run out!" she managed past a mouthful.

"You've got to admit it, that was a decent prank," Finn said, nudging me playfully. "They got you good."

I frowned. "Fishing line? I'm not buying it. How did we not notice it before? Surely someone would have spotted it or tripped as people carried the pumpkins to the tables."

Bella leaned in and lowered her voice. "Maybe that was just something to tell the tourists." She wiggled her fingers mysteriously to emphasize her point.

Alex chimed in. "If I had any magic worth mentioning, I'm not sure I'd be above a little Halloween trickery. 'Tis the season and all that." He bounced his eyebrows up and down with a mischievous grin.

"I thought the whole point of Havenwood was to *hide* the magical elements from the tourists," I muttered nervously, thinking back to what happened at my shop during the grand re-opening.

Bella wavered a hand back and forth. "Not necessarily hide. More like obscure. After all, the Silverthornes founded this town as a sanctuary for magical beings to exist without fear. That's why the charms exist. So that the humans who visit us are more susceptible to accepting magical encounters. Exhibit A," she said, gesturing at the crowd who was happily returning to their carving. I overheard a pair retrieving their runaway pumpkin as I walked over to grab my own.

"That was a good one," the middle-aged woman said.

"I didn't even see the fishing line! How'd they do that?" her partner responded.

"I keep telling you to get your eyes checked," she chided.

"You've made your point. I'll book an appointment for tomorrow when we go home," he said in good-natured surrender as they moved out of earshot.

The Silverthornes' charms must be working in overdrive if they could convince these tourists that Lara's shaky story was the truth. I looked around at the chatting, milling crowd, trying to guess who might be responsible for the prank. Everyone was laughing off the incident. No one seemed the least bit suspicious. Maybe I shouldn't be either. After all, even magical folk weren't above temptation. Perhaps a young witch or wizard was feeling rambunctious and decided to lean into the season? However, I didn't see any likely suspects as I headed towards the porch where my pumpkin had rolled to a halt.

As I stooped to collect the runaway jack-o'-lantern-to-be, voices drifted through the open kitchen window of the farmhouse. I paused, knowing eavesdropping wasn't polite, but something about the conversation caught my attention.

"...going on here, Lara?" The voice was female and muffled. It sounded familiar, but I couldn't quite place it.

Lara sounded nervous. "We're still not sure. Obviously, it was a spell of some sort, but no one saw anything. Clark is telling the helpers to be extra vigilant though, in case someone tries any other pranks tonight."

"There will be no further shenanigans, of that I promise you. I'm addressing the matter personally," the other lady responded.

"There's really no need for that, Vivienne. We're taking care of it." Lara sounded nervous through the open window.

"Yes." The single word was sharp enough to slice through silk without snagging.

Vivienne? I thought to myself. *The only Vivienne I know is Vivienne Silverthorne.*

If she was the one talking to Lara, no wonder the owner of the pumpkin farm sounded nervous. I empathized with her. After my run-in with Vivienne Silverthorne last month, I'd do just about anything to not be on her bad side again.

My thoughts had distracted me, and I missed whatever was said next until Vivienne sniffed and spoke louder. "The Harvest Festival is a very important time for Havenwood. It brings in a significant number of tourists and we cannot afford for magic to be running amok. I'll be monitoring the situation closely. If you discover who is responsible, bring them to me directly. I'll ensure there are no more of these so-called pranks disturbing the peace. By whatever means necessary." The coldness in her tone made me shiver.

"Of course," Lara murmured. The sound of voices faded as the women moved away from the window.

I scooped up my pumpkin, heading back towards my table as the two women stepped out onto the porch. It wouldn't do to be caught listening at the window. Especially not by Vivienne Silverthorne. She was a formidable force. One not to be trifled with. And then there was what happened during Spellbooks' grand re-opening. Let's just say I never wanted to be on her bad side. Never again. Whoever this prankster was, I wished them either a great deal of luck if Vivienne Silverthorne ever caught up with them or the good sense to stop while they were ahead.

I returned to the table, my thoughts consumed with magic, spells gone awry, and retribution from the most powerful mage in town. Finn, Bella, and Alex kept up the amiable chatter, leaving me to my carving and my thoughts.

We all finished just in time to enter the jack-o'-lantern contest. Finn and Alex bantered good-naturedly about who would win as they went to put their pumpkins on the table. I'd opted to keep mine, already dreaming up how I could arrange a witch's hat or a broomstick around the pumpkin as an extra bit of Halloween flair on Luna's side of the shop's front window. Bella also kept hers to display at her parents' bed-and-breakfast.

Bella leaned over as the guys took their pumpkins to the front. "Are you okay? You're awfully quiet."

"Just thinking. Do people pull pranks like this a lot around town?" I looked around and dropped my voice. "Magical ones, I mean."

Bella shrugged. "It happens, but usually only around other paranormals. You'll get little flashes in front of the tourists every once in a while. A young shifter needing to be extracted from a tense situation before they turn or a witch new to her powers shooting sparks out of her fingertips, that kind of thing. But rarely on purpose and never at a big town event like this."

"Yeah, Vivienne Silverthorne didn't seem pleased," I murmured.

Bella grabbed my arm, digging in her nails as she stared at me urgently. "What did she say to you? Is she still mad about that thing at Spellbooks from last month? I thought that blew over."

I frowned and shook my head. "No, I mean, yes, I think it did. I overheard her talking to Lara, that's all."

Bella blew out a sigh of relief. "Well, that's good."

I nudged her with my elbow. "Did I just hear you condone eavesdropping?"

Bella smiled anemically at me. "Vivienne Silverthorne isn't someone you want to mess around with. There's a reason more magical, violent beings don't bother us here in Havenwood. Reason, singular."

"Vivienne Silverthorne?" I guessed.

Bella pointed at me. "Got it in one. She'll do whatever it takes to protect this town, and I do mean *whatever* it takes. I hope that whoever was responsible for the pumpkin thing has the good sense to keep their head down and let this whole mess blow over."

Finn and Alex meandered towards us, holding steaming cups of hot apple cider in both hands. Finn handed me a paper cup covered in a brilliant red apple design. I murmured my thanks and sipped my cider cautiously as Lara's voice rang out over the microphone. "Our judges have told me they've never seen a more intriguing, well-carved set of jack-o'-lanterns in their lives, and, based on what I see before me, I have to agree with them. However, there can only be one winner. Before I announce the grand prize, I want to give some honorable mentions." She rattled through a list of names, some of whom I recognized, but most I didn't. Neither Finn's nor Alex's names were called.

"What happens if neither of them wins?" I whispered to Bella.

She opened her mouth to respond, but Alex cut her off. "We've already talked about that and thought it would be a shame to deprive you ladies of a pizza night so if neither of us wins, Finn has generously offered to buy the supplies," he said, dipping his head at the druid next to me.

"And Alex here is going to whip up an Italian feast to wow the senses," Finn jumped in. "We were thinking maybe the day after tomorrow? After the Zombie Shuffle?"

"The Zombie Shuffle? What's that?" I asked.

"It's the race they put on every year," Bella explained. "Participants can run, walk, skate, whatever they like. There are also different distances.

Families usually opt for the 1k, but those who are more athletically inclined can do the 5 or even the 10k."

I snapped my fingers. "I remember now. I didn't realize they'd settled on a theme."

Bella nodded. "Last year, they called it the Witchy Walk, but I like this one better. It should be hilarious to see all those runners dressed as zombies."

"I can't wait!" I exclaimed. An icy breeze kicked up, sending my wavy hair into a tangle. I shivered as I tried to finger comb it out of my face.

Finn wound his arm around my shoulders, tucking me into his side and rubbing my arm for warmth. "For the zombies or the pizza?"

"Why can't it be both?" I asked. "Although, I should probably keep Spellbooks open a little later if there is a town event on."

"Fair enough," he chuckled, giving me a little squeeze. "Come on over after the race is finished. Everyone heads over to the town square after the race for photos and hot apple cider anyway, so I doubt there'll be any zombies around buying books."

"Perfect. Pizza trumps zombies any day." I snuggled into his one-armed embrace, thankful for the comfort of his touch and the warmth. The chill of the autumn evening settled into a cold night whispering of impending winter. Somehow, it reminded me of the ice in Vivienne's tone. I shivered again, and this time it wasn't just from the nippy autumnal weather.

Lara called for the crowd's attention. "And now, the moment we've all been waiting for. The winner of this year's jack-o'-lantern carving competition!" Applause met her words, and she waited a beat for it to quiet down. "Now that he's figured out how to tell time, our champion tonight is none other than Mason Forham himself!" She loudly led the applause as the dwarf climbed the steps to claim his pumpkin-shaped trophy. He beamed broadly and lifted the prize in both hands like he'd just won the Super Bowl instead of a small-town pumpkin contest. The crowd loved him for it. The cheers that erupted were almost deafening. Alex and Finn looked at each other, shrugged away the loss, and shook hands.

"Day after tomorrow?" Finn asked over the noise.

"I'll send you a list and don't skimp on the tomatoes, okay?" Alex said.

"Only the best for you." Finn winked at him and then turned to me. "I'm booked pretty solid with appointments, but I'll pick you up after we both close up. Say around six?" His warm smile and sparkling eyes chased all thoughts of pranksters and Halloween magic from my head.

"It's a date," I said, already looking forward to it.

Pranks and Pests

As I settled into the passenger seat of Bella's car after saying goodbye to Finn and Alex, I decided to test the waters.

"So, *Bells*," I began casually, "it seems like you and Alex have a history. Anything you want to share with your best friend?"

Bella shot me a mischievous grin. "Oh, we've had our adventures," she said, her eyes twinkling.

I raised an eyebrow, intrigued. "Adventures, huh? Do tell!"

She sighed, her smile turning wistful. "Alex was my boyfriend back in the day. We were together for a while, but then life happened."

"What do you mean?" I asked, genuinely curious to hear her version of events.

"Long distance," Bella said with a shrug, keeping her eyes on the road. "We tried to make it work, but it was tough. Then he left for Europe for this cooking opportunity. It was incredible, don't get me wrong. I was happy for him. But then he decided to stay longer, and we just...drifted apart. He was there, I was here. Different lives, you know?"

I nodded, understanding. "That must have been hard."

"It was," Bella admitted. "But we tried to stay friends, albeit friends who didn't talk all that much."

"It happens when there is a literal ocean between you," I said, sympathetically, thinking of all the friends I'd lost touch with over the years in similar circumstances.

"I guess. And then, out of the blue, he's back in town. I didn't know he was coming back. He never said anything."

"So, how do you feel about that?" I asked gently.

Bella laughed softly. "I don't know. It's weird, you know? Seeing him again after all this time. It's like all those old feelings are rushing back, but it's been so long. We're both different people now."

I smirked. "Do you think there's a chance for a rekindled romance?"

She rolled her eyes playfully. "You've been reading too many cheesy romantasy books! I don't know what to think. I'm just trying to figure things out. Starting with pizza."

"Hey, I'm just saying, sometimes sparks fly again," I teased. "And who knows? Maybe he developed some incredible pastry skills at culinary school too. Think of it. Pizza followed by a tiramisu? Now that's a relationship worth pursuing."

Bella giggled. "To be fair, he makes a mean chocolate chip cookie. If things go well with the pizza, maybe I'll invite him over for a bake-off. Against me of course. It wouldn't be fair to pit him against Mama, even with European training."

She was right. Honey's magical gift involved baking enchanting treats. I swear, she could create something magically delicious out of just about anything.

"Now that's a plan I can get behind. I'll be the judge, of course," I said with a wink. My baking skills were far inferior to those of Honey and Bella. Not that I minded in the least. I still got to sample all their delectable treats, so it was a win in my books.

"Of course," Bella agreed, laughing. "But seriously, it's strange. One minute, he's a part of my past, and the next, he's standing right in front of me, looking just as handsome and charming as ever."

"Handsome and charming, huh? Sounds like a recipe for sparks to fly," I joked.

"The only flying sparks will be coming from the wood-burning pizza oven if there is one," Bella retorted with a grin. "But seriously, let's not get ahead of ourselves. For now, I'm just trying to navigate this unexpected twist without doing or saying something stupid."

"Well, whatever happens, I'm here for you," I said sincerely. "What are best friends for, right?"

"You've got a point," Bella agreed, her smile warm. "Thanks, Harper."

We both laughed, and the conversation shifted to lighter topics. We shared stories about our Halloween costumes from previous years, each tale more hilarious than the last. Bella's anecdote about a costume malfunction involving a witch hat, a rubber chicken, and her elderly neighbor's missing nightgown had us both in stitches.

"Remember the time you dressed up as a pumpkin and got stuck in the door?" Bella teased.

I groaned but couldn't help but laugh. "Don't remind me! I was orange for days after that fiasco."

As we continued down the road, I tried to surreptitiously coerce more information about Alex from her, but Bella's attempts to evade my questions about him became more creative. Each time I thought I had her cornered, she would deftly change the subject, leaving me more curious than ever.

By the time she dropped me off outside Spellbooks, I was yawning from a mix of exhaustion and laughter.

"Thanks for the ride, Bella," I said, waving goodbye.

"Anytime! And good luck with setting up your treasure hunt!" she called back with a wink.

As Bella pulled away from the curb, I said a quick hello to Gideon before letting myself into the darkened shop. I didn't have the energy to fiddle with the treasure hunt or any more decorating tonight. Besides, it looked like Luna and Mr. Wigglesworth were fast asleep in their respective windows for the night. Rather than disturb them, I set my very first jack-o'-lantern on the counter. On a whim, I put the candle Finn had bought for me through the hole in the top and lit it, just to see what it looked like when it was illuminated.

For my first time, it wasn't a bad carving. The light flickered spookily within the grinning face, but it wouldn't have stood a chance against some of the incredibly elaborate designs on display tonight. Oh well, there was always next year. I blew out the candle and headed upstairs.

After brushing my teeth, pulling on pajamas, and reading a couple of chapters in bed, sleep didn't come as quickly as I had hoped. I sighed and rolled over in exasperation. I'd been up early, and it had been a busy day. Sleep shouldn't be so difficult.

I contemplated starting the treasure hunt for my customers to find the statues downstairs when the little lavender journal on my writing desk that Spellbooks had given me caught my eye. If sleep wouldn't come, then at least I could finish the story of my first week in Havenwood. Writing in the journal had become somewhat of a ritual. I liked following in Granny Bea's footsteps, and there was something therapeutic about recounting everything that had happened since I moved to Havenwood.

With the journal open in front of me, I began to write. I don't know how long I sat hunched over my journal, scribbling away, but my hand was cramping by the time I wrote the final few lines detailing the end of the events surrounding my grand re-opening.

> *I wonder what sort of secrets are yet to be uncovered in my magical bookshop, and I'm already looking forward to seeing what the next chapter with my handsome new neighbor holds, but all of that can wait for now. This is a moment for celebration, for new friends and old, as well as for new beginnings. I plan to take Granny Bea's advice and savor the start of my next grand adventure.*

I sat back in my chair, massaging my hand. Maybe someday, my heir would read these words and feel connected to me in the same way I did to Granny Bea. A yawn escaped my lips as I closed the journal and placed it back on the desk.

Finally, feeling the weight of the day, I decided it was time to call it a night. I slipped into bed, pulling the covers up to my chin, and within moments, I was drifting off to sleep, eager for whatever tomorrow might bring.

Sometime later, but much earlier than I would've liked, I half woke from a very pleasant dream involving Finn and pizza. I blinked into the darkness, wondering what had woken me. Usually, I was a sound sleeper. So sound, in fact, that my mom claimed it would take an entire Fourth of July celebration in my bedroom to wake me, and even then, I'd only get up for my dad's stuffed burgers. I never argued with her because his burgers were always awesome and well worth missing some sleep over.

However, with my parents miles away and no scent of sizzling patties on the grill, something else must've woken me. There! Through my sleep-hazed brain, I detected the faintest quiver through my bedframe. I laid a hand on the wall next to my bed. The wooden panel shivered and shuddered rapidly under my touch, which was something I'd never felt from the shop before. I sat up in bed, instantly alert.

"Spellbooks? What is it?" I demanded. A ripple passed along the wall under my fingertips, swelling like an ocean wave rushing towards the stairs. I jumped out of bed and jammed my feet into my slippers. As soon as I reached the top of the stairs, I saw a faint orange glow from the shop below. That was strange. I'd turned off all the lights when I went upstairs to bed. Hadn't I?

I rubbed at my eyes, and I headed down the stairs as quickly as I could manage without tripping over my slippers. Maybe Gideon had turned on a light? No, that was ridiculous. The gargoyle didn't need more than a faint beam of starlight to see perfectly in the darkest gloom. I yawned, sucking in a lungful of air and on it the strangest scent. Realization hit me a moment later just as Gideon's voice rang up the stairs.

"Fire! Fire in the shop!"

Panic roared through me. That's what Spellbooks had been trying to tell me! I took the rest of the stairs two at a time. I froze in my tracks for a moment as the shop came into focus. Gideon flapped madly around the room, carrying a mug that he'd filled with water from the sink in the back room. He dumped the cup on the small pile of papers smoldering on the front counter. Mr. Wigglesworth yowled in his window, back arched and fur standing straight up. He faced away from the blaze, focusing on something in the stacks of fiction books. What was he looking at?

Luna thumped her foot loudly. "Carrot calamity! Don't just stand there gaping, Harper! Help Gideon!"

Her words jarred me into action. I rushed to the back room, filling a small bucket I kept on hand to clean up coffee spills. I was back out in the main room within a minute. The water flooded from my bucket, over the wooden counter, splashing down the sides, and dousing the small fire completely. I breathed out a sigh of relief. A charred and now waterlogged book sat in the middle of a huge scorch mark on my counter next to my soaking wet jack-o'-lantern. The pumpkin tipped over on its side, the smiling face leering at me crazily as it wobbled back and forth. It might have been my imagination, but the pumpkin's smile looked a little more disturbing than it had when I went to bed.

Luna's whiskers twitched. "Fluff and furballs, that was close!"

"Too close!" Gideon agreed, sinking onto the counter.

"What happened?" I demanded, righting the pumpkin. The small candle rolled out of the top hole. Mr. Wigglesworth yowled again and hissed, but I ignored him. The cat might live in a magical bookshop, but there was nothing supernatural about him. Unless it was his ability to eat. Regardless, I wouldn't get any answers from him.

Luna thumped her hind foot rapidly. "I don't know. I finally got to sleep and was in the middle of a very pleasant dream. It was a world with absolutely no cats and all the lettuce one could eat."

"Some people like cats," I observed, my heart rate returning to something resembling normal.

"Well, they obviously haven't had to put up with that mangy excuse for a feline howling his head off, or they'd know better," Luna said, putting her nose in the air with a little sniff of derision.

"I didn't hear him," I said, honestly.

"Well, he stopped eventually, didn't he? Good riddance too. Can't get any decent sleep around here with him caterwauling at all hours," Luna griped.

"*Cat*-erwauling? Was that a joke?" I asked with a smirk. Luna glowered at me, but before she could offer a retort, Gideon chimed in.

"He *was* loud, which is why I spent most of the night outside. I didn't come in until I felt Spellbooks' call of distress and by then, the fire had already consumed most of that book."

I glanced at the charred remains of the spine. "*Name of the Wind*?" I asked. I'd been reading it in the few quiet moments I had between customers and had really enjoyed the world building so far. Now, I'd have to buy another copy. That was a shame.

I shook my head. Not the point. Fire. In the shop. While I was asleep. A feeling of dread settled in the pit of my stomach. What would have happened if Spellbooks hadn't woken me?

"How did this start?" I asked, wanting a distraction from the dark turn my thoughts had taken.

Neither Luna nor Gideon answered immediately. Finally, the gargoyle cleared his throat with the sound of gravel being run through a blender. "There is a candle on the desk," he ventured, pointing at it with a stone talon.

"What? Oh that? I wanted to see my jack-o'-lantern lit up before I went to bed, but I blew it out before going upstairs," I said.

"Beatrice never allowed candles in the shop," Luna said with a haughty sniff.

"It was out!" I protested, but immediately second-guessed myself. Had I forgotten to extinguish it? I grabbed the candle, examining it closely. The wick was singed, but the surrounding wax had barely melted. Exactly what I would expect from a candle used in a momentary test for my first jack-o'-lantern, but surely not the cause of a small fire hours later. I gingerly touched the wax near the blackened string. It was cold and hard.

I held up the barely used candle. "This didn't cause the fire; I'm sure of it."

Luna's ears swiveled towards me, and she hopped over, holding out an imperious paw. I handed over the candle. She inspected it, sniffed the wick, and then passed it back. "I'm inclined to agree with you. However, if this wasn't the cause, what started the fire?"

Mr. Wigglesworth hissed at the shelves again as if they were to blame. I looked around nervously, remembering the strange giggling runaway pumpkins. Did the cat sense something? Was someone back there? Had the prankster targeted me specifically? Had they followed me home, just waiting for the perfect moment to strike? Setting fire in a bookshop was a far cry from some giggling pumpkins, but maybe someone didn't like the fact I'd taken over Spellbooks and was using Halloween as a cover to show me their displeasure?

Silently, I raised a finger to my lips and motioned for Gideon to follow me towards the shelves. He nodded. Without a sound, we crept down the aisles of books. I jumped around the corner, hoping to surprise the culprit, but there was no one there. I sighed, not knowing if I was happy or disappointed to find an empty shop.

"Well?" demanded Luna as we came back to the front.

"Nothing and no one," I said.

"Well, then it must've been the candle. Perhaps a spark escaped, and you didn't notice it. There's no other explanation. You should know better than to have an open flame in the middle of a bookshop! Get rid of it and never bring that little waxy cylinder of literary death back in this place ever again!" Luna chastised me.

"I won't," I said, dropping the cold candle into the trash can next to the desk. If the candle hadn't started the small blaze, I could only think of one possible scenario, but even that seemed like a stretch. The prankster *had* struck again, after all. The feeling of unease burbled like a boiling cauldron in the pit of my stomach. Knowing I wouldn't be able to rest until I'd checked every door and window on the ground floor, I asked Gideon to accompany me. We found absolutely nothing. The shop was locked up tight, and there were no signs of forced entry.

I sighed as we returned to the front counter. "Well, there goes that theory."

"What theory?" Luna asked.

"Someone pulled a prank at the pumpkin farm tonight. A magical prank. I thought maybe they'd struck again."

"But there's no sign that anyone was in the shop," Gideon protested.

"I know," I said, not sure if that made me feel better or worse.

Luna's whiskers twitched. "You two!" she exclaimed.

"What?" I asked.

Luna thumped her back foot twice. "Really? You can't see the flaw in your logic? We live in a *magic* town. You think the prank was done by *magic*. Who says they'd leave behind a clue? Or that they'd even enter the shop at all? You can cast a spell just with line of sight, you know."

The feeling of unease spiraled upwards, catching in my throat. I spun around, searching the darkness outside the front windows for…I don't know what. Someone watching me maybe? But with the lights on inside, it was impossible to see the street clearly.

"Gideon? Do you mind—"

"Doing a fly-over?" he finished for me. "Not at all. Be back in a jiffy." He snapped a smart salute my way and then sprang into the air, disappearing through his little revolving doorway above the main entrance.

I fidgeted with the hem of my pajama shirt as I waited and noticed the box on the floor by the counter. The one which had held the little statuettes. I needed to take it back upstairs before I opened the shop tomorrow. I bent to pick it up and set it on the counter, but when I did, the bottom collapsed.

"Woah!" I exclaimed as the box shifted under my hands. I juggled it awkwardly to the floor. My fingers came away damp. I glanced down to see the entire bottom of the cardboard box was a darker shade of brown than the upper part. Had water splashed down onto the box when I put out the fire? I didn't think so but hadn't really been paying attention. My entire focus had been on dousing the flames before they could do more damage.

"What's the matter?" Luna asked.

"This box is wet. I think I might need a new one or the bottom may fall out completely," I said, nudging the box with my toe.

"You definitely need a replacement, but not just because of the water," Luna said, hopping over. She stuck a paw through a hole in the bottom corner. "It looks like you have a mouse problem."

I groaned. "Are you serious? I thought that the magic of Spellbooks would keep all pests out."

Luna snorted. "Magic only extends so far when it comes to pests. Exhibit A." She pointed as Mr. Wigglesworth padded across the floor towards his food bowl.

"Hey! He's not a pest!" I exclaimed.

"Says you," Luna muttered.

Gideon flew back through the revolving door before I could answer her. "No one is around that I could see."

"Which means no one is around," Luna said with an air of assurance I didn't quite share.

"Oh. Well, okay." I didn't know what I'd been expecting, but absolutely nothing wasn't it. But with no culprit in sight, what could I do? "I guess I should... go back upstairs and try to get to sleep," I said, somewhat lamely.

"You do that. I'll stay on extra-high alert," Gideon said seriously. "No one will get by me. I swear it."

I smiled reassuringly at the little gargoyle. "I know you will. Thanks for watching out for us all."

He sprang into the air and disappeared through his door a moment later. Luna hopped off, muttering about patrolling the back of the shop. I chewed on my lower lip and looked around as Mr. Wigglesworth finally padded back over to his usual spot in the window. There was nothing to see and even less I could do other than return to bed, unless I wanted to talk to my cat. Unfortunately, he wasn't much of a conversationalist. Unless it involved a treat or a good cuddle, Mr. Wigglesworth wasn't interested.

Before heading upstairs, I decided to take some practical steps. I took out the trash, including the candle and the book. I even considered getting rid of the pumpkin, just in case. Better safe than sorry, right? However, looking at it tipped over on its side, I didn't see how a pumpkin could be responsible for a fire. I moved the jack-o'-lantern, sans candle, from the counter to Luna's front window, reasoning that the rabbit wouldn't mess with it as much as Mr. Wigglesworth might. He was usually pretty good about the shop rules, but the last thing I needed was the cat assuming the pumpkin was some new-fangled litter box and doing his business in it. I spun it around so it could smile crazily out at the moonlight illuminating Arcadia Avenue.

With nothing else to do, I switched off the lights and headed upstairs to bed. Despite my best efforts to get back to sleep, questions danced around my head, keeping me from the land of slumber. What had happened tonight? Was it just a freak occurrence, or was someone targeting me? Was it the prankster from the pumpkin patch, and if so, why target me? Or was there another prankster running around Havenwood? Or perhaps was there something more sinister at play?

I shook my head, trying to slow the racing train of thought that seemed to career crazily from one worry to the next. It was as if my mind refused to let me rest, replaying the events of the night over and over. I needed to focus, to ground myself somehow.

Taking a deep breath, I forced myself to think practically. I'd check the shop first thing in the morning and make sure everything was in order. Maybe I'd even talk to some neighbors to see if they'd noticed anything unusual. If pranks were common this time of year, perhaps they'd have some insights. Either way, I definitely needed to look into why the sprinkler system hadn't turned on and maybe invest in an extra fire extinguisher. I couldn't afford to have another close call with a fire. The damage to the books or the structure of the building would be awful, but I didn't know what kind of impact fire might have on Spellbooks itself, and I didn't want to find out.

Unable to sleep, I returned to my little writing desk and flipped to a new page. If sleep wouldn't come, then at least I could organize my thoughts. I started jotting down the events of the night, beginning with the prank in the pumpkin patch and then the fire. Was it connected somehow? Or just a series of unfortunate coincidences? I wasn't fully convinced yet that I wasn't jumping to conclusions, but after what happened with the stolen books, I valued getting it all written out. It helped me clear my mind and maybe, just maybe, get back to sleep.

Unfortunately, no answers presented themselves. Gray fingers of dawn streaked the horizon before I finally surrendered to a fitful sleep plagued by dreams of flames and charred words burning to nothing.

Candy Catastrophe

THE NEXT MORNING, I was on edge, jumping at shadows and fidgety after my restless night. The two cups of coffee on an empty stomach probably didn't help matters, either. I could really do with something to eat. I glanced through my nearly bare cupboards, already knowing what I'd find. Stale cereal, an unopened jar of strawberry jam, tea, coffee, peanut butter, and half a loaf of bread. I swung the fridge open. There was some milk, butter, cheese, and apples. I wouldn't starve, but the limited supplies didn't make for a very appetizing start to my day. An unexpected parcel caught my eye.

"Oh, bless you, Honey!" I whispered, pulling the pumpkin spice bread out and cutting a generous slice. I popped it in the microwave and then plopped a generous dab of butter on top. The smell of cinnamon and nutmeg filled my small apartment with a heavenly aroma. I took a bite. Tender crumbs melted in my mouth, and the autumnal spices did a better job of comforting me than the coffee had. I polished off the first piece and cut myself a second. Maybe today wouldn't be so bad after all.

After breakfast, I felt positively cheerful. For about two minutes. As soon as I went downstairs, the ugly, black scorch mark on the front counter reminded me of last night's incident. Unless I wanted to explain the scorch to every customer who entered the shop, I needed to deal with it. I sighed.

Restoring the counter would take more expertise than I had. I picked up my phone and dialed Grimgor.

The carpenter-slash-fix-it-man picked up immediately. "Good morning, Harper. How are you? Do you have that new order of poetry books in yet?"

"They're due in today," I assured him.

Despite what most people might assume about the lumbering half-giant, he was as dexterous with his thinking as he was with his hands. He loved poetry and spent hours chatting away in the little garden I had behind the shop. Sometimes he talked to me, but mostly he enjoyed the company of a certain tree nymph who lived in the large oak tree. Thistle was a shy creature. She liked the garden, the birds, and no disturbances. However, Grimgor seemed to have bridged the emotional moat she'd built around herself. They regularly enjoyed hours in the garden, discussing various planting techniques or bird watching together. I'd even seen him read to her as she worked. It was very sweet.

Grimgor's voice rumbled over the connection. "That's good. Thanks for letting me know."

"Actually, that wasn't the only reason I was calling," I said. "There's been a bit of an accident at the shop. A small fire, in fact."

Grimgor's tone instantly turned sharp and worried. "Is everyone okay?"

"Yes, everyone's fine here," I said quickly, trying to reassure him. Naturally, he'd be worried if there was a fire anywhere near Thistle's leafy home. "The only things damaged were a book and my counter. Any idea how to remove a scorch mark?" I asked hopefully.

"Tell you what. I'll come by later today and take a look. If the damage isn't too deep, I should have it fixed for you in no time," Grimgor said.

"Thanks. I appreciate it," I said, already feeling better about the direction the day was going. I said my goodbyes and then got to work.

I hurried through my list of chores and opened the shop. In between helping customers, I created the clues for a mini-treasure hunt to locate the statues I'd hidden strategically next to my top sellers around the shop, printed cute little cards customers could check off when they found one, and finished digging into the remaining boxes of decorations from the attic, adding more bits and pieces until I was satisfied the shop was Halloween and Harvest Festival worthy enough to suit even the demanding nature of Vivienne Silverthorne.

As I stood back to admire my handiwork, I felt a sense of satisfaction. The shop looked festive and inviting. Mentally, I gave myself a small pat on the back before moving on to the next task. I pulled up a new tab on my laptop, planning on working through the next module of my online business course since the shop was empty of customers for the time being. That's when I noticed something was off.

The little dragon figurine on my counter. It was gone.

A sudden, uneasy chill ran down my spine. I scanned the counter, my eyes narrowing. The dragon had been there, right next to the register. I distinctly remembered placing it in that exact spot. My stomach tightened with a sense of foreboding. Did it get moved in last night's fiasco, and I just didn't remember? Maybe Gideon picked it up, or Luna moved it out of the way?

I crouched down, peering under the counter, my pulse quickening. The small space was empty. Straightening up, I looked around, feeling a prickling sensation at the back of my neck. I even checked the trash can and the back room for good measure, but the little dragon was gone.

Frowning, I searched through the last box of decorations. Maybe it had somehow ended up there. At the bottom of the box, I found a few more odds and ends I wanted to examine more closely later, but no dragon. I also found a small ledger written in Granny Bea's distinctive penmanship. Knowing her penchant for writing, I flipped through it, momentarily distracted by my curiosity about what was inside.

At first glance, it looked like more of Granny's notes and some lists. I set it to one side on the counter, intending to examine it in greater detail later, after I found the dragon. My unease from earlier crept back in, stronger now. The dragon had been here on the counter. Right here. And now it was gone.

My mind raced with possibilities, none of them comforting. Had a customer moved it? Unlikely. Was it the prankster from last night? More likely. Was that what the prankster had been targeting? The dragon? But why? And how? Had the fire just been a diversion for the theft? Standing alone in the quiet shop, I felt the hairs on my arms stand up. The idea that someone had illicitly entered my shop while I'd been asleep upstairs made my skin crawl.

I chewed on my lip, trying to quell the growing anxiety. I called out, my voice loud in the empty shop and a little shakier than I intended, "Hey Luna? Have you seen the little statue? It was on the counter yesterday, and now it's missing."

The rabbit hopped into view and peered up at the counter. She shook her head. "Is this part of your bookshop treasure hunt? Why are you young folks always trying to bring newfangled traditions into vogue? Isn't knocking on strangers' doors and threatening to trick them unless they give you candy enough of a radish ruckus? No need to go overcomplicating an already bizarre holiday, am I right or am I right?"

"I, um, don't know how to answer that," I said.

"Obviously, there's only the one correct answer," Luna said primly.

I ran a hand through my hair, trying not to upset the grumpy rabbit any further. "Well, if you see a statue lying around the shop, please let me know. I found it in the box of Granny Bea's decorations I got from the attic."

"How am I supposed to know which statue you're talking about when you scattered them willy-nilly all over the place?"

"The little purple one. I put the statuette right here, and now it's gone," I said, laying my palm on the counter.

Luna's whiskers twitched, and she rolled a shoulder in a little shrug. "Maybe a ghost took it?"

"Wait. Is that even possible? Can ghosts do something like that?" I asked. This was *Havenwood,* after all. I'd heard people talk about hanging out with ghosts like it was an everyday occurrence, but I'd never experienced a real life haunting. At least, not that I knew of.

"Don't be ridiculous. Ghosts can rattle windows or thump in an attic, but that's basically the extent of their ability to influence the physical plane unless you run into a really unique one. But moving a statue?" Luna snorted. "Fluff and furballs, I was joking! What do they teach you in school these days?"

"Sorry, I must've fallen asleep in my introduction to ghost behavior class," I said dryly.

"Well, that was rather irresponsible of you, don't you think?" Luna said with a haughty sniff.

"What? No. What I meant was—"

The door to the shop burst open, and Finn rushed in, cutting off my protests. "Harper! Something is happening over at the Candy Cauldron!" he exclaimed, naming the candy store located one street over from Spellbooks on Fairydust Lane.

"What's going on?"

"Apparently the prankster from last night has struck again. C'mon! We've got to help poor Poppy!" He grabbed my hand and dragged me towards the door. As quickly as I could, I flipped the sign over on the door to say I'd be back soon and locked up behind me. Finn grabbed my hand again, and we rushed across the street, between two buildings and onto Fairydust Lane. The Candy Cauldron was three shops down on the left. There was already a substantial crowd clogging the sidewalk outside for this time in the morning.

Laughter and surprised, delighted shouts filled the air as we hurried over. Tourists guffawed and pointed at each other as they clutched small paper bags filled with various sweets in their hands. I saw a pair of twins each pop a gummy bear in their mouths at the same time and burst out in outrageous giggles. Their big brother had a huge wad of bubblegum wedged into his cheek. I watched in amazement as he blew a bubble as big as his head and, with a small piece still in his mouth, started to float away. I hoped he'd bump back to earth after a moment or two, but he kept floating higher and higher. I tugged on Finn's arm, genuinely concerned for the kid's safety if the bubblegum balloon popped. However, one of the nearby adults noticed his ascent. She stopped giggling long enough to pop a chocolate bonbon into her mouth. In a moment, she was bouncing off the sidewalk like a super ball. She flew high enough to grab the boy's sneaker and pull him back down before he floated off into the sky. He sucked in the pink bubble and started chewing again furiously.

Poppy Zucker, the owner of the Candy Cauldron, appeared in the doorway, wringing her hands. Finn and I waded through the giggling crowd to get to her.

"What's going on, Poppy?" Finn asked.

She was a striking woman in her mid-thirties with a cheerful smile and bright blue hair that always looked vibrant enough to be fresh from the salon or made entirely of cotton candy. Maybe she spent a great deal of time in the chair or, the more likely conclusion, in my opinion, she was part fairy. However, a worried frown marred her beautiful features as she looked out on the street.

"Someone is messing with my sweets! Giggling gummies and bouncing bonbons! What's next? Munchkin marshmallows?"

At that moment, the twins pulled the pillowy sweets from their bags. They bit down on the fluffy confection and immediately shrank to half their original size, laughing uproariously and sounding like they'd just inhaled helium or whatever was holding their brother's bubblegum balloon aloft.

"Oh no!" Poppy moaned as the two munchkin-sized children ran in circles around their bouncing mother, dodging under her feet whenever she hovered in midair, only to dash out of the way just in the nick of time as she crashed back to earth again.

I noticed two men skirting around the edge of the crowd, working their way toward us. Something about their smiles looked forced and almost plastic, but other than that, I'm not sure they would've caught my attention amidst the rest of the chaos had I been one of the giggling tourists. Both were good-looking enough to earn the description of devastatingly handsome if they hadn't been so seriously focused on the chaos in front of the candy shop. They were obviously related. They had matching wide-set brown eyes, dimpled smiles, and the same curly black hair. If I had to guess, the taller one was the older of the two, but that was only a conjecture based on his more purposeful stride and the self-assured way he held his shoulders. The shorter one paused next to the door, keeping his eyes fixed firmly on the crowd and his lips moving without making a sound. The first man, the one I assumed to be older, leaned close to Poppy, keeping his voice low, but I was close enough to overhear his words despite the noise of delighted laughter from the tourists.

"What's going on here, Poppy? You know magic in the open is forbidden," he murmured through his smile.

"This isn't me, Lucas. I swear it! Someone must've tampered with my candies while I was making them last night." Poppy looked on the verge of tears.

I couldn't help myself. "Or maybe someone is playing a prank like they did at the Moonshadow Farm," I added, as I moved closer.

Lucas swung a probing gaze towards me. He considered me thoughtfully and then nodded. "My mother mentioned something about that."

Finn leaned over and whispered out of the corner of his mouth as the boy with the bubblegum balloon started to float away again, "Perhaps we could discuss this after the *agic-may* in the street is contained?"

Lucas snapped his fingers and pointed at the man I assumed to be his brother. "Gabriel? You've got the first part. I'll take care of the second." The other man, Gabriel, gave him a thumbs up without ceasing the unintelligible muttering. Lucas turned to Poppy. "Quickly now. I need some water or chocolate milk or soda. Anything liquid and drinkable will do really," he said, steering her into the shop.

I glanced at Finn. "What do we do?"

"Stay alert and out of the way. They'll get it under control again, I'm sure," he said with a confidence that hadn't been there before.

"Okay. Who are they exactly, and why are we trusting them to handle everything?" I asked under my breath.

"They're Silverthorne brothers." Finn tipped his head towards the shop. "That's Lucas with Poppy. He's going to give his mother a run for her money in the power department in a decade or so. That's saying something because Vivienne is no one to be trifled with. The younger sister might be his equal for power, eventually. She's an elemental mage but is out of town at some super elite private school for magic users. Gabriel is the one working the containment magic. He's the middle child. He's not quite the all-rounder or the powerhouse when it comes to magic that his brother is, but from what I hear, no one can match him for illusions."

Just then, I felt a pressure on my ears like I'd cannon balled into the deepest end of a swimming pool. A shimmery haze surrounded everyone on the street, including the candy shop.

Lucas reappeared in the shop's doorway carrying a tray of small cups filled with an effervescent red liquid. Poppy followed closely on his heels, balancing a matching tray.

"Free samples!" Lucas called with a jovial smile, offering the cups to the tourists.

Poppy's smile looked forced. "Limited supply! Get them while you can," she called.

I moved forward as if on instinct, but Finn grabbed my arm. He put his mouth next to my ear and breathed, "You don't want to drink those. Trust me. But let's lend a hand passing them out."

We grabbed some samples and helped Lucas and Poppy distribute them. The tourists crowded around, tossing back the samples with excited speculation of what the newest concoction would do. Bewilderment replaced excitement and confused murmurs crescendoed throughout the crowd. Lucas raised his arms, commanding attention, as Poppy dashed back inside.

"Excuse me!" Lucas called, drawing all eyes to him. "Poppy, the owner of the Candy Cauldron would like to thank you for testing out some of her newest recipes. However, one of her employees made a mistake and doubled the amount of sugar in some of this morning's batches. In extreme cases, the excess sugar can wreak havoc with the imbiber's system, including but not limited to increased heart rate and strange hallucinations. If you don't mind returning the candy in your bags, Poppy has already prepared replacements. Free of charge, of course," Lucas finished with a flourish of his hands as Poppy reappeared holding a new tray laden with striped paper bags stuffed full of treats. We joined in, passing the bags out to the tourists, murmuring apologies for the fictitious employee.

I overheard some tourists as they traded out their "overly sugared" sweets for the normal ones. "Strange. I've never heard of sugar causing those kinds of symptoms. Even in high doses," one woman said.

"Well, they are always telling us sugar is bad for us," a man who I presumed to be her partner said.

"And who is they exactly?" she quipped.

"I don't know. Doctors. Teachers. Hairdressers. You know? Them." He gestured widely with a piece of fudge before popping it in his mouth.

She raised an eyebrow. "Taking that advice to heart I see."

He grinned a chocolatey grin. "You only live once, babe. Better enjoy it."

She shook her head and passed him her bag. "I don't think so. I thought I saw those kids shrink and that boy float away on his bubblegum. No, I'm swearing off all sugar for a while."

"Your loss," the man said with a shrug, snagging her bag with an unrepentant grin.

The rest of the tourists, returned to their normal size and gravity, drifted off to find other shops to explore. No one seemed bothered by the overt use of magic, and most laughed it off as completely impossible. I shook my head in amazement. The Silverthornes' spells were no joke.

Once the tourists dispersed, Poppy blew out a relieved breath and turned to the Silverthorne brothers. "I can't thank you enough," she said in a rush.

Gabriel smiled, making his dimples appear. "Think nothing of it. It's what we're here for."

I raised a hand, unable to stop myself. "I'm confused. What just happened?"

Lucas eyed me speculatively. "And who are you again?"

I stuck out my hand. "Harper Sullivan. Beatrice Sullivan was my great-grandmother."

Recognition lit his face. "Ah, so you're the new owner of Sullivan's Spellbooks? My mother mentioned you. It's nice to make your acquaintance," he said, shaking my hand. "You're a witch like your grandmother, I presume."

I paused, rather shocked that he'd asked outright. Most people waited until that type of information was freely offered. It was kind of an unspoken etiquette among paranormals, but Lucas was waiting expectantly for an answer.

I settled on a dodge. "Yes, but not as talented," I finally said. The truth, but not the whole truth.

Rather than press the issue of my magic, Lucas gestured with his free hand. "As for what happened here, Gabriel wove an illusion spell to keep anyone else from noticing anything abnormal while I enchanted the punch to wash away any memory of magic in the last hour. In conjunction with the spells around town, that's more than enough to convince the regular folks nothing of note happened here." He spoke freely of his magic, like it was no big deal. To someone as powerful as Lucas Silverthorne, perhaps it wasn't.

"Is that really what you think happened?" Finn asked.

Lucas shook his head grimly. "Mother told us about the pumpkin farm. It looks like we have a serial prankster in town. Hopefully whoever it is will get bored soon before they cause any real damage."

"Or makes a mistake and we can catch him," Gabriel added.

"I wouldn't want to be in his or her shoes when Mother figures out who's behind the mischief. She doesn't like anyone messing with town events. Especially the Harvest Festival," Lucas said seriously.

"That's like saying the weather in Siberia is a little brisk this time of year." Gabriel's voice was dry. "If these kinds of pranks continue, I don't want to be anywhere near Havenwood when Mother rains down her retribution. Maybe not even Connecticut. I hear the Bahamas are nice. Although still possibly not far enough."

"I agree, little brother. However, you and I are on containment duty for now. Then we need to check all the charms around town," Lucas said, clapping his brother on the shoulder. "No escape to tropical paradise for us. Not today at least."

Gabriel groaned. "That's going to take all day."

Lucas nodded. "But it's better than rumors of magic in Havenwood getting splashed all over the internet with the video evidence to prove it. Don't worry. We'll get Mother to help, but yeah. You'd better cancel any plans you had."

Gabriel sighed. "Fine. I'll head north and sweep the street for anyone who might have seen the candy catastrophe. You head south. We'll meet in the town square in thirty minutes?"

"Sounds like a plan," Lucas said and then turned to Poppy. "Just so you know, I enchanted the whole carton of punch. If something like this reoccurs, give the affected tourists a sample and call me immediately. Do you have my number?" Poppy nodded, clutching her empty tray like a life preserver.

"What can we do?" I asked.

Lucas considered me thoughtfully before speaking. "For now, just return to your normal routine, but keep your eyes open for this prankster. The sooner we catch him or her, the sooner we can get back to making this the best Harvest Festival ever. C'mon Gabe. We've got work to do."

Gabriel nodded and shook Finn's hand, then mine. "Thanks for your help. We appreciate it. And it's good to meet you Harper. Welcome to Havenwood."

"Thanks," I murmured.

The Silverthorne brothers set off with the easy swagger of the overly confident. Despite their obvious magical gifts, I wasn't sure that level of self-assurance was entirely warranted in this situation. Rolling pumpkins across the grass as evening fell was quite another thing to openly enchanting tourists in the broad light of day in the middle of town.

Maybe I should've said something about the fire in Spellbooks to the Silverthornes, but if the prankster had openly enchanted Poppy's candies, then they couldn't be targeting only me, could they? The other two instances, first at the pumpkin patch and now at the Cauldron, were quite public and not at all destructive. Maybe the incident in Spellbooks really had been caused by the candle, after all. A mundane explanation for last night was almost preferable to being the mark of a magical prankster. But there was still the matter of the missing dragon statue to address.

Part of me felt a fleeting relief that the fire at Spellbooks might not have been a malicious attempt at destruction. However, that relief vanished quickly as I considered the broader implications.

If I wasn't the only target, then what did the prankster want? And what would they do to get it?

Blink

As Finn walked me back to Spellbooks, I asked tentatively, "So, who do you think is responsible? The same person as pranked the pumpkin farm?"

Finn shrugged. "Perhaps. It stands to reason, I guess."

"What do you think they want?"

"I've been trying to figure that out, and other than disrupting the relative order of Havenwood, I can't think of a thing. Maybe to elicit a response from Vivienne Silverthorne? I don't know. I mean, pranks like this aren't unheard of. They're just usually contained to the magical population of town," he said.

I chewed on my lip as I thought it over. "Bella said something similar. But these are more public?"

Finn nodded seriously. "Much more so than anything I've ever heard of happening. The gifted who live here like to keep the whole magic thing quiet."

I paused, letting his comment roll around in my head as we walked. Finally, I asked, "Do you have any guesses who might be responsible? Or where they might strike next?"

Finn chuckled and wove his fingers through mine, tugging my hand up and tucking it in the crook of his arm. "Are you planning on playing detective again? Should I give Sheriff Jackson a heads-up? Perhaps call

Officer Johanna and let her know that a number of fictitious cats are on the loose and could turn up in anyone's closet?"

I bit my lip, ignoring the reference to my less-than-legal snooping last month. Maybe he was right. Perhaps I should try thinking like a detective again. The last time, I'd succeeded in recovering the stolen books, after all. Maybe I could do it again.

Finn was looking at me curiously. I realized the silence had dragged on, so I hurried to say, "No. I'm just curious, that's all."

He pulled me to a stop in front of my house. "I'm curious too. About what you like on your pizza. Let's leave the prankster to the Silverthornes, shall we?"

"I suppose," I murmured, not entirely convinced that I was willing to give this up just yet.

"Are we still on for tomorrow night or should I cancel on Alex to stake out the candy shop in case they return?" Finn teased.

My stomach rumbled at the thought, letting me know that the morning pumpkin spice bread wouldn't sustain me much longer. I spoke over the gurgling, hoping Finn didn't hear. "If Alex is cooking, I'm game for whatever he wants to make."

"Sounds like a plan, and it also sounds like you need some lunch." Finn's eyes twinkled. He'd obviously heard my stomach complaining.

I blushed and pressed a hand to my midsection. "Yeah, I may have forgotten to stock the kitchen, but I'm sure I can find something to throw together," I said with more confidence than my cooking skills and kitchen supplies warranted.

Finn pulled out his phone. "I'll tell you what. I could use an early lunch myself and was going to order something from the Hobbit Hole. Could I add something for you to the order?"

The Hobbit Hole was a local restaurant that did remarkable food. I opened my mouth, but my stomach took control of my words before my brain could. "That sounds great! Thanks!"

"Wonderful. What's your pleasure?"

I thought back to the tasty pizzas Finn and I'd shared on our first date there, but we were having pizza tomorrow. That, combined with my delicious yet decidedly not nutritious breakfast, I decided to do something kind for my body. "Better make it a salad. Something with chicken please."

"Got it. Anything else?"

I bit my lip and wavered for a whole three seconds before giving in. "And an order of their truffle Parmesan fries." A girl couldn't be sensible all the time, could she?

Finn chuckled and nodded, pressing a few buttons on his screen with a flourish. "Done. It should be here in about thirty minutes. I'll swing by, and we can eat together."

Food delivery service *and* a good-looking date for lunch? How had I gotten so lucky in a next-door neighbor like Finn? "Thanks. Can I pay you back?"

He waved a hand. "Don't worry about it. If it really bothers you, you can get lunch for us another day."

"Don't think I won't!" I said as he started to walk towards his shop.

"I'll hold you to it," he said with a wink.

I re-opened the shop, but there was always an afternoon lull just before lunchtime. In the quiet moments, I decided to use the time to jot down my thoughts. I dashed upstairs and grabbed my lavender journal from the writing desk in my apartment before returning to the shop. Perched at the counter, I added what happened at the Cauldron with the enchanted candies to my notes.

I tapped the pen against my lip, pondering who might be behind the mischief. I reluctantly started a "persons of interest" list with the Silverthorne brothers at the top. They were powerful and obviously knew the town very well. Besides, they'd shown up before the Sheriff could even get to the Cauldron. Suspicious much?

I hesitated, but then added Alex. After all, there hadn't been any pranks in town before he showed up. I suppose that could apply to several other people as well, but I remembered that he'd been purposely vague about his magical gift. Was he like me, trying to keep his powers under wraps to avoid causing drama, or was there something more nefarious going on with Bella's ex?

Thinking of Bella stirred a mix of protectiveness and guilt within me. I didn't want to see her hurt, and Alex's actions were suspicious. But he was her ex, and there were clearly still feelings involved. Adding him to the list felt distrustful and a bit judgmental, but also necessary. His presence was too coincidental to ignore. I decided not to tell Bella about my suspicions—at least, not yet.

Switching gears, I decided not to include the business owners who had been targeted. It just didn't feel right, but I made a note about possible connections between the pumpkin patch and the candy store. Perhaps someone was jealous of the successful businesses or held a grudge against the owners. Either way, I felt these were legitimate leads that a real detective would pursue.

Just as I finished updating the journal, Finn brought my lunch over. The salad was delicious. Juicy, roasted chicken nestled on a bed of wild greens and colorful, crunchy veggies adorned with a sprinkle of toasted pecans, and the perfect amount of a delectable forest berry vinaigrette. To top it off, the truffle fries were the ideal salty complement to the meal. As delicious as the lunch was, Finn's company was even better. He had a way of making me laugh from the center of my soul. He even helped man the counter so I could finish my lunch when a swarm of tourists crowded into the shop. The mischievous pranks faded quickly from my memory as I finished my lunch.

After Finn returned to his shop for an appointment, a steady stream of customers kept me busy. I tried to keep my mind on the business, but my thoughts kept returning to the pleasant lunch with my handsome neighbor and wondering what the future might hold.

Grimgor showed up around an hour after Finn left, toolbox in hand. He examined the scorch mark on the counter. "This shouldn't be too hard to polish out. Some toothpaste and baking soda ought to do the trick."

I blushed. "That seems so easy. I should've thought of checking for a solution before calling you. I bet it would've been one of the first things to pop up online. Sorry for dragging you out here."

Grimgor smiled easily. "Not a problem. My day was light, so it wasn't an issue. Besides, this gives me an excuse to check out that latest poetry book. You said it would arrive sometime today?"

I pulled out the slim volume by Amanda Gorman. "I'm so glad you introduced me to her. She has almost a musical style to her writing."

"I agree. Since I'm here, would you mind if I read a couple pages out in the garden? Perhaps I could bother you for a cup of coffee as well?" Grimgor asked hopefully.

I smiled, knowing the reason he wanted to stay had little to do with either my coffee or the book. My guess is he wanted to visit with Thistle.

"Of course, not a problem," I assured him.

Grimgor tugged out his wallet. "What do I owe you?"

I waved my hands in front of my body. "Nothing. It's the least I can do to say thank you for taking the time and for the advice with the counter."

"But I didn't do anything," he protested.

"You showed up. That counts," I pointed out.

"Harper, this is no way to run a business," he said. His face was stern, but his eyes sparkled with merriment. I think he enjoyed being treated as a normal person even though the half-giant towered over me and could have probably smashed an entire bookshelf to smithereens with a careless flick of his hand.

"Says the handyman who rescheduled his afternoon to help a friend?" I asked. He shook his head. I brushed away his impending arguments. "Look, if you're really wanting to pay me back for the coffee, do me a favor and keep an eye out for a little dragon statuette? I thought I left it on the counter, but it seems to have gone missing. I can't find it anywhere!"

Grimgor furrowed his brow at me. "You mean, that one?" he asked, pointing a thick finger at the cute statue curled up on top of the cash register.

I blinked in surprise. "That's the one," I murmured in disbelief, taking a closer look. I was sure I'd left the dragon next to the register, not on it. And I was nearly positive it hadn't been there earlier today. Unless sleep deprivation was getting to me. It had been a restless night. Maybe I'd just overlooked the little guy somehow?

Grimgor scooped up the poetry book. "Glad I could help then."

"Yeah, thanks," I said softly. I shook my head and made shooing gestures with my hands. "You go ahead. I'll bring your coffee in a minute."

Grimgor nodded and headed out the door. A few minutes later, I carefully balanced a tray with a black coffee in a mug big enough to classify as a small pool. I'd bought it especially for Grimgor. I wanted to make him feel comfortable when he came to visit. Also, drinking out of something that was relatively the size of a thimble didn't seem appealing. I'd added an herbal tea for Thistle and a small plate of the last of Honey's almond and vanilla biscotti to the tray just in case.

Grimgor and Thistle were sitting on the bench under the last few leaves still desperately clinging to the branches of the oak. Grimgor read aloud in his basso rumble as Thistle closed her eyes and turned her face towards the autumn sun, soaking up the last of the warm rays before winter really sunk its chilly bite into the region. Briefly, I wondered what tree nymphs did in the winter. Did they hibernate or bundle up warm and enjoy hot chocolate by the...wait. Thistle probably didn't have a fire. It would be dangerous inside her tree, wouldn't it? But without a fire or electricity hooked up to the oak tree, how did the nymph stay warm in the winter? Did the cold affect her? If so, how? Did she have to wear a coat made of leaves and a scarf made of woven branches? Neither of those sounded comfortable or warm. What about snow? Did she get frostbite on her feet or catch a cold with the chilly weather setting in?

I bit the inside of my cheek. Perhaps these were questions to be approached with more tact at another time. I slid the tray onto the bench as silently as I could so as not to disturb the reader or his audience. Grimgor nodded his thanks without dropping a word. I tiptoed away, not wanting to intrude on their moment.

When I returned to the shop, I headed upstairs to my apartment for the toothpaste and baking soda. Grimgor was right. With a little elbow grease, the scorch mark disappeared as if by magic. I was wiping the last of it up as the half-giant came back in, carrying the two mugs.

"Did you have a nice visit?" I asked.

He nodded, an uncontainable grin stretching from one large ear to the other. "She is truly a light in my world," he said in a soft rumble as he glanced toward the door.

"I agree. Thistle is a special lady. Oh! How did you like the book?"

Grimgor slid the blue volume across the counter to me. "Ms. Gorman has a talent with words. They fall upon the ear with the easy restoration a gentle summer rain has upon a field."

I smiled fondly at the big man. He loved poetry but was afraid to be ridiculed, especially by his peers in the giant communities. I thought it was a shame for anyone to be embarrassed by their reading preferences. I always kept my door open and my shelves ready for the Grimgors of the world. In my mind, Spellbooks was a safe place to explore any literary road one wanted to walk, and I wanted people like Grimgor to feel the same. "I haven't read it yet, but I'll have to find some time to take a look. Poetry always says so much with so few words. I find myself contemplating the meaning of a single poem for far longer than it took me to read it."

Grimgor closed his eyes and recited, "In words we weave, in verses bright, inspiration takes its flight. A song of hope, a tale of grace, a vision of a better place."

The words reverberated around the shop, filling cracks in my soul that I hadn't realized were there. When his deep voice faded to silence, I let out a breath. "That was beautiful. Gorman's work?"

"Only my poor imitation. I'm sure she'd take my words and polish them until they shone with deeper meaning. Speaking of shine, it looks like you solved your problem." Grimgor pointed a finger at the unmarred surface of the counter.

"I did. Thanks for the tip," I said with a grin.

His shaggy brows drew together as he considered the counter critically. "Any idea what caused it?" the half-giant asked, obviously noting my lack of candles.

I frowned and shook my head. "No. I thought it might be the prankster running around town, playing a trick on me. But it wasn't a very good one."

"I heard about that. Someone pulling pranks on the tourists, right? Something about pumpkins?"

"And also candy, but what happened here wasn't mischievous or funny. If Spellbooks hadn't woken me up, things might've been much worse than a mark on the counter or some rolling pumpkins."

Grimgor's expression darkened. "If it was the prankster, he's going to have more than just Vivienne Silverthorne after him. No one messes with my friends."

A warm feeling sprang to life inside my heart. It was the first time I'd heard Grimgor call me his friend out loud. I'd only been in Havenwood for a short time, but it was feeling like home more and more each day. Grimgor's protective response made me feel even more like part of a community. Like I was finally putting down roots.

Afraid of getting too sentimental, I leaned my hip on the counter and folded my arms. "That's not the first time I heard Vivienne would be upset by these types of shenanigans. I get why she doesn't want anyone messing around at the Harvest Festival or spilling the beans about Havenwood, but everybody seems concerned that she's irritated. I know she's supposed to be mega powerful, but just how much power are we talking here?"

Grimgor glanced around at the empty shop but lowered his voice despite our obvious privacy. "Vivienne's power isn't just about magic, Harper. Sure, she's got a lot of that—more than most around here—but it's also about influence. The Silverthornes practically own this town. They control a lot of the local businesses, real estate, and even most of the politics. If Vivienne's unhappy, she can make life very difficult for anyone who crosses her. Rent hikes, legal trouble, business retribution—you name it."

"Yes, I had an inkling," I said, my mind flashing back to my encounter with Vivienne during my grand re-opening. I never wanted to get on her bad side again, but I also needed to know exactly what she was capable of. "But what about her other powers? The magical ones? All I've ever heard people say is that she's incredibly powerful, but no one elaborates. What's her gift?"

Grimgor stroked his chin where a five o'clock shadow covered his jaw, even though it was barely past noon. "As you know, most people in Havenwood are magical mundanes or humans. The magic users can do one, maybe two spells well and that's it. Bake a great loaf of bread, sing to the birds, that type of thing. Nothing that's going to be world-shattering. Vivienne is...different. She was offered one of the nine seats on the North American Mage Council. Those only go to the most powerful, experienced mages."

"She turned them down?" I breathed, engrossed by his story.

Grimgor shook his head. "No. She served. For a time. Then she walked away. No one knows why but what's more fascinating is the aftermath of that decision."

"What do you mean?"

"Serving on the mage council is a lifetime tenure. At least, it is for everyone but Vivienne Silverthorne. She left an un-leaveable post, moved back here, and has been a leading figure in the Havenwood community ever since. To top it off, the mage council has done absolutely nothing about it."

I bit my lip, considering his story. Finally, I asked, "So, what does that mean?"

Grimgor lifted a shoulder noncommittally. "Don't mess with Vivienne." He paused, considering. "Or the rumor mongers in this town have really exaggerated over the years. However, I'm more likely to go with the former than the latter. No one can make up stories that consistent or detailed and few have the imagination to apply them to a lady like Vivienne Silverthorne." He glanced at the clock on the wall. "Sorry to read and run, but I need to get on my way. See you later." He grabbed his toolbox and headed towards the door.

"Bye," I called after him as I flipped the sign to say 'Closed' and locked the front door of the now empty shop. I needed a moment of peace and quiet to think this through. I didn't want to be in the prankster's shoes if, no, *when* Vivienne caught him. To be fair, I'd prefer to not even be in a four-block radius. I drummed my fingers on the counter as I considered what Grimgor had said. Was Vivienne a force to be reckoned with? No doubt. However, was she the type of woman to scare an entire council of powerful mages into leaving her alone? I wasn't entirely convinced. However, I wasn't *not* convinced either. I just didn't know enough about her. The little dragon statuette caught my eye.

I ran a finger down its scaly back as I mused aloud, "Regardless of Vivienne's past, I'd be more concerned with her present. Between her and her sons, that prankster better stop making mischief in town, don't you think?" I paused as if waiting for the inanimate object to respond so I could politely carry on my one-sided conversation.

When I opened my mouth to do just that, the little stone figurine wriggled under my hand. I yelped and jumped back, immediately chastising myself for the worst kind of idiot. Statues didn't move. I pressed a hand to my racing heart and shook my head at my utter foolishness.

"Spellbooks? What are you doing?" I called out to the shop, assuming the sentient building was playing its own little prank.

Which is when the tiny dragon rotated its head and blinked at me.

Statues, Sloths, and Snickerdoodles

I JUMPED BACK AND may have screamed. Possibly. Probably. It was all a blur for a few moments as the *dragon* woke up and stretched languorously in the middle of my *counter*.

Luna's ears pricked up from the front window and she sprang towards me. "What? What is it? Who do I need to kick?" Her whiskers twitched violently, and her back foot thumped an aggressive staccato on the floor.

The little dragon cocked its head to the side and considered me thoughtfully. It might have been my imagination, but it looked like a toothy grin curled the corners of his lips up, revealing tiny, wickedly sharp teeth. Then he dropped his head to the countertop, stuck his tail in the air, and waved it rapidly back and forth. It reminded me of...a puppy. A cute, tiny, very scaly puppy.

I held up my hand to halt Luna's incoming attack. "No need for kicking, I think. I was just surprised."

"Hopscotch on a haystack! I think you took years off my life!" Luna exclaimed, pressing a paw to her chest. "What's got you so excitable?"

"Well, there's a statue on the counter for one."

"Yes. The statue. The one that was missing. If I overheard correctly, Grimgor found it for you. I remember."

"Right. Except he's moving."

"Fluff and furballs, I can't believe you got me out of bed for that! I thought we already solved this. Statues can't move!" Luna exclaimed.

"Well, tell that to the smiling, blinking dragon looking at me right now," I said without taking my eyes off the tiny creature.

"Wait. Did you say *dragon*? Oh, for the love of Peter Cottontail, don't tell me that's Ignatius." Luna jumped up onto the counter, took one look at the little dragon, and let out a long-suffering sigh. "Oh, it *is* you. Well, I suppose it had to happen someday, but why this week? I've just gotten my whiskers tinted and really don't want hours at the salon wasted when you singe them off. Again," she said, glaring at the little dragon who didn't look the least bit perturbed to be the source of Luna's ire.

"You take hours to tint your whiskers? Wait. That's not the point. The point is... The point is..." I trailed in shock, completely taken aback by her unexpected response and distracted by the fact the dragon was still wagging his scaly tail like an adorable, over excited puppy.

"The dragon," Luna prompted.

"Right. The dragon."

"His name is Ignatius, by the way. Bea didn't tell you when you visited?" Luna asked, patting at her whiskers to put them back in order.

Now that the excitement calmed down, Mr. Wigglesworth stuck his head out of his front window and then padded over. The big cat was a beautiful orange tabby with piercing green eyes. If I hadn't known, aside from his stunning good looks, that he was a normal cat, I would've sworn *he* was the witch's familiar, and Luna was the pet. Until she opened her mouth. After that, no one would've doubted she had been Granny Bea's magical companion.

Mr. Wigglesworth sprang up on the counter, landing with a thump, and sniffed at the tiny dragon. The little dragon placed a clawed talon on the cat's furry cheek. I held my breath, readying myself to leap forward and stop the impending attack. By which creature, I wasn't sure. A low sound rumbled around the shop. It took me a moment to realize it was the cat. He was purring. Suddenly, Mr. Wigglesworth leaned forward and ran his long pink tongue along the dragon's hide. The cat curled around the tiny creature and shut his eyes, the deep purr only intensifying.

I blinked in surprise, my muscles slowly uncoiling, and looked at Luna. "No. Granny Bea didn't tell me anything about a *dragon in the shop.*"

"Oh."

I stared at her. When she didn't elaborate, I prompted, "Care to explain what's going on?"

Luna ran a paw over her whiskers again. "Of course. Beatrice adopted all kinds of strays. Questionable taste if you ask me. But she always said a bookshop without a cat was like a garden without carrots," she said, shooting a dark look towards Mr. Wigglesworth.

"No, I'm not talking about the cat. I meant the *dragon*!"

"Right. Well, Beatrice had a fondness for dragons. She thought they were fascinating."

"That still doesn't explain why there's one in the shop," I said, trying not to lose my cool.

The rabbit twitched an ear dismissively. "Oh, that. Ignatius is like most of the rest of Havenwood. A bit of a misfit with his own kind and wanting a quiet life. He turned up here about six...no, wait, seven years ago, now. Beatrice took him in, as she was wont to do."

I waited a beat, but when it was obvious Luna wasn't going to continue, I prompted her again, "And? How did he turn to stone? Is he part gargoyle or something?"

"No. Beatrice did that."

"She did what now?"

"Turned. Him. To. Stone. Really, Harper. Try and keep up," Luna said in exasperation. "You're usually much quicker than this."

I folded my arms and took a deep breath, keeping one eye on the dragon and the other on the talking rabbit. Usually, the trick with Luna was getting her to stop talking, but today? Today it was like pulling stubborn weeds out of a garden to get a straight answer out of her.

"I'm going to need more details. *All* the details in fact," I said, fighting to keep my voice calm.

Luna sighed dramatically. "It was Beatrice's choice to invite him to stay at Spellbooks, against my sage advice, I might add. Ignatius, like most dragons, likes to hoard things. Except instead of gold, he likes to hoard books, which is why he visited Spellbooks in the first place."

The dragon's tiny, scaled head poked up from the fluffy mountain of cat fur. "Books!" he exclaimed.

My jaw dropped open. "He can talk?"

Luna sniffed. "When he chooses to. It's difficult for his kind. Too many teeth, don't you know. But I suppose it's impressive that he manages as well as he does. Anyway, it took Beatrice a little while to figure out why he kept flapping around the shop. Once she did, she invited him to stay, under the premise he understood the books weren't his to keep, but he could read what he liked. For a few days, everything was lovely. And then the burnings started."

"Burnings?"

Luna nodded. "It turns out that Ignatius here gets a little over-excited when he reads, especially if it's epic fantasy or a thriller. When that happens, it prompts his fight or flight reaction which, in his case, is more of a fire or flight reaction. Apt for a dragon, I suppose."

"He sets the books on fire?" I asked, glancing at Ignatius. "Like the one last night?"

Ignatius hung his head, looking so sad that my heart lurched in response. "Accident. I sorry," he murmured.

Luna spoke up. "Unintentionally, and he always is quite remorseful afterwards, as you can see. Fire isn't a problem for him. Being a dragon, he's fireproof, of course. But the same can't be said of the magical bookshop situated precariously close to a forest."

The ramifications hit home of how dangerous the tiny dragon could be, not only to Spellbooks, but possibly all of Havenwood and beyond. "What happened then?" I asked.

"Beatrice couldn't have him burning down Spellbooks or the surrounding countryside of course, so she went to her friend Agatha. Together, they created a ritual to turn him to stone until they could find a better solution."

"Stone?" I echoed.

Luna narrowed her eyes at the interruption. "Yes, stone. Apparently, it's like taking a nap, except you don't know what century you'll wake up in. Anyway, every year or so, they'd splash some water on him to dissolve the spell. They'd try out one magical solution after another, but nothing ever worked. He kept setting books on fire. To be honest, I didn't even know she'd turned him back. I thought he was still stone somewhere."

"Apparently not! I found him in a box with the Halloween decorations and thought he was a statue. How long has he been hanging out in the attic?" I asked.

"He couldn't have been up there for long or something else would've burned. Cabbage catastrophe! Spellbooks! What are you playing at?" Luna thumped her back foot repeatedly on the floorboards. They vibrated under our feet, but I couldn't tell if it was an apologetic or amused rumble.

"What's going on?" I asked.

Her cute little pink nose wrinkled, and her head whipped up, one ear standing erect and quivering slightly. "Beatrice was kind of like a raven. Except instead of collecting shiny objects, she went for the magical and mysterious. Which Spellbooks. Is. Meant. To. Protect!" she said, with loud thumps of her powerful hind foot punctuating her words as she glared at the floorboards. "Why did you dissolve the stone spell?" she demanded of the shop.

A soft scraping sounded on the chalkboard behind the counter as Spellbooks painstakingly wrote out a terse message.

NOT ME.

As if offering an apology for not keeping the statues safe and tucked away, Spellbooks rumbled and nudged out Granny's ledger from the box across the counter, flipping it open to a specific page.

"What's this?" I asked Spellbooks, who just bumped it closer.

At first glance, it seemed to be an itemized list of the contents of the boxes of decorations. Four plastic pumpkins, two bags of leaves, one skeleton hand. I dragged a finger down the list, checking off the items in my mind. When I reached the last entries on the page, I was surprised to find an asterisk by each and an additional note at the bottom of the page.

Do not, under any circumstances, expose to fairy dust, liquids, trolls, or grape jam. Strawberry is fine. Oh, and the wizard is partial to honey in his tea.

That was odd and more than a touch confusing. What sort of statue liked tea? I checked the listed items marked with an asterisk. A wizard and a tiny stone dragon.

Luna peered at the ledger and tapped it triumphantly. "See! I told you it was Ignatius! But how and why you dissolved the stone spell is beyond me."

"I didn't!" I protested instantly, but then I paused. I *had* splashed water all over the counter to put out the fire. Had that done it? No, Ignatius must've been animated before then if he'd been the one to set the book on fire, which still left the question of how the stone spell got dissolved in the first place? Before I could figure it out, Spellbooks rumbled under my feet, obviously trying to communicate something.

"Or sure, now you want to share!" Luna exclaimed, glaring at the floorboards. "If you've got something to say, why couldn't you have warned her earlier?"

The rumbling intensified, taking on what I imagined to be more than a hint of frustration.

My phone rang, interrupting the brewing argument between the talking rabbit and the sentient shop. I held up a finger as Luna opened her mouth again, silently asking her to wait as I checked the caller ID. It was Bella. I frowned. We didn't have plans this afternoon that I'd forgotten about, did we?

I tapped the screen to accept the call and held the phone up to my ear as I wandered a few steps away for a semblance of privacy. "Hey Bella. What's up?"

"Are you okay?" she demanded instantly.

"Yeah," I dragged the word out, confused by the undercurrent of panic in her tone. "Are you?"

"I heard about the fire," Bella said in a rush. "Please tell me it didn't spread."

I blinked in surprise. I hadn't told her about the fire at the shop. Had I? No, I'd definitely forgotten to call her. It wasn't an intentional omission, of course. I just hadn't gotten around to it yet, what with the customers, the prank at the Candy Cauldron, lunch with Finn, Grimgor, more shop stuff, and then this whole thing with Ignatius. I cleared my throat. "No, everything's fine here. Gideon caught the fire early, and I put it out before it spread too far. I lost a book, and there was some damage to the countertop, but Grimgor came over and helped me with that and—"

"What are you talking about?" Bella demanded. "There was a fire in Spellbooks?"

"Only a little one. Wait. What are *you* talking about?" I asked.

"Papa just told me that there was a fire last night in the woods near your shop. It was small, and they caught it early. Thank goodness that we've had a lot of rain lately or it might have spread faster. However, as soon as I heard it was close to you, I had to make sure you were okay. I mean, you're basically all alone over there."

"I promise, everything's fine. And I'm not alone. I've got Luna, Gideon, Thistle, Mr. Wigglesworth, and…" I trailed off, realizing what I had almost let slip. Bella didn't know about Spellbooks' magical abilities, and maybe she shouldn't know. Granny Bea had kept Spellbooks' nature a secret from almost everyone. A part of me really wanted to confide in Bella, to share the secret, but could I? More importantly, *should* I?

"Harper, are you there? I think we've got a bad connection."

I quickly answered, "I'm just fine. No need to worry. I was just saying that with Luna and Mr. Wigglesworth around, I never feel truly alone here."

"I know he's huge, but I'm not sure the cat counts in this scenario," Bella said doubtfully.

I chuckled. "You're probably right. But this is the first I'm hearing about any fire in the woods. What happened?"

Bella spoke in a rush. "Papa is friends with the chief of the fire department. The official story is that a group of teenagers with bad fire safety training wanted to roast some marshmallows and things got a little out of hand."

I frowned, pacing down the mystery aisle. "The official story? What's the real one?"

"That's the thing. They don't know. According to Papa, there was nothing at the scene. No matches, no evidence of a campfire, no footprints, no clues at all."

"So, what do they think? Someone purposely set the fire?" I asked, my stomach sinking.

"At the moment, that's the theory, but they still don't know why or how. It's like the culprit vanished without a trace. I mean, how can you walk out into the woods and not leave any footprints?"

"No footprints? How is that possible?" I asked.

"Well, magic is the obvious answer, but I'm not sure that is the case here. There are a lot of rocks out there. Theoretically, someone could jump from rock to rock or, if they were light enough, not make any noticeable prints," Bella said logically.

I rounded the corner of the aisle, and my eyes fell on Luna glaring at Ignatius, who was curled up on my counter again. The tiny nerves all the way up my spine tingled with warning, and a sense of dread sprang to life in my stomach.

"What if he flew in?" I asked softly, pitching my voice not to carry.

"I mean, as a hypothetical, yes that would solve the conundrum but, between you and me, I think they probably just missed the signs. I'm sure Sheriff Jackson will turn something up, however. He's good at tracking people down. It's the werewolf in him."

"I suppose," I said, my eyes still fixed on Ignatius.

"I thought you were all about the business books lately. When did you switch over to fantasies?" Bella teased. "How many people do you know can fly around town or *would* fly with all the tourists around? No one is that crazy, especially not with Vivienne Silverthorne threatening to rain retribution down on the head of the people responsible for disrupting the Harvest Festival."

"Not people. Dragons. Specifically, one tiny purple dragon."

Bella paused, a beat of silence filling the airwaves. "The statue?" she finally asked. "You're saying you think *the statue* from your granny's storage room started a fire? Not exactly plausible, Harper. Be serious!"

"I am! Besides, he's not exactly a statue anymore. His name is Ignatius, and he's the one who started the fire in Spellbooks last night." As quickly as I could, I filled her in on the pertinent details related to the fire in the shop.

I hesitated as I neared the end of my story, recalling my confusion about the stone spell being dissolved. "I'm not sure what happened. According to the notes in Granny's ledger, Ignatius was supposed to be a statue, but somehow, he turned back. I don't know what could have caused that," I finished.

Bella gasped over the phone. "Oh my gosh, Harper, I think it might have been me. Yesterday, I accidentally spilled some water on the statue when I broke the glass. I dried him off, and he didn't seem damaged, so I didn't think it was a big deal. I'm so sorry!" Her voice trembled, and I could hear the guilt and worry seeping through. "I didn't mean to cause any trouble for you, I swear!"

I nodded slowly, the pieces of the puzzle coming together. The timing made sense. That must've been the catalyst for Ignatius' animation but knowing how it happened didn't help me solve the problem of his fire-breathing existence in my shop. I scrubbed a hand through my hair. "I know, and I'm glad you told me. At least that mystery is solved, but I'm not entirely sure it explains the fire in the woods. Do you think, maybe…" I trailed off, not sure I wanted to accuse the little dragon of causing havoc around town.

Bella sucked in a breath and then blew it out in a rush. "You think this Ignatius is responsible for that too?" Her voice was shaky, and she sounded like she was on the verge of tears. "I'm responsible for almost burning down your shop and all of Havenwood!"

"Don't be so silly. Of course you're not! It was an accident and there's no way you could've known. If we're playing the blame game, then I share as much blame as you do. I should've checked Granny Bea's ledger before putting the statues out. But knowing about Ignatius gives us an idea of what could've happened in the woods, doesn't it? No footprints. No sign of a campfire. Exactly the way a tiny dragon with limited control over his fire-breathing abilities would accidentally start a forest fire."

Luna's ears pricked up, catching the last of my words despite my attempts to stay quiet. "What was that?" she demanded.

I closed my eyes and sighed. No way to avoid it now. I pointed at the phone. "Bella says someone started a fire out in the woods behind the shop last night," I whispered.

"And you think it was Ignatius?" she asked.

"Wasn't me!" The tiny dragon protested. Tears welled in his eyes and started to spill down his scaly cheeks. "Never set fires on purpose! Never ever *ever*!"

"That's right, only when you're reading," Luna snapped.

Ignatius threw back his head and let out a mournful wail. "Accident!"

"Luna!" I hissed over the dragon's cry. "Be nice!"

"Is everything alright? What's going on over there?" Bella asked.

"Too much. I'll call you back later, okay?"

"Sure. Glad you're safe. I'm sorry again. Let me know if I can help," Bella said softly before she ended the call.

I jammed the phone in my pocket and hurried back to the front of the shop. I scooped up Ignatius, stroking the warm scales on his back as he let out a little hiccupping sob. "It's okay, no one thinks you set the fire in the woods," I murmured, keeping my voice soft.

"Except you," Luna pointed out.

I glared at her as Ignatius fluttered his wings and let out another wail. "You're not helping here, Luna. Besides, we checked the shop last night. There was no way he could have gotten out. All the doors and windows were locked up tight. The only way to leave the building is through your door or Gideon's. Granny had those runes installed so only you two could pass through them," I pointed out logically.

Luna narrowed her eyes at me, and her ears twitched rapidly back and forth as she considered my logic. "Fine. I'll admit you have a point," she finally allowed. Ignatius drew in a shaky breath but seemed to calm down now that he wasn't being actively accused of arson. Luna wrinkled her nose. "What are you going to do about the fires though? Word will spread about the fire in the shop, and someone will link the two. It's only a matter of time before they jump to the same conclusion I did and blame the fire-breathing dragon."

I felt Ignatius tense up and his tiny claws dug into the skin of my palms, not breaking the skin but definitely letting me know his time as a statue hadn't dulled his talons. I closed my eyes and ran through the options in my head. There weren't many good ones. If Ignatius was really that bad at controlling himself, it was only a matter of time before he set fire to something really important. Like a float during the Pumpkin Parade. Or Vivienne Silverthorne's hair. My stomach dropped right down to my toes as I envisioned the matriarch of Havenwood running around the town streets, flapping at her burning hair, her Silverthorne sprint forming the most horrendous end to the Harvest Festival ever. A blush of embarrassment burned my cheeks as I imagined all the accusing eyes in town turning towards me.

Luna interrupted my horrible day-mare. "Hello? Ears up, Harper. What are you going to do?"

I shook my head, letting out a little shudder as the image of Vivienne as a human torch faded from my mind's eye. "I've got to tell someone. Not Vivienne though. Maybe I could reach out to Lucas or Gabriel? I met them this morning. They seemed...less intense."

And less likely to eviscerate me for inadvertently loosing a dragon on the town than their mother. I didn't verbalize that last thought, though.

"The Silverthorne boys?" Luna shook her head. "Trust me, you don't want to do that."

"They aren't exactly boys, but why not?"

"When you're my age, everyone your age gets younger by the year. Besides, you *have* met their mother, right? Terrifying woman? Doesn't suffer fools? Actually, I have quite a lot of respect for Vivienne, but I doubt she'll look favorably on you in this instance."

"You're probably right," I admitted as the feeling of dread started to re-manifest in the pit of my stomach. Unable to contain myself, I began to pace.

Luna pointed a paw at me. "You've got to listen to me. Vivienne Silverthorne is a hard woman and doesn't tolerate people messing with her town. If she gets even a whiff you might be involved in something that could jeopardize Havenwood, she'll shut you down so fast it'll make a vampire running from the sun seem like a sloth on tranquilizers."

"Speaking of vampires, how does my lawyer hang out in the daytime without turning to ashes?" I asked, weeks of curiosity finally bubbling to the surface.

"Fluff and furballs, is that all you heard? Focus. *Vivienne.* Shutting down Spellbooks like she threatened to do at your grand re-opening. If she thinks you're ignoring the most important rule in Havenwood for a second time, things will end badly. That I can promise."

"But I'm not telling the world about the town's great secret that magic exists. Quite the opposite. I'm trying to stop the magical pranks before someone else spills the beans. Besides, I'd be talking to Lucas or Gabriel, not to her."

"It amounts to the same thing in my opinion, and I've lived here long enough that you should listen to what I am saying," Luna said, her back foot thumping a quick staccato rhythm.

I furrowed my brow, Luna's agitation finally breaking through my hastily made plans. "She might be upset, but you can't possibly be suggesting that Vivienne Silverthorne would hold me accountable for an overly excited dragon who was a statue only yesterday."

"Oh, she can, and she would. Trust me, that woman will make your life here in Havenwood a living nightmare if she thinks you're the one responsible for disrupting one of the biggest festivals of the year," Luna said seriously. "If she even lets you stay that is."

"But it was an accident!" I protested. "And he didn't have anything to do with the fire in the woods. Or the runaway pumpkins for that matter. Did you?" I lifted the dragon, so he was level with my eyes.

"Nuh-uh." Ignatius shook his head seriously.

Luna folded her front legs and tipped her head to the side in an impressive imitation of a not-angry-just-disappointed teacher. "Vivienne doesn't believe in accidents. Only incompetencies."

"Wow. Ouch," I said. Luna just shrugged in a manner that screamed *doubt-me-at-your-peril*. What that rabbit could communicate without words rivaled what she could say with them, which was impressive.

I sighed. "Okay, okay. I hear you. What do you suggest I do?"

"Find Agatha," Luna instantly. "She's the one who helped Beatrice with the stone spell last time. If you explain the situation to her, I'm sure she'll help you."

"That's actually a fantastic idea."

Luna's eyes narrowed. "Why do you sound so surprised?"

I didn't need a warning to avoid that verbal trap. Instead, I said, "I probably shouldn't re-open the shop, not until I take care of this."

"Agreed. You need to go see Agatha," Luna repeated.

"Okay, I hear you. It's been a while since I visited her place. The last time I went, it was with Granny Bea. I must've been, fourteen? Maybe fifteen. Any idea where she lives now?"

"Like most respectable witches apart from your great-grandmother, rest her soul, Agatha lives in the forest. Follow the mossy path until you reach a small hut."

I raised an eyebrow at the description. "Really? She moved out of town? I didn't know."

Luna thumped her back foot on the floor in irritation. "Yes, really. Last time I was there, there was a garden full of flowers and a small wishing well in the front, but Agatha embraces Havenwood's festivals with an almost unhealthy fervor, so I wouldn't be surprised if she redecorated to fit the Halloween theme."

"Well, do you have her number so I could check if she's home?"

"She doesn't really do phones and today, she's likely out playing mahjong with some of the other ladies from town. They rotate locations, so you'd probably be best to wait a few hours and then try her at home," Luna said.

"Great. Any other advice for surprising a witch in the middle of the forest?" I said dryly.

Luna tipped her head to the side. "Bring cookies. She's partial to snickerdoodles if I remember correctly. Oh, and take that winged lizard with you." The floorboards vibrated under my feet in a manner I took to mean Spellbooks agreed with her. Luna continued as she hopped off the counter. "I'm not about to get my fur charred or worse. Not after I've just been to the salon for a tint and trim."

Now I had more questions to add to my ever-growing list. Aside from my wonderings about vampires, how much time *did* Luna spend at the salon? More importantly, where could I get snickerdoodles?

Tricks and Talons

DESPITE EVERYTHING WEIGHING ON my mind, I decided to re-open the shop while I waited for Agatha to return home. Otherwise, I feared I would drive myself crazy in the meantime. I gave Ignatius a stern talking to about the expectation in Havenwood of keeping magic a secret. Then I made him a little nest behind the counter before flipping the sign to read 'Open' once more. It was a good decision too, because I sold a surprisingly respectable number of books. More than enough to give me hope I was getting the hang of this whole running-a-bookshop thing.

During the lulls in business, I took the opportunity to start the set-up of my new inventory management system and spent some time creating social media advertisements for events I wanted to host at Spellbooks.

It would've been a perfectly productive afternoon if not for Ignatius. I didn't want to let the dragon out of my sight in case there was another accidental book burning, but with all the tourists browsing the shelves, I couldn't let him roam the shop either. Ignatius napped contentedly for a couple of hours until a group of noisy children looking for the latest graphic novel woke him. He kept trying to poke his head up and look around at the bustling shop. In between customers, I attempted to convince him to stay safely hidden away, but his curiosity kept getting the better of him. I didn't have time to take him upstairs and wasn't sure I wanted to, anyway.

What would happen if he got lost in one of my books and set the bed on fire? My anxiety grew by the minute as I tried to think of a solution while I rang up a middle-aged couple.

I felt the tug of tiny claws on my jeans and froze. Both the woman I was helping and I looked down to see Ignatius' head pop over the counter. The dragon looked up at me, then turned to the woman and blinked. My heart raced, and my mouth went dry. How could I explain a dragon in a bookstore? How would the couple respond? Would they run away screaming? Post it on social media for the world to see? What if Ignatius set the place on fire again?

"Ooh! What a nice trick!" exclaimed the wife, surprising me.

"Very good," chortled the husband. "Animatronics, I assume? Did you trigger it manually, or is it on a motion sensor? Are we on camera?" he asked, craning his neck to find the supposed recording device.

I blew out a silent breath and smiled weakly at them. "Something like that." The answer seemed to satisfy the couple, and they moved off with their books in hand, chatting about the "robot" dragon.

Ignatius swiveled his head to look up at me and blinked hopefully. "Out now?" he asked.

I quickly weighed my options. Having him on the counter would make it easier to keep an eye on him and avoid any incendiary incidents. "Fine. We'll give it a test run. But you stay on the counter and look cute. No teeth, no flying, and absolutely no fire."

Ignatius nodded his little head rapidly. "Teeth, flying, fire," he echoed.

I held up a finger. "*No* teeth, flying, or fire. Can you do that?"

He clambered up the wooden counter and curled into a ball next to the cash register, pretending to go to sleep. Then he opened his eyes and blinked dramatically, winked and feigned going back to sleep. After the mini performance, he sprang up. "*No* teeth, flying, fire. Ignatius do," he said seriously, as he leaned back and drew a tiny 'x' over his chest with a single talon. The sincerity of the action surprised me into laughing. Ignatius kept his lips closed, but they curled into the broadest grin he could manage without putting his mouthful of teeth on display.

"Perfect," I said.

I don't know if it was the expectation of getting tricked this time of year or the Silverthorne spells woven around town, but the tourists loved the "clever animatronic dragon in the witchy bookstore." Other than comments on how cute he was, no one remarked on Ignatius' presence on my counter. Slowly, the tension in my shoulders released with every seemingly normal interaction with the customers. Ignatius appeared to love the attention from the customers and played up his cuteness factor. They all were delighted with the moving dragon and, to my great relief, not even one asked if he was real.

The flow of customers I'd grown accustomed to seemed to increase by the hour. I was busy for the rest of the day, helping people find the perfect book with subtle assistance from Spellbooks and ringing up sales while Ignatius startled clients with his cuteness. No one questioned the dragon's presence on my counter beyond asking how the robotics worked. I just smiled enigmatically whenever the question arose. Everyone knew real dragons were majestic creatures, soaring across the sky to mysterious realms and hording treasures in fantasy stories. They weren't the size of your hand, curled up on the counter in a bookshop in Connecticut. Not a chance.

By the time I closed Spellbooks for the evening, I was exhausted. But at least we'd avoided burning anything other than my energy. I really needed to eat more than a salad in the day to keep me going. I locked the door, flipped the sign to say 'Closed', and collapsed into one of the comfy arm-chairs I kept in the shop for browsers to peruse books before purchasing. Mr. Wigglesworth padded over and jumped into my lap, surprising me. The cat usually only moved himself if the angle of the sun shifted in his window or for food. I smiled and smoothed his fur with soft strokes as the sun sunk lower in the sky. Life in Spellbooks was like my dream come true. I closed my eyes to savor the moment.

Luna hopped up, ruining my peace. "Fluff and furballs, this isn't the time for sleep! You've got to find Agatha and figure out how to turn that adorable scaly menace back to stone before he fries us all in our sleep!"

I sighed; the moment effectively shattered by the rabbit's sharp tongue. "Yes, Luna. I'm on my way."

"Don't forget to take the dragon with you. I'm not a firefighter, you know, and calling Chief Flint is much too hard without thumbs," Luna said, waving her paws at me.

I dislodged the cat gently and grabbed my coat and purse, opening it wide for Ignatius. "Come on then, buddy. We're going on a field trip."

"Where?" Ignatius asked excitedly, settling himself in my bag.

"To find a witch in the woods. I just need to stop by the Enchanted Oasis first."

"Whatever for?" Luna demanded.

I winked at her. "Snickerdoodles."

Friendship and Flames

AFTER I LOCKED UP Spellbooks, I headed straight over to the B&B. When I walked through the door, Bella was sitting behind the front desk, idly scrolling through her phone. As soon as she saw me, she jumped up and ran over, wrapping me in a tight hug.

"I am *so* sorry!" she immediately exclaimed, her voice trembling. "I feel like it's all my fault. If I hadn't knocked that water over—"

I hugged her back, gently patting her shoulder. "Accidents happen, Bella. Besides, there's no way you could've known. What matters now is that we handle the situation as quickly as possible. Preferably without Vivienne Silverthorne finding out about Ignatius."

Bella pulled back, her face pale and eyes wide with worry. "I hadn't even thought about that."

I squeezed Bella's hand reassuringly. "Hey, we'll figure this out. We've faced worse, right? We'll just take it one step at a time. And remember, we're in this together."

Bella nodded, a bit of color returning to her cheeks. "Thanks, Harper. I don't know what I'd do without you."

"You don't have to worry about that," I said with a smile. "We're best friends. We've got each other's backs, no matter what. Even if life throws a dragon at us."

As if on cue, Ignatius, who had been hiding in my bag, poked his head out. He flapped his wings and perched on my shoulder, using his tiny talons to stabilize himself on my coat. Bella's eyes widened in surprise, and she let out a soft coo. "Oh my gosh, he's even more adorable in real life!"

I smiled; glad she was feeling a bit more at ease. "Yeah, he's pretty cute when he's not causing chaos."

Bella reached out gently, and Ignatius nuzzled her hand. "You've got a little troublemaker here, but he's a sweet one."

"Sweet," Ignatius agreed, his voice a bit garbled. "Like...honey...buzz buzz."

Bella giggled, clearly charmed. "He can talk?" she asked in surprise.

"Sort of," I said with a grin. "But all the teeth make it difficult I think."

Ignatius then did a little twirl and puffed out a small, harmless ring of smoke that floated up and gently dissipated. He looked up at Bella with big, innocent eyes and wiggled his tail.

"Oh my gosh, he's too precious!" Bella exclaimed, her face lighting up with delight.

We shared the brief, light-hearted moment as Ignatius showed off. However, it wasn't long before Bella's face clouded over again, and she started to spiral.

"But this is bad. They might think we're to blame for it all. I mean, if Vivienne thought we were responsible for all the pranks at the pumpkin farm, the candy shop, the forest, and the orchard, I don't know what she'd do!"

"Wait. What happened at the orchard?" I asked, concern creeping back into my voice.

"Didn't you hear? Someone pranked the trees in Bert's orchard and hid caramel apples among the real ones."

"At least that doesn't sound too bad," I said.

"It was, and it wasn't. Bert's orchard was packed, and everyone loved the idea of finding sweet treats among the trees. The guests that came back to the Oasis couldn't stop talking about the clever way to incorporate a trick and a treat at once. Although, they couldn't figure out how the sticks of the candy apples seemed to grow directly out of the trees. At least they were wrapped, or Bert might have had a real issue with bugs."

"At least there's that," I said weakly. If the human tourists were commenting on the inconsistencies of the locals' stories to explain away the pranks, how long would the obfuscation spells hold? Were the Silver-thorne's charms strong enough to withstand repeated, substantial doubt? I didn't know, but I hoped so. "Any news on who was responsible for the fire in the forest?" I asked.

Bella shook her head. "According to Papa, the fire department and police are stumped. Hopefully whoever is responsible for these pranks needs to chill out before someone gets hurt. Could you imagine what would've happened if it hadn't rained recently? The entire forest could've gone up!"

"I don't even want to think about it!" I exclaimed with a shudder. Spellbooks was way too close to the tree line for comfort if a fire were to happen. It's one thing to think about a quick evacuation of people or animals, but how do you save a living building? I kept the thought to myself, feeling a quick pang of loneliness and guilt for not being able to tell Bella the full truth about Spellbooks.

Bella blew out a breath, her eyes wide. "I never thought I'd say this but thank goodness it's been so rainy! I won't complain about thunderstorms ever again!"

"Now don't go making promises you know you can't keep." I grinned at her. "But speaking of the forest, do you have those cookies for Agatha I texted you about? It's getting dark, and I don't want to get lost in the woods."

Bella nodded and hurried back to the kitchen. She returned with a small tote bag filled with goodies. "Here you are. Mom packed up some extras for you just in case. She also threw in some leftovers from the breakfast buffet."

I looked inside at the white boxes in surprise. "These aren't leftovers! This is enough to feed a small nation. Or Mr. Wigglesworth for lunch."

Bella chuckled and pointed at the small box on top of the pile. "Mama made those snickerdoodles like you asked but also packed a sandwich for you. She said to remind you that you can't exist on sugar and coffee."

I peeked inside and saw a delicious-looking wrap. My stomach growled loudly at the sight, reminding me I'd forgotten to eat dinner and that the salad Finn had brought over had been hours ago. "Your mom is too good to me. What did she make this time?"

"Just some leftovers she threw together. A smoked turkey wrap with bacon, avocado, and some sun-dried tomatoes on a spinach tortilla."

"Your leftovers are better than my genuine attempt at cooking," I said, only half-joking. "What's in the rest of these?"

Bella pointed at one white box after another. "You've got some rocky road bars with homemade marshmallows. Those are in that tiny one on top. There are also some toffee and chocolate chip cookies. But, believe me, you haven't lived until you've tried them. The large box on the bottom has a half dozen of the caramel apples from Bert's farm. Some guests brought them back because there were just too many for them to eat."

I stared at the hefty tote bag and then up at my best friend. "Are you sure I'm not depriving you?"

Bella snorted. "Please. You're doing us a favor. Mama loves the fall and wants to try out some new recipes, but Papa won't let her until there's room in the kitchen. You're simultaneously saving me from parental squabbles and empty calories if you take these. Really. I swear."

"Well, if you insist. I promise to share them with the witch in the woods," I said.

"That's not how the story goes," Bella replied with a wink.

"Hopefully, it's how mine goes. Followed by a solution to my dragon problem. Wish me luck!" I said as I gently re-situated Ignatius back into my purse to keep him safely out of sight.

Bella waved as I walked out the door, carefully hoisting the tote onto my shoulder. Ignatius stuck his nose out of his hiding spot in my purse and sniffed loudly. "Chocolate?" His voice was hopeful.

I glanced around and then dug out the small box on top, flipping open the lid. I broke off a small piece of the rocky road bar and passed it to him. "Just don't get crumbs all over my bag, okay?" I said.

"Crumbs," Ignatius said, pronouncing the word carefully through his mouthful of teeth.

"No. No crumbs," I reminded him sternly.

"No crumbs," Ignatius promised.

I headed towards the woods, sharing the delicious treat with the tiny dragon as I went in search of a witch to help me stop him from accidentally burning down my shop. Or the forest. Or potentially the whole town.

Was this how everyone went trick or treating or was I just special?

The Witch in the Woods

It was dark by the time I stumbled down the mossy lane. The weak moonbeams trickling through the clouds weren't enough to illuminate the path clearly, so I used my phone's flashlight to avoid any disasters. Like falling on the boxes of goodies. I'd already eaten the wrap, sharing bites of it with Ignatius as I went, but with only the cookies and treats left, I felt a little like Little Red Riding Hood. At least there weren't any wolves near Havenwood. At least, not any regular wolves. I knew of a couple of werewolves in town, but the ones I knew were friendly folks. Even so, I jumped at every strange sound I heard in the forest.

The lane finally ended in front of a small cottage with smoke coming out of the chimney. Instead of the idyllic, sweet getaway Luna described, this cottage looked like it belonged in a fairy tale, but not the happily ever-after kind. The Grimm brothers' versions. One of the really creepy, twisted ones.

I shivered as I peered at the house. The wishing well was covered in spiderwebs. Glowing candles lit the windows of a dark, crooked little house that was nearly falling down. Dead and withered flowers decorated the overgrown garden. Scraggly branches scraped and clattered ominously as a chill wind blew through the tiny meadow, making me shiver. What had happened? The place looked like it had been abandoned years ago and left to rot. Did Agatha even still live here?

The door suddenly banged open, revealing a hunched silhouette in a tattered black robe. "Who dares intrude on this dark night?" The elderly female voice was shrill and commanding.

I almost turned around and ran right then. However, a hat I recognized appeared in the window next to the door. A distinctive red and purple hat and under it, a familiar face.

"Madame Fontaine?" I asked, surprised to see the fearless leader of my book club here, of all places.

"Harper Sullivan? Is that you?" The old lady hurried out the door and took a couple of steps down the path, peering into the darkness.

I turned the flashlight on my face. "Yes, it's me. I didn't know you lived out here," I said, assuming I'd taken a wrong turn somewhere.

Madame Fontaine waved a hand covered in chunky rings through the air. "Oh, I don't. I was just visiting my good friend Agatha here. I told her to expect more visitors, but she dismissed me." The old fortune teller turned her nose up and shook her head regretfully at the foolishness of the notion.

I let out a relieved sigh and walked closer, so I wouldn't have to raise my voice over the wind gusting through the skeletal branches. "I was trying to find her, but I thought I'd gotten lost. This isn't anything like the house Luna described."

The breeze sent the clouds scuttling across the moon, lighting the small clearing better as the first figure came out of the house to stand next to Madame Fontaine. The woman looked to be roughly the same age as the fortune teller, but her silver hair was a wild white cloud around her head, matching the witchy ambiance created by the tattered robes and her spooky abode. But in the darkness, it was hard to get a clear look at her face.

The woman waved at the house. "You mean all this? This is for the tourists, dearie. Decorations to scare the little ones just enough. It is the season after all," she said, flicking her wrist. The image before me wavered like a heat mirage. I gasped as the scene transformed into a beautiful garden and a perfect little house adorned with adorable, homey touches everywhere. Standing right before it was Aunty Agatha, beaming widely at me.

The image wavered again and popped back to the decrepit, creepy hut it was before. My jaw dropped. This magic was so much bigger than Agatha's small gift for brewing excellent tea that I remembered from my childhood. Had she been hiding her more powerful abilities all this time?

"Wow!" I breathed out the word without meaning to.

"Just a small illusion spell. It's easier than putting out real decorations at my age," Agatha chuckled.

"Well, you fooled me!" I exclaimed. "Can I come in or is something waiting to jump out at me?"

"See! I told you there would be guests arriving," Madame Fontaine said.

Agatha folded her arms and frowned. "Did you forget how to count, Charmaine? There's only one guest. If you want me to believe in your predictions, you're going to have to get it *all* right." She turned to me. "What brings you all the way out here, dearie?"

"I was hoping you could help me. I stumbled across an old ledger of my great-grandmother's and—"

"This sounds like a long story," Madame Fontaine interrupted me. "One that should be told indoors. Besides, I really should be on my way. I'll see you later for mahjong, Agatha?"

"Only if you want to lose again."

Madame Fontaine chuckled. "I believe the score is tied at the moment." She turned to me. "And I'll see you on Monday at the library for book club, won't I?"

"I wouldn't miss it."

"Fabulous. I'm off then! Rhys Bowen's latest cozy mystery won't read itself, you know. I can't wait to see what Lady Georgiana has gotten up to this time." Madame Fontaine strolled down the lane, leaving me alone with the witch in the woods.

Agatha considered me thoughtfully for a moment before spinning on her heel. "You'd better come in and tell me what this is all about then."

Ignatius popped his head out of my bag and made a little whimpering sound. I ran a fingertip along his scales. "I know, buddy. However, this is the only way to get some answers." I took a deep breath and followed her into the house.

I'd been expecting an interior as ramshackle as the exterior, despite Agatha's claims of illusion spells. However, the inside of her cottage was bright, cozy, and surprisingly roomy.

"Tea?" Agatha asked, waving a hand. A teapot floated out of the kitchen, followed by a little jug of milk and a bowl of sugar, giving me *Sword in the Stone* vibes from when young Arthur met Merlin. I stared in awe as they arranged themselves on the small round table while Agatha rummaged around for cups and saucers.

I finally remembered my manners. "Thank you. Oh, I brought you some cookies." I dug into my bag and handed her the correct box.

Agatha's eye lit upon the label. "These are from Honey, aren't they?"

"Yes. You're favorites. Snickerdoodles."

Agatha frowned and shoved the box back across the table. "I bet Luna told you that."

I furrowed my brow in surprise. "Yes. She said you loved them."

"I *hate* them. Ridiculous cookies if you ask me. Give me a good old chocolate chip any day. A brownie. A blondie. Sugar straight out of the bag. Anything but *snickerdoodles.*"

"Why would she tell me the opposite?" I asked, confused.

"I suspect she's getting back at me for bringing her a bunch of rhubarb instead of radishes before I went to visit my grandchildren two months ago, but I couldn't find radishes anywhere! How was I to know she hated rhubarb so much? Everyone loves rhubarb, don't they?"

I suppressed a chuckle and tucked the offending box back in my bag. "Well, it just so happens that I also brought some caramel apples, a few of Honey's delicious rocky road bars, and her secret recipe chocolate chip cookies." I pulled out the other boxes.

Agatha's eyes lit up. "Now *those* sound delicious." She snapped her fingers, and three plates sailed out of the kitchen to clatter onto the table in front of us. The boxes lifted out of my hands, and the treats floated out of them to settle onto our plates.

"There," said Agatha with a self-satisfied smile. "All set. Now tell me what's on your mind." She bit into a large cookie laden with an ample amount of chocolate chips, gesturing with it for me to get on with my explanation.

The floating dishes and the abrupt change in Agatha's demeanor startled me. I remembered her having a knack for brewing tea, but this, combined with the illusion spell on the house, seemed to operate on a level of magic far beyond that minor talent.

"I'm so confused," I blurted out. "These aren't minor spells or have to do with tea at all! This isn't how I remember your gift from when I was a child."

Agatha chuckled, waving her hand dismissively. "Oh, dear, most of these are just enchanted items I've accumulated or made with Bea over the years."

I nodded, the pieces falling into place. When I was a child, I thought Granny Bea's magical power was selecting the perfect book for the perfect person. It was only after I inherited the bookshop that I discovered that talent came from Spellbooks, and Granny's gift was amplifying the magic of those around her. I didn't know the ins and outs of how her gift worked, but it sounded plausible that she'd helped Agatha create enchanted items.

Agatha misinterpreted my silence and tried to explain. "It's like having a clapper light or a dishwasher, but with magic."

"Okay. But I'm not sure I get it," I said honestly.

"Do you need to build the dishwasher to know how to run it? Or personally wire the lights in your house before using a light switch?"

"Well, no, I suppose not," I allowed.

"The same premise applies to magic. Why stand up to turn on the lights or wash the dishes by hand when you can simply activate a spell someone more powerful has wrought? The rest of the magic is woven into the walls of this old house itself. It's not quite Spellbooks, but it's not far off either," she said with a wink.

I blinked, trying to process what she was saying. She knew about Spellbooks? As soon as I thought it, the answer was obvious. Of course she knew. She was Granny's best friend and had basically come right out and admitted it to me a time or two.

"So, you're not actually creating the spell, just triggering someone else's magic? Did you buy all these items?" I asked.

"Some, yes," she nodded. "I've picked up quite a few treasures at magical flea markets and the like. Others, I've enchanted myself through rituals, usually with the help of your dear Granny Bea. Her true gift lay in amplifying magic, you know. She had such a knack for enchantments and rituals as well. That's how Spellbooks came about in the first place.

But even she couldn't do anything super-powered without some help. She often needed an extra boost required for the bigger spells."

I leaned forward excitedly. I'd been dying to ask Agatha about Granny's real power. "So, she focused on amplifying magic in enchantments?"

"Exactly," Agatha replied. "She knew creativity and collaboration were her strengths and worked to stretch her limits where she could. She asked for help whenever she needed it. Her enchantments were always clever and well-crafted, even if they didn't have the flash and bang of some other magics. Most of the really clever things around this old place stem from one of Bea's ideas."

I nodded slowly, starting to understand. "So, it's not just your magic, but the magic you and Granny Bea wove into all of these items together."

"Exactly, although we didn't do all the work here. Some things, I just bought because I'm old, and I deserve the perks that come with living this long," Agatha said with a wink. "Now, tell me what brought you all the way out here at this time of night."

I recovered myself quickly. "Well, I was up in the attic searching for Halloween decorations, and I found something unusual." I dug into my bag, lifting out Ignatius as I talked. Agatha groaned as she saw him. "What's wrong? Should I not have brought him here?" I asked.

Agatha rolled her eyes and shook her head. "No, nothing like that. It's just that Charmaine was right. She said 'guests' and there are, in fact, two of you. There'll be no living with her now." She flicked her fingers, dismissing the comment. "Never mind that now. So, you dissolved the stone spell, and you want some help restoring it before Ignatius burns Spellbooks down in the middle of reading a Pratchett book?"

My mouth dropped open. "It was Rothfuss, but how did you—"

Agatha grinned, extending her hand towards Ignatius. He scrambled up her arm, curling up on her shoulder. "It isn't my first rodeo with this little troublemaker," she said. "Although I thought of some new spells to try since the last fiery outburst. Now, where did I put them?"

She flicked her fingers, and random papers covered in scribbles that might generously be called writing floated out of drawers, from behind curtains, and even from under the sofa. She glanced at them one by one as they floated in front of her face, finally snatching up a bright blue post-it from the middle of the line of fluttering paper.

"Ah ha! Jackpot! Yes, some good ideas here." She nodded as she examined the writing before finally looking up at me. "I'm happy to keep him here for a few days while I run my tests if that works for you. Much easier than trying to trek back and forth to town, don't you think? The only thing is, I'm leaving soon to go on a cruise with some friends. Sailing around the Caribbean and enjoying some sun, but I'm happy to have Ignatius stay here until I leave."

"That'd be great," I said and then hurriedly added, "If it's okay with both of you." I looked over at Ignatius. He grinned at me, his long tongue flicking out through his teeth, and nodded.

"Oh, we'll get along just fine," Agatha said.

Ignatius let out a happy rumble and rubbed his nose against her cheek. "Agatha friend."

"See?" the old witch said.

I let out a sigh of relief. "Thanks Aunty Agatha."

That was one problem off my plate. At least while Ignatius was here, there was no chance he could burn down my shop. Now all the town had to deal with was the fire-starting, pumpkin-rolling, caramel-apple-loving prankster.

Agatha's eyes sharpened. "Ignatius isn't the only reason you stopped by, is he?" she asked, reading my expression.

My shoulders slumped. "He is, and he isn't. There's someone pulling pranks in town. Magical pranks. Rolling pumpkins, making caramel apples grow out of trees, that type of thing. Apparently, there was even a small fire in the forest, just outside of town, but the fire department caught it before it spread. It's like someone took a 'how to wreak havoc magically' course and decided to use the Harvest Festival as a practical exam."

"That's not good at all," Agatha said, her face serious.

I nodded, my mind racing. "Yeah, it's causing quite a stir. Any idea who or what could be behind them?" I asked, hoping for some insight.

Agatha shook her head. "No clue. The number of pranks is troubling, though."

"Number? How about type? It's the fire in the forest that's really bothering me. If it had gotten out of control, who knows what could have happened? I mean, Spellbooks is close to the forest, and you live in the woods. Who knows what might have happened if it had gotten out of control? Thank goodness they caught it in time! It could've been so much worse than it was."

Agatha patted my hand. "Don't worry your head about me. I've got more fireproof wards up on this old place than you could shake a wand at."

"What about Spellbooks?" I asked.

Agatha lifted a shoulder. "I never asked Bea about her precautions with the shop, but you're right, whoever is behind this seems to be getting bolder."

"That's partially why I'm so worried. Do you have some insight or advice on how to handle this?" I asked.

Agatha nodded thoughtfully. "First, we need to keep an eye out for anything unusual. We'll get to the bottom of this, I'm sure."

"I just hope we figure out who's behind it before Vivienne Silverthorne finds out about Ignatius. Even though I'm pretty sure he wasn't to blame, who knows how she'll respond to a fire-breathing dragon in the local bookshop, even if he is a miniature one."

Agatha raised an eyebrow. "You're right. Vivienne won't be thrilled about her precious festival turning into a magical circus."

I nodded in agreement. "Nope, she's definitely not pleased. I overheard her talking with Lara Moonshadow, and she seemed... let's say, perturbed."

Agatha nodded knowingly. "I believe it. Just be thankful she's not after you again. Especially after that Spellbooks incident last month. I'd hate to see you get on her bad side. That girl can nurse a grudge."

I swallowed back a giggle at the stern Vivienne being called a girl. "That's why I'm here. I know Ignatius is innocent, but convincing the town might require more than just a cute dragon and my word."

"You may have a point," Agatha leaned back in her chair, her eyes flicking back and forth like she was running through potential scenarios in her head.

My thoughts started spinning out the possibilities. "What happens if none of your brilliant ideas work, and you leave on vacation? I can't watch him twenty-four seven. Leaving him alone in a sentient bookshop also seems like an extraordinarily bad idea."

"I agree. That is a problem."

I spoke slowly, not liking what I was about to say. "As much as I hate to say it, maybe we should reinstate the stone spell before you go. Just as a temporary fix until we figure out a more permanent solution."

Ignatius whined and hid his face under a wing. My heart wrenched. I didn't want to turn him to stone, but what choice did I have?

Agatha's face fell. "It's not that easy, I'm afraid. The ritual to turn a being to stone is understandably complex otherwise everyone would be doing it."

"Why can't these things ever be easy?"

"Because then it wouldn't be magic, dearie."

I sighed. She had a point. "Okay, tell me about this ritual. What do you need?"

Agatha settled back in her chair and started ticking items off on her fingers. "A carved pumpkin, a silver dagger, a piece of moonstone, some honey, salt, and moonlit dew collected under a full moon. A thimbleful should be enough for your needs."

"That seems oddly specific. How do you collect dew?" I asked.

"Slowly," Agatha said with a long-suffering sigh. She added another finger to those already marking my list. "Oh, and a candle infused with a drop of your blood."

I blinked in surprise. "Why *my* blood?"

Agatha frowned at me. "Because it's your mess. Your shop, your dragon, your responsibility. Besides, I'm too old to be chasing after all the supplies. My hips won't hold out, and the Silverthornes don't approve of me flying around town, regardless of the season. Doesn't mean I don't do it, of course. But even I know not to go poking at Vivienne when she's already on edge."

My eyebrows shot towards my hairline. I couldn't help it. This was the first time I'd heard of Agatha, or any other witch I knew, actually flying. My eyes flicked towards the broom neatly leaning behind the door. What would the obfuscation spells make Agatha look like to unsuspecting tourists? A very large bat? Some kind of drone?

"You, um, fly?" I said, trying to keep my voice casual and failing miserably.

"Yes." Agatha caught my shocked gaze and rolled her eyes. "Of course on the enchanted broom I picked up at the Witch's Bazaar, not that old thing. Really. What did you think? That I could just click my heels and my band of flying monkeys would appear?"

"I don't think that's what—"

Agatha snapped her fingers to regain my attention. "Focus! We have a job to do, and you'd better take notes, so you don't forget anything. Even a witch with the most innocuous magical gifts can prove quite powerful in a ritual, but it's far too easy for that power to go awry if one is unprepared or distracted. Have you ever performed a ritual before?"

I shook my head. I couldn't imagine what my dad would've thought of practicing magical rituals in the middle of an army base. However, knowing him, he probably would've sat next to me and made me do it again and again until I had it perfect. Then he would've told me to do it ten more times because there's no such thing as perfect. Only relentless discipline and unwavering dedication until a skill becomes so ingrained it's like second nature. Speaking of dedication, I pulled out a pen and my journal where I'd been making notes on the mystery of the prankster. I flipped to a new page and quickly entered the list of ritual items before they disappeared from my memory.

Agatha sighed and pursed her lips. "What was Beatrice thinking? She really should've trained you better. But I suppose you didn't have much time together, all things considered. Well, no time like the present and all that. Besides, I find most people flourish under pressure."

"What do you mean?" I asked.

"Well, given the nature of the ritual, you only have one chance to get it right, on Halloween. If you can't manage that, you'll have to figure out how to keep Ignatius from burning down the town until the next mystical power surge which won't be until the winter solstice."

"What! Why?" I demanded.

"Magical rituals are always governed by seemingly arbitrary rules. It's a rule." Agatha said, as she sipped serenely from her teacup.

When she didn't crack a smile, I sighed. "Fine. I'll gather all the things, and then you can show me how it's done."

Agatha raised an eyebrow, seemingly unimpressed by my newfound bravado. "Oh no, that's not how this works."

I crossed my arms. "Why not?"

Agatha started ticking off items on her fingers with a sly grin. "One, because, like I said, it's your dragon, not mine. Two, it's high time you learn how to do rituals. That's where a witch's real power lies, not just in whatever mystical talent your magic threw your way. Three, and this is the most crucial part, I'm embarking on a cruise in two days. You'll have to do this on your own or wait until I get back."

Panic started doing the cha-cha in my stomach, and I momentarily lost control of my tongue. "What?! Why? I mean, what happens if I mess it up, can't turn him back to stone, and he burns down the entire town just because he read something by Douglas Addams?"

Agatha chuckled. "I suggest you avoid unleashing the dragon's inner decorator. Besides, like I said, Vivienne can hold a grudge. Ever been on the wrong side of a resentful mage? It's like being stuck in a reality TV show directed by Shakespeare – full of drama, mistaken identities, and curses." She shook her head and closed her eyes. "So many curses."

"No," I said, my voice dropping to a whisper.

"I wouldn't want that either, so listen up!" Agatha leaned forward, beckoning me closer. "Ritual magic is unique to the caster. Each witch brings her own unique flair to a spell, by changing a word or swapping an item that feels right to her. However, as this is your first ritual, I'd suggest sticking to the tried-and-true recipe, or you could risk dire consequences that go far beyond a little bit of accidental fire damage."

"This really doesn't sound like something I should do unsupervised. Wouldn't it be better to find a witch to coach me? Especially this first time around? Kind of like driver's ed, but for magic?"

"Stuff and nonsense! I'm already helping you. What more do you need? Besides, there might be other witches in town, but I promise you, no one knows this ritual. Beatrice and I kept it very hush-hush."

My leg started jiggling of its own volition as I searched for a better solution. "Well, could you perhaps reschedule your vacation? You know, in the best interest of Havenwood?

Agatha chuckled wryly. "Young people, always looking for the easy way. If you really want to honor Beatrice's legacy, you need to step up. She might not have handed Spellbooks to you on a silver platter, but the shop chose you. Spellbooks doesn't trust just anyone. The fact that it picked you *means* something. Now, it's time to prove you're worthy of the responsibility it has bestowed upon you."

"Great," I said, the word jumping off my tongue before I could phrase my response more delicately.

Agatha's eyes sharpened. "I don't need any of your sass. I've got plenty of my own, thanks. Now, I'm going on my Caribbean cruise, and nothing is going to keep me from those beaches. I'm willing to help you with your ritual, but only if you're going to listen. Are you?"

I modified my tone to a more respectful decibel. "I'm listening," I said sincerely, turning the page so I had more space to write.

Agatha nodded her approval. "Fabulous. Now, you need to gather all the items and take them to a secluded location, preferably one that has very little chance of catching fire. Somewhere outside usually works best, I find. Draw a large circle with the salt, making sure there are no gaps. The circle will keep the magic in one place for the duration of the ritual but make it big enough that you won't scuff it accidentally. Even the smallest break in the ring will release the binding magic."

"Got it," I muttered, scribbling away furiously in my journal.

"Place the carved pumpkin in the middle of the circle but hold on to the top. Mix the honey and moonlit dew into a cup. This will anchor the spell. Place the cup and candle inside the pumpkin. Once you've prepared everything, prick your finger with the dagger and allow a drop of blood to fall on the moonstone. Your blood starts the ritual. Place the moonstone in the pumpkin and speak the spell loudly and clearly. It is important not to mumble." Her voice dropped to a mystical, echoing resonance. "By the light of the moon, in the depths of the night, I summon the powers to set things right. Ignatius, your sparks must cease. With this spell, I bring the town peace."

Quickly, I scribbled the spell into my journal. Agatha paused with her eyes closed, silence hanging heavily in the room. I wasn't sure if she was pausing for dramatic effect or had fallen asleep. When the moment stretched uncomfortably, I cleared my throat. "Umm, is that it?"

Agatha shook herself with a little snort and blinked at me. "No, not quite. As soon as Ignatius flies into the pumpkin, put the top on. Light the candle and, badabing, badaboom, he turns to stone."

I felt myself frown in confusion. "How am I supposed to light the pumpkin if the candle is inside?"

Agatha glared at me. "That's why I told you to *carve* it. It doesn't have to be pretty. Just something to hold the magic in and still give you access to the candle."

"What if it's raining? Or extra windy that day?" I asked, pointing out the most obvious problems I could see. I really didn't want this to go wrong, especially if there was no alternative but to wait until the winter solstice and hope nothing burned in the meantime.

Agatha's expression turned serious, her gaze piercing. "If there's one thing I've learned, it's that magic is a dance with the unpredictable. Rain or wind, you'll have to make it work or wait until I get back. If you don't complete the ritual on Halloween, you'll have to wait until the winter solstice."

"What should I do with Ignatius if that happens?" I asked, panic rising in me.

Agatha patted my hand. "I'll look after him until I leave, but if you don't complete the ritual, Ignatius will be in your charge. Think of it like a pass or fail exam. I always thought those were easier anyways."

I gulped, the weight of responsibility settling heavily on my shoulders. As I left Agatha's, her instructions echoed in my mind. The night felt colder, the shadows more ominous, as I hurried back to Spellbooks. My mind raced through the possibilities. I couldn't help but picture myself in the middle of a magical circus act, desperately trying to pull off the dragon-stopping ritual amidst the chaos of weather and hiding the ritual from the prying eyes of Vivienne Silverthorne. Could I walk this tightrope without falling?

The Zombie Shuffle

As Bella and I walked towards Finn's apartment the next evening, I turned my collar up against the chilly wind. Apparently, there'd been a problem with the oven at Alex's place, and Finn had kindly offered his home for pizza making. I was thankful it was a relatively short walk from Spellbooks; otherwise, I might've insisted Bella drive us over to Finn's place, given the chilly weather. Secretly, I was glad at the change of plans because I was excited to see his apartment. We had always met in public spaces, and I always felt a person's home said so much about them.

My mind wandered back to Alex and how little I knew about Bella's ex. I felt a sudden pang of disappointment as I realized I wouldn't get a chance to snoop around his place tonight in the hopes of discovering a little more about him. For no good reason, I didn't trust him. Maybe it was general paranoia, or maybe it was because he was new, but something about him just didn't sit right with me. I'd even put him on my list of persons of interest. Maybe I was just hoping to find some reason for my distrust, but maybe there was something more to it than that. My gut was telling me—

"She wants you to do what?" Bella asked, interrupting my thoughts and pulling me back to the present. We'd been discussing my visit to Agatha and her advice on how to deal with my dragon/fire problem.

"Complete my first ritual on my own with little more guidance than a shopping list and the words to say."

"That seems a little irresponsible. Why can't she do it?"

"She's going on a cruise and the ritual has to be done on Halloween. But she said she'd watch Ignatius for me until she left. Then, I'm on my own."

"And you're sure you can't ask another witch for help?"

"I don't make the rules," I said with a shrug. "Besides, I don't know any other witches in town. You know how it is here. Volunteering information about yourself is fine. Asking someone else about their gifts is not."

"Why is magic never easy?" Bella asked, echoing my thoughts from earlier. "Whatever happened to waving a wand and everything just magically fixing itself?"

"Apparently, that never works out."

"Depends on what kind of stories you're talking about. Princesses on the big screen? Always. Grimm brothers? Never, with a ninety-eight percent chance of gruesome death."

I hitched the collar of my jacket up higher as a stiff wind gusted down Arcadia Avenue. "Let's hope that I can pull off my first ritual without making a mess of it."

"Well, I'm cheering for you if that helps. What do you need to complete the ritual?"

I rattled off the list as best I could from memory. "Honey and salt are easy enough," I said as I finished.

"The pumpkin should be too. You could use yours, and there were plenty left over after the carving competition at Moonshadow Farm. What about this moonlit dew?" Bella asked.

"I checked out the lunar cycles, and it's a good thing I did because the full moon is tomorrow. Can you imagine if I missed it? The whole ritual would be ruined before it even started, and we'd have to wait until the winter solstice."

"Lucky you. Maybe doubly lucky," Bella said, shooting me a sly glance. "You, the moonlight, a little magic? Sounds like the perfect time to invite a certain druid out for a midnight picnic." She nudged me with her elbow and winked.

I chuckled and shook my head. "I told you, we're taking things slow. I like him and am enjoying his company, but I don't want to rush into anything. Especially with the guy next door. Can you imagine what might happen if things didn't work out?"

"Can you imagine what could happen if they do? C'mon! Live a little. Ask the cute guy out for some one-on-one time. What's the worst that could happen?"

"Something with fire-breathing dragons springs to mind," I said dryly.

"You're looking for excuses to avoid him when you should be looking for excuses *to see him*. Besides, you said it yourself. Aside from gathering all the things on your list, nothing can be done until Halloween. You have to get the dew anyway. Why not multitask?" Bella cajoled. Her smile went a bit wicked. "After you finish collecting your ingredients, I bet Finn would be up for some Halloween treats," she said with a wink.

I rolled my eyes and bumped her with my shoulder. "You're incorrigible."

"No, *encourage*-able. Mostly, *encouraging* you to go out with the handsome man who is totally into you," Bella said as we walked up the steps of Finn's building. Through the ground-floor window, I could see Alex standing in the kitchen, chopping tomatoes on the island as Finn tossed a salad. Alex must've said something funny, because Finn threw his head back and laughed. Butterflies sprang to life in my stomach as I watched his face light with joy. I bit my lip. Finn was good fun and, if I was being honest with myself, I wanted to be more than friends. So why was I pumping the brakes?

"Speaking of 'just friends,'" I said, deciding to avoid addressing the issue of Finn by turning the tables on Bella. "What's going on with you and Alex?"

Bella blushed slightly, clearly caught off guard. "Oh, nothing. We're just friends, really."

"Uh-huh," I said with a knowing smile.

Bella balled up her fist and knocked on the door, interrupting my thoughts. I saw Finn start towards us. Bella spoke out of the side of her mouth in a rush. "Just so you know, you should ask him out, or I'm totally setting up another double date."

"Bella!" The door swung open as I hissed her name. We both straightened up quickly, trying to look casual and composed.

She turned up the full wattage of her smile. "And Harper! We brought wine. Oh, something smells delicious," she said. Finn greeted us with a warm smile, making it even harder for me to hide my feelings. Bella gave Finn a perfunctory hug and breezed into the kitchen, her nose leading the way.

His smile broadened as he ushered me into his cozy apartment. It wasn't the change in temperature or the comforting smell of cooking pizza that chased away the autumn chill. It was the warmth in his eyes as he wrapped me in a longer, tighter hug than he'd given Bella. "I've been looking forward to this all day," he said, speaking softly for my ears only.

"Hey you two! The pizza's ready!" Alex called.

Finn took my hand and escorted me towards the kitchen. I felt a flutter of excitement and nervousness at being in his apartment for the first time. As we walked through, I couldn't help but admire how well-furnished it was for a single man. The rooms seemed to flow seamlessly, with tasteful accents that complemented the warm tones of the natural wood. Someone with a good eye for color had clearly influenced the decor.

A part of me wondered if it had been an ex-girlfriend. A brief flare of jealousy shot through me. I blinked in surprise. I didn't have any right to feel jealous. We all had a past, didn't we? But the thought of another woman holding Finn's hand and sitting at the round kitchen table with him over wine and pizza raised feelings I hadn't realized ran so deep. Maybe Bella was right. I should ask him out. If not for a moonlight ritual hunt, for something else. Something more fun. Something...

"Dinner is served!" Alex said with a flourish, sliding two crispy, thin-crust pizzas onto the table. Bella carefully added four glasses with generous pours of wine to each place setting. A large, colorful salad balanced out the meal.

"Wow! You went all out," I said, my mouth watering at the delicious smell of oregano and pepperoni mixing with the rich scent of tomato sauce and slightly bubbling cheese. We quickly settled around the table as Alex explained his culinary offerings.

"Nothing but the best for you ladies. Now here, we have a trattoria amore. I wanted to do a true testament to the classic flavors of Italy. Thin crust with a slow-simmered tomato sauce, topped with a creamy mozzarella di bufala, some thinly sliced prosciutto di Parma, fresh basil and a hint of black pepper. The second pizza is what I like to call a Mediterranean Sunset. The dough has a hint of rosemary to compliment the sun-dried tomato pesto. On top are roasted red peppers, caramelized onions, Kalamata olives, and a mix of feta and Parmigiano-Reggiano. Oh, and some fresh arugula brushed with a lemon vinaigrette for my own special twist."

"I am so glad you came back from Italy," Finn said sincerely, passing me a slice of each.

"Me too," Bella said as she reached over and squeezed Alex's hand. He looked slightly dazed in the face of her brilliant smile but recovered himself quickly.

I gave Bella a knowing look, raising an eyebrow and smirking slightly. "*Just friends?*" I mouthed.

She caught my eye and winked back; her expression mischievous. The slight, unrepentant shrug of one shoulder spoke volumes without her needing to say a word.

The guys were completely oblivious to our silent exchange. Alex continued explaining his dishes, and I did my best to focus on the meal.

"This is my Tuscan Harvest Salad. The base is baby spinach leaves, topped with heirloom cherry tomatoes, some ribbons of prosciutto, shavings of Parmesan cheese, and toasted pine nuts. The dressing is a blend of olive oil I brought back from Italy, aged balsamic vinegar, and a touch of honey."

"Make sure you save any leftovers of that honey for Harper," Bella said as Alex served the salad for everyone. I scooped up a large forkful. The contrasting flavors danced in harmony across my tongue, and I almost sighed in pleasure. I'd definitely be asking for seconds.

"Oh? Are you planning on taking up baking?" Finn asked me, curiously.

I swallowed quickly and chuckled. "Not with Bella's mom around. I'd be too embarrassed! No, it has to do with a ritual."

Alex perked up. "Ritual? What kind of ritual?"

"Umm, nothing?" I said, shooting Bella a desperate look. Maybe my suspicion of Alex was paranoia, but then again, maybe it wasn't, but I should've watched my words! I didn't know how much I should trust him.

Bella sensed my hesitation and jumped in. "Harper had a little run-in with Vivienne during her grand re-opening event. Some magic went haywire, and a tourist or two might've noticed. If it hadn't been for Harper's quick thinking, the whole thing could've ended really badly. But now, she's understandably shy about the m-word."

I grimaced. Bella had misinterpreted my hesitation and shared more than I would've. Besides, she was dramatically under reporting what had happened. Alex looked interested and leaned in excitedly.

Before he could ask a question, Bella waved her hand. "Anyway, that's a long story for another time. But Harper's trying to toe the line. You know? Keep her nose clean."

"And not spill the beans on Havenwood's secret magic population. I get it," Alex said with an understanding nod. He shot his eyes back to me. "Look, I won't ask you about your powers, but I have some of my own that I don't usually like to talk about. Mostly because they don't do anything special."

"I wouldn't say that," Bella protested.

"I'm not sure predicting the weather is a fantastic magical gift. Unless I wanted to go into meteorology. Besides, I can only tell you what the weather will be, not influence it at all," Alex said with a rueful shake of his head.

"At least we'll know if we need an umbrella with you around," Bella said.

"And you make a mean pizza." Finn lifted his slice for emphasis. A chuckle rolled around the table.

Even with Alex's confession, I wasn't sure I trusted him enough to get into the entire story about Ignatius' appearance. Maybe I shouldn't have said anything. I didn't want to get into my powers, but I definitely didn't want word spreading back to the Silverthornes about Ignatius, especially with the fire that had been set in the woods. It might've been that Alex was still a relatively new acquaintance, despite his history with Bella, or maybe it was just my suspicion talking, but something in my gut told me I shouldn't share everything. Especially since I already considered him a person of interest in the pranks around town and had discovered nothing to dissuade me from that notion.

Looking at Alex's expectant face, it was too late to avoid the topic completely. I sighed, opting for a dodge. I quickly recounted my visit with Agatha, but omitted the reason for the ritual. While I admitted to being a witch, I glossed over my gifts. I didn't like people knowing that I could open any lock I wanted.

Finally, I ended with the list of ingredients. "I think I've figured out most of them, but where am I going to find a silver dagger or moonstone?

And how do I infuse a candle with my blood?" I took a moment to steal a bite of the Mediterranean pizza. I had to hand it to him. He might still be a suspect, but Alex really knew his way around flavors.

Finn's eyes lit up. "Oh! I can help with that!" He pulled his phone out of his pocket and tapped on the screen a few times before passing it over to me. "Look at the library's event on Sunday."

I zoomed in on the orange and black schedule decorated with smiling spiders and grinning ghosts. "Is this for real?" I asked.

"Is what for real?" Bella managed around a mouthful of pizza.

"The library is hosting an educational event of historic New England, including candle making?" I read from the flyer.

Bella groaned and smacked the heel of her hand against her head. "I totally forgot about that. Martha Morningstar is a history buff, as you might imagine a librarian to be. Every year, the library hosts the colonial costume parade, takes tourists on haunted historic tours, provides colonial games and crafts for the kids, that type of thing. Candle dipping is one of their big draws. Not my favorite because it means I lose out on time I could be spending in the food stalls. Why anyone would want to repeatedly dip a string in hot wax when they could be eating lobster rolls and apple cider doughnuts is beyond me."

"Why anyone would want to eat anything other than this pizza is beyond me," I said. "Alex, you have a gift." Our chef for the evening performed a little bow from his chair to a round of applause.

"And we're happy to take advantage of your talents anytime you choose to share them," Finn chimed in, raising his wine glass.

"Cheers to that." I raised my own wine, and the four of us clinked our glasses together.

"You know, we should make this a—hold on. What's that?" Bella exclaimed, peering out the window.

I turned around and glanced outside to see a crowd of people on the street. Most wore glowing necklaces or bracelets, illuminating disfigured faces and ragged clothing. My jaw dropped open, and I pointed. "What's going on?"

Finn glanced over his shoulder and shrugged. "It's the Zombie Shuffle. Some people put a lot of effort into their costumes for the race." He glanced at the time. "Hmm, that's strange. They usually finish a little earlier and head to the town square."

Alex waved at the window. "I don't think it's the race. Look! They're all moving in unison."

"Maybe it's some kind of flash mob?" I ventured.

"It'd be a shame for their performance to go to waste," Finn said, standing and heading towards the window facing the street.

As the four of us watched the costumed runners shamble along, their movements seemed familiar somehow. "Wait. No. Is that...the Thriller dance?" I asked.

Alex snapped his fingers. "It is! This is hilarious! What a great idea to promote Harvest Fest. I just wish someone had told me. I totally would've joined in."

"Or filmed it," Finn added, pulling out his phone to do just that.

Bella lowered Finn's phone before he could start filming and pointed at the two figures running up behind the crowd of dancing zombies. Lucas and Gabriel Silverthorne looked concerned as they drew even with the crowd. "I don't think this is a promotional gimmick," she said, as Lucas started weaving his fingers through the air in complex patterns. Gabriel spun around, searching the darkness for...something.

Or someone.

Lucas broke his hands apart sharply, and the zombie runners halted their dance mid-step. Gabriel strode forward, waving his arms to gather everyone's attention. I couldn't hear what he was saying, but the looks of confusion on the runners' faces melted into relief. Many of them pulled out cellphones as they drifted off in different directions. I closed my eyes and groaned to myself. Normally zombies dancing to Michael Jackson would've been the highlight of my day, but not when they were obviously enchanted by some magical mischief maker.

Finn blew out a breath, reading my thoughts. "So, not a flash mob then. It looks like the prankster strikes again."

"Whoa. That's a bold move. Charming that many people at the same time is no small feat of magic," Bella said.

"What do you think their endgame is?" Alex asked. "Is it just Halloween mischief or is there something more?"

"I don't know, but I wouldn't want to be on the wrong side of Lucas and Gabriel," Finn said, pointing out the window at the two brothers. They looked livid and on edge as they searched the dispersing crowd for any hints of the perpetrators. "I hope they catch this guy before these pranks cause problems for all of us."

"Yeah, and soon," Bella added.

The Silverthornes finished their futile inspection of the street, and Lucas' gaze snagged on us in the window. He raised a hand in a grim, silent greeting.

I flinched, instinctively wanting to duck. The last thing I needed was to be seen at yet another 'scene of the crime.' But it was too late to avoid detection, so I returned the gesture with the others, even as my stomach sank. Was I just drawing more unwanted Silverthorne attention? I hoped not. Maybe Lucas would understand that I apparently had a penchant for being in the wrong place at the wrong time. I wondered if he kept a person of interest list like I did. If so, there was a fairly good chance I was on it.

My hand trembled slightly, and I sipped my wine to cover my nervous reaction as I watched the Silverthorne brothers continue their search for the person responsible for the magical pranks. I doubted they would catch the prankster tonight. Whoever was behind the Halloween havoc was proving to be a sneaky opponent with a weird sense of humor. I couldn't fault their taste in music, though.

Was there a way I could turn that to my advantage somehow? I pondered the possibilities throughout the rest of the evening, but somehow, I doubted playing MJ on a boombox held over my head would Pied-Piper the pranksters out of hiding.

However, I filed the idea away as a last resort.

What You Need

ALEX ACCOMPANIED BELLA BACK to the Oasis while Finn walked me back to Spellbooks. He held my hand as we strolled through the crisp October evening. I took comfort in the warmth of his touch and the solace of his calming presence, but my mind was racing faster than any zombie had ever run down the streets of Havenwood.

Finn cleared his throat. I blinked, realizing he'd said something, and I'd missed it entirely. "Sorry, what did you say?"

"I asked how you liked the pizza, but it seems like you've got something else on your mind. Want to talk about it?"

"Yes. No. I don't know." I blew out a breath.

"You seem conflicted," he said with a chuckle.

I ran my free hand through my hair. "It's complicated." We walked a few more paces in silence as Finn let me sort out my thoughts. I'd lived my whole life keeping my magic under wraps. Advertising that you had a paranormal control over metal, no matter how small, wasn't a great idea on a military base. So, I tucked that part of me away and only brought it out on very rare occasions when I was one hundred percent sure I was alone. But it was different in Havenwood. Magic was not only accepted here, but it was also celebrated. At least, away from the eyes and cameras of tourists. However, old habits were hard to shake. I hadn't told Finn much about my powers and definitely not that Spellbooks was sentient. So how would he react to the news that I had a fire-breathing dragon to manage on top of all the ruckus going on around town?

As if he could read my mind, Finn asked, "This is about the pranks, isn't it?"

I shrugged a shoulder, not really sure how to communicate everything going on in my mind.

Finn nodded, as if he didn't need me to say the words. "They're getting to me too. I moved to Havenwood to get away from all the drama that comes with magical powers. It might not be for everyone, but I like the small-town life. I'll leave the epic adventuring to others while I grab my morning coffee and a blueberry scone from Pixie Pastries, thanks very much."

"Don't let Bella's mom hear you say that," I warned, only half joking.

Finn chuckled and squeezed my hand. "Let's just say I have everything I want right here. But if these pranks continue, I don't know what it'll do to the balance in Havenwood."

"What do you mean?"

Finn shrugged. "Magic is like anything else. It runs out eventually, even for mages as powerful as the Silverthornes. If these pranks keep pulling power from the obfuscation spells, they will break. Maybe not today or tomorrow, but soon. That's why Gabriel and Lucas keep running around town to charge them up, but they're only human. They have to sleep sometime. What happens when the magic powering their protection spells peters out?"

"People get more tricks than they bargained for this Halloween?" I ventured, but it sounded lame, even to my ears.

Finn shook his head. "Beyond that. What happens when someone catches Agatha flying around on her broomstick? Or Martha flying full stop?"

I frowned. Martha, the librarian, could fly? What *was* she?

Before I could ask, Finn continued, "The pixies at the pastry shop won't be able to pass their ears off as prosthetics or their wings as intricate tattoos. Mark my words, if the charms fail, video evidence of who and what lives in Havenwood is going to leak out, and then this won't be a haven for our kind anymore."

The potential repercussions of the pranks crashed home. This wasn't just about dodging Vivienne Silverthorne's wrath. All the mundane magic users here could be in serious trouble if they lost their sanctuary and hordes of tourists, not to mention news vans, descended. Where else in this world could people like Grimgor or Thistle find a peaceful home without being constantly badgered or hunted down? Not to mention the ripple effects! Disclosing the supernatural world actually existed would be catastrophic for all paranormals. Sure, it worked here in Havenwood. Magical creatures lived alongside normal humans, more or less in harmony. I had my doubts that would be the case if more powerful paranormals were shoved into the spotlight, front and center on the world stage.

"We have to figure it out!" I blurted out.

Finn looked over at me, his brow furrowed. "Come again?"

"The pranks? We have to solve it. Figure out who's behind the pranks and stop them before they ruin Havenwood for us all." My breath came short and fast. All I could see were phantom video cameras and eager journalists swarming Havenwood in search of the career-making scoop that magic really did exist, and it was right here in our own backyard.

"I agree, but I don't think you see the full picture here," Finn said, his voice low.

"What do you mean?" I asked, feeling the nervous energy that usually preceded my fight-or-flight response bubble inside me.

"Do you think the Silverthornes will let it get that far? When they feel the wards weaken to that point, they could start banishing anyone who might be responsible," Finn said grimly.

I shuddered at the thought. "Anyone? What about people like Grimgor or Thistle? They wouldn't be able to live out there in the real world. Not without avoiding people altogether or sticking out like a sore thumb. And what about people like Bella and her family? This is their home."

"And what is that worth when measured against the safety of everyone else in Havenwood?"

I opened my mouth and then shut it again with a snap. His words sounded harsh, but he was right. One person could endanger this sanctuary for everyone. Banishment might be the only way to protect Havenwood in that case.

"Would they do that to someone who was innocent? The people who call this place home? They don't deserve to lose their sanctuary," I said, my voice trembling with emotion. I didn't voice it, but what I really wanted to say was that I didn't want to lose my sanctuary, either.

Finn's expression softened slightly, but his tone remained serious. "I don't think they take banishment lightly, but they'll be looking for a way to shut this pranking nonsense down quickly."

"Like what?" I asked, feeling the nervous energy swell and crest like an impending emotional tsunami.

"Well, if it were me, I'd look at people who might possess the type of magic to pull off these pranks. Or those who've been present at most of the events."

"But that's nearly half the town, isn't it? Between the pumpkin patch, the orchard, the candy shop, and the race, there must be a ton of people who've been at most or all of those events, right?"

"Including us," Finn said softly, gripping my hand and turning me to face him. "Harper, we've been present at nearly every prank scene. There's a very real possibility they might consider us suspects too."

The idea of being banished or possibly even worse by the Silverthornes made my stomach churn, and I felt like I was about to vomit. I'd worked so hard since I arrived in Havenwood to put down roots, to make this place my home. To be banished now? The thought was inconceivable, and a knot of dread tightened in my chest. "We have to stop this," I said, my voice steadying as determination took over. "We can't let one prankster ruin everything Havenwood stands for."

Finn nodded seriously. "I agree with you. The pranks need to stop, but I think we should probably leave it to the Silverthornes. You saw the Zombie Shuffle tonight. That type of enchantment takes powerful magic. I don't think either of us should deliberately go hunting this prankster down. Leave the pumpkins, the candy, and the fire to the Silverthornes."

"You heard about that? The fire in the woods, I mean?"

Finn chuckled wryly. "This is a small town, and it was supposed to be a secret. So, naturally everyone's talking about it."

My heart plummeted. I had a secret of my own. Ignatius. How long would it take before people started whispering about him? Would harboring a dragon who winked at customers be cause for banishment in the eyes of the Silverthornes?

Finn squeezed my hand. "Harper? Are you okay? You look like you've seen a ghost."

"Ha!" The laugh burst out of my mouth, expelled on the nervous energy and worry about Ignatius.

"You can tell me, you know. Whatever it is that's bothering you?"

The genuine concern and warmth in his eyes had me talking before I realized it. Once I started, it seemed like I couldn't stop. In a rush, I told him everything that I'd been holding back. From the dragon, to accidentally dissolving the stone spell, to the visit to Agatha and the real reason behind my sudden interest in rituals. "So, you see, I'm to blame. It's all my fault. And now, if I don't successfully turn him back to stone, Ignatius is going to start more fires. With my luck, the wrong tourist will see him and Havenwood won't be safe for our kind anymore," I said in conclusion.

To my dismay, I felt my lower lip quiver and tears burned in my eyes, making the world go blurry. I tried to turn away, but Finn tugged my hand, pulling me into him. I gave in and let the tears fall as I buried my face in his shoulder. "This was starting to feel like home. Somewhere I could really put down roots. And now, I've ruined it all!" I gasped out through the uncontrollable sobs wracking my body.

Finn's arms wrapped tightly around me, and he murmured comforting shushing noises into my hair. I'm not sure how long he held me, but by the time my tears ran out, my fingertips were going numb, and my coat wasn't thick enough to keep the rest of me warm in the cool night air.

I pushed away, hurriedly brushing away the last of my tears with the back of my hand. "Sorry. This isn't what you need right now."

Finn smiled warmly down at me. He ran the pad of his thumb across my cheekbone, flicking one last tear into the night. Then he leaned down and kissed me. It was gentle and sweet and over too quickly for my liking. I looked up at him in surprise. "You're wrong," he said, his voice coming out a little huskily. "This is exactly where I need to be."

My knees went weak. I wasn't sure if it was from the look in his eyes, the kiss, or the relief that washed over me. Maybe all three. Finn tucked my hand between his two large ones and blew gently on my cold fingertips, warming them up. He repeated the gesture with my other hand.

"There. That's better," he said with a smile. "Now, what's the plan and how can I help?"

"Plan?" I repeated, somewhat dazed by the seemingly abrupt change in conversation.

Finn chuckled. "We may not have known each other very long, but I do know you well enough to guess that you already have a plan in place. What do you need?"

I hesitated, then decided to take a leap. "Well, I put together a suspect list," I admitted, feeling a bit embarrassed. "I've been trying to figure out who might be behind all of this.

Finn raised an eyebrow. "A suspect list, huh? That's very... thorough of you. Do you moonlight as a detective in your spare time?"

I blushed and looked away. "Only once. When my granny's rare books were stolen. I even considered you a suspect then, but only briefly," I said, looking up at him from under my lashes to gauge his response.

He put a finger under my chin and gently raised my face, so I was looking him squarely in the eye. To my amazement, he looked more... amused than anything else. "Given the circumstances, I might've suspected me if I'd been in your shoes. Don't worry about it. That's all behind us. Now, we need to figure this out by working together. But first, let's focus on the ritual and Ignatius. We can deal with the rest later."

"You won't tell the Silverthornes about him, will you? Ignatius? The dragon in my shop?" I asked in a rush, unable to stop myself.

Finn stroked my cheek with his thumb and shook his head. "Not if there's a better option. Besides, if Agatha says this ritual is the best way to turn him back, then that's what we'll do. We'll handle the dragon and leave the Silverthornes to deal with the shenanigans." Reluctantly, he dropped his hand from my face and set his shoulders. "Now, what do you need me to do?"

I smiled up at him, feeling a weight I hadn't realized I'd been carrying slide off my shoulders. "First, I need to collect all the things for the ritual."

"*We* need to collect them. You're not alone, remember," Finn said, weaving his fingers through mine once again.

"Okay, we need to collect them. The biggest priority is the moonlit dew. Agatha said it needs to be collected under the light of a full moon which, according to Google, is tomorrow."

"That's lucky. You could've had to wait almost a month for a full moon," Finn said.

"Yeah. Something had to go our way."

"How much do you need?" Finn asked.

"Agatha said we needed a thimbleful. However, I'd rather be over-prepared. I don't want the ritual failing because I didn't get enough of each ingredient."

"*We,*" Finn corrected with another gentle squeeze of my hand. "Sounds like an adventure. I've never been dew-harvesting before."

I laughed. "It doesn't sound all that exciting, if I'm being honest. When does dew even form? How much can you get at a time? A drop?"

"More like a droplet."

I groaned. "This is going to take all night, isn't it?"

"I can't think of better company for my first dew-hunting expedition. You bring something to collect the dew. I'll bring the snacks."

I peeked at him from under my lashes again. "Snacks?"

"Well, this *is* a date, isn't it? Good dates always have snacks. Great dates have moonlit picnics. At least in my experience."

My heart did a little fluttery dance. Maybe this wouldn't be so terrible after all.

Trouble in the Winds

THE NEXT DAY, THE shop was even more crowded as word of the animatronic dragon had spread. I had to make up an excuse about circuits not working properly in the tiny "robot" and having to send him out for tech support. Most people bought it and then bought some books as well. I was surprised when I looked up and realized it was already six o'clock. Somehow, the day had flown by, and I'd completely forgotten to eat lunch, which was a rarity for me.

Finn should be closing Wildwood Ink soon. We'd agreed to meet up and then walk over to one of the town's parks after work. According to Finn, the dew should settle on the vegetation sometime around eight. I took his word for it. He was a druid, after all. If anyone would know about nature stuff, it was him. My stomach rumbled. Eight o'clock meant there was plenty of time to enjoy his company and some snacks before getting to work collecting ritual ingredients. I won't lie; the snacks almost took top priority. Almost.

Luna thumped her back leg, sending an irritated staccato pattern echoing through the empty shop and interrupting my thoughts. "Fluff and furballs! I can't believe you're leaving me alone at a time like this!" the rabbit exclaimed, her whiskers twitching wildly.

I rolled my eyes but was careful to do so when she couldn't see me. "For the third time Luna, you aren't alone. There's Mr. Wigglesworth—"

"Hardly a viable protector in the face of a prankster on the loose, let alone a companion. He barely qualifies for a half-tolerated roommate."

"—and Gideon," I continued. "Not to mention Thistle is just outside, and Spellbooks will always be around." I patted the wall of the shop and felt a small vibration under my fingertips.

"Radish ruckus! Have you heard what those scallywags did today? Broomsticks were flying down Hocus Pocus Lane. By themselves! The Silverthorne boys finally caught them all, but not before they flew all the way over to Cauldron Circle."

"Wow. That's almost half the town," I murmured. I rummaged in my purse and pulled out my journal, adding the new prank to my list. I frowned at my scribbles. The pranks started at the pumpkin patch, then went to the orchard, candy store, Zombie Shuffle, and now broomsticks. Not to mention the two fires. On second thought, I crossed the fire in Spellbooks off my list. That had been Ignatius, but I still didn't think the dragon was responsible for the fire in the woods. That had to be the work of the prankster.

"Exactly. Everyone is on edge and trying to brush off any suspicions from the tourists, but it's getting harder by the day. Not to mention there's a fire-breathing dragon running around Spellbooks! Oh, I think you're turning my fur white," she said, slumping back and resting the back of her paw against her forehead dramatically.

"It's already white," I said distractedly, as I turned to my list of suspects. The Silverthorne brothers topped the list still. Contemplatively, I circled their names. Finn's logic had been sound when he said people might suspect us because we'd been at the scene of several of the pranks, but the same could be said of the Silverthorne brothers. Sure, it seemed like they were helping to control the pranking, but what if one or both were actually behind everything? Setting themselves up to look like heroes and swooping in to save the day?

"Carrot crunching chaos, that's not the point!" Luna snapped, glaring at me and pulling me back to the present.

"What?" I asked, confused and distracted.

"You and that terrifying dragon are making me old before my time!"

I shot her a skeptical look. "He's a miniature dragon, and you really don't have anything to worry about. Besides, Ignatius is staying with Agatha for the time being while she runs some tests. You're perfectly safe here."

"Harrumph!"

"Everything is going to be fine," I assured her with more confidence than I felt. "It's not like anyone is going on a cabbage rampage."

"Who's going on a rampage and why are they after cabbage?" Finn asked as he pushed through the door, carrying a large canvas bag and a blanket.

"Because they have excellent taste," Luna sniffed. "What's all that then?"

"Preparations," Finn said seriously. He winked at me over Luna's head.

"For what? It looks more like you are going on a date than working to catch that fluffernutting prankster."

"Fluffernutting?" Finn asked, looking between us in confusion.

I caught up my coat and hastily shoved the journal back into my purse, a little embarrassed by my attempt to discover the prankster's identity. What would Finn think of my suspect list? Especially if he was close to either of the Silverthorne brothers or Alex, all three of whom currently topped my list.

I grabbed Finn's arm and steered him towards the door. "Well, we've got to run! Don't want to be late, especially with the whole town counting on us to ensnare the fluffernutter responsible for all the, um, radish ruckus."

I flipped the sign over and locked the door behind us before turning with a rueful smile to Finn. "Sorry about that. Luna can be a little... grumpy."

"Don't worry about a thing. Everyone has their bad days, even rabbits. But I've got to admit, she's got a way with words. I've never heard of 'fluffernutter,' but I'm going to add it to my lexicon."

I chuckled and pointed towards the bag. "What's all this?"

"Like I said before, the best dates come with snacks. I stopped by Thandor's for some treats before he headed over to the town square to set up his stand for the fashion show."

I raised a hand. "Newbie here. Who's Thandor? I haven't met him yet."

Finn explained as we started strolling into town. "Thandor Willowbrook is his name. He owns Feyfare Delicacies."

"I've never heard of it."

"Well, after tonight, you'll understand why he's known as the go-to guy for delicious food. When I first moved to town, we bonded over our love of nature. Gnomes tend to prefer living with their own kind, but Thandor likes life here in Havenwood. After you taste his food, you'll see why Havenwood likes Thandor living here," he said, hefting the bag to emphasize his point.

"I don't think I've ever met a gnome before. What do his delicacies taste like?" I asked, my mouth already watering. Breakfast was a distant memory, and this sounded much better than anything I could have hoped for. I was grateful Finn had offered to bring the snacks, because I felt like I could eat my way through a five-course meal at the Hobbit Hole and still have room for the entire Mount Doom lava cake that usually fed two people.

Finn took my hand as we walked down the street, sending a warm thrill through me despite the chill in the air. "He makes the best gourmet finger foods I've ever tasted. I don't know if it's just because he's a whiz at flavor combos or if he enchants his recipes, but they are seriously next level," Finn said as we strolled down Arcadia Avenue.

"I can't wait," I said, and meant it with every rumble of my stomach.

"Speaking of Thandor, there's his stand," Finn said, pointing as we walked towards an already bustling town square. The small wooden counter looked to be a popular choice, even this early.

Next to the unassuming stand piled high with gourmet finger foods was a brightly colored sign I recognized as Pixie's Pastries. The bakery's stall was already doing a brisk business. Honey and Antonio DeLuca, Bella's parents, even had a booth. I waved as we strolled past, but Honey barely had time to flash me a quick smile in between serving her famous treats to customers. As we walked by, I saw a few more locals I recognized. I waved at a couple of people I knew.

"I can't remember, what's going on tonight?" I asked, wracking my brain for the details of the town's event list even as I took in the festive atmosphere. Small stands filled with food, drinks, and crafts ringed the communal open space that was liberally decorated with pumpkins, dried corn in various colors, and brightly colored signs welcoming everyone to Haven-wood's Harvest Festival. The entire scene reminded me of the Christmas markets I'd visited with my parents in Germany, but Halloween-themed.

"Tonight's event is the festive fashion show," Finn reminded me.

"Right," I said as fragments of a half-remembered conversation reconstituted themselves in my head. Now that he jogged my memory, I realized several people were setting up a sound system near the large gazebo in the middle of the square. Raised walkways extended out from the gazebo, forming what I now realized were catwalks decorated with leaves and more pumpkins. "Something about reclaimed fabric?" I said, my memory failing to produce any more details.

Finn nodded. "This year's theme is EcoEnchant. It's meant to showcase upcycled fashion. Many locals participate, but several designers from the surrounding area also showcase their designs."

"That sounds so cool! Too bad we're going to miss it," I said sincerely. If I had the choice, I'd much rather eat treats and look at new fashion creations than scavenger hunt for a ritual spell.

Finn looked at his watch. "We might have enough time to catch the end of it if the weather cooperates. I checked the forecast, and we're in luck. Given the changes in temperature today, dew should form within the next hour or so. Otherwise, we'd have to wait until the wee hours of the morning."

"I didn't even think about that. I'm glad you did, or I'd be sitting in a field all night staring at the grass waiting for dew to form."

"Is that better or worse than watching the grass grow?" Finn teased.

"About the same, I imagine," I said with a chuckle. "Speaking of, where are we headed?"

"I know a place," Finn said mysteriously.

"Oh? Do tell."

"I find showing is better than telling."

Finn refused to say another word about where he was taking me, and I gave up trying to convince him, enjoying the atmosphere of the bustling square as we skirted the edge of the ring of stands. The stroll through the quieter streets of town was a pleasant change, and Finn led me down some streets I hadn't yet explored.

"I didn't know these shops were even here," I said, peering at the signs as we walked.

Finn nodded amiably. "Havenwood might be a small town by most people's standards, but there are a lot of hidden gems here if you're willing to look for them. Speaking of, that's Thandor's place." He pointed out a quaint little building that exuded a gentle charm, even though it was closed and the lights were off. Ivy crawled up the brick walls, and a small sign in a flowing script welcomed visitors to Feyfare Delicacies. I paused to look at the weekly menu in the illuminated frame outside the door. The food sounded incredible. Thandor's offerings included tartlets filled with an herby goat cheese, smoked salmon pinwheels, brie and raspberry phyllo cups, and savory stuffed dates. Looking at the list, I didn't know which ones I hoped Finn had tucked away in his bag because they all sounded so good.

Finn must've read my mind. "Don't worry. I've selected plenty to sample. But we've got to get going, or we're going to be late."

We turned off the small street, and I caught my breath as I took in the sight before me. A large, ornate gate stood open and waiting for us. Twinkling lights gleamed in the majestic oaks, framing the entryway to what looked like a tranquil oasis of natural wonder.

"What is this place?" I asked as we walked toward the beautiful garden.

"Welcome to the Elderwood Botanical Garden. This is one of my favorite places in all of Havenwood."

"I can see why," I said, peering through the gate and into the garden beyond. Soft lights from solar-powered lamps illuminated the footpath and some of the plants beyond. I could imagine that in the daylight, the garden must be bursting with life. Even in the relative darkness, it looked like a magical, beautiful oasis from the modern-day hustle and bustle.

A form detached itself from the shadow of one of the massive oak trees as we approached. I jumped in surprise, but Finn raised his hand in greeting. "Hello Jeremiah."

"Good evening, Finnegan," an elderly man's voice creaked from the shadows. "It's good to see you."

"Likewise," Finn said, stepping forward to shake the man's hand before turning to introduce me. "May I present Harper Sullivan? Harper, this is Jeremiah Rowan."

"Ah, Beatrice's great-granddaughter. A pleasure. Beatrice was always the sunlight in our forest, bringing joy to this community for as long as I can remember. My condolences on her passing," Jeremiah said, stepping out of the shadows and into the glow of the streetlight.

I caught my breath. He was a tall, lanky man with long limbs and a shock of silver hair, but that wasn't what caught my attention. It was the gnarled bark covering his skin. It looked like he might have stepped directly *out* of the tree rather than from under it. Even in Havenwood, where the fantastical mingled with the everyday, meeting someone like Jeremiah was beyond anything I'd ever imagined. He looked like he could've stepped straight out of the pages of some epic fantasy adventure. I was suddenly reminded how many of Havenwood's citizens, like Jeremiah, would have a hard time leaving or living elsewhere if the wards protecting the town fell.

I must've stood there staring with my mouth open for too long as thoughts whirled through my head because Finn cleared his throat and gave a subtle warning look over Jeremiah's shoulder, a silent reminder to be respectful.

"You're..." I trailed off, searching for the right words as Jeremiah shook my hand warmly, his skin rough under my fingers.

His dark eyes gleamed with wisdom and ancient secrets as he winked at me. "You're correct. I am a botanist, for all my sins. But being a treant does give me a certain bond with my plants."

"A botanist? Rowan? Are you related to Jeremy Rowan by chance?" I asked, naming a member of my book club. The gangly man was quiet and very shy unless talking about plants. He and Stella, another member of the book club and owner of the local florist shop, often got lost in their own conversations during our meetings. I think more than half the reason Jeremy attended the book club was to see Stella.

"Ah, you've met my grandnephew. A bit of a black sheep in our family, but he's finding his own path."

"Aren't we all?" Finn said.

"Indeed," Jeremiah replied. "A true path is sometimes difficult to find and even more challenging to walk, but the view at the end is well worth the effort in my experience." His voice was low and deep, seeming to impart wisdom with every syllable. I felt my breath slow, and my shoulders relax as I listened to him.

"Speaking of paths, thanks for keeping this one open for us tonight," Finn said, gesturing towards the gate.

"For a friend like you? Anytime." Jeremiah held out a large key attached to a wooden keychain in the shape of an oak leaf. "Just remember to lock up. There's a chill in the air tonight."

"Winter is coming," Finn said seriously as he accepted the key.

"It is, but I don't think this has anything to do with the weather. No, there's trouble on the wind, and I'd prefer it stay out of my gardens."

His words sent a tingle of ice down my spine. Did this have something to do with the prankster? Were treants precognizant as well as having power over plants? Or was he sensing something else? Maybe Jeremiah just getting into the Halloween spirit and attempting to be spooky? I hoped it was that simple, but something in his kindly old face told me it wasn't.

Defying Gravity

Finn locked the gate to the botanical gardens behind us and took my hand before leading me past weathered stone benches nestled among delicate ferns. Towering oak trees marked the edges of the garden and a babbling brook meandered lazily through the greenery, its gentle song harmonizing with the rustle of leaves in the evening breeze and the distant calls of woodland birds.

Finn followed the footpath winding its way through the garden and finally came to a halt near a graceful arbor that was probably covered in beautiful blooms in the summer months. Now, the plants were trimmed back, awaiting the chill of winter to set in. Finn spread the blanket he'd brought over the plush moss in the soft glow of the full moon. As he arranged the gourmet treats he'd selected from Feyfare Delicacies, I took a heartbeat just to breathe in the moment, to savor the beauty and the peace of the garden. Havenwood didn't have the hustle of some cities where I'd lived, but this was another level of calm. I hesitated to say anything lest I break the spell.

Finn turned to me, two plastic flutes of something pale gold and slightly effervescent in his hands. "Care to join me?" he asked with a smile.

"Absolutely." I accepted a flute and settled down on the blanket. "This looks amazing!"

"Thandor really knows his stuff." Finn pointed out different boxes. "Over here we have dates stuffed with blue cheese and wrapped in bacon."

"Because everything's better with bacon," I said sincerely.

"Exactly. These are sweet mini peppers filled with a creamy spinach and artichoke mixture. Next, we have caramelized pear and walnut crostini topped with a drizzle of wildflower honey. Because it's the season, I couldn't pass on the mini pumpkin and sage tartlets or the pecan pie bites."

"Wow! I don't know where to start," I said honestly.

Finn raised his glass to mine. "My recommendation? Start with the wine. Thandor's twin, Zandor, owns a little wine emporium which is basically a treasure trove of unique wines. This one seemed to be ideal for tonight. It's called the Moonlit Chardonnay."

"Very apt," I said as I tapped my plastic flute against his and took a sip. The wine tasted of green apples with a hint of vanilla. It was light, sweet, and delicate bubbles danced across my tongue. If I'd been alone, I probably would've moaned and indulged in another long sip or three, but I didn't want to embarrass myself in front of Finn. Besides, there were treats to be enjoyed.

As if Finn could read my mind, he passed over the box of the stuffed dates. I helped myself to one of the succulent morsels and took a bite. The savory bacon paired wonderfully with the sweet date and the creamy, tangy blue cheese.

This time I did moan. "Oh, my goodness!"

Finn chuckled. "Yeah, that's how I responded the first time I tasted Thandor's food."

"How did you meet him? More to the point, why have you been holding out on me? This tastes incredible," I said, popping the rest of the date in my mouth.

Finn laughed and took a date for himself. "Thandor's actually the reason I discovered Havenwood. Do you remember I told you about the archdruid I trained with?"

I nodded. "You said he was a good guy but kept getting pulled into dangerous situations."

"Precisely. Druids are unique because we don't have to have innate magical talent. We train, study, and eventually become bound to nature through our tattoos." He held out his arm to show me the curling Celtic knotwork disappearing under his sleeve. "Once that happens, we can do some pretty amazing things."

"Like what?" I asked, fascinated. This was the first time Finn had talked so openly about his magic, apart from his ability with runes.

"Well, for example, I can encourage plant growth, influence the weather, and manipulate elements by drawing energy from the earth. But my magic takes a lot of time, preparation, and focus. Not to mention how tiring it is."

"That sounds really impressive!" I exclaimed.

"Well, it's about power levels. What I can do isn't really all that much in the druidic world, and it takes me a ton of time and energy. Right now, even the simplest spells drain me physically and mentally. It's a lot to handle. However, if I'd continued my studies, things would be much easier. I also might be able to bond with an animal companion by now or possibly even shapeshift."

"You can shapeshift?" I asked, my jaw dropping open.

Finn chuckled and shook his head. "No, I can't. But if I'd kept up my training, my magic would come more easily, and I could do more. Like I said, druidry is a long process. The more you study, the more you can do. However, when I saw the kinds of things my master got pulled into, I decided to take a different path. The problem was developing druids are isolated from the rest of the magical population of the world because we're basically as fragile as normal humans until we are bound to the earth. When I left after my binding ceremony, I had very few contacts and even fewer friends outside of the druids, most of whom didn't understand my choice to walk away from all that potential power."

"Power can be seductive and not in a good way," I observed, the words spilling out of me before I could think of a better phrasing. I helped myself to a pear and walnut crostini as I felt a blush creep up my cheeks at the words and hoped Finn didn't read too much into it or think I was weird. Quickly, I took a bite of the crostini, which thoroughly distracted me from my poor word choices. If possible, it was better than the bacon wrapped date.

Finn didn't seem the least perturbed. "Exactly. From what I saw during my studies, it was a cycle. Learn more spells, cultivate more power, have more problems. Repeat until something tries to take a bite out of you. That wasn't a life I wanted. I was content with the basics. So, I left."

"What happened next? Was your archdruid angry?"

"Well, he wasn't happy, but he couldn't exactly stop me from leaving after I was bound because I was a druid in my own right. Just a low-level one. When I left, I didn't know what to do, so I decided to take a sabbatical from real life. I packed a bag and lost myself in the wildest part of the Superior National Forest between Minnesota and Canada in a place called the Boundary Waters."

"I've never heard of it, but I didn't spend a great deal of time in the north when I was growing up."

"It's beautiful. There are over a million acres of unspoiled wilderness up there. As you can probably guess by the name, there's a whole system of interconnected lakes and rivers winding through dense forests between the two countries. I spent my time there soul-searching to figure out what I wanted to do with my life. And fishing. A lot of time fishing." He shrugged with a charming smile and took a sip of his wine.

"It sounds like the perfect place to do both."

"It was." His eyes went distant, and it was obvious he was reliving that part of his life. Abruptly, he brushed a hand through the air as if dispelling the memories. "Anyway, that's where I met Thandor. I was hiking to find a new campsite when I smelled the most amazing thing cooking. I was curious and went to investigate. That's when I found Thandor happily creating a feast from foraged berries, mushrooms, and other vegetables. I offered to add my day's catch to the meal, and he accepted. While we ate, he told me a little of his background and his home in Havenwood. I was fascinated. A town where mundane magical beings could live with little fear of discovery by the outside world? That was something I needed to explore. Besides, I already had my bag packed." He selected a tartlet and crunched through the flaky crust as he concluded his story.

"So, you traded away a chance at phenomenal cosmic powers for a peaceful life in Havenwood?"

"Better than having them and being forced into an itty-bitty living space," he said with a grin.

My eyes went wide. "You know *Aladdin*?" I demanded.

"Of course. Robin Williams as a big, blue genie was a staple in my house growing up."

"Mine too. My dad did his best to make sure I had as normal a life as I could growing up on military bases all around the world. *Aladdin* was always a favorite."

"Ah, but have you seen all three?" Finn raised an eyebrow.

"Naturally," I scoffed. "Although the sequel wasn't as good as the first one."

"They rarely are. It's hard to capture that kind of magic a second time.

"Agreed." I said, tapping my plastic flute to his.

He ran a hand over the nearby grass. "Speaking of capturing magic, I think we might be able to start doing just that."

I touched the plush greenery as well and my fingertips came away damp. "That was fast," I said in surprise.

"The weather conditions are playing in our favor right now, and the botanical gardens are a great place for dew to accumulate."

I rummaged in my bag and withdrew a couple of old jam jars I'd rinsed out and saved. "Do you think these will work?" I asked.

"Perfect."

"Then let's get to work!" I handed one to him, settled my wine in a safe place and started to run my jar over blades of grass. It didn't take long for me to realize the problem. I held up my jar after a few minutes to see one fat drop of dew roll down the smooth interior of the jar. I groaned and turned to Finn, lifting the jar to show the fruits of my efforts. "Even though the ritual only required a thimble full of dew, collecting it could take hours," I grumbled. Hours of crouching over grass and moss wasn't my idea of a good time, but what choice did I have? If I wanted to avoid Ignatius burning down Spellbooks once Aunty Agatha left, I needed this dew, and I had to collect it tonight.

"I thought that might be an issue which is why I came prepared with a backup plan," Finn said, grabbing a dead twig from the ground near the blanket.

"How is a twig going to help us?" I asked skeptically.

"I'm a druid, remember? Watch and learn." He walked over to the dirt path and crouched down, using the twig to scratch at the earth. I frowned and headed over so I could peer over his shoulder.

"What are you doing?" I asked.

"Druidry is all about bindings. That's what Celtic knotwork designs are, you know."

"Bindings?"

He continued scratching, creating an intricate design in the dirt. "Yeah. They're basically empty receptacles for a spell. Draw the right symbols, infuse them with a bit of magic, and everything should work. It's the old Irish equivalent to runes." He added an extra flourish with the twig and pushed up from his crouch. I looked around expectantly, but nothing happened.

"Umm, what should work exactly?" I asked.

"Give me a second. Like all good things, this takes time." He moved towards the opposite end of the clearing, and I followed, feeling very confused. He repeated the sketch in the dirt three more times, forming a square around our picnic site with his Celtic knot drawings at each corner.

When he finished the final drawing, he pushed to his feet with a self-satisfied air. "There, that should do it. Now for the final piece." He took me by the hand and led me back to the picnic blanket. From the tote bag, Finn withdrew a smooth wooden object that fit easily in the palm of his hand and looked somewhat like a very large acorn. He lifted the carved top to show me the empty cavity inside. In the light of the full moon, I could barely make out faint scratches along the bottom, along the inside of the cup.

"What's that?" I asked.

He handed it over so I could examine it while he explained. "It's the last piece of the spell. I've already carved the correct binding in the bottom of the cup."

I squinted, turning the cup this way and that to get a better look at the design in the moonlight. "It's so tiny! And intricate. Wait. What happens if you make a mistake drawing the binding? Does that mess up the spell?"

Finn nodded. "In theory, yes, but this one is a relatively easy binding to create."

"It doesn't look easy," I said, doubtfully. The twists and turns in the carving were already making me go slightly cross-eyed.

Finn chuckled. "Trust me, after some of the tattoos I've done, this is a walk in the park. No pun intended."

I handed the cup back to him. "Okay, so what happens now?"

"Now, I say the command words, and, if everything goes to plan, you'll have the first ingredient for your ritual. Are you ready?"

I looked around, a fluttering starting in my stomach. "Ready for what exactly? What does this spell do?"

Finn winked at me. "Magic." He took my hand in his and held the open wooden container cupped in his opposite hand. In a deep, clear voice, he said, "*Ceangail drúcht!*"

The unfamiliar words startled me. It sounded like he said, "kang gal drookht." Despite sounding completely foreign, it somehow gave me the impression of an ancient sentient tree. I couldn't tell you why. However, I didn't have much time to ponder as the binding activated. Within the square of bindings Finn had drawn, the entire clearing looked like it was filled with rain. Slow-moving rain. Rain that inconceivably floated up instead of down. I watched in fascination as droplets of dew merged to create drops and then a dribble of water. Finally, a full-on trickle wove its way lazily through the air, defying all laws of gravity and logic until it settled gracefully in the wooden bowl with a small splash. After the last droplets added themselves to the cup in Finn's hand, he said a single word in a commanding voice. "Lán!"

The pressure that I hadn't realized had been slowly building in the clearing suddenly vanished, and my ears popped. A moment before, the garden appeared magical, mystical, and full of ancient secrets. Now, it just looked like a mundane garden. Full of plants and moonlight, but normal.

Finn turned to me, looking worn and tired, but he managed to smile and even gave a little bow, extending the cup in my direction. "Your dew, milady."

I accepted the smooth wooden cup, cradling in carefully with both hands. It was maybe three-quarters full of dew sparkling in the moonlight. Much more than I needed for the ritual and collected in a fraction of the time. Magic was so cool. Scratch that. *Druidic* magic was so cool. But it also might've been that I was enamored by the practitioner as much as the spell work.

I looked from the cup in my hand to Finn and back again. "How did you...What did...I mean, thank you, this is amazing. But..." I trailed off with a helpless shrug.

He laughed and took the wooden cup from me, carefully pouring it into my old jam jar and sealing the lid as he explained. "The drawings around the clearing acted as border for the spell, and the carving in the cup was the focus. When I said the words, it triggered the spell."

"Yeah, speaking of, what language was that? I didn't recognize it."

"Old Irish. One of the first languages druids learn. *Ceangail drúcht* roughly translates to 'bind dew' and 'lán' means finished or complete. If I hadn't ended the spell, there would've been a constant trickle of dew attempting to find this cup until the bindings were disturbed."

"That would've been bad," I said.

"Especially for the plants," Finn agreed. "When working a binding, it's not only the drawings that have to be done with care, it's the words too. For instance, if I'd replaced dew with water in the spell, all of the water within the clearing would've been affected. Everything from the water in our cells to the water in the wine would've been bound."

"Not the wine!" I joked, but inside a little shiver of apprehension tingled up my spine. If Finn had misspoken or not drawn the correct symbols, things could've gone very badly. I decided there and then to leave the druidry to the trained professionals.

I carefully tucked the jam jar back in my purse as Finn scooped up our glasses. He held mine out to me with a warm smile. "Thankfully, disaster has been avoided. How do you feel about resuming our moonlit picnic? I could use some food after that spell."

I couldn't help but return the smile, feeling a warm flutter in my chest. "I'd like nothing more," I said. But just as I was about to take my plastic flute from his hands, an anxious voice cut through the darkness.

"Finnegan!"

Finn frowned, his body tensing. "Jeremiah?"

"He sounds worried. Did the spell hurt the garden?" I asked, my own concern rising.

Finn shook his head. "Not possible. We just borrowed a little dew."

"Finnegan!" Jeremiah's voice rang out again, closer this time, and even more urgent.

"Jeremiah, we're in the clearing by the arbor!" Finn called loudly as he jumped to his feet, inadvertently bumping into me as he did so. The sudden movement jarred the glass from my hands, splashing wine all over the grass.

I watched the wine soak into the ground, feeling a pang of disappointment. Our moment of happiness, like the spilled wine, was slipping away.

"What's going on?" I asked softly as I rose to stand next to Finn, searching the shadows for the treant.

"I don't know, but something's off," Finn said, scanning the darkness. He looked concerned and on edge; his usual calm demeanor replaced with unease. Tension crept into my shoulder blades and worry settled in the pit of my stomach. Seeing Finn, typically so composed, on edge only heightened my apprehension.

Jeremiah appeared on the path a moment later, the moonlight making deep shadows in the craggy wrinkles of his face. "Ah, Finnegan. There you are. Tell me the fire hasn't reached the garden."

"Fire?" Finn and I demanded in unison.

"What fire?" Finn continued. "Jeremiah, what's going on?"

The old treant spun and started back down the path. "No time. I need to check the rest of the garden."

"Wait!" Finn held up a hand and knelt, digging his fingers into the earth. He closed his eyes, a frown of deep concentration furrowing his brow. After a moment, he shook his head and stood, dusting off his hands. "I asked the earth to check. There's no fire within the gardens."

Jeremiah blew out a breath of relief. "Roots and branches, that's good to hear!"

"What's happening?" I asked, my voice tight with worry.

"There was a fire in the town square. One of the food stalls. The decorations went up in a blaze. The fire spread to three different stands before they got it under control."

"Was anybody hurt?" Finn demanded, his eyes wide with panic as he started gathering up our picnic supplies. I crouched to help him, my mind immediately flashing to Bella and her family. Were they okay?

"No, by the forest's grace," Jeremiah said. I closed my eyes and let out a little sigh of relief.

As Finn and I frantically packed up the picnic, my mind raced. What about the rest of the stalls? Had the fire spread to the shops surrounding the square? I couldn't put my finger on why, but this felt too intentional to be an accident. Like someone had planned to disrupt the gathering on purpose. The realization that our town, our sanctuary, was under attack, hit me hard. We had to figure out who was behind this before it was too late.

I bit my lip, remembering how far we'd walked to reach the botanical gardens. "If the fire was contained, why did you think it had spread all the way here?" I asked.

Jeremiah turned his ancient gaze to me. "Because the sparks drifted on the wind. Two shops and a nearby home also caught fire."

Finn frowned, panic rising in his voice. "That's not possible. The town square is large and surrounded by streets and sidewalks. For a single spark to travel that distance and be able to light a building on fire, it must be..."

"Magic," Jeremiah finished for him. My stomach dropped and then twisted into a knot. The old treant nodded seriously, confirming my suspicions. "This was no accident. Whoever started the fire did it on purpose. Worse, whoever is behind all this is one of us."

The Heat of Suspicion

JEREMIAH STAYED IN THE gardens, wanting to reassure himself that the magically spurred fire hadn't spread despite Finn's reassurances. In the light of recent events, our plans for a leisurely moonlit picnic had shifted dramatically. Panic rose in me as we hurried back towards the town square and my mind raced with worry about our friends, their homes, and businesses. The thought of losing everything we held dear because of some malicious prankster made my heart pound even faster. We needed to see if we could help, to check on everyone and ensure no one was hurt.

As we rushed through the streets, another realization hit me like a punch to the gut. Whoever was behind these escalating pranks wasn't just causing mischief anymore—they were putting lives and our entire community at risk. The fire in the woods, the blaze in the town square, it was all connected. This wasn't a harmless prankster; this was someone with malicious intent, someone who could bring down the very fabric of our sanctuary. Not just metaphorically, but literally. My heart pounded as I thought about all the people who relied on Havenwood for their safety. We needed to find and stop the prankster. The sooner the better.

I took a deep breath, trying to steady my racing thoughts. If the truth about Ignatius came out, the Silverthornes could easily blame me for everything. The thought of being banished, of losing the place I was starting to call home, made my blood run cold. I had to solve this mystery. I had to find out who was really responsible for the fires and stop them before they caused any more damage. Ignatius needed to stay hidden, away from prying eyes that might use him as a scapegoat. The stakes were higher than ever, and failure wasn't an option. We had to figure out who was behind all these pranks. The safety of Havenwood, and everyone in it, depended on us.

"Do you think this fire was started by the prankster?" I asked, my breath coming quickly as we ran towards the center of town, our picnic paraphernalia thumping awkwardly against our legs.

"I think the faster we get there to help, the better," Finn said grimly as we ran.

A sudden thought occurred to me. "Can you use your powers to make it rain and help put out the fires?"

Finn shook his head and kept running. "Something like that would take a lot of set up time and a strong connection to the earth. Neither of which we have time for right now."

With nothing left to say, we both focused on running as fast as we could.

As we approached the town square, we slowed our pace. Chaos reigned, but there were no fires that I could see. I let out a sigh of relief and paused to catch my breath. Tourists either drifted away towards their evening abodes or crowded around under the pretext of offering help when, for all appearances, they just wanted a closer look at what was going on. None of them looked injured or dangerous. If Jeremiah's assessment of the situation was accurate, a normal arsonist wasn't responsible, anyway.

I turned my attention to the locals, scanning their faces for signs of distress or suspicious activity. Firefighters in their red uniforms clustered around two buildings on the edge of the square that looked singed. To my untrained eye, the damage looked more cosmetic than structural. They must've caught it early. Other firefighters were forming a barrier around some stalls that looked significantly more damaged. Smoke still spiraled up from the furthest one, and a spurt of sparks jumped skyward. The firefighters reacted instantly, spraying the building liberally with water.

People I recognized rushed around the square, looking agitated and anxious. Others gathered in clumps, muttering in low voices as they shot suspicious looks at their neighbors. A short, pudgy man with a large mustache stood next to a tall, slim woman with a pinched face at the edge of the square. They looked up as Finn and I approached. The man's eyes flared in recognition when he saw me. He pushed his glasses more securely up his bulbous nose as he marched over to intercept us.

"And just where have you been?" he demanded, his tone accusatory.

I bit the inside of my cheek, reminding myself to be civil despite the upheaval. "Hello Mr. Puddleton. We heard something happened here. Is everyone okay?"

"No, everyone is *not* okay!" Oswald Puddleton replied brusquely, his voice raising and his mustache quivering. He owned a bookshop called the Dusty Tome just down the road from Spellbooks. I don't know if it was the inherent competition of owning similar businesses or part of their natures, but Oswald and his wife Hortense never hid their displeasure at seeing me.

"What happened?" Finn asked.

"Isn't it obvious? Someone has it out for us! They want the Dusty Tome to fail. If you ask me, the prime suspect is standing right here." Oswald glared up at me. "Just where were you between six and ten tonight?"

I forced myself to chuckle. "I think all those mysteries from the book club are getting to your head."

Hortense narrowed her eyes, making her pinched features contract into an unpleasant scowl. "We led a normal, happy life until you turned up in town. First there was that nasty business with the police, then the mysterious and unexplained happenings at your sorry excuse for a shop, and now this? Trouble like this didn't exist in Havenwood before you moved here, Harper Sullivan!" She shook a finger aggressively in my face, causing me to back pedal a few steps.

My mouth dropped open at the vitriol in the unexpected verbal attack. Her words stung, and I bit back a retort. As much as I hated to admit it, she had a point. My arrival had coincided with an uptick in strange and unsettling events. The thought sparked a new suspicion in my mind. What if someone new to town was behind all this? Someone who had arrived under the radar, like Alex, or maybe even a supernatural hiding out amongst the tourists? My thoughts raced as I considered the possibilities. Hortense's accusation, though harsh, gave me a new direction to explore.

However, before I could formulate an appropriate response to address the allegations of my distasteful neighbor, Finn slid an arm protectively around my shoulders. "Harper's been with me all evening, and, other than a brief stop, we haven't been anywhere close to the town square."

Hortense sniffed loudly; her pointed nose thrust into the air. "A likely story. You should choose your companions with greater care, Finnegan Oakheart."

"Indeed," Oswald added, his jowls quivering in rage. "Troublemakers like her are not to be trusted. Why I wouldn't be surprised if she started the fire that almost burned down our stand." He thrust a finger my way. My heart thundered in my chest, and the edges of my vision turned red. I'd never done anything to the Puddletons to warrant this kind of accusation. I would've given them both a piece of my mind, along with the sharp edge of my tongue, if Finn hadn't cut off my retort before I opened my mouth.

"Fire? Where did it start?" he demanded.

Oswald whirled, pointing a sausage-like finger towards the opposite side of the park. "Over there. One of the food stalls."

I looked over his head in the direction he'd indicated and furrowed my brow as a familiar sign caught my attention. "Wait. Isn't your stand right here? On the other side of the square?" I asked, seeing the boxes with the Dusty Tome's logo piled behind the nearest wooden stall.

Hortense put her hands on her narrow hips and glowered at me. "Yes, what's your point?"

"Just that your stall seems about as far away as it could be from where the fire started," I said, trying to keep my voice mild. I'm not sure I succeeded.

"Well, fire spreads, doesn't it?" Hortense demanded shrilly.

Oswald folded his arms over his chest and stuck out his head, attempting to appear wise but really looking like a judgmental chicken. "And who knows what kind of flammable materials were in that stall? That gnome's decorations went up pretty quickly. A fire hazard obviously, and one he really should've anticipated."

"The gnome? Which gnome?" Finn asked, his voice tight with concern.

"You can't expect us to remember every gnome's name," Hortense said with a sniff.

"I think it was Sandy? No, that's not right. Thandy?" Oswald said, stroking his moustache.

"No one would use the name Thandy, Oswald. It was Andor. Obviously," his wife chastised him.

We looked at each other as realization sunk in. "Thandor!" we said in unison. A heartbeat later, we were both rushing through the crowd, urgency propelling us forward. The Puddletons' undoubtedly disapproving looks burned at our backs, but neither of us cared.

We navigated through the throngs of people with purpose, our worry mounting. While the fire was mostly under control, the implications were serious. Thandor's stall could've been damaged, or he could've been hurt. Finn's usually calm demeanor cracked, replaced with a sense of anxiety that matched my own. My heart pounded as we made our way to the scene, the gravity of the situation weighing heavily on us.

A bustle of activity surrounded Thandor's stall. As we neared, I could see the side of the building was scorched and blackened. Someone had dealt with the fire quickly before it could do more than that. I saw a small man who I thought might be Thandor through the crowd. He was talking seriously with Gabriel Silverthorne and an older man with dark hair and silver at his temples who was wearing a fireman's uniform. Other than a smear of black soot across one cheek, the gnome looked unharmed. I breathed out a sigh of relief.

Finn touched my elbow and leaned down so I could hear his words over the hubbub of the crowd. "I'm going to check on Thandor. He looks okay, but I want to make sure."

"Good idea. I want to find Honey and Antonio and make sure they are all right too."

Finn squeezed my hand, looking serious. "I'll find you later. Be safe."

"You too," I said.

He started weaving through the ring of gawkers surrounding Thandor's place while I turned to find the DeLuca's stand. It'd been far enough away from the fire to escape any damage, but Honey still looked shaken up. Antonio wrapped his arms around her, whispering into her hair as he rocked her gently from side to side. Honey hid her face in her husband's shirt, but I saw her shoulders shake. Bella hurried over as I approached.

"Bella! Are you okay? Are your folks hurt?" I asked, grabbing her hands and doing a quick visual inspection.

Bella pulled me into a hug. "Yeah, everyone is fine. The fire didn't spread this far. Mama is just rattled. Papa's going to take her home while I clean up here."

"Do you need a hand?" I asked.

Bella pulled back and gave me a tight smile. "That'd be great, thanks." She walked towards her parents, and I followed. "Mama? Papa? I've got this. Harper's going to help me."

Antonio looked over Honey's head. "You sure?"

Bella nodded firmly. "You take care of Mama. We've got the rest."

Antonio shot us a relieved smile as he led Honey away. As soon as they were out of earshot, Bella spun and grabbed my arm. "Where is he?"

I frowned. "Finn? He's checking on Thandor."

Bella shook her head. "No, not the druid. The dragon," she hissed the last word in an urgent whisper.

"I left him with Agatha. Why?" I asked,

"A dragon who can't control his fire breathing? An unexpected fire in the middle of town? It doesn't take a genius to connect the dots," Bella said in a rush.

My mouth dropped open. I'd been so busy assuming that the prankster was responsible and protective of Ignatius that I hadn't even considered the possibility the little dragon might actually have caused all the chaos. If Ignatius was in town, I needed to find him before he set more accidental fires.

"I've got to call Agatha. Right now." I was already pulling out my phone.

"You do that," Bella said, making hurried, shooing gestures with her hands.

I dialed her number as I walked towards a quieter area of the park near the street where I couldn't be easily overheard. Trees interspersed with benches ringed the edge of the square. I headed towards an empty bench, tapping in Agatha's number. She answered on the second ring.

"Agatha? Is Ignatius there?"

"Hello to you too, Harper," the old witch's voice was sharp with a reprimanding edge. "Yes, he's here. We're watching a movie and having some popcorn. Well, he's attempting to pop the corn, but hasn't quite managed not to char it yet."

"And you're sure he's with you?" I pressed.

"Yes, I'm looking right at him. Why? What's going on?"

I paced back and forth along the sidewalk. "Someone set fire to one of the stands in the town square. I wanted to see if it was an accident or—"

"Or if Ignatius lost control of himself. I see." Agatha's tone lost the sharp edge. "No, it wasn't him."

"So, it was the prankster. I knew it!" I exclaimed.

"Or the fire and the pranks are completely unrelated except for the unfortunate coincidence of timing," Agatha countered. "Either way, Ignatius has been with me all day, and he's truly the most delightful companion. I'm going to miss his company when I have to go."

"Any luck on finding a solution for him so we don't, you know, have to turn him to stone?" I asked.

Agatha clicked her tongue. "Unfortunately, not, but I've got a few ideas left. I'll let you know if something works."

"Please do," I said.

"In the meantime, I think it'd be best if you find those ingredients for the ritual quickly. We don't want someone to assume Ignatius is responsible when he's innocent."

"Agreed," I murmured.

Aunty Agatha's tone shifted, all joviality gone. "Arson isn't a prank. Whoever's behind this has taken a step too far. I'll watch after Ignatius, but you be careful, Harper."

"I will," I promised before bidding her goodbye and ending the call.

Agatha's suggestion that the fire and the pranks could be unrelated sparked a shift in my thoughts. I leaned against the tree, trying to piece everything together. I pulled out my journal, flipping through the notes and adding my latest observations. The pattern of the pranks had changed, becoming more dangerous and erratic, but was that the original prankster escalating, or because there were now two people wreaking havoc in Havenwood?

Regardless, I needed to do this ritual as soon as possible so that no one could accuse Ignatius of being involved. If only I didn't have to wait until Halloween! Who knows what kind of trouble could occur in the next few days?

Lost in my thoughts, I didn't hear the approaching footsteps until an unfamiliar voice cut through the noise of the town square.

"Some welcome home!"

Instinctively, I pressed closer to the shadow of the tree trunk and froze as two people strode past me and onto the sidewalk. If I wanted to solve this mystery, I needed every advantage I could get. Tipping off the responsible party would only make it that much harder to catch him or her. Keeping my investigation secret was more important than ever, so I huddled in the shadows and watched.

The man grabbed the woman's arm, spinning her to face him. The streetlight spilled across both of them. I drew in a silent breath as I recognized Lucas Silverthorne. The woman was a stranger to me. She looked to be about my age but had thick wavy hair that was dyed a brilliant pink at the ends. It was a style I wasn't bold enough to consider for myself. She put her hands on her hips and glared up at Lucas. He held his ground, frowning sternly at her.

"What am I supposed to think, Isadora? You turn up out of nowhere. No word of warning. Nothing."

"Yeah. I got here a few days ago. It's called a surprise, Lucas. I grew up in the same house as you did, remember? I know Harvest Festival is Mom's favorite. At this time of year, I thought she'd like to have the family together again," the woman, Isadora, snapped.

"I'm sure she will, but if you came home to see family, why haven't you been to the house yet? Or told Mom?"

"I'm just...waiting for the right time."

"Oh? How are things going with your training?"

Isadora glared at Lucas. "Just what are you implying, big brother?" she asked, her tone icy.

Lucas refused to back down. "You know the whole reason Mom found you that special school was to help you."

"You mean, the whole reason Mom sent me away because she was too busy with controlling the town to help me herself," Isadora spat out.

"She thought she was doing the right thing. C'mon Isa. Even you have to see that."

"No. What I see is my family assuming the worst of me. Again." Isadora whirled around and marched down the street, her voice rising with each step. "I knew coming back here was a mistake!" she yelled over her shoulder.

Lucas started to follow her; his jaw clenched with determination.

"Lucas!" a voice called from behind me, causing him to stop in his tracks. I turned to see Gabriel running up, his face flushed with urgency. "Lucas, I need your help!"

Lucas scrubbed a hand over his face. He looked towards where Isadora was disappearing into the darkness. His voice was low but still carried clearly to my ears. "She just doesn't get it."

Gabriel patted his brother's shoulder. "I'll talk to Isa, but for now, we've got to smooth things over here. I'm hearing whispers from tourists about some *unexplainable* things they've seen around town. Things Mom wouldn't want to leak out. I'm worried the spells are running low. We need to power them up again. Especially after what just happened."

Lucas sighed, turning away from where his sister disappeared into the night. "You're right. We can focus on Isa after this has calmed down. Let's go."

The brothers hurried back towards the center of the town square, leaving me alone to ponder what I'd just overheard. Was the prankster behind tonight's fiasco? If so, what caused the escalation from trick candy and rolling pumpkins to arson? On top of that, if the Silverthorne brothers were any indication, the tourists weren't all buying whatever explanations the obfuscation spells were generating. Everyone was jumpy and on edge. Rumors were starting to fly—rumors that could bring unwanted attention to what really went on in Havenwood at Halloween.

I touched my bag, feeling the jam jar shift under my fingers. With pranks going haywire and now escalating into dangerous, destructive behavior, I felt like I needed to do my part to stop it before everything spun out of control.

I watched the brothers disappear into the crowd and took a deep breath, steeling myself. It was time to get back to Bella and see if there was anything I could do to help her tonight. After that, I had to channel my inner detective. I found the thieves who stole the rare books from Spellbooks before, and I could find this prankster now. I had to. The safety of Havenwood depended on it.

Whispers and Wicks

THE NEXT DAY WAS Sunday, and even though the town was busier than normal, I closed Spellbooks a little early so I could head over to the library. Partly because I wanted to know more about Havenwood's history and the library seemed like a good place to learn, but mostly for the opportunity to get one more item for the ritual. Sometimes doing your part was taking the little steps only you could, I reminded myself. For me, that meant ensuring I could complete the ritual to turn Ignatius back to stone and keeping my eyes and ears open for anything that might be a clue to help me discover the identity of the prankster.

The locals helping at the library's historical event were subdued, despite the clear skies and sunny weather. It almost seemed like everyone I knew was wearing a mask, even though it wasn't Halloween yet. The façade the locals showed to the tourists was happy, inviting, and genial. However, when the tourists weren't looking, the locals looked apprehensive and distrustful of everyone, but especially each other. The prankster really seemed to be getting on everyone's nerves.

I sighed and resumed dipping the long candle wick in the cauldron of melted wax. "Do you really think this is going to work?" I asked Bella.

"The candle? Sure, they've been made this way for ages. Doing it by hand really makes you appreciate electricity though, doesn't it?"

I rolled my eyes. "Not what I meant. You know—"

"Whoops!" Bella's wick slipped through her fingers and fell into the cauldron of heated wax.

Martha Morningstar, the town librarian and volunteer in charge of the historical candle making, hurried over. "You didn't get splashed by the wax, did you Bella? It can cause a nasty burn."

"No, I'm okay. All that's hurt is my pride."

"I can fish it out for you, if you like," Martha offered sympathetically. "However, the candle rarely turns out very well after it's been dropped in completely."

"No, thanks though. I guess I'll have to start over," Bella said with a sigh, looking forlornly into liquid wax. "Thanks for checking though, Martha."

The librarian rummaged in a basket filled with display candles and pulled out a half-finished one. "I know it's not exactly your project from start to finish, but at least it will save you some time," she said, handing it over to Bella.

"Thank you," Bella said, accepting the candle.

Martha settled on the ground next to us. "Other than historical candle making, there's a lot of things on display today that are interesting. You should really check them out."

"Like what?" I asked, keeping my eyes focused on the candle. I didn't want to drop mine and start all over as well. Not with the special modification I'd made to the wick.

"Well, there's the colonial costume parade focusing on the history of Connecticut this year. Mason is great at telling ghost stories, but only from history. Not from his drinking buddies," Martha said with a wink. It was well known in town that Mason liked to have a beer with the local spirits on occasion, although no one quite figured out how that worked from the ghosts' point of view.

A thought sparked in my mind. Mason's camaraderie with the spirits was notorious, and it reminded me of allegations of a prank he'd played on the vicar. Could Mason be escalating his tricks from harmless pranks to something more dangerous? He had a sense of humor that fit the bill and had won the pumpkin carving contest—were the rolling pumpkins a distraction so he could get a head start on his carving? I made a mental note to add him to my suspect list.

Martha continued. "Other volunteers are running traditional colonial games such as apple bobbing, sack races, and Halloween crafts for the kids. As the culminating event of today's activities, Madame Fontaine is leading the haunted historic tour this evening."

"That should be fun. Madame Fontaine always tells the most interesting stories," I said, thinking about my encounters with her at the book club.

"She certainly has a flair for the dramatic," Martha said with a small smile.

Bella leaned over. "It's the food that should really be your first priority. Bert makes these cinnamon and sugar apple cider doughnuts with apples from his orchard that will make you forget the word 'diet' ever existed in your vocabulary."

"They're that good?" I asked, dipping my candle again. Bella was right, the layers of wax were building so slowly that it was hard to see progress from one dip to the next. I was glad candle-making wasn't part of my normal chore routine.

Martha cleared her throat. "I don't have much of a sweet tooth myself. Personally, I'd recommend the lobster rolls from the Hobbit Hole. They donated some trays this year. I'm sure I could set one or two aside for you, if you like."

My stomach rumbled. Amid all the excitement and the increased traffic in the shop, I still hadn't set aside time to get to the grocery store. Living off the oatmeal in my cupboards and takeaway probably wasn't great for my health. I knew it wasn't good for my wallet, but there was no denying my stomach. "Lobster rolls sound great," I said to Martha.

"I'll grab you two that I set aside in the back before they disappear," the friendly librarian said as she pushed to her feet and headed towards the backdoor of the library.

My mind returned to Mason and his ghostly friends. I couldn't dismiss the possibility that he was involved. Perhaps he'd even recruited the spirits to help. If he collaborated with the ghosts, could they have moved the pumpkins without being seen or assist him in the other pranks? That would explain a lot, but I wasn't sure how ghostly interactions could've accounted for the flash mob at the Zombie Shuffle or the enchanted candies. However, the prankster seemed to have an insider's knowledge of the town's events, and Mason fit the profile. The idea made my stomach churn with unease. If he was behind this, I needed to keep an eye on him, find out what he was really up to, and come up with a plan to stop him.

Bella cleared her throat, breaking the silence. "Are you almost done?" she asked, tipping her head toward the candle.

"I think so. Just the finishing touch." I glanced around to make sure no one was watching me and then used the small knife I'd put in my bag to slice open my thumb for the second time today. The first time I'd done it, I'd smeared my blood along the wick of the unmade candle. Now, I ran my thumb around the circumference of the narrow wax tube four or five times, making irregular rings of red against the smooth white wax. Quickly, I dipped the candle a few more times, sealing my blood inside layers of wax.

I held up the finished candle for Bella's appraisal. "What do you think? Will this work for the ritual?" I asked.

"I think it's perfect. What did Agatha say?"

"She hasn't returned my calls today. I might swing by her house later to check on her and Ignatius." I carefully hung the finished candle on a nearby rack to allow the wax to set.

Bella nodded. "Probably a good idea. We don't want anything to go wrong with the ingredients for the ritual before Halloween. What else do you need?"

I put pressure on the slight cut on my thumb to stop the bleeding as I ran through the list in my head. "I've already got the pumpkin, the salt, and the moonlit dew. It's all back at Spellbooks in my apartment upstairs so a curious customer doesn't walk off with it."

"What kind of a customer coming into a bookstore would want salt?" Bella asked.

I rolled my eyes. "None that I know of, but what if they thought the dew was complimentary water or something?"

Bella raised an eyebrow. "In a jam jar?"

"You never know," I said with a shrug. A rustling sound from behind me caught my ear, and I turned. There was nothing there. I frowned, annoyed with myself for jumping at shadows.

"You're worried that they'd give you a bad review online for grassy-tasting water?" Bella asked, drawing my attention back to her.

I shook my head. "No. There's not another full moon before Halloween. Without that dew, the ritual to turn Ignatius back to stone can't happen."

"Well, at least you don't need special honey that was made by a legendary bee high in the mountains of a remote island or anything."

"No, thank goodness. Normal store-bought should be fine. Thanks for bringing some along today by the way," I said, patting my bag.

Bella lifted a shoulder. "What are friends for if not borrowing their mother's baking ingredients for a magic spell?"

"Good company? Witty banter?"

Bella batted a hand through the air. "Oh, go on. Now, what else do you need?"

"Just a silver dagger and a piece of moonstone. Any idea where I could find either of those?"

Bella opened her mouth to respond, but Martha cut in as she walked over. "I couldn't help but overhear. You're looking for moonstone? Have you gone by Stardust Gems and Charms?"

I shook my head. "No. I haven't even heard of it."

Martha explained as she handed us each a small, napkin wrapped parcel. "It's Elowen Wispdale's boutique jewelry shop. She's one of the fey." She lowered her voice and pointed discreetly to her ears. Bella and I exchanged a knowing glance. Most fey had pointed ears, making it harder for them to blend into the normal world without something like the protective charms around Havenwood.

Martha continued, "Elowen has a knack for creating unique jewelry. She always does a limited-edition charm to mark big town events. I happen to know that this year's Harvest Festival charm is a moonstone set inside a pumpkin carriage setting, kind of a Cinderella-meets-Havenwood vibe."

My eyes lit up. "That sounds perfect!"

"And pretty," Bella added.

"Thanks for the candle making, the tip, and the lobster roll," I said, feeling more positive than I had for the past few days.

Martha grimaced. "I don't mean to pull a bait and switch, but I had to grab one of the Hobbit Hole's mini mushroom and hazelnut pies for you. Someone replaced all the lobster meat in the back with plastic toy lobsters. Can you imagine?" She shook her head sadly. "It seems that no town event is safe from these pranksters. I'm all for a good joke, but this is getting old. And it's scaring away the tourists."

I frowned. Plastic lobster tails seemed like a step down from lighting a food stall on fire. I pulled my journal out of my purse and added the new prank to the list, as well as Mason's name with a star next to it on my suspect list. Speaking of suspects, I quickly scanned the nearby crowd to see if there was anyone acting suspiciously, but everyone seemed to be enjoying the activities.

Bella patted Martha comfortingly on the shoulder. "I have a feeling that by the time the pumpkin parade rolls around on Halloween, everything will have calmed down. The season for tricks will have passed."

"I hope so," Martha sighed. "Know anyone who wants a couple dozen buttery plastic lobsters?"

I shook my head as I tucked the journal away. "Sorry, Martha, I don't."

However, I did know a girl who wanted to follow up a lead on a pumpkin carriage charm. Hopefully, the jeweler would be a fairy godmother of sorts and put me one step closer to completing the ritual.

Secrets in Stardust

THE CANDLE IN ITS paper wrapping and the pot of honey from Bella made my bag noticeably heavier on the long walk across town to Elowen's jewelry shop.

"How come we've never been to this Stardust jewelry place before?" I asked, gesturing to Bella's typical array of accessories. Today, she wore some carved wooden earrings, a chunky bracelet, and a distinctive crystal pendant hanging from a gold necklace.

Bella shrugged with a smile. "Because it's not a place I normally visit. My budget stretches to the craft section of the local farmers market, not limited-edition fairy charms."

"I'm not sure I've ever met one of the fey," I said honestly.

Bella shrugged. "In this town, you probably have and didn't even realize it. They're pretty much the same as everybody else here. Except for the pointed ears. Those are always a dead giveaway someone has fey blood, but around town they usually wear a hat or keep their hair long. Although, now that I think about it, I've noticed a few being more open and claiming prosthetic work when pressed about it. You know, like they're Tolkien super fans who just really, *really* love Legolas."

"So, what's this Elowen like? Do I need to watch out for inadvertently making deals or watch my words like they do in the old fairy tales?" I asked.

"No, nothing like that. Those types of rules from fairy tales seem to be greatly exaggerated from what I've seen of the fey in Havenwood. I've never had an issue with any of the fey in town. Elowen wouldn't try to trick, coerce, or hurt anyone. You're as safe as can be in her shop. Unless you are metal and adverse to high temperatures, that is. Even then, she'd just remake you into something lovely, so it might be worth it."

"Is that why you wanted to tag along? To look at the jewelry? Not that I'm mad about the company. It just seems like you'd have better things to do than to go on a scavenger hunt with me."

"I've always been a sucker for treasure hunts. And I enjoy looking at Elowen's jewelry. It's always so pretty. Just because I can't afford it doesn't mean I can't look."

"Well, there's no buried treasure at the end of this hunt. Only a stone dragon. Hopefully." I crossed my fingers and squeezed my eyes closed for a moment.

Bella nodded in agreement. "He could really make a ruckus around town, and, with the prankster on the loose, we don't need any more upheaval. But the truth is I feel partly responsible for this whole mess."

"None of this is your fault," I said firmly.

"Maybe, but whatever I can do to help, you just say the word. In the meantime, if part of my penance means that I have to examine beautiful jewelry, then so be it!" Bella pressed the back of her hand dramatically against her forehead.

I chuckled. "Well, I don't know about penance, but I appreciate the support."

Bella nudged me with her shoulder. "I've got your back, girl. We're a team, remember?"

I linked arms with her as we walked. "Just like Agatha and Granny Bea. They always had each other's backs, and so do we."

"Always," Bella said, giving me another little nudge.

A pang of guilt hit me. Bella had been nothing but supportive, yet I still hadn't told her everything. I looked at her out of the corner of my eye, wondering if we could be like Granny and Agatha. Perhaps I could even share the secret of Spellbooks with her someday. The thought filled me with both hope and anxiety. What would she think?

"Look! There it is," Bella said, interrupting my thoughts and pointing ahead.

I squinted, shading my eyes against the late afternoon sunshine. Sure enough, a small stone building with elegant whorls carved along the façade displayed a sign in graceful calligraphy announcing this was the home of Stardust Gems and Charms.

As Bella and I pushed through the door, a small bell tinkled to announce our arrival. A beautiful woman looked up from behind the counter and waved at us.

"I'll be with you in just a moment," she called. I blinked in awe as she returned to assisting the woman perusing the jewelry in the case between them. Beautiful didn't do Elowen justice. Lavender hair cascaded to her shoulders in loose waves, framing a heart-shaped face. Her porcelain skin seemed to carry a faint, iridescent sheen that was reminiscent of moonlight on a still lake. However, the most striking thing about her was her eyes. They were a deep, enigmatic emerald that, even in the brief look she'd sent our way, seemed to hold a timeless wisdom and otherworldly sparkle, hinting at her true nature.

Bella nudged me from behind. "Are you just going to block the door, or can I come in?" she asked.

I shook my head. "Oh. Right. Sorry. I got...um...distracted."

Bella nodded knowingly. "The fey will do that to you if you're not careful."

"This one, I think," the lady at the counter said, pointing at a black velvet display pillow on top of the glass jewelry cabinets.

"Excellent choice, but I thought I'd already sent over this year's charm for you," Elowen said, a quizzical frown marring the smooth porcelain of her skin.

"Oh, you did. This is for my daughter, Isadora. She's due to arrive back from college tomorrow, and I'd like to surprise her." I sucked in a breath as I recognized the customer.

Elowen's frown turned into a gentle smile, which seemed to make her striking emerald eyes sparkle. "Well, that's very thoughtful of you. Would you like me to gift wrap it for you?"

"Please."

I gripped Bella's hand and tugged her towards the nearest display case, pretending to examine the bracelets on display as Vivienne Silverthorne glanced over at us. With the prankster on the loose, Ignatius in the mix, and the Silverthorne brothers already involved, I didn't need to draw any more attention to myself. Especially not from the powerful matriarch of that family. I frowned as I pretended to be intrigued by the elegant bracelets; her words sinking in. Vivienne said that Isadora was arriving *tomorrow*? But I'd seen her talking with Lucas *last night*. Why the discrepancy? If Isadora was surprising her family, surely her presence at the town event last night would've given her away. I peeked at Vivienne without turning my head. Why would Isadora lie to her mother about her arrival?

I hadn't told Bella about the incident between Lucas and Isadora I'd observed. My mind raced, wondering if I should share it now. Probably not. I didn't know exactly what gifts Vivienne or Elowen might have. Some paranormals had abnormally sharp senses, including hearing. No, it was better to catch Bella up on everything later, when I was sure we were alone.

"There you are," Elowen said brightly, handing the gorgeously wrapped box with an elegantly curling silver ribbon to Vivienne. "I hope she likes it."

"I know she will. Your work is always of the highest quality and so unique," Vivienne said, tucking the gift inside her purse carefully. "Once the Harvest Festival is over, I'd like to sit down with you to discuss this year's Christmas Eve Ball. I'm thinking about commissioning some special pieces."

"I can't wait," Elowen said, walking with Vivienne towards the shop door.

"Excellent. I'll be in touch." Vivienne swept out of the jewelry store, accompanied by a swirl of expensive perfume.

Elowen turned to us. "My apologies for the delay. My assistant called in sick today so we're a bit short staffed. Do you like the emberite?"

I reminded myself not to be dazzled by the fey's beauty, but even with the conscious reminder, it was difficult. "Emberite?" I managed lamely.

Elowen moved gracefully behind the display case and withdrew a golden bracelet set with gemstones that looked like crystalized flame. The gems glittered in the sunlight with a fiery glow reminiscent of smoldering embers. "I think this piece really shows the gemstone off to its full beauty. Emberite is a rare gemstone. It has a unique crystalline structure that gives the appearance of flickering fire and has the capacity to absorb and retain heat for extended periods. Ancient stories tell of its ability to enhance the wearer's connection to the element of fire." She laughed, waving her free hand in a gesture that could have been interpreted as dismissive. "But who believes in such tales these days? It is beautiful, nonetheless. Shall I pack it up for you ladies?"

I stared at the bracelet, mesmerized by the fiery depths of the gems almost as much as I had been by Elowen's beauty. Bella elbowed me in the ribs, which helped jar the words out of me. "Moonstone. I'm, I mean, we're looking for moonstone. Do you happen to have any?"

Elowen's smile was as gracious as it was luminous. "You're in luck. I have one more of my limited-edition Harvest Festival charms left." She tucked the emberite bracelet back into its case and led the way to the display case where she'd been helping Vivienne Silverthorne. She pulled out a black velvet pad with a single gorgeous charm in the middle.

Elowen pointed at the oval moonstone cunningly wrapped in a delicate swirl of curling pumpkin vines forming the frame of a magical silver carriage and finished with a heart-shaped leaf. "The moonstone is the perfect centerpiece for this year's charm. The natural adularescence of the stone causes the unique play of light within the microstructure of the gemstone, giving it an ethereal and almost mystical appearance." She gave a charming little smile and shrug. "I was inspired when working with it to create this whimsical Cinderella carriage with the moonstone playing the role of the magical pumpkin."

"It's stunning," I said sincerely. The delicate carriage looked like a fairy could've conjured it into existence. In a manner of speaking, I supposed one had been.

"Thank you," Elowen said, a faint blush coloring her cheeks. "It's always nice to have one's work appreciated."

"How much is it?" I asked, almost afraid to hear the answer.

Elowen named a price that made my jaw drop. For that amount of money, I could keep my bare kitchen stocked for a month. Maybe more. But I needed the moonstone for the ritual. I started doing some quick mental math, trying to figure out if I could sell a kidney before Halloween.

Bella read my dismayed expression and interjected. "I don't suppose you have something a little less fairy-tale, but more economical? We're not looking for any princes today."

"I'd need a prince to be able to afford that charm," I said, my tongue running away with me before my politeness-filter could halt the words. I hastened to add. "But it's lovely."

Elowen chuckled. "I understand completely. However, I don't have any other moonstone pieces ready at this moment. In fact, the only moonstones I currently have in the shop aside from this one are leftover fragments from the carriage charms."

"Could I see those?" I asked eagerly.

Elowen looked at me strangely. "Sure. I guess." She replaced the charm in its case and locked it. "I'll be back in a moment." She hurried through a door at the back of the shop and returned shortly, cradling a small square of black cloth in one hand. She spread it out on the glass case, clearly showing three irregular fragments of unfinished moonstone. "These are too small to polish down into the circular shape for the pumpkin, so I hadn't finished them yet. I don't know what I would use them for, but I don't like to waste materials. I'm sure I'll think of something for them eventually."

"How much for one?" I asked eagerly.

Elowen frowned at me. "You want an uncut, unpolished fragment of a gemstone? Why, may I ask?"

Bella interrupted me smoothly. "It's for a project at Sullivan's Spellbooks. Harper stumbled across something in her granny's attic, and we need the moonstone to finish it as a...a way of wrapping up some of Beatrice's unfinished business."

Elowen's features softened. "Like a memorial?"

"Something like that," I hedged, a blush coloring my cheeks. Lying didn't come naturally to me.

Elowen grabbed a tiny velvet bag from behind the counter and rolled all three moonstone fragments inside. "Beatrice did me a favor once that I was never able to repay before her death. Consider this my way of balancing the scales," she said, handing the bag over to me.

"What? Are you sure?" I asked, feeling even worse as I accepted the moonstone.

"Paying one's debts is important where I come from," Elowen said with a little wink and a smile. "Please. I insist."

"Well, thank you then," I said, adding the moonstone to my bag with the candle and the honey. A sudden thought occurred to me. "I don't suppose you make anything like a knife, do you? I need a silver knife for the, uh, memorial."

Elowen gave me a strange look and shook her head. "Beatrice always had eccentric taste. But no, I don't make anything like that."

I felt my face fall. Ah well. At least I secured the moonstone.

Before I could say goodbye, Elowen added, "If you are interested in weaponry, you should visit Mason Forham. He dabbles in such things although I don't know if he works with silver. It's worth a try though."

"Thanks for the tip," I said, feeling hopeful.

Bella and I left the shop with a wave to Elowen. As we walked, I took advantage of the quiet moment with my best friend to fill her in on all my current thoughts and suspicions about the case, except for my thoughts that Alex might be involved. Bella listened intently, nodding in agreement.

"Finding the prankster is crucial, but I'm not sure it's the Silverthorne brothers or Mason Forham. I can't imagine any of them doing anything like this," she said. "I'll keep an ear out at the Oasis for any idle gossip that might give us a clue."

"Let me know the instant you hear anything," I said, already feeling like I was gaining traction on solving the mystery of the prankster.

I felt a spark of optimism for the first time in days. I had all the elements for the ritual in hand except for the dagger, and I had a solid lead on where to find that as well. The prankster seemed to have scaled back to mischief again instead of dangerous antics, and, with Bella's help, I was confident we could uncover who was behind all the pranks. Things were looking up. All I had to do now was wait for Halloween, complete the ritual, and turn Ignatius back to stone. In that time, hopefully, the prankster might grow bored or get caught. Maybe we wouldn't even have to figure out who it was and could focus all our attention on Ignatius.

I should've known it couldn't be that simple, but I was naïve enough to let myself believe luck was turning my way. I should've known better.

Plane Pizazz

MY PHONE BUZZED IN my pocket as Bella and I walked away from Elowen's jewelry store. It kept vibrating as I pulled it out and glanced at the screen. Martha Morningstar? What could the town's librarian want with me? A merry little tune jangled from Bella's phone as I answered mine.

"Martha? Hi. What's up?" I asked as Bella answered her phone.

"Papa?" she said, stepping away so we could each talk without distraction.

"Harper?" Martha's voice sounded business-like, but there was an undertone of something else in her tone. Worry? Stress? Before I could put my finger on it, she continued. "Vivienne Silverthorne is calling an emergency town meeting at the library this evening. She asked me to help reach out to as many business owners as possible, given the short time frame. Are you available?"

I frowned. Town meetings were always a combination of town business, small town gossip, and jokes. But they were always planned. An emergency meeting? And called by Vivienne Silverthorne no less? I just saw her at the jewelry store. I looked around quickly to make sure everything looked normal. As far as I could tell, there wasn't any magic running amok in the streets of Havenwood, but it didn't take a large leap of logic to figure out the meeting might be a response to the prankster. However, what kind of response was Vivienne planning?

"Thanks for letting me know, Martha. I'll be there. Just let me know what time," I said.

The librarian sounded relieved. "Good to know. Vivienne wants to start at six o'clock on the dot. A few residents like Madame Fontaine will be running tours for the visitors, but most businesses close by then anyway on a Sunday. I just didn't know what hours you were keeping at Spellbooks during the Harvest Festival."

"Don't worry about it. I'll be there," I said.

"Okay, I'll make a note for Vivienne. I've got a list of other people to call, so I'm going to say goodbye for now. See you later," Martha said before hanging up.

"Bye," I murmured as I turned to Bella. She was just finishing up her phone call as well.

I held up my phone. "I just got the strangest phone call from Martha Morningstar."

Bella wiggled hers at me. "I think I just got the same message. An emergency town meeting?"

"Yeah. Is this normal?" I asked.

Bella shook her head. "Nothing about this is normal. The last time they called an emergency meeting was when a massive thunderstorm blew through about ten years ago. Parts of the town were flooded, and some people lost power. Without the town pulling together, things could have gone very badly for a lot of people."

"So, what you're saying is that a magical prankster is equivalent to a weather-related emergency?"

Bella tucked her phone back in her pocket and nodded seriously. "It is for Vivienne Silverthorne. And if she thinks it's an emergency, then all of Havenwood falls in line."

I really didn't want to give Vivienne an excuse to suspect me of anything but compliance, what with the small matter of dissolving the stone spell on Ignatius. I glanced at the time. We could make it back to the library with time to spare, but not much. "It looks like we'd better head back over then," I said.

"Agreed. I told Papa I'd go on behalf of our family," Bella said, looking nervous. "Do you think they'll have word on the prankster?"

I linked arms with her. "I'm hoping it's all good news. They've caught him. Life is returning to normal. Everyone can relax," I said with a smile. Even as I spoke, I didn't believe my own words. We started walking briskly back to the library. In my heart of hearts, I knew news like that could be delivered and received via text message. An emergency meeting meant something more dire. I just knew it.

As the clock struck six, the room became a sea of hushed whispers, and small groups of locals huddled together, shooting suspicious glances around. The air was thick with anticipation and nervous energy, mirroring the collective unease that gripped Havenwood. I could feel the same unease creeping over me, amplifying the questions racing through my mind as I stood near the back of the crowd with Bella. Was the prankster among us? Was he hiding in plain sight? Or were they taking advantage of the chaos, plotting more disruptions while we were gathered here, trying to devise a plan to deal with him or her?

Just before the tension could reach its peak, Mayor Flavian Featherfoot, a small man in a charmingly old-fashioned suit, raised his voice above the murmur of the crowd. Instantly recognizable, his smile attempted to bring a sense of calm to the room, but the urgency in his words betrayed the gravity of the situation.

"Friends, please excuse the abrupt nature of our meeting. However, given the circumstances, it's of the utmost importance we all act together on this matter. To that end, allow me to present Vivienne Silverthorne, who will spearhead this town initiative."

The applause he led was a scattered, uneasy acknowledgment as he made room for Vivienne to step forward. Her mere presence commanded the attention of the entire room.

"Good evening, citizens of Havenwood," Vivienne began, her voice cutting through the room like a razor, silencing any lingering whispers. "As you're all well aware, our quaint town has recently fallen victim to a mischievous prankster. A disruptor of our peace, a disturber of our traditions."

Vivienne's intense gaze swept across the room, as if she was piercing through each person's intentions, her eyes locking on to the collective conscience of the community. "To the one responsible for these antics, let me be clear. We know this juvenile trickster is one of our own because of their unique... gifts. Hear me when I say that your actions will not be tolerated any longer. This town has thrived for generations, and we won't let the likes of you tarnish its reputation."

Even with her carefully chosen words, Vivienne hinted at the hidden magical nature of Havenwood. Her eyes glittered with fierce determination, each word resonating with a weight that hung heavily in the air. "To the prankster, heed my words. Cease your activities immediately or face the consequences."

As Vivienne spoke, the room fell from quietly attentive to a collective silence, broken only by the anxious shuffling of feet. The tension in the air became suffocating, and I, like everyone else, nervously scanned the room, attempting to decipher the faces of our neighbors. The weight of suspicion seemed to press down on us, creating an atmosphere of uncertainty and unease that permeated every corner of the library. Havenwood, usually tranquil and harmonious, now stood at the precipice of a crisis. Who would come out on top? The powerful Silverthorne mage or the audacious prankster?

As if in response to Vivienne's authoritative message, the room was suddenly filled with an unexpected and whimsical display of paper airplanes. The enchanted planes danced through the air, performing acrobatic loops, swirls, and dives that made it nearly impossible for anyone to predict their trajectory. Tied to their tails were messages in bold writing. I craned my neck to read the one on the nearest plane.

Vivienne's Smiles: A Myth or a Miracle?

A surprised laugh I barely disguised as a snort escaped me. Another plane flew by, the message on its tail reading:

Vivienne Silverthorne's Guide to Grumpiness: A Bestseller in Havenwood!

Bella tugged on my arm, pointing out a large paper plane with a huge banner proclaiming:

Local Mage or Sourpuss Sorceress? Vivienne's Identity Crisis Exposed!

The room erupted in a mixture of laughter and surprised chatter as the whimsical airplanes darted around, prompting people to dodge and duck to avoid being dive bombed by the paper projectiles.

I glanced to the front of the room to see how Vivienne would respond. Her stern expression transformed into one of fury as she read the messages. With a snarl and a snap of her fingers, the amusing paper planes burst into flames, disappearing one after the other in brilliant flashes that reminded me of the flaming paper stage magicians used. One by one, the planes turned to fine ash, the remains of the lighthearted prank drifting down onto the upturned faces of the crowd replacing the earlier laughter with a hushed, uneasy silence.

Amid the dissipating laughter, a movement caught the corner of my eye. I glimpsed two small figures in pointed hats dashing out the doors of the library and making a quick escape. The mischievous duo, who I assumed were the architects of the prank, vanished into the lengthening shadows outside, leaving only a lingering giggle behind them. I raised my hand to point them out.

"I saw—" I began, but my voice was lost in the chaos as a loud outburst from the back of the room drowned out my words.

I spun around to see what looked like a holographic image of a giant mouth hovering in midair and grinning down at the assembled townsfolk. Suddenly, the mouth stuck out an enormous tongue and blew a massive, noisy raspberry. The thunderous sound was accompanied by a spray of confetti and glitter, showering everyone in the room. The unexpected and immature prank caused even more of an uproar.

Some townsfolk gasped in shock and a few shouted in displeasure or annoyance, brushing confetti and glitter off their clothes. Groups of people started angrily grumbling, their voices blending into a hum of confusion and irritation that filled the room.

"Enough of these childish antics!" Vivienne declared, her voice cutting through the remaining echoes of chaos. My eyes snapped up to her. Vivienne stood with her hand upraised and her eyes still blazing with determination. She slowly lowered her arm. "We won't be distracted from the task at hand. The prankster may revel in his momentary victory, but mark my words, we *will* prevail, and peace shall once more be restored to Havenwood."

Vivienne swept through the crowd, heading outside to where the pranksters had disappeared. Something about her earlier words struck me. She'd spoken in singular, but I'd definitely seen two figures running away. Should I tell her? As she approached, I opened my mouth to pass along the tidbit. However, her expression made me snap my teeth closed with a click. Based on the storm clouds gathering on Vivienne's face, there was no way

I was going to get between her and her quarry. Not now. Preferably not ever.

Let Vivienne do her thing; I'd focus on doing my part. Get the ingredients, turn Ignatius back to stone, keep my head down, and not draw any undue attention my way while I tried to discover who these pranksters were.

I was just about to tell Bella what I had seen when my phone buzzed with a new message. Glancing down, I was surprised to see Officer Reggie's name pop up on my screen. I thumbed my messaging app open to see I'd missed several texts and two calls from him and some from Finn as well. My eyes widened as I read the last one from Officer Reggie.

Urgent: Break-in at Spellbooks. Need you here ASAP.

Panic shot through me. I turned quickly to Bella, who was still brushing confetti out of her hair. "Bella, I have to go. There's been a break-in at the shop."

Her eyes widened, and she immediately nodded. "I'm coming."

I glanced around at the chaotic aftermath of the pranksters' latest tricks. "I appreciate the support, but the police are already on the scene. Someone needs to stay here and keep an ear out for any useful information." Quickly, I filled her in on what I'd seen just before the explosion of glitter. "See? We need to cover all our bases if we're going to catch them," I finished.

Bella hesitated, then reluctantly nodded. "You're right. I'll see what I can find out. Be careful, okay?"

"I will. Thanks, Bella," I said, giving her arm a quick squeeze. The knot of anxiety in my stomach tightened as I turned and sprinted towards Spellbooks. Each step felt heavy, burdened by the weight of worry and fear about what I might find when I arrived.

Break and Smash

I CLUTCHED MY BAG as I dashed down Arcadia Avenue towards Officer Reggie standing in front of Spellbooks. The friendly policeman wore a serious expression as he waved people by. "Nothing to see here. Police business. We've got this under control."

If I hadn't been so worried about Spellbooks, I might've pointed out that his choice of words sparked more curiosity than it quelled, but this wasn't the time to argue pedantically over word choice. "What's going on, Officer Reggie?" I asked through gasps of air as I tried to calm my racing heart after the sprint over here. I craned my neck to look over his shoulder. My mouth dropped open. A pane of glass in my front display was broken and the door to the shop stood ajar. "Oh, my goodness!"

"Nothing to see here. Nothing at all. Noth – oh, Harper. Good to see you."

"Is everyone okay? Where's Luna? Mr. Wigglesworth? Thistle? Please tell me no one is hurt!" I said, a sense of dread solidifying and dropping like a boulder in the pit of my stomach.

"Just wait here. The boss will be back in two shakes. He's inside making sure all's clear," Reggie said, his tone comforting. However, the lack of information was not. My mind raced with worst-case scenarios, and the uncertainty gnawed at me.

What had happened here? It looked like someone took a golf club to the front window. I was suddenly glad Officer Reggie's boss was handling the situation. I'd never seen Sheriff Jackson shift into his werewolf form, but if someone was still inside Spellbooks, the gruff lawman was the man for the job. Standing out on the street like this reminded me of how I'd re-met Sheriff Jackson when I moved to town back in September. He'd been investigating the theft of the rare books from Spellbooks. He'd intimidated me then but seemed like a fair and competent lawman. After that incident, though, I'd asked Grimgor to build some more secure display cases with gnomish glass and enchanted locks. Perhaps I should've asked him to do the entire shop, regardless of the cost.

I was running calculations of replacing all the windows in my shop with the expensive gnomish glass when Sheriff Jackson appeared in the doorway. He took one look at the handful of curious tourists gathered around and frowned deeply, his bushy eyebrows drawing together and his large moustache drooping downward.

"Nothing to see, folks. Move along now," he growled.

Although his words held no threat, something in his tone or aura warned the primal, subconscious part of my brain that this was a predator, and it would be best for my survival to be somewhere, *anywhere*, else. Apparently, I wasn't the only one. The people surrounding my shop scattered, leaving me alone with the two police officers for a moment.

"What happened, Sheriff?" I asked. The tension in the air was palpable, my heart pounding in my chest as I waited for Sheriff Jackson's report.

"Better come with me," Sheriff Jackson said. "Reggie, you stay here and keep the lookie-loos out."

"Got it, boss!" the cheerful officer replied.

I followed the sheriff into the shop, placing my hand on the frame of the door as I entered. I didn't know if Spellbooks could read my mind, but I wanted to offer what comfort I could at the moment.

Sheriff Jackson put his hands on his hips and sighed. "The sooner we catch this guy, the better. For everyone."

"What guy? What's going on?" I asked as I looked around frantically, starting with the rare books in their specialized display case. No broken glass there. In fact, other than the broken window, it didn't look like anything else had been disturbed. I let out a little sigh of relief.

"As far as I can tell, your shop has fallen victim to the prankster wreaking havoc around town. However, I checked in with Luna, and both she and the cat are fine. Your neighbor, Finn Oakheart, offered to take them in until we could find and inform you what had happened."

I let out a little sigh of relief. I was glad to know that Luna and Mr. Wigglesworth were okay. As soon as I could, I'd go over and check on them. "Wait. Prankster? How did they get here so fast? They were just at the emergency town meeting," I said without thinking.

Sheriff Jackson's eyes sharpened. "They? Town meeting? Tell me everything," he ordered.

As quickly as I could, I explained what had happened. Sheriff Jackson had a good poker face, but the downward tilt of his lips under his massive moustache let me know the chaos plaguing his town displeased him greatly. When I finished, Sheriff Jackson excused himself and stepped to the front door, speaking to Officer Reggie.

"There's been an incident down at the library. Give Bill a call and tell him to get down there as fast as he can to preserve the scene and keep everyone calm. We'll head over as soon as we can."

"Got it, boss," Reggie said, giving the sheriff a thumbs up.

Sheriff Jackson turned back to me, his tone brisk and efficient. "I know it looks bad down here, but it seems to be just the window. You'll have to run an inventory to be sure, but it doesn't look like anything's been disturbed in the shop."

I let out a sigh of relief. "Well, that's good."

Sheriff Jackson continued. "Upstairs is another story. But it looks worse than it actually is."

"What are you talking about?"

He pointed towards the stairs leading to my apartment. "It's easier to show you. Come on."

The sheriff led the way, and I followed, senses tingling. Why had the prankster targeted my shop? My home? This wasn't anything like the light-hearted use of magic at the library, the candy store or even the pumpkin farm. This was vandalism. Why such differences in the mayhem? And why were they escalating? What had changed?

The sheriff spoke over his shoulder. "We've had a number of these types of petty crimes. Someone breaks into a property, tosses things around, and then leaves through the front door. As far as we've been able to tell, nothing's ever missing, but they do cause a mess. Between the break-ins and the pranks at the town events, we're run off our feet. I want nothing more than to sniff out this prankster, apologies, *pranksters*, but I don't have the time with all the shenanigans they're pulling."

"Do you think the pranks and the break-ins are two separate perpetrators or are they working as a team like at the library?" I asked, a little surprised. This was the first I'd heard about any break-ins.

"Too soon to tell, but I wouldn't rule anything out yet," the sheriff said. The set of his jaw told me I wouldn't get any more out of him. I made a mental note to ask Officer Reggie later. He was always more talkative than the taciturn sheriff and might let a clue slip.

Sheriff Jackson pushed open the door to my apartment, and I gasped. It looked like someone had turned the entire place upside-down and shaken it to look for loose change. My jaw dropped as I scanned the chaos. Books were strewn haphazardly across the floor. Pillows were tossed across the room. All the cupboards in my kitchen were opened and every one had been emptied. Thank goodness I hadn't found the time to go grocery shopping, or the mess would've been much worse. As it was, cans and boxes were scattered across the counter and floor. I saw at least one broken jar of strawberry jam, and the small packet of sugar I kept on hand to sweeten tea had exploded all over the sink.

"What...?" I trailed off, words eluding me.

"It looks worse than it is," Sheriff Jackson said from behind me. "Most of this is messy and just downright annoying, but you'll have to be careful sweeping up that broken glass in the kitchen. However, if it's anything like the other places, a broom and a vacuum will solve most of the problem. Keep your eyes open and let me know immediately if anything is missing here or in the shop, but if this is like the others, it's just irritating tomfoolery rather than a robbery."

"Just how many more break-ins have there been?" I asked, looking around at the mess in disbelief.

Sheriff Jackson pushed his hat back and scratched his head. "This makes five in the last three days, but nothing's ever taken. We've tried to keep it all under wraps. Vivienne Silverthorne doesn't want anything to interfere with the Harvest Festival. It would be bad for the town to have a series of petty crimes ruin one of our biggest events of the year. However, I'm not sure how much longer I can keep this news from spreading."

"This isn't good," I murmured.

"Not at all," the sheriff agreed grimly. "And whoever is behind all the commotion in town seems to be escalating. First, it's rolling pumpkins and now it's fires and broken windows. What's next?"

I bit my lip, wondering if I should warn him about Ignatius. After all, the little dragon could add immeasurably to the mounting problems. However, it might not be wise to draw the sheriff's attention away from catching the real culprits, and the entire town needed these shenanigans to stop. Warning the sheriff might put me not only on his bad side but also on Vivienne Silverthorne's. Besides, the dragon problem was contained for now. My best bet was still the ritual, and I didn't need the sheriff for that. I decided not to mention it. "I don't know, but I hope you catch the culprits. They caused a real mess at the library too with the paper airplanes and the glitter and confetti."

The sheriff nodded seriously. "I need to get over there as soon as I can, but—"

Officer Reggie clattered up the stairs, interrupting Sheriff Jackson. "Sheriff? Joe is here with that wood."

"Thanks Reggie," the sheriff said. He turned back to me. "I hope you don't mind, but I've asked my buddy, Joe Hawkins, to bring over something to cover the window for you until you can get someone out to fix it. He's an excellent carpenter and a better neighbor. He'll get that window secured for you until you can get it fixed. Feel free to look around. We've already cleared the scene. It's just like the others. No fingerprints, no clues as to who's behind everything." He turned and headed towards the door.

"Thanks, Sheriff. I'll look at everything and see if anything's missing," I said, feeling a mix of frustration and helplessness as I surveyed the chaos in my apartment. At first glance, I agreed with the sheriff—it seemed more of a mess than any actual damage. But why would someone do this? As I examined the disarray, a deep sense of violation washed over me. Someone had been in my home, my sanctuary, and turned it upside down. Why?

A sudden thought occurred, and I spun to Reggie. "How long ago did this break-in happen?" I asked.

Officer Reggie paused, his brow furrowing as he considered my question. "Somewhere between an hour or two ago, based on our best estimate. We got here as soon as someone called it in."

My mind raced. The timing made sense; it gave the pranksters just enough time to travel from Spellbooks to the library. But why target my home of all places? What had I done to draw their attention, or was this a random act of vandalism?

Officer Reggie looked around, shaking his head. "I'm sorry you have to deal with this, Harper. And the second time since you moved here. I'd like to say this isn't the way things normally go here in Havenwood, but this week hasn't been a great one for our town, has it? I mean, this little prankster has really got everyone up in arms."

My ears perked up. I bit my lip, trying to decide if I should try to press Reggie for clues. Curiosity got the better of me and I asked, "Little? Did someone see something?"

Reggie nodded and stuck his thumbs in his belt loops. "People haven't seen anything properly, but they've caught glimpses. A shadow here. A flash of movement there. That type of thing. However, from what everyone's told the sheriff, it seems like this guy is the strangest perp I've heard of in a while and living in Havenwood, that's saying something. Not that there's much crime here, but our population isn't exactly normal, now, is it?"

Reggie had the habit of veering off on tangents, so I gently redirected him, hoping for a clue. "You said he was strange? How so?"

"Oh. Right. Well, everyone who's caught a glimpse says he's on the short side and has a weird fashion sense. He wears a pointed hat instead of a ski-mask, which is a new one for me. Although, it is the Halloween season so maybe he just picked something up at a costume shop."

My mind flashed back to what I'd seen at the emergency town meeting. Two shadows with pointed hats ran out into the night. It had to be the same rascals. But who would break into my shop and then dare to mess with the matriarch of Havenwood almost immediately afterwards? I cast my mind back. I didn't remember seeing the sheriff or Officer Reggie at the town meeting. Perhaps that's why the police hadn't attended. Was it a calculated plan to keep the police from the emergency meeting? If so, why target Spellbooks?

"Officer Reggie," the sheriff called up the stairs. "A moment please!"

Reggie shot me an apologetic smile and clattered noisily downstairs.

I picked up some pillows, tossing them back on the couch and then shoved books haphazardly onto the nearby shelf. I'd reorder them later, but for now, it made me feel more in control to start tidying. The floorboards under my feet shook strongly enough that a small book fell off the shelf.

"Spellbooks!" I exclaimed, stooping to pick it up. I recognized it as the ledger in which Granny Bea had kept track of the Halloween decorations. I tried to set it back on the shelf, but Spellbooks pushed it off again. "What's going on? I'm trying to clean up," I said as I barely caught the book before it fell. Rather than fight with my sentient bookshop, I set the ledger on the couch next to my purse. The floorboards underfoot vibrated in seeming displeasure.

"Hey! There are still police downstairs," I hissed. "Let me make sure they've gone before you get all rumbly."

The sullen silence that descended on the apartment let me know that Spellbooks was acquiescing. For now. I hurried downstairs, my thoughts still racing.

At the front of the shop, I found a man who had to be Joe Hawkins already at work, efficiently securing the broken window with a sheet of plywood. His golden eyes flickered with a faint, supernatural glow as he nodded at me, a silent acknowledgment of the chaos inside.

"Harper, this is Joe Hawkins. Joe, Harper Sullivan," Sheriff Jackson said by way of introduction.

Joe put down his hammer and held out a calloused hand. "Pleasure to meet you Harper. Sorry it had to be under such circumstances."

"Nice to meet you too," I said, my voice tight with residual tension as I shook his hand. "I appreciate you coming out so quickly."

"Any friend of the sheriff's is a friend of mine. Nice place you got here. Shame about the window though. Let me know if you need any help fixing it up," he said, digging into the pocket of his flannel shirt for a business card and passing it over.

"Thanks," I murmured as I accepted it. I turned to Sheriff Jackson and Officer Reggie, who were preparing to leave. "And thank you both for your help. I appreciate it."

Sheriff Jackson gave me a curt nod, his demeanor as stern as ever. "We'll head over to the library to deal with the pranksters now. Stay safe. We'll catch whoever's responsible for this."

Officer Reggie gave me a small smile and a thumbs-up. "Hang in there," he said, and then jogged to catch up with the departing sheriff.

Joe packed up his tools and nodded at me. "You take care now. Lock up tight and don't hesitate to call if you need help with that window."

As they all left, the shop felt eerily quiet. I closed the door behind them, making sure the lock clicked into place. Alone in the silence, a wave of insecurity washed over me. I checked the lock again, ensuring it was secure.

Feeling lost and a little alone, I pulled out my phone and sent messages to both Finn and Bella, updating them on the situation. Neither responded right away, which probably meant they were busy. I should be too. I had a lot of unexpected cleaning to do and even more desire to catch the pranksters.

Imperil

WITH A DEEP BREATH, I turned back towards the stairs and the mess waiting for me in my apartment, ready to start putting things back in order. This was my sanctuary, and I wouldn't let anyone take that from me.

The kitchen needed some serious attention. There was more stuff there, even in its depleted state, than the rest of the apartment. After all, I was just settling in. Knickknacks and pictures accumulated with time, but a girl couldn't live without chips, salsa, and peanut butter. Not all at once, of course. That would be a gross combo. But I loved a good PB&J. It was cheap and delicious. Too bad my last jar of jam had been smashed.

My breath caught. Jam jar. Smashed. No, no, no, *no*.

I hurried into the small kitchen, picking my way through the mess. I stretched up to reach the open cabinet next to the sink, peering up at the top shelf. The shelf where I'd put the moonlit dew and the salt I needed for the ritual. My breath caught. Both were gone. I looked at the floor. A damp splotch sank into the hardwood floor underneath shards of broken glass and scattered piles of what I now realized was salt, not sugar. My stomach dropped. The salt was easy to replace, but the dew? It was impossible! There wasn't another full moon before Halloween. Without the dew, I couldn't complete the ritual to turn Ignatius back to stone. I stared at the broken jar in disbelief as all my hopes for a quick and easy conclusion to this mess with the dragon shattered as completely as the jam jar on my floor. What was I going to do now?

There was a clatter behind me. I spun to see my purse and Granny's ledger laying on the floor. Spellbooks had somehow managed to push them both off the couch.

"Spellbooks!" I groaned, frustration boiling over. "I'm trying to clean up and solve the mystery of the pranksters. You causing more of a mess isn't helping!" I started picking up the scattered items, my irritation clear. "Do you even realize what I'm dealing with? The pranksters have been causing nothing but chaos—annoying mischief, but still. And the fires? Those aren't just pranks. They're dangerous. I have this list of suspects, but none of them seem to fit all the crimes. I'm getting so overwhelmed, and none of the pieces fit together!"

As I ranted, Spellbooks seemed to hum in response, the floor vibrating gently beneath me. I sighed, feeling a bit foolish for losing my cool.

"Sorry," I sighed, plopping onto the floor. I pulled my knees up to my chest and hid my face in my hands, both embarrassed and overwhelmed. A warmth accompanied the gentle vibrations in what I imagined might be Spellbooks' version of a hug, making me smile.

I patted the floor. "Thanks. I needed that. It's just—a lot, you know? I'm doing my best, but I can't figure this out and then this..." I trailed off, waving an arm helplessly at the apartment. A sudden thought occurred. Maybe the pranksters hadn't been keeping the police away from the town meeting. Maybe they'd been targeting the dew. As soon as I thought it, I shook my head. That didn't make any sense. The dew was for the ritual to change Ignatius back to stone. Why would the pranksters be interested in disrupting that? Besides, how had they even known about it? Bella was the only other person who knew where I was storing it. No, my paranoia was getting the better of me.

A scraping sound drew my attention across the room to the chalkboard I hung on the wall. A word was slowly forming there. I held my breath. Spellbooks occasionally used the chalkboards in the shop and my apartment to communicate with me, but from what I could tell, it was an arduous process that seemed to drain Spellbooks of its energy. It only used the chalkboard on rare or important occasions. I tried to wait patiently as the single word formed on the board.

JOURNAL.

"Journal?" I read in confusion, scooping up the one that had fallen out of my bag. "That's what I've been trying to tell you. I've been making notes of everything that's been happening around town lately to try to figure out who is behind the pranks."

A thought occurred, and I laid the journal on the floor, knowing that Spellbooks had some sort of magical ability with books. I didn't fully understand how it worked, but if Spellbooks had taken the time and effort to write to me, maybe it thought it could help.

Apparently, I'd done the right thing because the pages started flipping faster and faster. Suddenly, it stopped, the pages falling open to the last notes I'd made about the pranksters. After the furious page turning, the sudden silent stillness felt simultaneously on edge and oppressive.

Tension crawled up across my shoulders, leaving an itchy, unsettled feeling behind. Unable to withstand the building pressure, I broke the silence that had descended on my apartment. "That's everything I know so far about the prankster, but it's no use. I still haven't been able to figure out who's responsible, but I could really use some help to—"

Before I could continue, the pages of Granny's ledger on the floor next to me started flipping, seemingly of their own accord, which made me jump. My mouth dropped open. What was going on? Obviously, after the journal, Spellbooks was behind the ghostly page turning, but why? As suddenly as it started, it stopped, the book falling open to a specific page.

"What is it, Spellbooks?" I asked, retrieving the book and looking at a familiar warning and list in Granny's distinctive penmanship.

Do not, under any circumstances, expose to fairy dust, liquids, trolls, or grape jam. Strawberry is fine. Oh, and the wizard is partial to honey in his tea.

I double checked the listed items marked with an asterisk. A small dragon statue and the wizard. There was even a small sketch of each item in the margins. I spotted Ignatius now that I was taking the time to look at the drawings. Next to him was the wizard, cradling a cup of tea.

"I don't get it, Spellbooks." Realization dawned, and I jabbed a finger at the wizard with his teacup. "Wait a second! Are you saying that the wizard is responsible for everything? I suppose he could have gotten splashed with water as well, dissolving his stone spell, and he is wearing a pointy hat."

A stronger vibration met my words, and, without a second thought, I dashed downstairs, heading to the spot on the shelves where I'd hidden the statue of the wizard. If he wasn't there, that would confirm he was the one behind the pranks, wouldn't it?

I skidded to a halt in the fantasy section, my hope at solving the case suddenly deflating like a pricked balloon. The wizard was still on the shelf, just as stony and enigmatic as ever. I doubted he would've turned himself back into stone willingly, especially after causing so much trouble in town. If I were in his curly wizard slippers, I certainly wouldn't do that. With a sigh, I reached out and patted the wall.

"It was a good idea, Spellbooks, but the wizard is here. He can't be the one causing all this mayhem. Besides, I saw two of them at the library tonight. It was a good try though."

A vibration along the wall seemed to ripple back towards my apartment. I was getting better at interpreting Spellbooks' non-verbal communication, but I couldn't quite figure out what this one meant, so I took my best guess.

"I enjoy working with you too, Spellbooks. And it was a good thought. Maybe if we put our heads together, we can figure this out. You know, like Watson and Sherlock Holmes or something? I'll go out and gather the clues, and then we can analyze them together. I bet you might see some connections I miss," I said, trying to use the moment to build on the developing bond of trust between the two of us. If we were going to be partners in running the shop, we were also partners in protecting it.

Another vibration traveled along the wall, stronger and more insistent this time, as if Spellbooks was urging me to follow. I felt a strange sense of urgency, a shared determination. "Alright, lead the way," I said, letting the vibrations guide me back upstairs.

As soon as I pushed back into the apartment, the sight of the mess made my heart sink. It wasn't just the unexpected disarray, but the violation of my sanctuary—the place I called home. Someone had done this deliberately, and it was more than just broken glass or upended cupboards. They had shattered the inherent sense of peace I hadn't even realized was woven into my concept of home in Havenwood. Sure, I could sweep up the smashed jars and reorganize the belongings scattered across the floor, but how did one piece together the fragmented shards of shattered tranquility?

The soft flutter of pages turning pulled my attention away from the mess. I glanced down to see Spellbooks was manipulating the ledger once more, making the paper fan out as it flipped from cover to cover. Obviously, Spellbooks wanted to show me something, so I forced myself to ignore the mess in the apartment and focus on what my magical partner had to tell me.

"What is it?" I asked, crouching next to the ledger. It fell open to the now familiar page with Granny's warning about the wizard and Ignatius.

I tapped the page. "Yes, it would make sense. If Granny turned the wizard to stone, she had a reason. She wasn't the type to just turn people to statues all willy-nilly. But he's still downstairs, and Ignatius is with Aunty Agatha. I don't think either of them are responsible for all the pranks."

To my amazement, the page under my finger tugged and strained. I lifted my hand, more in surprise than anything else, and the page flipped over. My heart stuttered and my breath caught.

There was one more entry on Granny's list. One that I'd missed entirely. Disbelieving, I traced a finger over the single word.

Imps.

A quick sketch revealed two figures, one tall and slender and the other shorter and rounder, wearing matching mischievous grins under hats. Distinctive pointy hats. And there were two of them, just like there had been at the library.

I frowned. Was I grasping at straws here? I didn't remember seeing any imps when I unpacked the Halloween decorations. Perhaps they weren't running around town causing havoc, but had simply been misplaced and put in a different box in Spellbooks' cavernous storage space? But then again, this was a magical bookshop in a magical town with a magical prankster problem. Could I really afford to ignore Spellbooks' theory just because it sounded implausible?

The short answer was no.

My feet were already moving by the time my brain reached that conclusion. I dashed to where I'd stashed the box to keep it out of the way of customers until I had time to deal with it. In all the hustle and bustle, I'd nearly forgotten about it entirely.

I found the box, and, upon closer examination, it looked more water-damaged than chewed up by mice, like I'd initially suspected. My mind flashed back to putting out the fire Ignatius had started. Water from my bucket had splashed onto this box. Could that have been the catalyst for everything that was happening now?

The box had been under the counter. It could have also gotten a good soaking. Not only that, but there was the hole in the corner. Large enough for two imps, newly freed from a stone spell to crawl through, perhaps? Two imps that had then escaped the shop. Two imps that wore pointed hats and might like to play pranks. Such as sending taunting airplanes zooming around the town library.

I frowned as I traced the discolored cardboard around the ripped hole near the bottom corner. The pranks had started before the fire in the shop. The pumpkin patch, the candy store, the orchard—all occurred *before* Ignatius set fire to a book and the subsequent dousing.

So, if I hadn't dissolved the stone spell, how did the imps escape? More importantly, where were they now?

Another thought popped into my mind. If the imps came from Spellbooks, I was the one responsible for the pranks around town. Sure, it might be indirectly liable, but I doubted Vivienne Silverthorne would see it that way. After tonight, she was on a crusade to save her town, and I doubted a little thing like a series of unfortunate and unpredictable events would persuade her to be lenient. With the imps or with me.

To top it all off, with the container of dew smashed to smithereens, there was nothing I could do to stop them.

Terror and Turmoil

I DID MY BEST to engage with customers the next day, but they all jumbled together into one, faceless blur as thoughts of Ignatius and the imps living in Havenwood full time whirred through my brain. In my spare moments, I used Granny's books to conduct research on imps and frantically discussed plans and options with Spellbooks. Everything we found confirmed my suspicions. The stone spell that had been cast on the imps had dissolved, and they were now wreaking havoc all over Havenwood. My stomach churned with a nauseating combination of guilt and urgency. I needed to fix this before things spiraled further out of control.

Spellbooks nudged a book across the floor once the last customer before lunch left and the shop was empty again. I crouched to retrieve it.

"Have you been doing some more research? What have you found?" I asked eagerly, setting the ancient-looking book on the counter. I didn't know where Spellbooks had found it, but if the information inside helped us catch the imps, I was happy the spirit in the shop had located it.

Spellbooks vibrated lightly under my fingertips, seemingly eager to help. Suddenly the cover flipped open, and the pages seemed to riffle themselves, falling open to a section on imps.

"Great work! Now, let's see," I murmured, tracing a finger down the page. "Imps are known for their mischief and trickery. They're attracted to places with high magical energy... like Havenwood." Spellbooks hummed in agreement. "It says here they particularly enjoy pranks that cause chaos but rarely cause physical harm," I continued reading aloud. I frowned and reread the section before tapping the page. "That fits the bill for the rolling pumpkins and the candy store antics. But the fires..." I paused, putting my hand on the wall to feel Spellbooks' reaction to my words. The vibrations slowed, almost as if the shop itself was contemplating the mystery.

I tried to force the pieces of the puzzle to fit together, but try as I might, they didn't click into place. Slowly, I shook my head. "The pranks around town are pure mischief. I can totally see two escaped imps making pumpkins roll or enchanted candy, but the fires don't fit that type of chicanery," I said. The wall rumbled under my fingertips in what I took for a surprised guffaw at my choice of words. "What? I read. I'd be a pretty poor bookshop owner if I didn't. But it's the fire thing that's throwing me. It doesn't make sense. The sheriff thought they might be entirely separate incidents. Maybe he's right. The imps might be behind the pranks, but something else could be responsible for the fires."

Spellbooks gave a gentle shudder, as if in agreement. The more I thought about it, the more I was sure the fires didn't fit neatly into the imps' repertoire of chaos.

"This doesn't make sense," I muttered. Spellbooks gave a light tremor, urging me on. "Alright, let's focus on what we know," I said, feeling a renewed sense of determination. "We've got two imps causing mayhem. We need to track them down and find a way to recast the stone spell. And while we're at it, we need to figure out who—or what—is behind the fires." I leaned back, feeling a strange sense of camaraderie with Spellbooks. "We're in this together, aren't we?" I asked softly. The shop responded with a warm, gentle vibration. I smiled, feeling a surge of gratitude. "Let's do this. Let's save Havenwood."

Despite my desire to hit the streets and stop the imps right now, I still had a business to run. I didn't need my online business course to tell me that shutting down the shop in the middle of a day wasn't a great idea. So, I kept it open, tried not to grow impatient when customers spent an inordinate amount of time browsing without buying, and conducted as much research as possible with Spellbooks in the quiet moments when the shop was empty.

However, my anxiety only grew as the day dragged on. It seemed like every local who came in whispered of more pranks plaguing the town. People were wondering if they would continue to escalate like the fire in the town square. Although that was of concern, what worried me more was what would Vivienne do in retaliation once she learned the imps came from Spellbooks. She'd threatened to shut down the shop once before for what was a relatively harmless bit of magic. What would she do if she learned I was responsible for the imps terrorizing her Harvest Festival, and what was worse, I had no way to stop them?

Six o'clock rolled around before I knew it, and I closed up the shop on autopilot. Based on my records, I'd sold a fair number of books today, but I couldn't remember a single one. Rumors and my own spiraling imagination had distracted me.

What was I going to do if I couldn't stop the imps? Throw myself on Vivienne Silverthorne's mercy, confess the whole mess, and hope she could help?

Perhaps not, but I could take certain steps to ensure the safety of Spellbooks. I sent a text to Grimgor to confirm when he was coming out to fix the front window. Then, for safety's sake, I wrapped up the little stone wizard in as many Ziplock bags, bubble wrap, and layers of packing tape as I could manage. I wasn't about to have another statue-coming-to-life incident.

With all that taken care of, I sighed and got myself a cup of coffee, my thoughts drifting back to Vivienne Silverthorne. What would her response be if she found out the imps came from Spellbooks? Make my life here unbearable? Turn me into a toad until the imps were caught? Banish me from Havenwood for endangering the town? To be honest, I probably deserved it.

"Harper? Harper!" A grumpy voice broke through my concentration.

"Hmm?"

"Fluff and furballs! You're spilling coffee everywhere!" Luna exclaimed, snapping me out of the horrible daydream of imps swinging from Christmas lights while singing naughty parodies of carols. I glanced down and hissed. A pool of dark liquid spilled across the front counter, stretching towards a pile of books I needed to return to their proper places in the shop. I scooped up the books, moving them out of the way of the coffee flood, and grabbed some paper towels to mop up the spill. At least the wizard was safely ensconced in layers of plastic under the counter.

"Sorry," I muttered. "I've got a lot on my mind." As quickly as I could, I explained the whole situation to her.

"Well, I suppose this explains your distraction, but it doesn't excuse it," Luna muttered. She hopped up on the newly cleaned counter, her little pink nose twitching in irritation. "You've got to take care of these imps and soon!"

I felt my heart rate rise as my stomach plummeted. Groaning, I buried my head in my hands, thankful the shop was empty. "I can't!"

"That's a rubbish attitude. Whatever happened to the mantra of that little green muppet?"

I frowned, thinking of my childhood. "It's not easy being green?" I asked, remembering watching Kermit the Frog sing a song with a guitar in a marsh. How the frog managed the complex instrumental fingering while covered in mucus and swamp slime boggled my mind, even as a kid.

Luna's ears flicked back and forth. "No. The other one. Something like quit trying and just do it?" She looked at me expectantly.

I stared at her blankly. What was the rabbit talking about?

Realization dawned a moment later. "Oh! You've remixed Yoda with a Nike commercial. Yoda said, 'do or do not, there is no try.'"

"Which is horrible grammar. How can he possibly expect to connect to today's youth with their attention span of less than a second if he can't even put words in the right order in a simple sentence?" Luna grumped.

I bit back a smile, despite the situation. "You're right. He should've just said, 'Yo, dude. Either totally crush it, or don't even bother, man! There ain't no halfway, ya dig?'"

Luna's eyes flashed dangerously. "What did you just say to me?"

I dropped the act. "Nothing. You're right. The imp problem won't fix itself. However, with the dew evaporated, I can't complete the ritual. I don't even know how they found out I had the dew in the first place. I suppose it could've just been a random break-in. The sheriff said there were several around town in the past few days, but I'm not sure I buy it. The coincidence is just too much, don't you think? Maybe they overheard me talking about it at the library with Bella? But even if they did, why didn't Spellbooks do anything to stop them? I mean, you'd think a sentient shop would—"

"Snap out of it!" Luna's tone was sharp, jerking my rambling to a halt.

"But how did the imps know—"

"Doesn't matter. They did. Move on. What are you going to do? Mope around here all day?"

The scathing tone in her words made me bristle. "No! I'm not moping."

"Well, you were putting on a fluffing good imitation then," Luna snapped. "You had a plan. It didn't work. Welcome to life, kitten."

"That's not really—"

"Fair? Ha! You thought *imps* were going to play by the rules? What do they teach you kids these days?" Luna thumped her back foot in a rapid, hollow rhythm on the counter.

"I'm not a kid," I protested.

"Then stop acting like one," Luna snapped. "Ears up! Be courageous. Meet your problems head on. Make a new plan and act on it. Or are you just going to hide away in the bookshop and hope your troubles magically take care of themselves?"

That had been exactly one of my plans. Admittedly, low on my list because I had been trying to find a solution all day, but I protested on principle. "What? No! I wasn't going to—"

"Good! I'm glad to hear it! Adapt, pivot, and, where you can, do it with some style. That's the difference between those who make things happen and those who watch life pass 'em by. Now, which are you going to be? A watcher?"

I glared at her. "No!

Luna sat back on her haunches. "Glad to hear it. So, what's Plan B?"

"Plan B?"

"Or Plan Double Q. Perhaps Plan Flibbertigibbet. What? I don't know your naming system," Luna said with a sniff.

"If this is going to work, it needs to be something better than just 'B'. I'm thinking...Plan Fluffernutter."

Luna smirked. "I like it. So, what's Plan Flutternutter?"

"At the moment? *Imp*-rovise until I have a solid plan," I said with a wink, already feeling better than I had all day. "Maybe Aunty Agatha can help. She hasn't left on her vacation yet."

"If anyone knows about adding a touch of flair to a backup plan, it's Agatha. I always thought she had the makings of a fine rabbit. At least from a psychological standpoint. The lack of proper ears will forever be an insurmountable obstacle for her," Luna said primly.

"What? You know? I don't want to know. I need to find Agatha right now. Can you keep an eye on Spellbooks and make sure no more imps break in?"

"Of course. You war paint your whiskers and don't let these imps push you around. Float like a butterfly and kick them in the head like a ninja rabbit!" She struck a martial art pose, scowling fiercely at the world.

"Yeah!" I said, caught up in Luna's fervor. I grabbed my coat and purse, locking the door to Spellbooks behind me as I hurried down the road towards Agatha's.

It took me two blocks to realize that Luna had goaded me out of my spiral of self-recrimination and burgeoning despair.

Wow! That rabbit was fluffing good.

Choices, Choices

A CHILLY WIND GUSTED through the trees and almost blew me down the path to Agatha's house. Dead leaves swirled around my feet as I rounded the bend, and her house came into view. I think it might have been the first time in history that anyone was ever relieved to see a spooky-looking witch's house. Thankfully, I knew what lay beneath the illusion spell, and I couldn't wait to make myself at home in her cozy abode, hopefully with a cup of delicious tea.

The door swung open even as I raised my fist to knock. Agatha smiled at me from the welcoming interior. "Ah, there you are. Right on time. Come in, come in. There's some spiced hot chocolate on the stove and ginger cookies waiting for you. That is, if Ignatius hasn't eaten them all," she said, half-turning to direct her words towards the small dragon perched contentedly on the round kitchen table. He smiled toothily at me and let out a little belch, complete with floating smoke ring.

Agatha's words sunk in as she closed the door behind me, and I slid out of my coat. "How did you know I was coming?"

"Charmaine told me. She's going to look after the place while I'm on holiday. Believe me, I can't wait to get away from this cold."

I frowned. "I thought her predictions were only right one out of every dozen. How did you know it was the true one? Do you have a magic spell for sensing when she's using her powers?"

Agatha pursed her lips and shook her head. "Not everything can be solved by magic. Sometimes the answer is simple. In this case, I counted."

"Oh," I said, feeling a little stupid.

Agatha grinned. "Not to worry. When you've been in this game as long as I have, you get used to looking at things a little differently. My best advice? Use what's right in front of your nose to get the job done." She held up a wooden spoon from the counter and waved it at me before walking to the stove. She stirred the silver pot of hot chocolate and then quickly poured the steaming liquid into mugs, handing me mine. "Then, when people assume you used magic, as they inevitably do when they discover you're a witch, let them. I find an enigmatic smile and a wink work wonders." She tipped her head to the side and gave me a knowing smirk, her eyes twinkling.

I chuckled and shook my head, more out of bemusement at her antics than a true understanding of what she'd said. My imp problem consumed too much of my mind.

Agatha must've read the distraction on my face, because she gestured to the table. "Come. Sit. Tell Aunty Agatha all about what's bothering you."

I sank into a chair and wrapped my hands around the mug of steaming hot chocolate. It smelled incredible. The rich scent of the cocoa was topped with an interesting and unexpected mix. Cinnamon, for sure. Possibly nutmeg. But there was a little something else that I couldn't quite identify. I sniffed at the mug again as Agatha carried over a small teacup of hot chocolate for Ignatius and settled at the table with her own cup.

"Now, tell me what the problem is," Agatha commanded.

I sighed and my shoulders slumped. "I messed it up," I confessed in a small voice.

"Messed what up?" Agatha asked.

"The ritual. I gathered all the things on the list. Well, almost all the things. I still needed the silver dagger, but I have everything else. *Had* everything else."

Agatha's eyes sharpened. "What happened?"

"The imps happened," I groaned. I filled her in on everything that had occurred in town, my hypothesis that Granny had cast the stone spell on the imps, and somehow, I'd accidentally dissolved it. "On top of everything else, they broke into my shop and smashed the jar holding the dew. Without another full moon before Halloween, how am I supposed to complete the ritual? For them or for Ignatius? I don't know if they just got lucky or they overheard me. Luna says it doesn't matter, but—"

"And she's right," Agatha interrupted. "Don't let the whiskers fool you. That's one smart lady rabbit, and you'd be wise to follow her advice."

"Well, she told me to adapt and pivot. Oh, and to do it with style. How does one pivot with style?" I asked, feeling despair rise in my chest again.

"Ballet training helps," Agatha said mildly.

Despite myself, I snorted out a small laugh, which I tried to disguise by taking a sip of the spiced chocolate. My eyebrows shot up, and I stared at the mug. The hot chocolate was sweet and rich. Combined with the nuanced spice mix, it was warming, comforting, and altogether delicious. It was hot chocolate and so much more, all wrapped up in a single sip. I took another, just to be sure my first taste hadn't been a fluke. It hadn't. If possible, the cocoa was even better the second time.

"What is in this hot chocolate? I've got to know. Cinnamon, nutmeg, and...what?"

"Oh, just a little something I like to throw in the pot on cold days," Agatha said, waving a hand vaguely towards the kitchen.

"I've got to know! I know the flavor. It's on the tip of my tongue, no pun intended, but I just can't place it."

Agatha shrugged. "Oh, just a little of this and that. My secret recipe, but I find it does the trick."

Sensing defeat, I raised my mug to her. "Well, whatever it is, I salute your potion making. This is a truly magical blend."

Agatha tipped her head to the side, a small, mysterious smile playing over her lips, and winked at me. Instead of answering, she nudged the plate of cookies closer to me. "If you don't have a ballet background, sugar and spice often help to get the ol' brain churning."

"What?" I asked, still distracted by the cocoa.

"For the pivot Luna advised you to make? Now, I have something else that might help." Agatha raised a finger and bustled into the adjoining sitting room, pulling a small plastic container tied shut with twine from the fireplace mantle. She returned to the table and set it in front of me with a flourish. A clear liquid sloshed around the bottom of the plastic dish.

I looked at the unassuming container in confusion and then up at Agatha. "Umm, thanks? I think. What is this?"

Agatha rolled her eyes. "It's dew, you ninny. Moonlit dew collected under a full moon."

My jaw dropped, and I stared at the plastic box in shock. "How did you know I'd need this?"

Agatha snorted and settled back with her mug of cocoa. "I didn't. Like I told you, the dew is necessary to turn Ignatius to stone as well as the imps. I was just being prepared. None of my experiments worked, you see, and I leave for my vacation tomorrow. I can't have him burning down my house while I'm gone."

"And I wouldn't want to," Ignatius chimed in.

"But you told me I was responsible for the ritual," I said.

"And you thought I wouldn't have a backup plan for a witch doing her first ritual?" Agatha asked, raising an eyebrow.

"Well..." I trailed off. That had been exactly what I thought.

"Look, rituals are easiest for a newbie to cast at the right time of year with the correct preparations. In this case, exactly how I told you to do it on Halloween night. However, *I* can use the same ingredients to turn a willing little dragon back to stone anytime I want. Ignatius and I were just having a little treat together before I started the stone spell," Agatha finished.

"But why make me go through collecting all the ingredients for the ritual then?" I demanded.

"How else are you going to learn?" Agatha asked. "Besides, did you really think I was going to leave you with a fire-breathing dragon unable to control his abilities while I went waltzing off to the Caribbean tomorrow?"

I glanced back and forth between them. Ignatius looked sad but resigned to his fate. Agatha's expression was a mixture of understanding and acceptance. I supposed for her, this was the solution that made the most sense. However, seeing Ignatius' face, a little part of me didn't want to see the tiny dragon turned to stone.

"Isn't there another way?" I asked.

Agatha shrugged. "Maybe, but I haven't been able to discover it. He can breathe fire on command, but it's controlling it when his emotions are running high that's still giving him problems. Once he gets swept away, there's no stopping it unless you have a fire extinguisher on hand," Agatha said, pointing over my shoulder. I glanced behind me and saw a familiar red cylinder with a black handle sitting on the floor next to the broom.

Ignatius nodded. "Got spark inside. Needs to get out. Stuff burns. Books burn. Don't want that. Maybe go 'way. Far, *far* 'way. No friends, no books." The effort of speaking so much looked like it exhausted him. His voice hitched up on the last few words, and a sparkling tear spilled down his scaly cheek.

Agatha stroked the spines along his back gently. "None of us want that, my friend. Don't give up hope. I'll keep searching for an answer. It has to be out there somewhere. We just need to find it. Please, be patient a little while longer." Ignatius turned a wavering smile towards Agatha and nodded silently, brushing a taloned forefoot at the tears glistening on his scaly cheeks.

Agatha turned back to me. "There's a problem though. Now that we know about the imps, we really need to wait until Halloween to attempt the ritual on them. The extra power from the holiday will make the ritual even more effective."

"But what about your cruise?" I asked.

"Oh, I'm still going," Agatha said firmly. "This one is on you, but-tercup. But I'm going to help you prepare. Think of me like your own personal Mr. Miyagi."

I sucked in a deep breath and blew it out. It would be easier if Agatha was staying, but I remembered that stubborn look from when I was a child. There'd be no changing her mind now that it was made up.

"Okay sensei. Train me," I said.

And she did. For the next two hours, Agatha made me repeat the steps of the ritual over and over again, using household items. I drew the salt circle, set the pumpkin, which was really her tea kettle, lit the birthday candles we used as stand-ins for the ritual candle, and said the words. On the third attempt, Agatha started trying to distract me. On the fifth, Ignatius joined in. By the last time, they were both howling and dancing around me as I calmly recited the words to the spell that would finally bring peace to Havenwood.

Agatha plopped back into her chair, looking tired but proud. "Now, do you think you can remember all the steps when you need them?"

I nodded my head. "I'll remember. And now that I've got this," I put a hand on the container of dew. "I just need to get the dagger and hope the imps don't cause too much mischief before Halloween."

"And what happens if the ritual fails for whatever reason?" Agatha asked.

"Have a backup plan," I recited, as I had done for the past couple of hours.

"Which is?" Agatha prompted.

"Go to Vivienne Silverthorne and tell her the whole thing. Leave nothing out and offer to help after the next full moon when I can collect the dew. Take responsibility, but don't let her blame me for what I couldn't have known," I recited.

"Good," Agatha nodded briskly. "Now, don't forget to include some meat in Ignatius' diet. Dragons need more protein than most and these powders you find at the grocery store just won't cut it. Steak is the best. He likes it medium rare and is getting pretty good about cooking it himself, I must say."

Ignatius beamed and wriggled happily under the weight of the praise, but I frowned in confusion. "What are you talking about? I thought you were...you know?" I tipped my head towards the tiny dragon and then froze, emulating a statue.

Agatha furrowed her brow. "Do you think I spend all my evenings outside gathering dew? No. I have a life you know." She tipped her head towards the plastic container on the table in front of me. "That's barely enough dew for the ritual to change both the imps."

"What do you mean?" I asked, already knowing I wouldn't like the answer.

"Isn't it obvious? You'll have to pick. Ignatius or the imps."

"How am I supposed to pick?"

Agatha shrugged. "Flip a coin. Make a pros and cons list. Channel the ancients and try to define meaning through the flight of birds. I don't know."

I glanced over at the little dragon. It wasn't really a question. Ignatius at least had a good heart and didn't *want* to hurt anyone.

"The imps," I said firmly.

Agatha nodded as if she'd anticipated my answer. "In a month, you'll be able to gather more dew and do another ritual. Either that or wait until I return. Easy peasey."

"No, not easy peasey. A *month*? What can we do about Ignatius, so he doesn't burn Spellbooks down? Can he go with you?"

Agatha shook her head. "No can do, sweet pea. I'm leaving tomorrow for my cruise, and I don't think a dragon, even one as cute as Ignatius, would be welcome aboard, do you? And before you ask, no, he can't stay here while I'm gone. I'd really rather not come home to the charred remains of my house." She glanced at the tiny dragon. "No offense."

"No 'fense. Agatha friend. Ignatius go hide in wild," he said, covering his eyes with his wings.

Agatha shook her head firmly. "We've talked about this, Ignatius. You've never lived in the wild. Survival can be hard and dodging detection even harder. Besides, what happens when you get startled or scared? You could burn down an entire forest! No, it's better that you stay with Harper. Right?" She shot me a pointed look over the dragon's head.

"Umm, right," I said past a dry mouth. "I'm sure we'll figure something out." The words sounded more confident than I felt. I toyed with the string securing the plastic lid of the container of dew. The imps were a growing nuisance, getting bolder every day. I needed to take care of them, for the sake of the greater good.

But then what was I supposed to do with the dragon who couldn't control his fire breathing? I lived in a building full of books, which would make the perfect kindling. I had a responsibility to keep Luna and Mr. Wigglesworth safe too, not to mention Spellbooks itself. Didn't I?

With Aunty Agatha leaving tomorrow, I felt the burden of responsibility settle squarely on my shoulders as I walked back to the shop. Not that I was completely alone—I had Ignatius with me. But how was I going to deal with both the dragon and the imps? Was I really up to the task? I hoped so, but only time would tell.

Soggy Pillows and Sleepless Nights

THE FLOORBOARDS VIBRATED URGENTLY under my cheek for the third time that night. I groaned and scrabbled for the bucket of water I'd filled before I fell asleep. Smoke drifted up from the small nest I'd built for Ignatius out of pillows. The tiny dragon tossed and turned, exhaling sparks as his tail whipped back and forth in his sleep. Another spark landed on the pillows as I watched. A small flame sprang to life among the charred, sodden pillows. It flickered twice and then died as another spark fell on the smoldering mess. I sighed and tipped my bucket over the pillows. Again.

Ignatius woke with a start as the water flooded his bed. He blinked around in surprise and then looked sorrowfully up at me. "Fire?"

I nodded and held up the bucket. "Sorry for waking you, but Spellbooks really doesn't like fire."

"I know." Ignatius said sadly. "But Buttercup and Westley—"

I interrupted when sparks began to form as the little dragon worked himself up again. "I like *The Princess Bride* too, but we really need to find a solution so we can both get some sleep. I thought the soaked pillows would help, but your fire is too strong."

Ignatius bobbed his head. "Dragon fire hot. Burns anything. Even wet pillows."

I sighed and sat back on my heels. "What did Agatha do when you stayed with her?"

Ignatius yawned widely and stretched his wings. "Slept in fireplace. Grate kept sparks inside. Nice. Cozy. I liked. You have lavastone fireplace?"

"Lavastone?" I asked.

Ignatius nodded his head eagerly, but a yawn interrupted him. The effort of speaking so much seemed to wear him out. "Best for dragons. Holds heat. Doesn't crack. You have some? Better than soggy old pillows." He caught my eye and glanced away. "Ignatius rude. Sorry. Soggy pillows nice. Very...squishy."

I sighed. "No, you're right. We need a better solution. You need someplace where your fire isn't a danger. Spellbooks can't be expected to wake me up every time a spark catches, and I need sleep too," I said with a yawn. "Let's make it through the night, and we'll brainstorm some options in the morning."

"Okay," Ignatius murmured, curling up in a ball in the middle of the soaked pillows.

I padded to the kitchen, filled up the bucket once more, and returned to the blanket and pillow I'd spread on the floor. I glanced longingly at my bed, but I couldn't feel Spellbooks' warnings through the mattress. As uncomfortable as the floor might be, it was better to develop a crick in my neck than it was to miss the rumblings of the shop and wake up to a conflagration. I sighed and pressed my hand against the hardwood floor. "Thanks for waking me again," I whispered. A slight tremor ran under my fingers, and I looked at the chalkboard where some words appeared as if written by an unseen hand. When Spellbooks took the effort to write, I knew to listen.

Need a better solution.

"I agree." A thought occurred to me. "Does Granny have anything locked away in the attic that might help?" I asked.

The words disappeared from the chalkboard, leaving only a dark, blank space in the middle of the small frame. I waited a minute or two more, but nothing appeared. The building seemed to prefer a series of various rumbles and vibrations to writing, but this time there was only silent stillness in answer to my question.

I sighed. "It was worth a try. Can you keep a lookout tonight please? Tomorrow, we'll find a better solution." The floorboards beneath my fingers warmed and a gentle vibration tickled at my palm. I took that as an encouraging sign. I yawned again and stretched out on my makeshift bed. If I was lucky, I might be able to get a few more hours of sleep before morning. I just hoped Ignatius didn't have any more dreams.

Despite my confident words to Spellbooks and the fatigue dragging at my eyelids, sleep proved to be elusive. Spellbooks was still the rest of the night, and Ignatius must've drifted into a dreamless slumber because there were no more sparks from his side of the apartment. Still, I couldn't sleep. Thoughts of Spellbooks burning and the cackling imps running all over town played in the cinema of my mind, keeping me awake. By the time the sun peeked over the horizon, I was no closer to a solution for either Ignatius or the imps.

Temper Tantrums

I WAS ON MY third cup of coffee by ten in the morning, but I still couldn't keep the yawns at bay. At least helping customers kept me busy. Ignatius did his cute, "animatronic" act by the register, which the customers loved. It was good to have him so close, but I was constantly on edge, ready to spring for the bucket of water I'd stashed under the counter. Between my fraying nerves, the disrupted night, and the overabundance of caffeine in my system, I was a jumpy mess. Which explained why I screamed when a large hand fell on my shoulder while I was re-shelving books in a rare quiet moment.

"Sorry, Harper," Grimgor said, backing up with a concerned look on his craggy face.

I pressed a hand to my racing heart. "No, I'm sorry. I didn't hear you come in."

The half-giant frowned at me. "You seem...stressed. Is everything okay?"

I forced a smile, running a hand through my hair. "Yeah, everything's fine. I just didn't get enough sleep last night."

Grimgor squinted at me, not looking entirely convinced by my response, but he didn't push. "I got your message about a broken window. I'm assuming you'd like it fixed as quickly as possible?"

"Yes please, if you can fit it into your schedule."

"For you? Anything. What happened?" Grimgor asked, pulling out his tape measure.

I sighed and folded my arms, leaning against the counter as I watched him get to work. "Apparently, Spellbooks was the target for a not-so-funny prank."

Grimgor pursed his lips and shook his head. "Someone needs to put a stop to this. Havenwood is a nice place. It's not the kind of place where these things are supposed to happen."

"I agree," I said, returning the last of the books to their proper places.

Mr. Wigglesworth appeared from where he'd been napping at the back of the shop and wound his way around Grimgor's legs. The big man smiled and crouched to give the cat a gentle scratch behind the ears. "I'd hate to think of what would've happened if this fella had been in the window when they broke in," Grimgor said, stroking the cat's fur.

"Me too." A thought popped into my mind as I watched the handyman pet my cat. "Hey Grimgor? I've got a weird question for you. What would you do if your pet started breathing fire?"

Grimgor stared at me in surprise and then slowly withdrew his hand from Mr. Wigglesworth's back. "Is this your way of warning me to not pet your cat? I thought he was a Maine Coon. Is there something more to him?" he asked cautiously.

I waved my hands in front of my body. "No. I mean, he is. A Maine Coon that is, not breathing fire. As far as I know, he's just a normal, albeit very large, cat. It was just a...hypothetical. I was asking because you know materials that are both mundane and paranormal. Is there some sort of fireproof pet carrier or a flame-resistant bed or something?"

Grimgor looked around nervously. He dropped his voice. "Is this for Luna? When did she start to breathe fire?"

I shook my head. "No, not Luna. That's a terrifying thought though."

Grimgor nodded somberly. "I've been on the wrong side of her sharp tongue a time or two. It's not something I wish to repeat with fire attached. She really doesn't need to add a flamethrower to her arsenal of insults."

"Agreed," I said and meant it. Although Luna appeared to be a cute little rabbit, she could be terrifying in her own right.

Grimgor pushed to his feet, appearing to give my question serious consideration. "Well, if I had a hypothetical pet that breathed fire and I couldn't figure out what to do, I'd probably get rid of it. Send it to a farm or something like that for, um, fire-breathing pets."

"What if that's not really an option for say, oh, about a month?" I asked.

Grimgor's bushy eyebrows drew together. "This hypothetical is oddly specific," he mused. "However, if getting rid of the flame-breathing beastie isn't possible and you don't want your house burning down, I'd recommend going to see an expert in magic like Vivienne Silverthorne."

"Umm. Okay. Thanks," I managed, but my stomach dropped at the mere mention of the severe matriarchal figure of the entire town of Havenwood. If I went to her for help with Ignatius, she might discover how the stone spell got dissolved in the first place. While that wasn't necessarily a problem in itself, she might eventually connect the dots. If she figured out that the imps were once stone and in Spellbooks as well, that would mean she'd know I was the one responsible for them ruining the Harvest Festival. Sure, it might be tenuous to assume she could deduce that much, but I preferred the lowest possibility of deduction if I got to choose. Which meant asking Vivienne for help was a non-starter.

Grimgor clapped his hands together and rubbed them briskly. "Right. If I can't help solve any other strange hypotheticals, I've got a window to repair."

"Of course. Let me get you a cup of coffee while you work," I said, hurrying towards the mugs.

"With a dash of cream, if you don't mind," Grimgor called after me.

"You got it! Do you want me to bring it out back when you're done? I can make Thistle a cup of tea too," I offered.

Grimgor glanced around the shop, his eyes lingering on the back door. "I'd love to go out back and see Thistle, but these prank repairs around town have me busier than a one-legged gnome in a kicking contest. I've got jobs lined up all day today."

"Maybe next time. Thanks for helping out, Grimgor. I really appreciate you fitting me in." I handed him the steaming mug.

"Always," he said, inhaling coffee's rich fragrance. "Now, let's get that window sorted for you."

By the time six o'clock rolled around, the shop window was fixed, Mr. Wigglesworth was on his fourth nap of the day, Luna was on her seventeenth haughty sniff aimed at the laziness of cats, and I was exhausted. I'd been busier than ever, selling books, answering questions, and re-shelving. Harvest Festival might be a boon to Havenwood's economy, but it wasn't doing my feet any favors. I stretched and groaned.

I locked the front door and flipped the sign over with a sigh of relief. I grabbed my bag from behind the counter, checking Agatha's plastic box with the all-important dew for the umpteenth time. It was still unclear if the imps had targeted the items for the ritual or if they'd just gotten lucky. To be fair, I wasn't even positive it had been the imps who broke into Spellbooks in the first place, although they could have, given the timeline the sheriff had told me. Regardless, I wasn't taking any chances. The rest of the ritual's ingredients were easily replaced, but if this dew spilled, I was really in trouble. Best to keep it close, just in case.

"C'mon Ignatius," I called wearily. "Let's go see what we can scrounge up for dinner."

The little dragon raised his head, a curl of smoke spiraling up from his nose. I noticed he'd been reading an urban fantasy novel in the *Smoke and Shadows* series, a personal favorite. Or it had been. The edges were singed and starting to smoke, which was a little too on point for my taste in literature.

"Hey now! None of that!" I exclaimed, rushing over and patting the book with a damp tea towel.

Ignatius hung his head. "Sorry. Got excited. Like living 'nother life but no go outside."

I sighed, finding it difficult to stay upset with the tiny bibliophile. "I get it. I feel the same way. But sometimes we have to leave the shop. For example, to find food."

Ignatius looked longingly at the scorched book on the counter. "You... drink more coffee? Like for breakfast and lunch," he said hopefully.

I shook my head at his ill-disguised attempt to stay in the shop a little longer to keep reading. "Sorry, buddy. I need some actual food, and so do you. Let's go." I stuck out my arm and Ignatius sprang aboard, clambering up my forearm to perch on my shoulder like a scaly, fire breathing parrot.

I headed up the stairs, but when I reached the top, the door leading to my apartment wouldn't open. Frowning, I jiggled the handle. Had I locked it? I couldn't remember. I pulled out my key and tried turning it in the lock. To my surprise, the key snapped as soon as I applied even the slightest force, leaving the majority stuck in the lock. I blinked and then frowned. Was the key worn? What had damaged it so that it broke that easily?

I was too tired to attempt to figure out the conundrum. Instead, I put my hand on the doorknob and channeled my magic. I closed my eyes and concentrated my small magical affinity for metal on the broken bit of key stuck in the lock. Slowly, it scraped free of the doorknob, moving seemingly of its own accord. The broken fragment dropped to the floor with a dull thud. I ignored it, focusing my energy on the tumblers inside the lock. One by one, I jiggled them into the correct position with my magic. A faint sheen of sweat broke out on my forehead at the exertion. When the tumblers were all in place, I let out a soft grunt of satisfaction, twisted the knob, and pulled.

Nothing happened. The door didn't budge. I frowned at the knob. Had I missed a tumbler?

"What's happening?" Ignatius asked.

"Give me just a second," I muttered, refocusing on the lock and searching for the misaligned tumbler. Except there wasn't one. Everything was perfect. The lock shifted easily in my mind's eye as I twisted the knob back and forth. So why wasn't the apartment door opening?

I placed my palm flat against the wall next to the door and spoke aloud. "Uh, a little help please, Spellbooks? The door seems to be stuck."

Nothing happened. Again. Not even the faint vibration Spellbooks usually used as an acknowledgement of my words. I gently tapped on the wall with my index finger. "Hey Spellbooks? Are you there?"

A faint thud sounded from the shop below. I glanced down the stairs. That was strange. I went to investigate. With Ignatius balanced on my shoulder, I crept back down the stairs. The urban fantasy novel, complete with dragon-induced scorch marks, lay on the floor. But when I looked around, neither Luna nor Mr. Wigglesworth were in sight.

I crouched to pick up the book and replace it on the counter. Perhaps I'd been more tired than I thought. I could have sworn I'd placed the book next to the register. It should've been impossible for it to fall to the floor.

A flicker of movement caught my eye. I turned to see a message slowly appearing on the chalkboard in bold, capital letters.

NO MORE FIRE!!!

I sighed. So *that* was the reason my door wasn't working the way a door should. My building was mad at me. I put a hand on the wall and spoke gently. "I know, I know. We feel the same way, don't we Ignatius?"

The little dragon gave an emphatic nod from his perch on my shoulder, which nearly sent him tumbling. He dug his talons into my shirt to steady himself. "I is sorry," the dragon said earnestly.

"There, you see? No one is trying to hurt you intentionally. Give me a couple more days. A week at most. After I turn the imps back into statues, I can give my full attention to helping Ignatius. Even if it turns out I can't find anything to stop the fire, Agatha will be back from her vacation soon, and she'll be able to help." I didn't know if that was precisely the truth, but what was I supposed to say? I couldn't turn Ignatius loose in Havenwood. He might accidentally set the whole town on fire. Surely, I could deal with a couple of sleepless nights if it meant no dragon fire in town, right? And if I could do it, then Spellbooks should be able to.

I bit my lip as new writing appeared on the board. A series of forceful underlines materialized one after the other, emphasizing Spellbooks' previous message. I stared at the chalkboard in dumbfounded consternation.

Move into a sentient building, they said. It'll be fun, they said. Like you're living in your own little fairy tale. But what they don't tell you is that when the building gets grumpy, it can throw an epic hissy fit, lock you out of your own home, and there is absolutely nothing you can do about it.

Of Dwarves and Dragons

WHAT COULD I DO now? Sleep on the floor of the shop? Push the armchairs I kept for browsing readers together to create a make-shift bed? But both options put Ignatius closer to temptation. What would happen when I drifted off and he crept over to read the latest thriller novel? Would Spellbooks even wake me in time? The shop had to, right? For its own survival, if nothing else.

But what if it didn't?

I ran a hand through my hair, forgetting Ignatius was perched on my shoulder. He hissed and flapped his wings, trying to maintain his balance.

"Sorry," I muttered as he dug his talons into my shirt, scraping the skin off my shoulder, but not breaking it. I stroked his warm scales. "I don't know what to do. Do you have any bright ideas?" I asked, dejectedly.

"Food?"

I chuckled despite myself. "You're like Mr. Wigglesworth. Any mention of dinner makes him instantly ravenous."

"Cat smart," Ignatius said.

I paused to consider my options. If we left now, there was no guarantee that Spellbooks would let Ignatius back in. However, my supplies in the shop were limited to coffee, tea, and an emergency candy bar I kept under the counter. Not enough to satisfy either of us. But where could we go if Spellbooks locked us out? Bella's? Maybe, but I didn't want to risk it with Ignatius, especially since the B&B was likely full of guests. Agatha's? The witch was already on vacation, so I knew her house was empty. With my magic, getting in the door wouldn't be an issue. However, Agatha and I didn't have that kind of relationship. I wasn't sure the old witch would look kindly on me Goldilocks-ing around her house with the dragon in tow. Not to mention that she might have some kind of magical wards or deterrents in place.

My stomach rumbled loudly, reminding me I'd been neglecting it far too often of late. I felt Ignatius flick his tail. "Harper hungry? Ignatius too. We eat."

"I can't argue with that logic," I said, grabbing my coat and purse. Thank goodness I'd left them in the shop versus my apartment. I'd wanted to keep the dew close in case the imps really had targeted it the first time, and it seemed silly to put the coat upstairs when my purse was downstairs. I never thought I'd say this, but I was grateful for paranoia. It was going to keep me warm tonight.

Ignatius glided down to the counter as I wrapped up against the chilly October evening. "What are you in the mood for?"

"Meat," came the instant reply, which made me smile.

"Okay, we'll get you some meat, but I don't think it's a good idea to go to a restaurant and eat it. What if someone sees you?"

"Shop?" he asked.

I chewed on my lip, considering the options. There was a little corner market about three blocks down from Spellbooks. It wasn't fancy, but it had all the essentials. I glanced at the clock and frowned. Unless they were staying open later because of the Harvest Festival, the market would be closed by now. Which meant an almost twenty-five-minute trek to the large supermarket at the end of town. I groaned inwardly. I'd been debating getting a bike or an electric scooter to make trips like this a little easier. However, with winter approaching, it didn't seem sensible. I couldn't afford a car at the moment, nor did I really want to deal with the headaches of parking, gas, and maintenance. Besides, it wasn't like I needed a car for my staircase commute to work. Havenwood was small enough that there weren't many ride-share options either, unless you got lucky or booked in advance. I pulled out my phone just in case. Sure enough, nothing popped up on my screen. I sighed and tucked the phone away.

"Well, it looks like we're walking. Do you want to ride in my purse or in my coat?" I asked Ignatius.

"Coat. Warmer." He sprang into the air with a flap of his leathery wings and wrapped himself around my shoulders like a living, fire-breathing scarf. I grabbed my actual scarf and tucked it over him, both for warmth and to protect the little guy from prying eyes. I'm not sure I could explain away my choice of necklace as an animatronic curiosity in the bread aisle of the supermarket.

"Comfy?" I asked as I turned up the collar of my jacket, hitching the shoulders of the coat into place over his scaly body.

I felt Ignatius bob his head up and down in the affirmative. "Warm."

"Great." I grabbed my purse and headed for the door. It swung open without me laying a hand on it and, as soon as we exited the building, Spellbooks slammed the door shut. I heard the locks click loudly into place a moment later. Well, I suppose that answered *that* question. In addition to getting dinner for a dragon, I needed to find a place for us to sleep tonight. I sighed. One problem at a time. I turned left on Arcadia Avenue and started walking.

The supermarket was surprisingly busy for this hour in the evening. I had to be careful when I held up packages of sirloin and ribeye in front of my jacket for Ignatius to choose from so that no one caught a glimpse of him. As it turns out, dragons can be quite picky when you treat them to dinner. Eventually, I found enough provisions to keep both of us going for a day or two and checked out.

I exited the building and was immediately faced with another problem. Where were we going to eat? It was cold in the evenings at this time of year, but we couldn't go back to Spellbooks. Restaurants usually frowned on patrons bringing in their own food. The town square at least had benches where I could sit while I figured out my next move. I'd just resigned myself to a cold trudge and even colder dining, when something across the street caught my eye. A line of businesses faced the street, their bright signs clear even at this time of day. Behind them, someone had cleverly lit the town's water tower to look like a grinning jack-o'-lantern, undoubtedly for the

Harvest Festival. I wasn't interested in the giant, grinning pumpkin, but something I saw underneath it.

"Where going?" Ignatius asked as I set off at a brisk pace away from the grocery store.

"Mason Forham's. I forgot his auto repair shop was out this way. Elowen Wispdale said he might have a silver dagger I could borrow for the ritual. It looks like there are some lights on. As long as we're in the neighborhood, I might as well ask him, right?"

"But...dinner..." Ignatius said, with just a hint of a desperate whine in his tone.

"It'll be two minutes, tops. Then you can have your ribeye however you like it, okay?"

"Okay. Hurry," he whined, nestling back under my scarf as the wind forcefully kicked up.

I pounded on the door of the auto-shop, hoping to be heard over Mason's blaring music. A pang of guilt shot through me. Mason had been on my person of interest list for the pranks, but now that I knew the real culprits, I felt bad for suspecting him. Especially since I was about to ask him for a favor. I made a mental note to officially cross him off my list.

The music suddenly switched off. A moment later, the door swung open, and a warm light coming from inside the shop illuminated Mason's stocky frame.

"Yes? What can I do you for?" Mason asked, looking up at me and then out at the small, empty parking lot behind me. He raised a bushy brow. "You know I fix *cars*, right? To do that, it's usually a good start to *have* a car. In my humble experience, that is."

"And when I have a car, I promise to bring it to you and only you," I said with a bright smile. "However, I have something else to ask you about. May I come in please?"

Mason frowned as he looked at the grocery bags. "Aren't you a little old to be selling Girl Scout Cookies? But if you've got 'em, I'll take four boxes of Thin Mints and a couple of Samoas."

"Sorry, I don't have any cookies tonight, but I'll make sure to send any wandering Girl Scouts your way."

Mason shivered. "Don't. They might be cute and come with snacks, but don't be fooled. They're terrifying."

"Girl Scouts?"

"No, the moms hovering over their shoulders. I swear, those moms have figured out how to convert a single dirty look into a weapon of mass consumerism. You go in with the best of intentions to only buy one box and end up leaving with a truckload."

"Ah. Well, I promise that I'm not hiding any Girl Scouts or their disapproving mothers. But it is a bit cold out here," I said as a chilly wind whipped my hair around my face.

Mason sighed and opened the door wider. "I suppose you're safe enough. Come in then."

"Thank you," I said as I hurried into the warm office area. It was small, with only enough space for a couple of chairs and a small desk. The desk looked cluttered with a computer and a stack of messy paperwork, but it didn't seem to bother the dwarf.

Mason waved at one of the two plastic chairs while he took the other. "Now, tell me why you need an auto mechanic even though you don't have a car."

I set the grocery bags down but didn't take off my coat. If I'd thought this through a bit better, I'd have asked Ignatius to hide in my purse. I knew Mason was a dwarf and was clued into the paranormal side of Havenwood. He even had a reputation for hanging out with ghosts, not that I'd ever seen the evidence of it with my own eyes. Although was it even possible to see a ghost? I shook my head. Not the point. The point, no pun intended, was to get a dagger.

I cleared my throat. "I don't know that we've been formally introduced. I'm Harper Sullivan. Beatrice's great-granddaughter." I stuck out my hand.

"I know who you are," Mason said, shaking it. His grip was firm, and he had the thick callouses of a man who worked with his hands every day. "The kerfuffle with the inheritance of Spellbooks was town gossip for weeks. Glad it's you and not that other guy. I didn't like the look of him."

"Me too," I said honestly. Mason was talking about Thaddeus, a distant relation. Granny had set up a test to see which one of us would inherit Spellbooks, and I'd won, despite Thaddeus playing dirty.

Mason folded his arms over his stocky chest. "So, why are you here? I don't need any books unless you also sell audiobooks."

The unexpected turn took me aback. "Umm, no. Sorry." And then because I couldn't help myself. "Are door-to-door audiobook sales a thing?"

"Not that I know of, but they should be. I go through at least two or three a week. Sometimes more. I love listening to them while I work, especially mysteries. I can't get enough."

"Well, I'll see what I can do about audiobooks then. But the real reason I'm here is about a dagger. A silver dagger to be precise. Elowen Wispdale said you were the man to talk to about such things."

Mason frowned and leaned forward. "And what would a nice young girl like you want with a dagger? Planning on doing something ill-advised?" He raised a bushy eyebrow.

I saw my error and immediately waved my hands in front of my body. "Oh no, nothing like that," I assured him hurriedly. "I need it for a ritual. My granny's friend Agatha is helping me perform my first one, and a silver dagger is on the list of ingredients she sent me to collect."

Mason stroked his beard. "I know Agatha. I also know she's finally gone on that cruise she's been talking about for ages. Left today, in fact." He glared at me suspiciously. "So, how can she possibly be helping you with a ritual if she's not even in town?"

I tried not to roll my eyes, but it took a supreme effort of will. After not getting much sleep last night and constantly being on edge to keep Ignatius from lighting any fires all day, the last thing I needed was a grilling by a skeptical dwarf. "She's, um, training me. I've never really been able to do magic openly. My dad's a master sergeant, and I grew up on army bases. We used our magic at home, but magic and the military don't really mix."

Was it my imagination, or had Mason's scowl relaxed slightly? I continued in a rush, stretching the truth a little. "When I came here, I wanted to learn more about my magic. I discovered some old magic books at the shop. Agatha was a friend of Granny's and offered to help me with the basics of this spell. She told me to practice while she's gone. You know? As a sort of a stopgap until she gets back?" I smiled, hoping to strike the perfect balance between hopeful and innocent. While nothing I'd said was technically a lie, I had omitted one rather *important* truth.

Mason considered me a moment longer, and then a wide grin broke across his face. "Knowing Agatha, she sent you on a wee scavenger hunt 'round the town, didn't she? You had to look for all manner of ridiculous things, didn't you?"

A surprised chuckle escaped me. "She's done this sort of thing before?"

"Sure! Anytime a young witch comes knocking on her door. I'll bet this ritual turns a hat into a flower or some such nonsense, doesn't it? And you have to complete it before she gets back, or she won't train you?"

"Something like that," I said with a weak smile, not wanting to get into the imp situation.

He scratched his nose, considering me. "I'll never understand witches. If you want a bouquet, why not sell the dagger, take the money, and go to the market?"

"Because then it wouldn't be magic," I said, the smart-aleck response popping out of me before I could hold it back.

"Ah, but it would be much simpler, wouldn't it?" He had a twinkle in his eye, like he was enjoying the debate.

"Maybe," I allowed. "However, Agatha told me that sometimes people don't always understand the nature of magic and when that happens, I should do this." I put on my best mysterious smile and winked at him.

Mason slapped his leg and chortled. "Sounds just like Agatha, that does. Looks like her too. Don't let her scare you, lass. She might seem a tad bristly at the start, but she's got a heart of gold. You can take my word on that. Now, seeing as you're a student of Agatha's, I'll *lend* you the dagger on two conditions."

My stomach dropped, and suspicion flared. He wouldn't make me go on a quest with twelve of his friends to reclaim a mountain or something, would he? If that was the case, I'd find another way to get the dagger. "Okay?" I said tentatively.

Mason held up a stubby finger. "First, this is a loan, not a gift. We clear? Bring it back when you are done. Second," he lifted another finger. "I want to hear the story of how it all went."

I blinked in surprise. "That seems...easy enough, I guess. You have a deal." I stuck out my hand, and we shook. I couldn't help myself and added, "But why do you want to know, if you don't mind me asking?"

"I'm a dwarf. We love a good story." His smile grew wider behind his bushy beard. "But mostly, it's because I know Agatha. Her rituals never seem to go exactly according to plan, and the results are usually worthy of a tale or two. Now, let me get that knife for you."

His comment about Agatha's magic didn't inspire a great deal of confidence, but before I could ask him what he meant, Mason sprang off his chair and headed through the door leading deeper into his shop. As soon as it banged shut behind him, I felt a tug on my scarf and Ignatius stuck his head out.

"What are you doing? He's going to be back in a second!" I exclaimed as Ignatius wriggled around so he could look at me.

"What's audiobook?" Ignatius asked.

The question took me aback. "Well, it's a book you can listen to. Please, can we talk about this later?"

He considered my words and then nodded. "Reads to you?"

I shook my head. "Not exactly. Someone records the book using technology. Then you can listen to it from your phone, computer, or whatever. Now, will you get back inside before Mason comes back?"

"No pages? No paper to burn?"

I stared at him in surprise and had the sudden desire to face-palm myself. Of course! Why hadn't I thought of that? But even if there wasn't something flammable inches from his nose, Ignatius still breathed fire when he got excited. Audiobooks might solve part of the problem, but not the entire equation. A wooden shop could still burn even if Ignatius got excited by listening instead of reading a paperback. I stroked his warm scales gently. "It's a good thought buddy, but please, can we talk about this later? Mason is coming back and—"

Mason banged through the door at that precise moment, holding up a small gleaming knife like it was Excalibur and he was leading knights into glorious battle. "Here we are! One silver dagger, as prom—wait. What's that?" He pointed with the knife at me and the dragon I was talking to.

Uh-oh.

Meat and Fire

My stomach dropped like I was on a roller coaster, and I froze, unable to think of the best course of action. No such reaction impeded Ignatius. The little dragon wriggled free of my jacket and flapped towards Mason, performing an elegant little aerial bow. "I is Ignatius. Pleasure meeting you."

Well, that was one way to handle it, I suppose.

Mason's jaw dropped as he stared at the dragon. The beat of silence lengthened into something almost unbearable. I was about to shatter the awkward moment with a loud explanation into new-fangled dragon-drones when the mechanic bowed in return. "The pleasure is all mine. It has been a long time since I've seen one of the fire-kin."

I stared between them in shock. "You don't hate each other?" The words slipped out of me before I could think better of them.

Mason scowled. "No. Why would we? We've just met."

I shrugged and tried not to shrink in my chair. "Isn't there a thing about gold? Don't both dwarves and dragons love to hoard it or something?"

Mason's glare faded, and he laughed a deep belly laugh. The dwarf gasped and wiped his eyes with his beard as I stared at him in confusion. When he finally got his breath back, he spread his arms to indicate his auto repair shop. "And just where do you think I'm hiding all this gold, lass? Under my wrenches? Or perhaps behind the oil cans? Besides, dragons hoard, not dwarves. But they don't always hoard *gold*. Common misconception." He looked back at Ignatius. "What do you hoard, then?"

"Books," the dragon answered instantly.

A grin split Mason's beard. "Oh, we'll get along fine then, although I don't have many of those lying around. I love a good story, that I do, but I come from an age when people swapped tales around a campfire. Never did learn how to read too well. Even when I tried, the letters danced all over the page like they had someplace to be other than making sense in my head. Which is why I love audiobooks so much. Lucky for us both, there are plenty of those to go around."

"I burn books. By accident." If a dragon could blush, Ignatius would be right now, but I could hear the embarrassment in his voice.

"Which is actually one of the reasons we went on a walk," I chimed in. "A fire-breathing dragon in a bookshop..." I trailed off and shrugged, not wanting to hurt Ignatius' feelings.

"Well, fire's not a problem here. In fact, if you can control it, it's the very best thing, in my humble opinion. Here, let me show you." The dwarf tipped his head and led the way towards the back of the shop. Curious, Ignatius and I both followed him.

When the dwarf swung the door to his workshop open, my jaw dropped. Never in a million years would I have guessed he had an old-fashioned forge in the corner, complete with an anvil and a rack of hammers ranging from the size of my finger to a massive war hammer. I guessed that the war hammer was just for display, given it was mounted slightly apart from the others. A worktable sat in the opposite corner from the forge and the heat from the banked embers was pleasant, but not oppressive. I couldn't believe all this was hidden in the back of an auto repair shop.

Mason waved at the room. "Welcome to my sanctuary. The Silverthornes helped me with the spell work ages ago to keep this place from being noticed by the humans, but it gives me a place to escape and do a little metalwork from time to time."

"Nice," Ignatius said, flapping over to examine the glowing coals. He settled on the stone edge and stretched his talons towards the shimmer of heat with a sigh of contentment.

"That's not the best part," Mason said with a wink. He grabbed a remote from the worktable in the corner and tapped a few buttons. A moment later, a deep, exciting voice filled the room, narrating a story I recognized.

"Wait, is that Stephen Fry?" I asked.

"It is indeed. I put the speakers in here especially so I could listen to my books when I'm not banging away on the anvil."

"This heaven," Ignatius breathed.

Mason looked around proudly. "Well, I don't know about that. It's not much, but it's home. I used to do this type of thing full time, but it's hard to pay the bills by making swords these days. People need a working car more than they need a sharp blade, if you know what I'm saying? But that's not what I wanted to show you. Come here," he said, waving us over to his worktable. Everything was neatly organized and ready to be used efficiently at a moment's notice, in stark contrast to the disorganization of his desk in the office. Tucked under the low table were several heavy-duty red shelving units on wheels. Mason pulled open one drawer after another, muttering to himself. Over his shoulder, I saw glints of glimmering stones, shining fragments of metal, and a slew of other items I couldn't identify immediately.

"Aha!" Magnus said, triumphantly. He pulled out some dark nuggets of what looked like ebony ore that had hints of fiery orange trapped within. In his other hand, he held fragments of a reddish gemstone that seemed to glow like the embers in his forge

"What's that?" Ignatius said, flapping over to get a closer look.

"It's an old family secret recipe," Mason explained. "You see, lavastone steel and emberite both have the ability to absorb heat and a bit of fire. Not enough to keep you safe in the middle of a forest fire, but enough to protect a careless child as they learn the dangers of the forge," he said with a rueful smile, rubbing his hand as if in response to an old memory.

"I've never heard of that combination," I said, peering closely at the items in Mason's hands.

"Perhaps because my great-granddaddy many generations ago developed the alloy to create this type of lavastone steel himself. It's too brittle for weaponry and not pretty enough for jewelry, so he never really found a use for it until he got an idea. He combined his new alloy with some emberite shards and made a wee bracelet to protect his curious young son as he learned how to craft alongside his da. The trinket worked. It absorbed any spark that landed on the young boy, allowing him to stay by his father's side without fear."

"Nice story," Ignatius said with a shrug.

It was, but I saw the deeper implications immediately. "You think the same thing could work for Ignatius?" I asked in excitement.

Mason shrugged noncommittally. "I know fire, but magical fire is a whole other element, no pun intended. However, from what I've seen over the years, lack of control leads to fear, and heightened emotions make it even more difficult to control the magic. Nasty cycle, and very difficult to break. Without help, that is," he said, holding up the lavastone and emberite once more.

Ignatius' eyes widened. "You help control my fire?" he asked, a little breathlessly.

Mason wavered his hand back and forth in a kinda-sorta gesture. "Only you can really control your fire, but I could make you something that could catch any stray sparks before they become a problem as you build confidence in your own abilities."

"You saying...I read? No burning?" Ignatius asked hopefully.

Mason chuckled and nodded. "I'm saying that you could fly into a library and spend the whole day there without fear of incinerating the literature. Once you have more practice and more control, you'll be able to do it without any assistance."

Ignatius let out a whoop of pure joy and sprang into the air, flapping in excited loop-de-loops and somersaults in the middle of the shop.

"I think it's safe to say you made his day," I said as I smiled at the elated dragon.

"My day? My life!" the happy dragon exclaimed excitedly.

Mason watched the aerial display as well, a small smile peeking out from under his beard. "We all need a little help now and then. The trick is finding the right help for the right person. Or in this case, dragon. The only thing is, he's going to need to come in regularly for fittings. Lavastone steel is finicky to work with, and the fit has to be just right. It would be better if he could stay here, but I don't want to make him uncomfortable," Mason said in a low voice, the words meant for my ears only.

"Aren't you nervous about the fire? What if he burns down your workshop by accident?" I asked.

Mason chuckled, the sound rumbling low in his chest. "Lass, this place was *built* for fire. Besides, with the number of spells built into the very rock of the walls, he'd be lucky to leave so much as the tiniest scorch on the floor."

I bit my lip, considering the options. I still felt a twinge of guilt for even briefly suspecting Mason, but this could be the perfect solution. Spellbooks had kicked us out based on Ignatius' lack of control with his fire, and despite his penchant for jokes, Mason was an upstanding member of the local community. However, I didn't want Ignatius to think I was trying to get rid of him just to make my life a little easier. On the other hand, the idea of a full night's sleep without fear of waking up to anything burning was appealing. But this wasn't about me. It was about Ignatius.

Mason cleared his throat, his expression turning serious. "Before I agree to do this, I need to ask you something. Have you heard about the fires around town?"

I nodded, a sinking feeling in my stomach. "Yes, I've heard."

Mason flicked his eyes pointedly towards Ignatius. "Has he...been involved in any way?"

I shook my head firmly. "No, he hasn't. He's been with Agatha. He's not responsible for the fires, I promise."

Mason studied me for a long moment before nodding. "Alright then. If you say he's not involved, I believe you. But you understand, this is serious business. If the Silverthornes catch wind of a dragon in town, they'll have questions."

"I understand," I said, feeling the weight of his words. "That's why I need to get him some help. I can't do this on my own."

Mason nodded. "Agreed. And that's what Havenwood is all about. Community coming together. Think he'll agree to stay with me while I try to find a solution for him?"

"Let's ask him," I finally said. "If he's comfortable staying here and you don't mind the company, then that seems like the most sensible choice. If he doesn't want to stay, then I suppose I'll have to figure out a way to bring him back and forth."

"Back and forth what?" Ignatius asked as he glided over and settled on the worktable after his burst of enthusiastic flight.

"Mason thinks he can make you something that will help you control your fire, but you need regular fittings to make it work. He's offered to let you stay here if you like, but if you'd be more comfortable coming with me, I'll figure out a way to get you over here whenever you need," I said with more confidence than I felt. I didn't know I could manage that while running Spellbooks by myself. However, if Spellbooks refused to open the door when I got back, I supposed I couldn't actually sell any books, anyway.

"I stay," Ignatius said, doing another happy somersault in the air.

"Are you sure?" I asked.

"Has fire. Books. What more I want?" Ignatius asked. He grinned at me and then glided over to the forge. He curled up on the warm stone next to the embers and tucked his nose under his tail for a nap.

Mason laid a hand on my arm. "Don't worry, lass. I'll keep a good eye on him. We all need to help a neighbor out when they're in need, don't we?" he said with a twinkle in his eye.

I didn't know if he meant Ignatius or me, but either way, I was grateful for the dwarf's help.

"I couldn't have said it better myself," I said.

A surge of relief mixed with lingering worry filled my heart as I left Mason's repair shop. This was a step in the right direction, but the journey was far from over. Ignatius was safe for now, but the imps were still out there, causing chaos. I needed to figure out a way to stop them before things got worse for everyone in Havenwood.

Sparks of Trouble

I LEFT THE BAG of groceries with ribeye and other supplies I'd purchased for Ignatius with Mason. After a quick discussion, the little dragon decided to roast his steak on an impromptu spit over the embers of the forge while Mason pulled a sandwich out of a refrigerator in the shop. Almost before I could blink, they were deep in a discussion about which audiobook Ignatius should listen to first. Mason was pushing for something like *Sherlock Holmes* as read by Stephen Fry, which was what he was currently listening to anyway, but Ignatius wasn't convinced by the time I left. Whichever way they decided to go though, I had a feeling the two would become very close friends.

As I walked home with my own bag of food looped over one arm, something Mason said stuck in my head. Something along the lines of finding the right help for the right person. Well, it seemed like fate had aligned to bring the two of them together tonight. Mason definitely seemed to be the perfect support for Ignatius. Who knew? Maybe the little dragon could bring some companionship into Mason's life in a sort of symbiotic relationship. Either way, I was glad that there was a solution on the horizon for Ignatius, and he might not have to be turned back into a statue. Speaking of statues, I pulled the little silver knife out of my bag and examined it. This, and the salt in my grocery bag, were the last of the ingredients I needed for the ritual. Except, of course, for the imps. I still had to find them before they could pull off more pranks and without getting caught by the Silverthornes. Easy peasey. I let out a sarcastic huff.

Today was Tuesday, and I needed to figure everything out before Halloween on Thursday. The clock was ticking, and the pressure was mounting. How was I supposed to find the imps? Was there some sort of imp-tracking spell out there or did I just stand in the middle of a cornfield, wave my arms, and shout at the sky until they showed up? I frowned. That part of the plan needed some serious work, but after I figured that out, it should be smooth sailing. I just had to follow the steps for the ritual and cross my fingers that Agatha's spell worked.

It had to, right?

I swallowed hard, trying to calm the growing panic. Failure wasn't an option, not when so much was at stake. The town depended on me, even if they didn't know it. I couldn't let them—or myself—down.

In the reflective sheen of the small blade, I caught a sudden glint of orange light. That was weird at this time of night. I looked around, searching for the source. There! One block over and through an alleyway, I saw the glimmer of orange again. I frowned. Was that firelight? It was near the edge of town. If I had my bearings right, that street should be...what was it? Oh! That's right. Grovekeeper's Trail. It was the last actual road on the western edge of Havenwood before the town surrendered to the dark forest. What was someone doing with a fire over there? It wasn't a residential area, so it couldn't be a pleasant campfire with a family roasting marshmallows or anything like that.

My common sense was telling me to walk away. No good could come from exploring a dark street leading to a darker forest by myself. Especially not when all I had for protection was what amounted to a bag of snacks and a knife that was barely bigger than a letter opener. However, there were the imps to consider. In addition to the pranks, they had also likely set fire to the stand in the town square. Could they be at it again? Maybe. But hadn't Mason just said that good neighbors helped each other out when they were in need? Besides, what if the fire spread? What kind of neighbor would I be if I just walked away? What kind of person?

A smart one! A little voice inside my head screamed.

But an unattended fire between a forest and empty business buildings? Who else would be out on this chilly October night to see it and stop it? I sighed and started jogging toward the gleaming light. I was hoping to find kids making s'mores, but I got out my phone just in case I needed to call the fire department.

As I approached the source of the glow, the tension in the air thickened. The smell of burning wood and the crackling of flames became more pronounced. The fire was too close to town to be a legal campfire, and the big town bonfire wasn't scheduled until the pumpkin parade on Halloween. My steps quickened, my heart pounding in rhythm with my footsteps, the growing trepidation clogging my throat.

The distant flickering light transformed into a fiery glow as I drew closer. As I rounded the corner, an empty street came into view, save for the warehouse where flames danced uncontrollably up the walls. The orange hues painted eerie shadows on the trees behind the warehouse, casting a terrifying otherworldly ambiance over the scene. My eyes widened as I spotted the silhouette of a human-looking figure within the flames racing deeper into the burning building. Panic sank its talons into my brain at the sight.

"Get out of there!" I shouted, my voice shrill with terror as the flames crackled and spat angry sparks into the sky. No answer came from the burning building.

What to do?

My mind whirred desperately as sparks spiraled skyward. My magic was no help here. A small affinity for metal wouldn't put out a fire. I needed help. Professional help. I clenched my fists. As I did so, I suddenly remembered the phone still in my hand.

Stupid, Harper! I thought to myself.

My first instinct should've been to call the fire department, not race towards the fire on my own, magic or not. As quickly as I could, I tapped in the emergency number, holding the phone to my ear.

"Havenwood Police Department. What is your emergency?" a tinny voice demanded.

"There's a fire! Please send help as quickly as you can," I said into the phone, rattling off my location.

The woman on the other end of the line stayed calm, but her tone took on a professional edge. "Are you or is anyone else hurt?"

"No. Maybe? I don't know. I thought I saw someone in the building, but no one came out, and the fire is too hot to go in after them."

"Don't go in. Leave that to the fire department. I've already sent the call out. They'll be with you soon," the woman said.

"Okay. What should I do?" I asked, looking around. Was it my imagination or was the fire spreading? What happened if it reached the tree line behind the building?

"Wait right there," the woman said confidently. "They'll be there soon, and they don't need to worry about you too."

She was right, but it wasn't my imagination. The fire *was* spreading. I looked around for any means to further contain the growing inferno. Was the water tower behind the warehouse a possible solution? With my magic, I could probably figure out how to open a valve to release the water. Worse came to worst, I could puncture the metal tank. But that presented a multitude of additional problems. How to redirect the water? The tank was too far away to attack the fire without a hose or something. That problem aside, assuming I could use the water inside to put out the fire, how would I close up the tank again? Would there be structural damage that would lead to a larger problem? I shook my head. No, the tank would be a last resort, but it came with too many unknowns to safely try now.

The crash of something falling inside the warehouse seemed to reverberate down the empty street. The fire department was taking too long. My heart rate spiked, and my vision tunneled. My breath came short and fast. I didn't need to be told that panic was the opposite of what was needed right now. I scanned the surroundings for additional resources. There was a gardening store that might have some tools that could help us. My eyes flicked back to the growing fire. A watering can wouldn't do much to dent the fiery inferno. No, we needed something bigger. Stronger. With more water.

I looked desperately down the street. I knew it had only been a minute or two, but what I wouldn't give to see a fire truck come flying around the bend right now. They'd drive up, attach their hose to that fire hydrant and use the hoses to douse the flames. Fire hydrant. I nearly facepalmed myself as my gaze settled on the brightly painted cylinder on the side of the road. It was too far to reach the flames, even if I managed to open it with my powers, and I still didn't have a hose to redirect the water.

I heard another crash from within the warehouse, sending a jolt of panic through me. Without thinking, I sprinted toward the base of the water tower. My hand reached out, fingers brushing the cold metal of the struts. I desperately tried to think of a way to use my powers to help without causing a bigger catastrophe. Could I weaken a strut and collapse the tower, sending a deluge of water to douse the flames? But how to control the aftermath? No, there were too many things that could go wrong. Maybe I could climb to the top and find a valve? But then I ran into the same problem I had with the hydrant of how to redirect the flow of water? Besides, all of that would take precious time I didn't have.

A blessed sound pierced through the chaos in my brain—the distant wail of sirens, growing louder with every passing second. I froze, hope mingling with fear. The fire department was finally here. They were trained for this type of thing. There was no need for me to destroy any part of the water tower. I let go of the metal support and turned, dashing back toward the street. As the scarlet fire trucks screeched to a halt, firefighters leaped out, their movements a blur of practiced efficiency. I watched, heart pounding, as they began to battle the flames, my breath catching in my throat as I prayed they could save the warehouse—and whoever was inside.

Even though I wanted to help, I knew I'd only get in the way. I stepped back, finding a spot on the curb to sit and wait it out. In a matter of moments, water from the fire hoses rained down on the flames. The intensity of the fire waned, and the potentially devastating blaze began to relent. The valiant efforts of the fire department saved the trees in the forest and the warehouse, leaving only the lingering scent of burnt wood in the air.

The warehouse, though scarred, stood defiantly against the night sky, and the forest, spared from complete destruction, seemed to exhale a collective sigh of relief. The immediate danger had passed, but the uncertainty of what lay ahead lingered in the air, combining with the scent of smoke from what could have been a disastrous end to the evening.

Lies and Suspect Lists

THE FIREFIGHTERS WERE THOROUGH and efficient. I sat on the curb, out of the way, as they swept the building to make sure the fire was completely extinguished and there was no one trapped inside. It was only when one firefighter exited the warehouse and gave the all-clear that a tall man with dark hair streaked with stony gray at the temples strode over. I rose as he walked up. He considered me thoughtfully from deep-set, granite-colored eyes that held a combination of stern determination and wisdom. The lines etching his face told the tale of countless challenges faced and overcome. Even under his uniform, it was obvious that he kept in shape, his strength undoubtedly an asset in his chosen field.

"I'm Chief Maxwell Flint," he said, extending a callused hand. His voice held the calm, comforting rumble of an authority figure in complete control of the situation.

"I'm Harper Sullivan." I said, shaking his hand. His grip was strong and firm, everything I would expect from a man such as him.

"Sullivan?" Chief Flint asked. "Any relation to Beatrice Sullivan? Of Sullivan's Spellbooks?"

"Her great-granddaughter. Nice to meet you, Chief Flint," I added,

Chief Flint nodded. "Beatrice was always an upstanding member of the Havenwood community. It's nice to see the apple doesn't fall far from the tree. Want to fill me in on what happened here this evening?"

I really didn't want to get into the ritual and the fire-breathing dragon I'd left at the auto mechanic's shop, so I opted for a partial truth. "I needed to go grocery shopping, but by the time I closed up for the night, all the shops nearby were shut. So, I decided to walk over and get something to eat," I said, pointing at my bag, which I'd dropped in my rush to get to the gardening store. I'd forgotten all about it in my attempt to put out the fire. Packaged food spilled out over the sidewalk.

"The grocery store?" Chief Flint folded his arms across his chest. "We drove past there on our way here, and I couldn't see the flames until we turned. How did you see them?"

"Well, I saw a light at Mason Forham's shop, and I wanted to, um, talk to him," I finished lamely. I felt a twinge of discomfort, not entirely comfortable with the half-truth. However, I didn't want to throw Ignatius under the bus, especially to a town official.

The chief raised an eyebrow. "Is your car in the shop? Is that why you needed to walk all the way from Spellbooks to the grocery store?"

"Well, no. I don't own a car." My face flushed. I really wasn't very good at this lying thing.

"So then why did you need to talk to Mason?" Chief Flint asked.

"It was...well, I...you see..."

"Yes?"

My stuttering brain finally landed on a plausible explanation that avoided all references to dragons. "I needed to talk to Mason about a project. I thought he, um, might have some insights that could help me." Not exactly a lie, but not the full truth, either. I hoped the chief would stop asking questions soon.

Chief Flint raised an eyebrow. "Sounds intriguing. What kind of a project could Mason help with? Nothing with ghosts, I hope," he said. Mason was known for hanging out with the local spirits and causing some minor mischief of his own, which was one reason he'd been on my suspect list in the first place.

I hesitated, feeling a flush rise to my cheeks. Lying definitely wasn't my forte, thanks to growing up with a father like Master Sergeant Edward Sullivan, who could spot a fib from a mile away. "I, um, needed to ask him about a silver knife," I finally blurted out, unable to think under the weight of the chief's stony stare.

Chief Flint's eyes narrowed slightly. "A silver knife? What kind of project requires a silver knife?"

I fumbled for words, feeling more awkward by the second. "It's...just something I'm working on. A little something I found in one of my Granny's books. You know, her. Always experimenting, am I right? Anyway, when I was leaving, I saw the glow of the fire and decided to investigate." I crossed my fingers behind my back and hoped he bought it.

Chief Flint studied me for a moment longer, and I felt like he could see right through my feeble attempt at obfuscation. My stomach dropped. He could tell something about my story was off. I just knew it. As the tension reached its peak, his radio crackled to life with urgent chatter.

"Chief Flint, we need you over at the north end of the building," the slightly distorted voice said.

The chief toggled his radio, keeping his eyes on me. "I'll be right there," he called. He lowered his volume and said to me, "I just have a couple more questions. The emergency line operator said you thought you saw someone in the building, but we couldn't find any evidence of someone inside. Did you see which way they went?"

I shook my head, grateful to be back on solid ground in the honesty department. "No. I saw a shadow that ran into the building when I came up. I couldn't tell you who it was or even if it was a man or a woman."

Or an imp. But I kept that last thought to myself.

"How tall was the figure? What were they wearing? Could you make out any details?" Chief Flint pressed, his tone sharpening.

I hesitated. "I didn't really focus on the height. The flames might have distorted the size anyway. All I saw was a dark figure. Honestly, it could have been anyone."

"Which direction did they come from? And did you see them leave?"

I frowned. "Leave? They didn't leave. At least I didn't see them. Didn't you see them inside?"

Chief Flint's expression hardened. "We found no trace of anyone inside. Were you watching the whole time? The firefighters said they didn't see you when we pulled up. Where were you then?"

Panic twisted in my gut. I didn't want to mention my powers or almost breaking the water tower. "I was around the side, looking for a way to help," I said, trying to sound casual.

"Looking for a way to help," he repeated, his eyes narrowing. "And how would you manage that? Do you have any firefighting expertise?"

I felt my face flush. "I just...I thought maybe there was something there I could use to put out the fire."

The chief nodded thoughtfully. "So, you don't know who could have started the fire, and there's no evidence of who might be behind this other than you glimpsing a supposed shadow. Have I got that about right?"

My stomach plummeted. When he said it that way, it made me look like *I* might've started the fire. "Yes, but I called it in as soon as I got here," I said, but the words sounded lame even to my ears.

The chief nodded, but his expression remained suspicious. "That you did." His radio crackled again, the voice on the other end more urgent this time. He glanced at it, then back at me. "Well, I think that's all we need from you this evening, but I might need to talk with you again soon. I can find you at Sullivan's Spellbooks, I assume?"

I nodded silently, not sure of what else I could say without unintentionally incriminating myself. The chief nodded, briskly shook my hand, and returned to his men without another word. I watched him go, dread building in the pit of my stomach.

In my effort to protect Ignatius with my shady story, had I just catapulted myself to the top of Chief Flint's suspect list?

Rascal Ruckus

I WOKE UP THE next morning, relieved and grateful that Spellbooks had let me back in, allowing me to sleep in my own bed. The comfort of familiar surroundings was a balm to my frayed nerves. As I stretched and reached for my phone, a veritable explosion of notifications filled the screen. I opened the long series of messages from Mason first.

Apparently, after I'd left Mason's the night before, the dwarf had managed to finish a rudimentary bracelet for Ignatius. It wasn't as refined as he would have liked, but the little dragon was ecstatic at what the emberite and lavastone steel item could mean for him and his fire breathing.

Mason wrote that he'd like to do some more tinkering which could take a day or two and would I mind if Ignatius stayed with him until then so he could make the most of his downtime between customers. I sent back a quick message saying that was fine with me as long as they were both okay with the situation and a heartfelt thank you to Mason for helping Ignatius.

Reading through his detailed updates, I couldn't help but feel a wave of gratitude. Mason had gone above and beyond. Despite my initial suspicions about him being involved in the pranks and fires, I knew now that he was on my side. Last night, he'd been working on the bracelet the whole time, giving him a solid alibi for the warehouse fire incident. I scooped up my journal and crossed him off my list of suspects with a flourish. I needed to focus on finding the real culprits behind the chaos in Havenwood, but after I did that, I made a mental note to bring over some more steaks for both of Mason and Ignatius. Mason even sent a little video of Ignatius flapping around the workshop with a band on his foreleg about the size of a chunky statement ring. I smiled to see him looking so exuberant. Even though I would miss the little dragon, part of me was relieved Ignatius would be staying with Mason.

As I got ready for the day, my mind raced with thoughts of what lay ahead. Today was Wednesday, and Halloween was just around the corner. With Ignatius' new bracelet, we might finally have a way to control his fire and keep everyone here at Spellbooks safe when he returned. That made me sigh in relief. Now, I'd be able to focus all my attention on tracking down the imps and finding a way to contain them before they caused more trouble.

But first, I had to deal with the barrage of notifications and messages. My mom had messaged, wishing me a happy Harvest Festival and filling me in on a few tidbits of life important enough to take the time to type out. I smiled as I read her messages and tapped out a quick response of my own.

There were messages from both Finn and Bella, as well as a couple from the book club group chat. I quickly responded to all of them before indulging in some mindless scrolling. A gentle but persistent vibration from Spellbooks propelled me out of bed about fifteen minutes later. I chuckled, but as I got ready for the day, my mind wandered.

After solving the issue of both the town's and my shop's dragon-related fire problems last night, along with securing the last of the ingredients I needed for the ritual to catch the prankster imps, I had to admit I'd been feeling pretty good. Even if I might've inadvertently made myself a suspect in Chief Flint's eyes. Ultimately, I trusted the fire chief would conclude I didn't have anything to do with the fire. Because I didn't.

Now, all I had to do was set up the ritual tomorrow and trap the imps by midnight, and I could put this whole crazy week behind me.

A wave of anxiety crashed over me. I had zero leads on finding or trapping the imps and no plan for how to do it. The weight of the task ahead felt overwhelming. How was I supposed to capture these mischievous creatures and keep the town safe from their pranks? And what on earth was I going to tell the town to avoid the Silverthornes' suspicions and without becoming the target of everyone's growing animosity? The thought of facing them all, especially Vivienne, made my stomach twist with unease.

I forced myself to take a deep breath, trying to steady my racing thoughts. "One step at a time, Harper," I muttered to myself. "You'll figure this out." But the words felt hollow. I needed a solid plan, and fast. Halloween was only a day away, and the clock was ticking.

Determined to make some headway, I got dressed and headed downstairs, hoping that a clear head and a fresh perspective might help me find a solution. Anxiety was still gnawing at my insides, but I had to keep moving forward.

"Cabbage catastrophe! Have you heard what happened?" Luna demanded almost as soon as my feet touched the shop floor.

"Good morning to you, too," I said, trying to keep my voice steady as I scooped up some food for Mr. Wigglesworth and tipped it into his empty bowl. The massive cat stretched luxuriously, allowed me to pet him for a split second to show his gratitude, then dove face first into his food bowl.

"There's nothing good about it. Nothing at all," Luna griped, her tone sharp and insistent.

I sat back on my heels, my earlier tension creeping back. "To hear you tell it, the sky is falling, the Mets are going to win the World Series, and all of Havenwood is going to be swallowed by a fictional, giant, spice-eating worm."

"Don't be so stupid," Luna sniffed. "The Mets have no chance this year, and everyone knows it."

"Well then, all is right in the world," I said, pushing to my feet and grabbing the crisp vegetables I'd brought downstairs for her.

"All is most definitely *not* right with the world! Whisker whammy! Pay attention!"

I set her breakfast down in her food dish. "Okay, what's got your tail in a knot?"

"Rabbits' tails do not get 'in knots.' They get poufed. But I'll forgive you your ignorance because there's much more pressing news. For starters, someone switched all the numbers on the mailboxes down on Whimsy Way."

"That doesn't sound too bad," I said, trying to keep my tone light as I filled up the water dishes for both animals, but my heart skipped a beat. The pranksters were at it again, and I was running out of time.

"Pay attention! I said, *'for starters.'* By the fluffy ears of the right honorable Biscuitwiggle, what do you think that means?!" Before I could answer, Luna plowed ahead. "It means I'm just getting started. The mailboxes were the least of the rumpus from last night. Those imps unleashed a veritable toilet paper tsunami all over the town square. Not only that, but they strategically sabotaged the entire square with confetti-filled balloons. It's a fluffed-up nightmare!"

"It sounds annoying for sure, but a *nightmare*? I don't think I'd go that far," I protested.

"You try getting confetti out of your fur and then we'll see whose tail is poufed. Fluff and furballs! I thought you were on *my* side."

"I am," I reassured the irate familiar, though my mind was already racing. The news of these pranks could either give the imps an alibi for the fire, or it could mean they had split up, making them culpable for all the mischief from last night. My thoughts spiraled, trying to piece together the timeline and locations of the recent chaos. Could imps be that organized? My gut churned with the realization that I had very little knowledge of the imps or how they operated. How could I catch them if I couldn't predict what they might do?

"Have you heard anything else?" I asked, attempting to mask my growing anxiety.

"The town is in an uproar," Luna replied, her nose twitching with agitation. "The Silverthornes are on high alert, and the townsfolk are getting restless. Everyone's looking for someone to blame."

I swallowed hard, feeling the weight of the situation pressing down on me. I needed a plan—and fast.

Luna continued, oblivious to my reaction. "Those fluffernutting imps crossed a line. They need to be taught a lesson in proper rabbit respect, I tell you! I'm wearing my ninja headband until they're caught!" Luna exclaimed, balling up her paws and jabbing them at imaginary, impish foes.

"I don't disagree," I said, struggling to stifle a laugh as Luna engaged in an impromptu shadow boxing session across the shop floor. The bell above the side door jangled, and I looked down the hall to see Bella push through, carrying the morning's delivery of pastries from the Enchanted

Oasis. Honey and I had struck a deal when I opened. We'd cross promote our respective businesses, and I'd pay her a small fee for a couple of boxes of whatever she made in the mornings to sell at Spellbooks. Personally, I felt like I wasn't compensating her adequately for the delectable treats my customers consistently bought out before noon, but Honey seemed content with our arrangement.

Today, however, Bella wasn't her normal bubbly self. She plopped the boxes down before leaning her elbows on the counter and resting her face in her hands with a groan.

"What's going on, Bella?" I asked.

"Have you heard what those pranksters did last night?" she replied, her voice slightly muffled by her hands.

"Yeah, Luna was just filling me in," I said.

"It's a carrot crunching calamity, that's what it is!" Luna grumbled as she munched on her morning cabbage.

"Calamity or not, I've got to do something," I said.

"I don't think I've ever seen Papa so upset before. He loves Havenwood and hates that someone is messing with the town. Mama is so distracted by Papa that she burned the cookies this morning."

"No way!" I exclaimed. Honey's magical gift for baking was the stuff of legends, and she never, *ever* burned anything.

Bella's eyes sharpened. "Wait a second. You said 'I'. You aren't going around town assuming responsibility for this mess, are you? I know you wanted to help solve the mystery of who was behind the pranks, but I don't think that's any reason to blame yourself. None of this is your fault."

Tears welled up in my eyes at my best friend's staunch belief in me. I had to swallow hard past the lump that rose in my throat. "What if it is?" I whispered.

Bella looked up, eyes wide with confusion. "What do you mean?"

I sighed and looked around the shop to make sure it was empty before I reached for Granny's ledger. "I was cleaning up after the fire Ignatius caused, and some water spilled from the bucket over the box with the statues. I didn't think much of it at the time, but now..." I trailed off, flipping through the pages until I found the section on the stone spell. "Look at this."

I handed the journal to Bella, who quickly scanned the page. Her eyes widened in surprise. "This is what we talked about before and I still feel bad about loosing a fire-breathing dragon in your shop even if he is a mini one, but really? Water dissolving a spell? Why didn't she wrap up the dragon in plastic or put it in a waterproof bag with a giant neon warning sign?"

"I have no idea. Maybe it was on her to-do list, and she never got around to it, or she thought the statues would be safe enough up in the attic."

"Wait a second. Statues? Plural?" Bella asked.

I nodded, turning the page so she could see the final entry, and explained what I'd witnessed at the library. "It looks like Ignatius wasn't the only one who was freed from the stone spell. There are two imps on the list and there's what I imagine to be an imp-sized hole in the box. By my best guess, water splashed them when I put out the fire and they've been causing mayhem ever since. The only thing I can't figure out is the timeline. Some pranks happened before the fire. So, is there more than one prankster out there or what?"

To my surprise, Bella's face fell, and she looked up at me with tears in her eyes. "I'm a horrible person."

"What? No. You're the best person I know," I said, grabbing her hand.

Bella shook her head. "It's my fault, not yours. Remember when I spilled water on the counter? Some of it splashed on Ignatius. I didn't think to mention it, because I'd never heard of a stone spell or knew a little water could dissolve it. However, I'm pretty sure some water landed in the box too, but not enough to make a big thing about then. Now? Now everything that is happening is all my fault, not yours."

I squeezed her hand. "Hey, don't say that. You didn't know. None of us did. We'll figure this out together. We'll find the imps and fix this. You're not responsible for this mess, okay?"

"Oh yeah? Who spilled the water that dissolved the spell?" Guilt contorted her face as tears streaked down her cheeks.

"If you want to play the blame game, I deserve more than you. Whose water was it? Where were the imps stored in the first place? Who didn't check the journal or triple confirm that there weren't any mischievous creatures lying in wait among the plastic pumpkins and the creepy cobwebs?"

"How would Luna know about mischievous creatures in the attic? Does she have an encyclopedic memory or something?" Bella asked, glancing at the leporine familiar.

"No, but—" I pulled myself up short. Bella didn't know about Spellbooks being sentient. Granny had kept that piece of information so closely guarded that not even her family knew about it. Only a few trusted members of the Havenwood community were clued in. Granny's lawyer, and Aunty Agatha, to name a few.

"But what?" Bella asked, curiously.

I swallowed, fearing how close I'd come to spilling my biggest secret. I needed to be more careful. "But, um, I really should've thought to read the ledger first. This is Havenwood, after all," I finished lamely.

Bella looked at me sternly. "If I'm not allowed to take the blame for spilling the water, then you're not allowed to take the blame for not knowing what your granny had tucked away in her attic."

"Well, that's—"

"Completely fair?" Bella asked, cutting me off.

"If you two are done trying to one up each other in the blame game, I might suggest you hop to figuring out a solution to the imp problem. Failing that, please lower your voices so I can enjoy my breakfast in relative peace," Luna said archly.

The rabbit's sharp tone proverbially slapped the guilt right out of me. Luna was right. Crying over who was more to blame was a waste of time when we should be figuring out how to catch the imps. Bella and I looked at each other, sharing a smile. I didn't need words to tell we were on exactly the same page at that moment.

"I don't care if the spell was dissolved by you or me or Winne-the-Pooh wandering through the shop with his little black rain cloud," I said honestly. "The fact of the matter is the imps came from Spellbooks. I don't think Vivienne Silverthorne or the other leading members of the community will look favorably on us if they find out what really happened."

"Agreed," Bella said instantly.

"How do you feel about helping me make a plan to catch the imps. According to Aunty Agatha, we've only got one shot tomorrow or we're going to have to wait a month."

"A month!" Bella exclaimed. "I don't think I can survive a month of pranks like this."

"Well, it's a good thing that I've got the gist of a plan worked out, but I could use your keen insight to make sure I didn't overlook anything major."

Bella perked up. "I'm in." Her face fell once more. "But I have to get back to the Oasis to help Mama and Papa. How about I come back over once things calm down?"

"Perfect," I said, even though I would've preferred to get going right away. Maybe, by the time Bella returned, inspiration would've struck, and I'd have a clear and well-organized plan for catching the imps.

Bella left Spellbooks with more of a bounce in her step than she'd had when she entered. The rest of the morning sailed by smoothly, which seemed strange because it was so normal. Customers came and went. Books were purchased. Luna glared at Mr. Wigglesworth, who predictably ignored her in favor of naps or food. It was nearly noon before I realized Bella hadn't returned yet.

In a quiet moment between customers, I checked my phone to see what was happening. Bella had messaged, but I'd obviously missed the notification. She'd called both Alex and Finn and drafted them into helping, which coincidentally meant a second double date except this time I was hosting at Spellbooks, and she was bringing the food. I sighed at her matchmaking attempt. Not so much because it bothered me, but the timing could've been so much better. Instead of focusing all my attention on not making a fool of myself in front of the cute guy next door, I needed to catch some imps.

Or, on second thought, maybe I was jumping to all the wrong conclusions. I still didn't fully trust Alex. He'd been at the top of my suspect list all along. Maybe all my suppositions about imps were entirely incorrect. On the other hand, perhaps I was being overly paranoid, but I still thought it was very suspicious that he showed up right before all the mayhem started. That, and he hadn't been exactly forthcoming about his powers. But if he was behind all the pranks, how could I explain the two figures I saw at the library and my missing imp statues?

I sighed again, dinner sounding suddenly much less appealing. Hiding my suspicions of Alex from Bella while simultaneously trying to plan an imp-trapment, all while not looking crazy in front of the guy I was crushing on.

That type of thing could only happen in Havenwood.

Un-brie-lievable Secrets

Bella arrived first, carrying two bags stuffed full of delicious looking breads, cheeses, and fruits. "Hope you don't mind, but if this is going to be a planning session, it'd be a crime for it to be under catered. I brought everything needed for the most epic cheeseboard you've ever seen."

"That sounds incredible!" I exclaimed, my stomach already rumbling in anticipation.

"Is it okay if I head upstairs and start setting up? The guys won't be here for about a half hour, but these weigh a ton," Bella said, hefting the bags and readjusting her grip.

I waved toward the stairs. "Help yourself. I'll lock up down here and then be up to help you in a second."

"Okay," Bella called over her shoulder as she headed towards the stairs.

I helped the last of my customers for the day and flipped the sign on the door to say Spellbooks was closed. After I locked the shop, I breezed through the most rudimentary closing I'd ever done. Even Luna sniffed in disapproval, but I figured I could come back down later to finish up. The closed laptop next to the register reminded me I had an assignment due for one of the online classes I was taking, but that could wait. For now, there was cheese to be eaten, plans to make, and imps to catch.

I trudged up the stairs to my apartment above Spellbooks, my mind heavy with thoughts of the impish chaos. Pushing open the door, I expected to find Bella cutting a block of cheddar into cubes. Instead, I was greeted by the sight of her holding a small cooking torch, caramelizing the top of a tray of melting brie.

"Bella, stop!" I shouted, my voice cracking with fear as I rushed toward her, my heart pounding in my chest. Seeing her casually wave a torch around my apartment almost gave me a heart attack.

Bella jumped, nearly dropping the torch. "Oh, Harper!" she exclaimed, pressing her free hand to her heart. "I thought I'd surprise you with something fancy. This brie with a caramelized sugar crust is amazing. Trust me! It's one of my mama's specialties and you haven't lived until you've tried it."

"What. Are. You. Doing?" I asked, trying not to shout despite the fear bubbling up inside me at the sight of the open flame. Underfoot, I could feel Spellbooks shudder, causing a couple of books to fall from the shelves.

"Whoa, what's happening?" Bella exclaimed, looking around in shock. "I didn't think Connecticut got earthquakes." She flicked the flame off and set the torch down.

My heart was still racing, the fear refusing to ebb away. "Bella, you can't use an open flame in here. Spellbooks is sensitive to that kind of thing," I blurted out, struggling to keep my voice steady.

Bella's confusion deepened into worry. "Spellbooks? The shop? How can a shop be sensitive?" she asked, her voice tinged with an edge of panic as she tried to make sense of my words.

Realizing my slip, I sucked in a breath, my mind racing. Bella's expectant look was like a knife to my gut. I was at a crossroads, the weight of my decision pressing down on me.

"Harper? What's going on?" Bella asked.

I thought about how fiercely Granny protected Spellbooks. It had been such a secret that I hadn't even known the shop's true nature until I inherited it after her passing. Nevertheless, Granny had told Agatha, her best friend in the world. Maybe I could tell mine. Scratch that. Maybe I *should* tell mine. After all, Bella had been the most steadfast friend anyone could ever wish for since I'd moved back to Havenwood.

"Harper? You're scaring me. What is it?" Bella said, laying a hand softly on my arm.

Her concern for me nearly caused me to break, but I'd also made my decision. I laid a hand on the wall and whispered, "I hope it's okay to tell her." A soft warmth and gentle vibration tickled my fingertips. I took that to mean Spellbooks was giving me the go-ahead.

"Who are you talking to?" Bella demanded, looking around anxiously.

I took a deep breath, meeting her eyes with a mixture of fear and determination. "Spellbooks. You're right that Spellbooks is the shop, but it's so much more than that," I began, my voice trembling. "It's sentient, magical, my partner, and it *really* doesn't like open flames," I explained, the words tumbling out in a rush, hoping she would understand.

Bella's eyes widened in realization and shock. She gestured to where I still held my hand against the wall. "Wait, was that the two of you... *communicating*?" she asked, her voice barely a whisper. I nodded, searching her face for any sign of reaction, be it good or bad.

Bella's eyes widened in shock and then narrowed in realization. "How? When? Why didn't you tell me?"

I sighed deeply, the weight of my guilt pressing down on me. "I'm sorry, Bella. It's a long story, but the secret of Spellbooks is so closely guarded that I didn't even know until after I inherited the shop," I admitted, my voice nearly breaking.

Bella's face fell, hurt flashing in her eyes. "You didn't trust me enough to tell me?" she asked, her voice trembling with the pain of betrayal.

"No, it's not that," I said quickly. "It's just...complicated. I'm sorry, Bella," I said, my voice filled with remorse. "I should have trusted you with this secret. You've always been there for me, but I was trying to walk in my Granny's shoes. Do things the way she did to honor her memory. I was trying to figure out how to handle, well, everything. Spellbooks and I are still learning how to work together, and I wasn't sure when or even if it was okay to share the secret with anyone. I haven't even told my parents yet. I didn't mean to keep it from you. You've always been there for me, and I should have trusted you with this."

Bella took a deep breath, her expression softening. "I get it, Harper. I really do. But I wish you'd told me sooner. We're a team, remember? No matter what."

"I know," I said, feeling a weight lift off my shoulders. "I'm so grateful for you, Bella. You've saved me more times than I can count, and I don't know what I'd do without you." Tears welled up in my eyes. I didn't deserve such a wonderful friend and yet, I was so glad to have her.

Bella pulled me into a tight hug, her own tears mixing with mine. "We'll figure this out together. No more secrets," she whispered fiercely, her words a promise and a comfort.

"No more secrets," I echoed, hugging her back.

The floorboards vibrated gently under our feet, startling us both. We looked down in surprise.

Bella recovered first. "Okay, okay, I hear you Spellbooks. No more torches either." I shot her a look of surprise. She was adjusting to the magical building so much faster than I had. Perhaps it was a perk of growing up in Havenwood.

A rumble sounded from deep within the walls, almost as if Spellbooks was chuckling. A rough sketch of a figure in a pointed hat slowly appeared on the chalkboard, surrounded by a crude drawing of a cage.

"I think... Spellbooks is offering to help us catch the imps," I said slowly. A stronger vibration met my words.

Bella shot me a surprised look and then laid one hand on the wall, keeping the other around my shoulders. "Well then, it's you and us, Spellbooks. Those imps don't stand a chance."

As we stood there hugging each other and talking to the wall, the door opened. Finn and Alex walked in. They took one look at us and exchanged puzzled glances.

"Are we interrupting something?" Finn asked, a bemused smile playing on his lips.

"How did you get in?" I asked, surprised. I quickly wiped away my tears with the back of my hand.

"Luna," Finn said, jerking a thumb down the stairs with a nonchalant shrug, as if it were completely normal for a rabbit to unlock a door.

"But if you two need a minute, that's cool," Alex said, looking a little uncomfortable as he realized, given the tears, they'd obviously walked in on a private moment.

Bella and I exchanged a knowing look, our bond stronger than ever. We were in this together, no matter what challenges lay ahead. I shook my head, laughing through my tears. "No, you're just in time. Let's get this planning session started."

Planning and Pepper Jack

My heart still pounded from the emotional rollercoaster of revealing Spellbooks' secret to Bella, but I turned to Finn and Alex. "Thanks for coming," I said, swallowing hard as I glanced at Bella. My chest tightened with the weight of everything that had happened. She gave me an encouraging nod before heading to the kitchen to work on the cheese board, sans torch this time.

"Anytime. Besides, Bella promised the smelliest blue cheese in town, so I'm already thrilled to be here, but if it involves some answers to what's been happening around town, all the better," Alex said with a grin. He tipped his head towards the shop below. "I love what you've done with the place. It really is giving Halloween-in-Havenwood without being too much, you know?"

"Thanks," I said, waving them inside. I forced a smile at Alex's seeming genuine kindness, but a lingering suspicion still hovered in the back of my mind. Why had he shown up in town just before the chaos started? Was it just coincidence? It had to be, right? I hadn't told Bella about my doubts, but the questions were like a relentless drumbeat in my head.

Finn held up a platter of sliced vegetables, interrupting my thoughts. "I didn't know what Bella was bringing, but I hope this will pair well."

"I'm sure it will, thank you," I said, accepting it and looking it over. Carrots, cucumbers, celery, and some cherry tomatoes were arranged neatly on the plate.

"I'll take that," Bella said, whisking the tray away to my small kitchen area. Alex followed her.

"Are you okay?" Finn asked, dropping his voice to a whisper meant for my ears only.

"More than okay," I reassured him. I raised my voice. "Why don't the two of you have a seat? It's kind of a long story."

Finn and Alex exchanged curious looks as they settled into the armchairs while Bella returned to her cheese board preparations. I took a deep breath and began recounting the events of the past few days, from the pranks to the imps. "So, it turns out the imps are responsible for most of the pranks around town. Bella and I pieced it together with some help from Granny's ledger," I finished, purposefully omitting mentioning Spellbooks' assistance.

Finn leaned forward; his brow furrowed. "Do you think the imps are behind the fires too?"

"I don't know," I admitted, frustration seeping into my voice. "The pranks are just mischievous, but the fires are dangerous. They feel like separate issues, but can we entirely rule out the imps being behind the fires?" The uncertainty gnawed at me, each question echoing the fear that we were missing something crucial.

Alex, who had been quietly listening, finally spoke up. "And what's the plan once we catch the imps? How do we keep them from causing more trouble?"

"I've been researching that," I said, pulling out my journal that held all my notes for the ritual. "We need to trap them, which means we need to find them first. Any ideas where to start?"

Bella spoke up from the kitchen area. "I brought a tourist map from the B&B that I've been using to keep track where the pranks have been happening. Maybe there's a pattern."

"Good idea," I said eagerly. My mind raced with the implications. If we didn't figure this out soon, what more damage could the imps do? How many more fires? How many more pranks? The weight of responsibility pressed down on my shoulders like a lead blanket.

Bella spread the map on the coffee table, and we all gathered around it. "Here," she said, pointing to various spots marked in red ink. "These are where the pranks have been reported."

We studied the map, and Alex traced a finger along the points. "It looks like they're moving in something like a spiral pattern, closing in toward the center of town."

"That's a good observation," I said, nodding. "If they keep following this pattern, perhaps we can predict where they'll strike next and set up a trap."

"These are all town events or prominent locations with lots of foot traffic," Finn noted.

"You're right," Bella said excitedly. "Maybe we could lure them to the next town event."

"That's the Pumpkin Parade, isn't it?" I asked.

Finn blew out a breath and shook his head. "Maybe that's not the best idea, if we're trying to keep a low profile. Wouldn't it be better to do this someplace a little less public? Speaking of, how exactly do we trap them?"

I flipped to the pages filled with my notes from my visit to Agatha's house and quickly explained the ritual. "We'll need to draw a containment circle and lure them into it. Once they're inside, the circle should hold them long enough for us to complete the ritual and turn them back to stone," I said in conclusion.

"Sounds easy enough," Alex said, leaning back in his chair. "Except they're imps and therefore completely unpredictable."

Bella smacked him lightly on the shoulder.

"What? I'm just calling it like I see it," Alex protested. "Imps are notoriously impulsive and known for behaving in completely erratic ways. Expect the unexpected, that's all I'm saying."

Finn nodded. "They do have that reputation, but I've never met one face to face before. However, we have something else to consider. Namely, what do we tell the town? Everyone's already on edge. Do we let them know what's really going on, or keep it to ourselves?"

"That's a tough one," I admitted, my throat dry. "If we tell them, it might calm some of the fear and suspicion, but what if it backfires?" My pulse quickened as I imagined Vivienne's stern face, the whispers of blame from the townsfolk, and the crushing guilt if they turned against us.

"And we could get some help from people like the Silverthornes," Finn said, oblivious to my inner turmoil.

"But it could also make it worse," Bella pointed out quickly, as if she could read my mind. "What if people start blaming us if we can't catch the imps? Or what if they blame Harper for letting them loose in the first place?"

"It wasn't her fault," Finn protested.

"You and I know that, but will everyone else believe it?" Bella asked.

All eyes turned towards me. Finn cleared his throat. "I think this is ultimately your call," he said softly.

My heart raced as I considered the options. The weight of the town's safety pressed down on me, and I couldn't shake the growing fear of what might happen to Spellbooks or to me if we didn't handle this perfectly. "We can't risk it," I said finally. "We'll keep this to ourselves. The fewer people involved, the less chance of something going wrong. Let's try to lure the imps out of town to minimize any further damage."

Bella nodded instantly, as if she'd expected this answer from me. "I agree. How about the corn maze at Moonshadow Pumpkin Farm? It should have fewer people tomorrow than the Pumpkin Parade."

"That's a good idea," I said, feeling a surge of relief at having a concrete plan. "We can set up the containment circle there and try to trap them."

"Let's work out the details so we ensure the best chance of success," Finn said, leaning forward.

"Great idea, but can we talk while we work. This cheese won't arrange itself," Bella said, waving at the half-prepared dinner she'd left in her excitement for the planning.

With all of us working together, we'd soon settled most of the details we could think of and arranged a beautifully displayed cheese platter that covered most of the surface of my small kitchen table, offering a variety of flavors and textures. Bella's half-toasted wheel of creamy brie took center stage, complemented by zesty pepper jack wedges and crumbly gouda. A delightful dragon fruit chèvre provided a colorful and tangy addition, while the strong Elven blue from the local fromagerie added depth with its savory notes. Fresh berries and a selection of nuts contributed a nat-ural sweetness and satisfying crunch, respectively. Accompanied by freshly baked bread and crispy fairy breadsticks, the spread showcased Bella's culinary expertise in pairing flavors and textures. I slid Finn's plate of vegetables onto the table and smiled. I couldn't have prepared a better meal for planning to rid the town of impish pranks if I'd tried.

As we nibbled, the room filled with the heady aroma of fine cheese. Laughter and camaraderie punctuated our discussion, but beneath the surface, I could feel my tension building. The success of the upcoming events hinged on my ability to flawlessly execute a ritual I'd never done before. Each bite of cheese felt like a small reprieve from the mounting pressure, but the responsibility of what lay ahead lingered at the edges of my thoughts, refusing to be ignored. Despite our planning session, I still had doubts as to my own abilities, and when it was all said and done, the magical entrapment was my responsibility to not mess up.

After we demolished the lovely cheese board, the conversation shifted to structuring contingency plans. Amid our strategic discussion, the clock ticked steadily. I felt as if it were counting down the minutes until either my debut as an accomplished witch or having to admit the debacle of releasing the imps to the entire town. Would I be able to withstand the pressure and uphold Granny Bea's legacy of being an upstanding member of the Havenwood community? Or would the imps be my undoing and the reason Vivienne Silverthorne unceremoniously threw me out of town?

For better or worse, it would all be decided tomorrow.

Back Where It All Began

As the sun dipped below the horizon the next evening, painting the sky in hues of orange and purple, Bella, Finn, Alex, and I were back at Moonshadow Farm, the site where the pranks all began. The familiar surroundings felt oddly comforting, even as my nerves buzzed with anticipation. I paced nervously, clutching the bag I had looped across my torso. Another bag was on the ground by my feet. The two contained everything I'd need for the ritual. If the imps actually showed up here tonight, we might finally put an end to the chaos.

I'd spent the day prepping, rehearsing the ritual in between helping customers at Spellbooks, and making sure I had every step memorized. I needed to be flawless tonight, or all our planning would be in vain.

Bella, true to her word, had spent the day spreading the word around town that there was a big to-do happening out at Moonshadow Farm. Finn and Alex also helped with the rumor mongering, hoping that the promise of a sizeable crowd would once more draw the imps out to the secluded farm. The imps seemed to have been targeting crowded places, so this was our best bet to lure them out without actually compromising the end of the festival parade.

The air buzzed with excitement as families enjoyed the kid-friendly Halloween delights. Wagons piled high with hay bales slowly trundled around a dirt path, much to the delight of the costumed children. The aroma of freshly popped kettle corn and warm apple cider enticed the waiting parents to grab a snack while their little ones enjoyed the ride. Stalls adorned with twinkling fairy lights showcased local artisans selling hand-made crafts, pumpkin carvings, and eerie but cute decorations. Laughter echoed from the children's corner, where face-painting artists transformed eager faces into whimsical creatures.

The main attraction tonight was the sprawling corn maze, its towering stalks casting long shadows as the sun sank. Groups of costumed attendees picked their way through the labyrinth, encountering friendly scarecrows, hidden surprises, and the occasional ghostly figure lurking in the shadows, which turned out to be recorded images from hidden projectors.

Nearby, a small campfire for toasting marshmallows crackled, casting a warm glow over hay bales arranged for seating. Revelers, adorned in costumes ranging from magical creatures to classic monsters, gathered around, sharing ghost stories and toasting marshmallows for s'mores. The night was alive with the sound of a local band playing familiar tunes, adding to the bewitching atmosphere.

An hour passed with no sign of the imps. My anxiety grew with each tick of the clock. What if they didn't come? What if we were wrong? Were the imps terrorizing the town while we were out at the Moonshadow farm? Were all of our careful preparations in vain?

I stationed myself near the entrance to the maze, my heart pounding with each passing minute. The sounds of laughter and excitement from the tourists contrasted sharply with the tension thrumming through my veins.

"C'mon, c'mon, *c'mon,*" I muttered, slamming my fist into my other hand repeatedly as I paced.

"They'll be here," Bella murmured, slowly turning in a circle to scan the busy farm.

"How can you be so sure?" I asked.

"Because this was your idea. You're the one who said the imps were targeting town events. If that holds true, they'll make an appearance here tonight," she replied confidently.

"But what if I'm wrong and they target the Pumpkin Parade instead?" I asked.

"That doesn't start for a while yet," Finn pointed out.

"A parade in the dark? I've been meaning to ask what's with that," I said.

"Well, it's not really all that dark. The local coven sets up a lot of witch lights that make the streets almost as bright as day," Bella explained.

"And it gives more of that Halloween ambiance," Finn said. "But the parade doesn't start for a while yet. For the time being, this is probably the best place to be to catch the imps, remember?"

"I'm not sure that's true," Alex said, as if a thought had just occurred to him.

"What do you mean?" Bella asked.

He pointed out at the corn maze. "Haven't the imps been rather fire-prone? I heard there's been a few unexplained fires around town. First in the woods, then at the fashion show, and, most recently, a warehouse nearly burned to the ground."

"I wouldn't say it was that bad," I muttered. How did Alex know about the warehouse? Was that common knowledge, or had he been there? I tried to superimpose Alex's figure over the silhouette I'd seen in the flickering flames.

"What was that?" Bella asked, interrupting me.

I froze. I'd forgotten to tell Bella about my part in saving the building in all the guilt about Spellbooks, hiding my suspicions of her ex-boyfriend, and ritual planning. Now wasn't the time to get into my brush with the fire bug, let alone anything else. Besides, I was trying to convince myself that the imps were responsible for the fires as well, and my lingering suspicions of Alex were unfounded. If that was true and everything went according to plan, we wouldn't have to worry about random fires around town anymore.

I cleared my throat. "Um, well, you see, I just heard that the warehouse was singed. Blackened maybe. But the fire department got there in time to save the building," I said in a hurry. Bella shot me a look that told me she knew I knew more than I was letting on. She opened her mouth to ask a probing question when a shout rose from near the maze, interrupting us. As one, we turned to look at what was going on. Lara Moonshadow, a professional smile that was just a tad too tight around the corners of her mouth and didn't even come close to reaching her eyes, waved people out of the maze.

"That's it, folks. The maze closes down at night. Besides, it's time to head into town for the Pumpkin Parade," she said loudly. Tourists started drifting towards their cars.

Bella shook her head. "This doesn't make sense. The corn maze always stays open late into the night. That's what makes it extra fun."

My eyes widened in understanding. "They're here. The imps are causing chaos in the maze," I breathed.

Finn grabbed my hand. "Now's our chance. Let's get them and end this." We fought the flow of foot traffic to reach Lara's side. She greeted us with a brief nod.

"What's going on?" I asked, keeping my voice low so as not to upset a nearby family of four. The older sister tugged on her father's hand, whereas the mother carried the little one who couldn't have been more than two or three. The little girl was nearly asleep but was valiantly fighting the fatigue of her long day. As they passed us, I saw the child pop her thumb in her mouth and start sucking, her eyes drifting closed once more and a contented smile lifting her lips. If I had my way, the rest of the night would be that peaceful for everyone in Havenwood.

"It's those pranksters again," Lara muttered. "Vivienne thought they'd target the Pumpkin Parade, but they're here. Somehow, they're creating hyper-realistic versions of ghosts to chase the tourists around the maze. One or two even got caught in a rain of ectoplasmic slime. I had to spin a story of how we were really embracing a Ghostbuster's theme this year and offer the family a box of free doughnuts. I'd really love to see the end of these pranksters, but, for now, I just want to get everyone back into town."

"Let us help," Bella offered. "Alex and I can stand guard here at the entrance of the maze and make sure no more tourists go inside."

"And Finn and I would be happy to make sure everyone is out of the maze," I offered with a bright smile.

Lara looked torn. "That would be helpful, but I don't want to take advantage of you. Not when you should be enjoying the last day of the Harvest Festival and heading toward the Pumpkin Parade."

"Nonsense! We're all part of Havenwood. If someone is messing with you, they're messing with all of us. Besides, what are neighbors for if not to help you when the going gets...um, spooky," I finished lamely.

"If you're sure you don't mind helping out, I won't turn you down," Lara said with a relieved smile. She pulled out a folded piece of paper and held it out to me. "This is a map of the maze, so you don't get stuck in there. I'm going to go tell the people at the refreshments stand to pack it in and hopefully we can usher all the guests out of here with no more slime-related pranks."

As Lara went off to organize the evacuation, Finn and I exchanged a glance, understanding the task ahead.

Finn said, "Bella and Alex, keep everyone out. I'll use my druidic magic and some well-placed runes to create barriers within the maze to drive the imps toward the center. Harper, you set up the ritual there. With all the tourists being guided towards town, it's the best place if you want to be undisturbed."

"Got it," I replied. I unfolded the map and traced the fastest path to the center of the maze with a finger. I tapped the map, confident that I could make it to the middle without additional assistance. Finn would need the map to put his runes in the best places possible. "Let's catch these imps and put an end to their mischief." I hefted the bags of ritual items and headed into the maze.

Finn paused at the entrance, crouching down to scratch some runes in the dirt as I hurried down the left-hand path, moving as fast as I could with my burden towards the center of the maze.

As I ventured deeper into the corn maze, the unexpected apparitions conjured by the mischievous imps unfolded before me. Friendly yet irritating ghostly figures, semi-translucent and donning comically exaggerated expressions, floated through the cornstalks. Their ghostly antics were accompanied by a symphony of sounds that oscillated between whimsical ghostly noises, playful laughter, and, to my disbelief, frat-boy-esque fart noises. The absurdity of the situation struck a peculiar chord, and despite the annoyance, I found myself stifling a mix of laughter and exasperation.

However, as I navigated the maze amidst the low-level humor, a sense of discomfort crept in. The echoes of the imps' juvenile pranks clashed with the gravity of recent events—the fire at the warehouse and the chaos during the fashion show. It was challenging to reconcile the incongruity between the crude humor of the ghosts in the maze and the potentially dangerous consequences of the fires. The juxtaposition of fart noises against the backdrop of recent calamities left me questioning the motives behind the imps' mischievous endeavors. A sense of unease lingered, reminding me that even in the midst of the bizarre and the absurd, there were consequences that transcended the realm of juvenile pranks. These imps needed to be dealt with, and they needed to be dealt with now. If everything went according to plan, this would be the last prank they played for a very, *very* long time.

Rituals and Responsibilities

THE BULKY BAGS BANGED against my legs as I jogged through the maze. They weren't heavy, but they were unwieldy. As soon as I reached the center of the maze, I breathed a sigh of relief and set them down.

Carved jack-o'-lanterns leered at me, seemingly from every nook and cranny. A scarecrow stood at the edge of the clearing, its clothes made of patched flannel, old denim, and a long trench coat. Someone had stuffed it with straw and stitched a crooked smile and button eyes onto its face. In the daylight, it might have been charmingly autumnal, but, in the darkness of night, the scarecrow looked ready to leap at me for intruding upon his inner sanctum of dry cornstalks.

I shook my head, chastising myself. This wasn't the time for flights of fancy. I needed to make sure everything went exactly according to plan. I focused all my attention on setting up the ritual. My hands moved with practiced precision, arranging magical components and creating a focal point for the spell. The air filled with the sound of ghostly laughter, as if the apparitions the imps had summoned were taunting me. I worked with a heightened sense of urgency, feeling as if the imps would jump out at me any second. Despite the eerie sounds, I did my best to ignore the apparitions and stay focused on the ritual.

Within ten minutes, I had everything set. Standing in the center of the circle I'd meticulously drawn with salt, the carved pumpkins sat patiently waiting to spring the trap designed to catch the imps. I'd cut the candle in half, making sure to smear my blood on both parts, and that the wicks were easily accessible for my long-handled kitchen lighter through the carved openings in the pumpkins.

Next to the candle in each pumpkin were two small doll cups I'd borrowed from Bella. Although I wasn't one to hang on to things, what with all the transferring between army bases as a kid, I was thankful Honey had never thrown out Bella's old toys. Each cup held a mixture of honey and moonlit dew. I wasn't sure how much dew it would take to trap the imps but didn't want to bungle the ritual because I was being stingy. If there were enough of the ingredients left over, then I planned to attempt the ritual again with Ignatius later tonight, but only if this one worked.

The tops for both pumpkins were lying in the grass next to the scarecrow, where I planned to hide. I took a deep breath, checking the salt ring one more time. Everything was in place. All that was left was to start the ritual.

"Here goes nothing," I whispered to myself as I pulled two chunks of unfinished moonstone from my pocket. Carefully, I pricked the tip of my finger with Mason's silver knife and smeared a droplet of my blood on each stone before placing them inside the pumpkins.

Clearing my throat, I began the invocation, my voice resonating through the night as I spoke the spell Agatha had taught me with a few last-minute wording substitutions to make the spell specific to my targets.

"By the light of the moon, in the depths of the night, I summon the powers to set things right. Imps, your pranks must cease. With this spell, I bring the town peace."

As the incantation echoed in the clearing, a shiver ran down my spine. Would this work? The dull thud of footsteps pounded closer. I looked up. Was it Finn coming? Or was it the imps? If it was the latter, I had to hide. If they saw me, they might run away before ever setting foot in the salt circle and ruining all our hard work. With the long, automatic fire starter from my kitchen clutched in one hand, I ducked behind the scarecrow, peeking through the effigy's spiky straw hair.

The seconds crawled by. With each passing moment, my nerves drew tighter until I was sure they'd snap from the mounting tension. So suddenly that I almost didn't realize it at first, two tiny figures poked their heads around the corner of the cornstalks of the right-hand path. The imps, drawn by the scent of honey and the magical allure, sniffed at the air.

In the dim moonlit clearing, I squinted as the two imps stepped into the clearing. The leader sported a shock of vibrant crimson hair that seemed to catch the faint moonlight. His lopsided grin, revealing pointy teeth, was visible even from a distance, and his attire, a patchwork of bright hues, made him stand out like an animated candy wrapper in the shadows. The second imp was slightly taller and had a mop of unruly green hair as bright as his friend's. If possible, his clothing was even more outlandishly garish than his companion's.

The red-haired imp sniffed loudly at the air again and exclaimed, "Well, lookie here, Snicker! What's this? A feast left outs for us? Honey or my nose is a rotten grape. Honey ripes for the taking!"

Snicker scratched at his armpit. "Whys would anyone wants a ripe rotten grape, Wizzle? 'Specially for a nose."

Wizzle reached out and smacked Snicker on the back of his head, batting the other imp's pointed hat onto the ground. "If brains was pennies, Snicker, you wouldn't have enough to buy a gumdrop."

"I loves gumdrops, Wizzle," Snicker said with a cheerful smile as he scooped up his hat and plopped it back on his head.

Wizzle sighed. "I *knows*, Snicker. You loves gumdrops, I loves *all* sweet. 'Specially honey. These big folks is being stupid again, leaving honey about all willy-nilly in a corn field."

Snicker chuckled, "Humans. You'd thinks they'd learn after the candy shop and the orchard that we likes sweet things. We ain't no garden gnomes, is we? Just standing around with stupid grins on our faces."

Both imps suddenly froze, posing in ridiculous caricatures of cheerful gnomes, their faces contorted into great grotesque grins. I held my breath as they stopped just outside the salt circle. Would they enter the circle? Would they break the ring? If they did, I'd have to figure out how to close it, and quickly.

Wizzle broke out of his pose first and nudged Snicker in the ribs. "See? We ain't no garden gnomes."

"Nah, we's much betterer than them. Funnier. Smartier. That we is."

Wizzle slapped Snicker on the back of the head again, this time propelling him into the salt ring. I sucked in a breath as the little imp stumbled across the line of salt. "Youse sound so stupid. Talk right. Funnier. Smartier. That we is, *for sure*."

"Sorry, sorry. You is right. For sure, we is smartier than stupid, sugar-free-candy-corn-for-brains garden gnomes," Snicker mumbled.

"Course *I* is," Wizzle said, puffing up proudly. "Who came up with the tricksy candy and the caramel apples growin' right out of the trees?"

"You did, Wizzle," Snicker said meekly.

"And I would've magicked those models' fancy clothes to candies if it ain't been for that fire in the town square."

Snicker whimpered softly, cringing behind Wizzle and looking around frantically.

"Don't be so scaredy cat. There's no fire here. Just honey and dew," Wizzle said, rubbing his belly.

"What? I thought you said it was yumminess. Not *melon*," Snicker whined.

"Not honeydew! Has you gots jellybeans rattling in that empty spot 'tween your ears 'stead of brains? Honey *and* dew! How does you even gets through the day without me?" Wizzle said, shaking his head and strutting forward into the salt ring. I held my breath, but he stepped neatly over it without scuffing the circle. I blew out a silent breath. One more hurdle crossed.

Just as I thought my nerves couldn't take it anymore, the imps scampered over towards the pumpkins in a rush and scrambled inside. I heard loud slurping noises and then simultaneous contented sighs.

"That's good, that is, Wizzle," Snicker's voice drifted out of the nearest pumpkin.

"I agrees, Snicker. Gives us a minute more, and then we'll heads to town. There'll be lots of mischief to stirs up at the Pumpkin Parade," Wizzle said, letting out a little belch.

I couldn't let that happen. Time was of the essence. I crept forward as silently as I could, clutching the tops of the two pumpkins in my sweating hands. The long kitchen lighter was in my back pocket, ready to finish the ritual and turn these two pranksters back into statues.

"Wizzle?" There was an edge to Snicker's voice.

"Yeah?" Wizzle replied with a yawn.

"Wizzle! Something's wrong. My feets won't move!"

"Are you sure you gots the right things? Not likes last time? Your feets is at the ends of your ankles. Your *ears* is on your head. Remember?" Wizzle said, not sounding at all concerned.

"I knows! I wrotes it on my hand for a month!"

"You wrotes it on your belly," Wizzle muttered.

"No, I didn't writes it on *jelly*," Snicker said, obviously mishearing his friend. "What do you takes me for? A nooble-headed lolli-sucker?" Snicker demanded.

"Some kind of sucker, that's for sure," Wizzle snorted.

"Wizzle! I is cerealious!"

"*Serious*, you nutty nooble muppet!"

"That too! I can't moves my feets!"

"Now enough's enough—wait! I can't moves my feets either," Wizzle said, his voice rising in volume as he suddenly realized his predicament.

But it was too late. In one swift lunge, I slammed the tops of the pumpkins down on the imps' round orange cages. The imps screamed in outrage as they realized things had just gone from bad to worse for them, but I paid no attention to their shouts. With only one more step, the ritual would be complete. Then all Havenwood would finally be imp-free and able to enjoy Halloween in relative peace. I pulled the kitchen lighter out of my pocket and jammed it through the carved openings in Snicker's pumpkin.

"Wizzle! It's a witch!" Snicker wailed. "I don't wants to be turned back to—"

His words cut off as I clicked on the trigger of the lighter, the popping snap of the mechanism sparking crackling through the air. The wick of the candle caught almost instantly. Through the carved pumpkin, I saw the change sweep over Snicker. The brightly clothed imp who had been joking with his friend a moment before was now frozen in the middle of the pumpkin, his mouth hanging open on a word he wouldn't say for quite some time if I got my way. Snicker was a small stone statue once more.

I turned to Wizzle's pumpkin, the lighter in my hand. One down. One to go. I clicked the lighter on, a flame flickering to life, and thrust it towards the second pumpkin.

That's when everything went wrong.

Pumpkin Predicaments

As I THRUST THE lighter into Wizzle's pumpkin, he met it with all the grace and maturity one might expect from a prankster imp. He leaned back as far as his trapped feet would let him go and then snapped his head forward, launching the largest loogie I'd ever seen right at the fiery tip of the lighter. The flame surrendered under the deluge of imp spit. I was left impotently clicking the useless kitchen gadget.

With some choice muttered words about imps, I yanked the lighter free and wiped off the worst of the mess on the grass.

"There's more weres that came from!" Wizzle cackled triumphantly.

"You're trapped in there. All I have to do is get that candle lit," I said, clicking the trigger again. I could hear it sputter, but there was still a globule of sputum lodged in the nozzle. With a vow to wash my shirt as soon as possible, I used the hem as an impromptu slobber serviette and wiped out what I could. I clicked the lighter again and this time, a tiny flame fought through the residual mess to flicker to life.

"Oh no youse don't!" Wizzle said with wide eyes glued on the flame. His cheeks bulged out once more, and he reared back like a snake ready to strike.

"Now just hold still," I said through gritted teeth as I tried to anticipate where the spittle assault would strike.

Wizzle shook his head violently, gently rocking the pumpkin from side to side. His eyes lit up and, before I could do anything to stop him, the imp had thrown himself to one side, sending the pumpkin rolling away from me.

Now, in most pumpkin rolling scenarios, this wouldn't have been a problem. The ground was fairly flat and surrounded by corn stalks. Where could it go?

When you add an imp to the mix, the answer to that question is anywhere it wants.

Wizzle must've channeled whatever imp magic was inherent to his kind because the pumpkin only gained speed as it scuffed the salt circle and rolled away across the bumpy ground. I caught my breath. The ritual only trapped Wizzle in place. It didn't freeze the pumpkin itself. Now that the circle was broken, what did that mean? Could he escape? Would the spell dissolve, freeing him?

The same thought must've occurred to the imp because the pumpkin started thumping along the ground, rising higher on each bounce before smashing down to the dirt. So, the spell was holding for now, but it was only a matter of time before he cracked the pumpkin open. Then who knew what would happen?! I had to do something, and quickly!

I dashed after the runaway pumpkin. Other than stopping Wizzle from escaping, I didn't have a solid plan in place yet. I just needed to catch that pumpkin. On the third bounce, Wizzle launched the pumpkin higher than I could have imagined possible.

I jumped, trying to catch it before it crashed to the ground and broke open, but catching sports had never really been my forte. Instead of cradling it into my chest and landing in the most bizarre replica of a touchdown ever imagined, I batted ineffectually at the pumpkin, sending it spiraling off on a new trajectory. I stumbled forward, trying to keep my balance as the pumpkin collided with the scarecrow, knocking the figurine's head off completely. For a moment, the pumpkin wobbled on top of the scarecrow's stuffed body. I sucked in a breath, just waiting for it to fall, crack open, and set Wizzle loose once more.

But what happened next was even worse.

The pumpkin stopped wobbling and spun to face me, its carved grin growing wider as Wizzle used his magic to animate both the scarecrow and the pumpkin. My jaw dropped as the scarecrow wriggled off the wooden posts holding it upright and, defying all laws of straw, physics, and yes, even pancakes, started running through the maze.

I was moving before I thought about what I was doing, giving chase to the fleeing pumpkin. Scarecrow? Imp. I chased the pumpkin/scarecrow/imp down the path, shouting at the top of my lungs for anyone to hear.

"He's getting away! Finn! Bella! Alex! Watch out!"

I heard a response from much closer than expected. "Don't worry! There're runes at every exit!" Finn's shouted response brought a renewal of hope.

Perhaps there was still a way we could put an end to this madness. All we'd have to do is box Wizzle in. That should be easy enough to do in a maze. Once we trapped him, I just had to figure out how to light the candle without the imp putting out my lighter again. Then, this whole mess would be behind us. I'd wrap the stone imps in plastic, then in duct tape, and stick them in a forgotten nook of Spellbooks' attic until I figured out what to do with them.

I rounded a corner to see my plans were going to come to a head much sooner than I'd imagined. Wizzle, still trapped in his pumpkin headed scarecrow, looked around wildly at the dead-end.

I skidded to a stop, holding out my hands. "It's over, Wizzle. No more pranks. No more jokes. Time to put everything back the way it was."

The pumpkin head swiveled a complete 180 degrees to look at me. "That's what you thinks! I is never going backs to stone. Not now, not never!"

"Yes, you are!" I said, inching forward. I wasn't about to let him get past me now that I had him trapped.

"Harper? Where are you?" Finn called through the maze. He sounded close, but that was deceptive within the maze. He might be stuck on the other side of the cornstalks.

"Here!" I called, hoping he could zone in on my voice.

"I'm coming!"

"Hurry! I've got him trapped!" I shouted, inching forward again. The tight span of the path played to my advantage. There was no way Wizzle could slip past me.

The pumpkin's carved face leered at me. "That's what youse thinks," Wizzle sneered from inside. With a mighty leap, he sprang at the densely packed corn stalks, the scarecrow's lightweight body able to scale the autumnal fence where mine would've crushed the stalks into spikey, jagged spears.

"You're not getting away!" I shouted, rushing forward and grabbing at his leg. Wizzle yanked it up and out of my grasp just in time, leaving me with a face full of dried corn stalks and empty hands.

"Haha!" he crowed. "You'll never catch me! Wizzle is smartier than any little witch!" he taunted. Then he blew a noisy raspberry and disappeared over the wall of corn.

"No!" I shouted again, kicking at the wall in frustration. There was no way I could shimmy up the way he had, not without doing damage to either me or the Moonshadow's property or both.

The pound of footsteps sounded behind me. Finn appeared around the corner. "Where is he?" Finn demanded.

"Gone," I said, hanging my head. What was going to happen now? Would the town be trapped with a mischievous prankster until the next time we could do the ritual? I didn't even know when that could be. Would I last in Havenwood that long, or would Vivienne Silverthorne throw me out on my ear long before Wizzle was caught?

Finn grabbed my hand and pulled me in the opposite direction. "C'mon!"

"Where are we going?" I asked, running after him.

"This isn't over yet. If this last week is anything to go by, that imp is headed straight for town. He won't be able to resist."

"The Pumpkin Parade," I gasped.

"Exactly. We still could catch him," Finn said.

"But I have to get the other one first. I can't leave him here."

Finn held up his hand, showing me the stone statue of Snicker. "Already got him. Let's go. We need to get to the Pumpkin Parade as quickly as possible."

We ran.

Finn dispelled his magic and scuffed out the runes at the entrance to the corn maze. Luckily, Bella and Alex could read the urgency of the situation and didn't demand answers until we were in the car and speeding back towards the center of town. Every so often, I caught glimpses of a strange-looking scarecrow running across the moonlit pumpkin fields of Moonshadow Farm, but he was too far away to catch. If we tried to chase him on foot, he'd probably give us the slip. Or pelt us with pumpkins.

Either way, our best bet was to get to town and head him off before he caused a bigger ruckus than he had already.

I tapped Bella on the shoulder and, being the good friend she was, she didn't need to be told twice. She stepped on it, sending the car practically flying over the deserted roads leading to town.

Spiders, Toads, and Snakes, Oh My!

Unfortunately, Bella had to slow her speed considerably once we neared the town. Because of all the congestion around the parade, it took us longer to travel three blocks than it had to get from Moonshadow Farm back into Havenwood in the first place.

"C'mon, c'mon," I muttered in the back seat.

"Doing the best I can," Bella gritted back, slamming on the brakes as a pair of kids dressed like pirates dashed across the road.

"Park the car," Alex suggested. "We'll make better time on foot."

"And we can spread out," Finn agreed.

"Fine by me," Bella said, inching forward carefully.

It took nearly five agonizingly slow minutes for us to realize there was absolutely no parking around. The town was jam-packed for the parade and most of the parking was either full or cordoned off.

Bella pounded on the steering wheel in frustration. "At this rate, I might as well just go back to the Enchanted Oasis. We're never going to find parking!"

"Let us out here then," I suggested. "Finn and I can start looking for the imp. You and Alex can catch up with us once you've found a place for the car."

"I suppose two of us hunting is better than letting him run around town while all four of us are trapped in the car," Bella said, pulling off to the side and popping on her hazard lights.

Finn and I scrambled out of the car, leaving the stone Snicker behind, wrapped carefully in a plastic bag to avoid anyone accidentally dissolving the stone spell for a second time.

Bella inched away as we scanned the crowd of happy costumed revelers. If it hadn't been for the sense of urgency to find Wizzle, I might've taken a moment to appreciate the effort that had gone into creating the festive scene.

Havenwood was on full display, bursting forth in a kaleidoscope of colors. Buildings glowed with jack-o'-lanterns and strings of twinkling orange lights, casting an otherworldly sheen. Houses and businesses were transformed into haunted wonders, adorned with skeletal creatures and friendly ghosts, while intricately carved and candlelit pumpkins lined the sidewalks, casting flickering shadows. People gathered along the parade route, claiming spots with anticipation. The distant strains of music could be heard from the town square, which was the end point of the parade and the location of the final Harvest Festival events: the crowning of the Pumpkin King and fireworks to end the night. The air was fragrant with the aroma of autumn spices, and the town pulsed with the lively energy of excited chatter and laughter as costumed locals and tourists alike shared in festive treats and the excitement of the upcoming parade.

Despite the lively atmosphere, tension gripped me as we searched for the elusive pumpkin-headed scarecrow in the bustling crowd. Struggling to catch a glimpse of him among the bright costumes, we craned our necks, trying to spot the scarecrow/imp.

"How are we ever going to find him?" I asked, hopelessness creeping into my mind. This was an impossible task! We didn't have a chance. Finding the imp-powered scarecrow among the crowd would be like trying to find a piece of hay in a haystack. It wasn't like we could lure him in again with rumors of an enormous crowd. He'd already lost himself in the biggest event of the season here in Havenwood.

"We need to split up," Finn said, his mouth set in a grim line.

I nodded and pointed. "Let's start with the streets closest to Moon-shadow Farm and use our phones to stay in touch. As soon as someone sees him, call. Bella and Alex will be here soon."

"What if he doesn't come?" Finn asked.

"He will," I said with more confidence than I had a right to feel. "A trickster like him won't be able to pass up the opportunity."

Finn and I parted ways. I clutched my phone, scanning the crowd with heightened intensity. Where was Wizzle? I headed down the crowd-ed street, narrowly avoiding crashing into excited costumed children as I continued the search. The minutes ticked by, amplifying the urgency. What if I couldn't find him? What sort of pranks would the imp play on Havenwood tonight?

As I hurried down the road and deeper into the gathered crowd, the Pumpkin Parade came to life. Colorful floats passed me one at a time, much to the delight of the crowd. It was my first Halloween as a full-time resident in Havenwood, and I wished I could've paid more attention as vibrant floats rolled down the illuminated streets of the town. However, I only caught distracted glimpses as I searched for Wizzle in his scare-crow costume. Each float boasted a unique theme, ranging from spooky graveyards to enchanted forests, capturing the essence of Halloween. Local businesses and organizations spared no effort, adorning their floats with intricate decorations, lively music, or dazzling lights.

I scanned the street, catching glimpses of the floats as I searched the crowd for a walking, talking, pumpkin-headed scarecrow. One float was decorated like an enchanted garden, featuring Stella, Havenwood's local florist, as a woodland fairy. She wore a crown of flowers and tossed brightly colored sweets to the children in the crowd. Next was Madame Fontaine's float. She'd leaned into her ability to predict the future by dressing as an outlandish fortune teller, complete with a crystal ball and flowing robes. She shouted obscure fortunes to the captivated audience as she tossed trinkets from her float.

As Madame Fontaine's float glided down the street, I thought I glimpsed a pumpkin moving amongst the costumed crowd on the other side of the road. Before I could get a good look, characters dressed in pastry-themed costumes danced down the street in front of a large cupcake float emblazoned with the recognizable Pixie Pastries' calligraphy. They handed out mini cupcakes and cookies to the crowd as they danced past.

I craned my neck to get a good look across the street, but with all the hubbub, it was hard to see clearly. I kept my eyes locked on the spot as I inched along the road, striving to get a better look.

My phone buzzed in my hand, and I glanced down to see it was Bella. I slid the green icon to accept the call.

"Harper? Alex and I just parked. Where are you?" she asked.

"I'm at the parade," I said as a tremendous cheer erupted from the crowd. One of the town's fire engines had been turned into a gigantic dragon. The firefighters, dressed as valiant knights, tossed candy from the dragon's "treasure hoard." I even saw Chief Flint driving the engine and waving at the crowd as the fire truck crawled along the parade route. Our eyes met for a brief moment, and I felt a flare of suspicion in his gaze. He held my stare for a second longer than necessary before he turned back to the cheering crowd.

"What?" Bella said over the phone.

I cupped a hand over my mouth as I shouted into the phone. "At the parade! I'm on, um, Enchanted Lane," I said, reading a nearby street sign.

"Got it. We'll be with you in a few minutes."

"Keep an eye out for the imp," I reminded her as I continued to scan the area where I thought I saw a pumpkin headed figure wearing a trench coat.

"Will do," she said and hung up.

It was so hard to tell from this side of the street what was a decorative jack-o'-lantern and what wasn't, especially with all the movement and shifting of the floats and the crowd. I really needed to get across to the other side, but how? I couldn't just run across the street in the middle of a parade. Not without drawing a lot of unwanted attention.

The next float to cruise down the street was shaped like an arcane bookshop, complete with an oversized magical spell book that radiated an eerie green glow from hidden lights. "The Dusty Tome" was emblazoned in large letters on the side of the float, along with a subscript that read "Havenwood's Premier Bookshop." I scowled at the moniker but couldn't waste more than a passing glare at the Puddletons' attempt to make unsubstantiated claims.

Mr. Puddleton, his short, pudgy frame adorned with an ostentatious wizard's robe and an oversized beard that could rival a broom, wore a scowl as if it was permanently etched on his face. On the other side, Mrs.

Puddleton, towering over him with a wicked witch's hat atop her pinched, annoyed visage, exuded disdain despite her forced smile. Maybe it was just me, but the candies they tossed looked like spiders and toads. There were even long rope marshmallows in the shape of snakes! More than one child screamed and refused to catch the sweets, despite their parents' laughing encouragement. I ignored the distasteful Puddletons, searching the crowd for any impish movements.

The cajoling reassurance suddenly turned to shouts of dismay. I looked back to see the pages of the enormous spell book turning as if fanned by an invisible giant. The glowing lights flickered wildly. The animated pages rebelled, spurting forth a chocolate fondue fountain that sprayed every-where, much to the dismay of the Puddletons. Mr. Puddleton attempted to slam the book shut, but only managed to get squirted in the face with chocolate for his trouble. Mrs. Puddleton screamed and threw the basket of candy she held onto the street. I saw what startled her a moment later as toads started hopping across the pavement and spiders scuttled away from the noise as quickly as they could. I even caught a glimpse of a snake disappearing down a grate on the curbside.

The chaos spread when all the Puddletons' candy turned into real crea-tures. Amid the pandemonium, I caught sight of the pumpkin scarecrow weaving through the crowd and away from the parade. I couldn't let Wizzle in his scarecrow costume slip away now! I glanced at the street, which was filling with locals and tourists alike. Lucas Silverthorne jumped up onto the Puddletons' float, shouting calming words as Gabriel stood off to the side, attempting to work his illusion magic on the scene.

Now was my chance. I took off at a sprint, running across the street and wading through the crowd in the direction the scarecrow was disappearing. Behind me, I heard Lucas' shouts for calm. The Puddletons' loud laughter and unconvincing guffaws at the "trick" soon followed. More locals joined in, awkwardly laughing at the supposed Halloween trick within the parade. Behind me, I heard an uneasy peace pass over Enchanted Lane, but I didn't have time to celebrate. I was on the trail of the runaway scarecrow, and he was not getting away this time.

I sprinted through the lively crowd, determined to catch up with the elusive pumpk*imp* scarecrow. The surrounding scene was chaotic, with Gabriel's illusion magic working to restore calm after the Puddletons' candy-filled mishap. Lucas' soothing words echoed, blending with the

Puddletons' laughter, creating a strange harmony of amusement and confusion.

As I navigated down the streets and away from the parade, I picked up the pace. Unfortunately, so did Wizzle in his scarecrow get-up. The pumpkin head bobbed through the revelers, moving with a more agility than a creature made of straw had any right to. I dodged costumed onlookers, my eyes never leaving the animated scarecrow.

Wizzle twisted suddenly, darting between two buildings. I sped up, my heart pounding in my chest, determined to close the gap. He tried to squeeze through a narrow alley, and for a brief, hopeful second, he got stuck. Seizing the opportunity, I lunged forward, my fingers just brushing the rough fabric of his sleeve. But in a swift jerk and twist, he wriggled free from my grasping fingers and darted out onto the street beyond. Desperation surged through me as I pushed harder, my foot catching on the uneven pavement. I fell, sprawling onto the pavement, and heard the sickening crunch. I groaned as I realized what had happened. The lighter—the one essential tool I needed to complete the ritual and turn the imp to stone—had broken when I fell.

Gasping for breath, I scrambled to my feet, my eyes darting around to take in my surroundings. I'd been so focused on the chase, so consumed by the need to capture Wizzle, that I hadn't noticed where we were headed. My heart sank as I recognized the brightly lit town square, filled with a cheering crowd. And there, in the center of it all, a young woman with shockingly pink tips in her hair was dragging Wizzle the imp, now disguised as a scarecrow, up onto the stage erected for the crowning of the Pumpkin King.

And to make matters worse? The judge on stage was Vivienne Silverthorne.

All Hail the King

THE GIRL WITH PINK-TIPPED hair presented Wizzle the Imp to Vivienne Silverthorne with a flourish. "Here you go, Mother. This is my choice for a costume so exceptional that it's worthy of the title 'Pumpkin King of Havenwood,'" she announced, her voice carrying clearly through the speaker system.

My jaw nearly hit the ground as I registered her words. *Mother?* That must mean that the pink-haired young woman was Isadora Silverthorne. As I placed her, my mind flashed back to the night of the fashion show. I'd stood under a tree and caught a quick sneak peek as Lucas argued with his sister about her surprise visit just after the imps had set the stalls on fire. I paused, furrowing my brow as the memory resurfaced. In the corn maze, Snicker had acted like he was terrified of fire. I remembered his reaction to the lighter. He was petrified. Come to think of it, Wizzle wasn't much better. A realization struck me, sending a chill down my spine.

If they hated fire so much, why had they started not one, but three fires around town? Were they really responsible? And if not, who was?

Now wasn't the time to get distracted. I frantically grabbed for my phone, nearly fumbling it as I tried to pull up my messaging app. Even with my fingers shaking, I managed to send a desperate message in a digital bottle to my friends. With the lighter broken and no way to complete the ritual, I needed all the help I could get. Even then, I wasn't sure that would be enough.

"Lass? Are you alright? You look like you've seen a ghost and not one of my drinking buddies," a male voice with a slight Scottish burr said near my elbow.

I nearly jumped and yelped until I realized who was talking. Mason Forham, the dwarven auto mechanic. I pressed a hand to my heart and closed my eyes. "Mason! You scared me."

"Apologies. Not my intention of course."

"What are you doing here?" I asked, falling back on the accustomed social norm of small talk as I fought for calm.

"Ah, well. I thought I'd take Ignatius out for a sort of a test drive of his new equipment," Mason said, holding out a small paper gift bag so I could look inside.

Sure enough, Ignatius poked his head out and grinned a toothy smile at me. "Harper! No fire!" the small dragon exclaimed.

"He's right," Mason said proudly. "It took us a bit of work to get the fit right, but we think we've cracked it. Now that we've got that down, the lavastone steel and the emberite will work together to help Ignatius control his fire. It'll take him some time to get used to it, but he's doing well, all things considered. Once he gets the hang of controlling his fire with the proverbial training wheels on, he'll be able to eventually manage it without my assistance at all."

A crazy idea popped into my head. I looked back at the stage where Isadora was smiling broadly for the audience, trying to convince her mother that her choice for the Pumpkin King was the best of all the costumed contestants on stage.

"...but of course, you can see the title should be his. I mean, he already has a pumpkin for a head. In all my years in Havenwood, we've never seen anything this clever," Isadora said, a mic amplifying her voice for the crowd. Enthusiastic cheers met her words. The carved mouth grinned wider as Wizzle ate up the crowd's adoration.

"I suppose he does have a sort of Headless Horseman look about him," Vivienne mused into a handheld microphone as she walked around Wizzle, getting a closer look at his costume. "And if I didn't know better, I'd say this is a real scarecrow body."

Isadora snorted lightly and did a dramatic little wiggle. "I doubt it, Mother. Could you imagine how itchy wearing straw all night would be?"

Wizzle's grin grew wider, and he did a shuffling little dance, ending with a click of his heels. Except there was no sound because his body really was made of straw, and he had no heels. The audience crowded around the stage loved it, however. They were eating up the show the two Silverthorne women were unwittingly performing with the prankster imp.

I had to do something. Luckily, I'd just acquired a secret weapon. I snatched the bag with the tiny dragon from Mason's hand. "Do you mind if I borrow Ignatius? 'Kay, thanks!" I said, dashing off towards the back of the stage as Mason stared at me, slack jawed.

"What..." Ignatius said as my pace jostled him in his tiny paper carrier.

"I need your help," I said in a rush, keeping my voice low in case those nearby grew suspicious of the woman having a conversation with her bag. Luckily, everyone seemed to be engrossed in the drama unfolding on stage, and no one seemed to notice me or my pet dragon.

"How?" Ignatius said, looking determined.

"That's the spirit," I said encouragingly.

Laughter and applause echoed through the square as I made my way around the edge of the crowd. I noticed other costumed participants on stage, each one vying for the title of Pumpkin King. The mayor and other committee members stood off to the side, evaluating each contestant with amused expressions. The brothers Silverthorne, ever the showmen, had also grabbed participants from the audience to join in the fun and were touting their choices, creating a chaotic and lively scene. It provided the perfect cover for me to slip backstage unnoticed.

A metal fence separated the backstage area from the general crowd, but the simple lock was no match for my metal magic. I was through the gate in a matter of seconds without even slowing my speech. "It's a long story, but you'll have to take my word for it. The prankster who has been causing all the mischief around town is an imp. I trapped him in the pumpkin, and he can't get out. That is, until the stroke of midnight. However, if we can light the candle that's trapped inside the pumpkin with him, the imp will turn to stone and this whole prankster nightmare will be over. Do you understand?"

Ignatius smiled for a moment, then his expression fractured, and he shook his head. "No. Um...fire good?"

I nodded emphatically. "Yes, in this case, fire very good." I crept up the temporary stairs at the back of the stage and held back the edge of the black velvet curtain. "You need to get to that scarecrow and light the candle inside the pumpkin. Preferably without anyone seeing you. Can you do it?" I asked urgently.

Ignatius looked back and forth between me and the scarecrow. He flicked his tongue out once, then twice, thinking hard for a moment. Finally, he bobbed his dragon head and grinned. "Fire good," he declared with a tiny nod. "I light pumpkin. Yes! Hold please," he said, wriggling around in the bag and holding up what looked like a dark metal ring studded with reddish gems the color of flames. I slid the emberite and lavastone steel creation onto my finger for safekeeping.

"Hey! What are you doing back here? Backstage is off limits!" a male voice behind me called.

I ignored him, making the best use of the precious few moments I had left to stop Wizzle once and for all. I crouched down, setting the bag on its side so Ignatius could wriggle free. As I turned to face the man striding toward me, I saw Ignatius scuttle along the edge of the stage, using the line of contestants as cover as he scampered toward the unsuspecting Wizzle.

"Harper?" the man said.

I turned fully to see someone I recognized. "Officer Reggie?" I said in surprise.

"What are you doing back here? I was told everyone backstage was supposed to have an official town badge," the friendly police officer said, tapping his chest where a bright orange badge proclaimed him to be an official town employee.

"Umm," I said, fumbling over my words. Mentally, I kicked myself. I really needed to get better at this lying thing. But fibbing to Officer Reggie kind of felt like convincing a child eating broccoli for the first time that the vegetable was a magical fairy tree that could grant superpowers. Someday, the kid would figure it out. I just hoped it wasn't today.

I feigned my most surprised, distressed look as I patted myself all over. "What? Are you saying I lost it?"

"Lost what? Can I help you find it?" Officer Reggie said, helpfully.

"My badge!" I spun around in a circle, pretending to search for the non-existent piece of official towns' wear. Out of the corner of my eye, I saw Ignatius leap onto the back of the scarecrow's pants and start to climb upwards. If Wizzle had been a real person instead of an imp masquerading as a scarecrow masquerading as a person in a costume, he might've felt the dragon's claws dig into his leg. As it was, the leg was made of straw. Wizzle didn't seem to sense a thing.

"You had a badge?" Officer Reggie asked, glancing around at the ground.

"I thought I did," I hedged. Would I be in as much trouble if I never outright lied to the policeman? "I can't seem to find it though. Do you see an extra one anywhere?"

"Oh! Well, why didn't you say so in the first place? I always have a couple of spares, just in case someone forgets theirs. Or I forget mine," Officer Reggie said with a chuckle, digging into the pocket of his coat and withdrawing one of the orange town badges. "It's happened more times than I care to admit, so Sheriff Jackson always tells me to bring an extra," he explained as he handed it over.

I ducked my head to hide the blush of shame creeping up my cheeks, feeling guilty for tricking the poor man. "Thanks," I whispered, accepting the badge and quickly pinning it to my shirt as I turned back to the drama unfolding behind the drama on stage. I couldn't afford to let my conscience interfere now, not when so much was at stake. I winced inwardly, vowing to find a way to make it up to Officer Reggie later.

Ignatius was nearly up to the scarecrow's shoulder now. Somehow, he had to clamber around the pumpkin, breathe fire into the carved gaps, light the candle, and turn the imp to stone. All while not being witnessed by the entire crowd who seemed to be utterly captivated by the crowning of a small town's Harvest Festival Pumpkin King.

What could I do? Storm out onto the stage, waving my arms and shouting? It would certainly get everyone's attention. But then, so would the dragon breathing fire. The whole point of this was to avoid drawing Vivienne's ire down upon my head. What would she say if I purposely wrecked the biggest event of the season? I glanced out at the crowd and had to swallow the sudden lump of terror that clogged my throat. Not to mention the fact that several people were holding up their phones, recording the whole stage, and making this monumentally more challenging.

How in all the magical kingdoms was I going to pull this one off? What I wouldn't give for a ninja bunny with the gift of invisibility right about now. But even Luna would be hard-pressed to avoid that many camera phones.

Vivienne's voice rang through my indecision, letting me know I'd stalled too long. My stomach sank. There was no way this Halloween was going to end in treats for me.

"I think we have found our Pumpkin King, wouldn't you say, Isadora?" Vivienne asked her daughter with a smile.

"Hey," Officer Reggie whispered into my ear. "What's that on the scarecrow's back?"

"I think we have, Mother," Isadora said cheerfully, turning to retrieve the crown that was nestled on a cushion of red velvet on a table at the back of the stage. She held it aloft for all to see. The Pumpkin King's crown gleamed with autumnal splendor, adorned with miniature pumpkins, golden leaves, and tiny flickering electronic lights that mimicked the warm glow of candle flames.

"Bring the crown and let us anoint this year's Harvest Festival Pumpkin King," Vivienne said grandly to her daughter, waving an arm to invite applause from the audience, which they readily provided. The town matriarch smiled benevolently at the imp dressed as a scarecrow. "Kneel, Sir Scarecrow, and receive your prize."

The scarecrow knelt gracefully in front of Vivienne Silverthorne, ducking its pumpkin head. From my angle backstage, I could see the pumpkin's mouth curl into a wicked grin and magical sparkles gather within the pumpkin's carved eye sockets. Wizzle was up to something, and I had no desire to find out what it was.

In a split second, several things happened all at once. Ignatius, taking advantage of the pumpkin head blocking him from most of the audience, slithered up the scarecrow's shoulder and expelled a spout of fire into the grinning face. Isadora, seeing something slither up the supposed man who'd just been named the Pumpkin King, screamed. Her unexpected shriek made Officer Reggie, along with several members of the audience, scream as well. The crown in her hands sparked and crackled as flames sprang out all over the autumn leaves forming the decorations. Was that Ignatius losing control of his fire breathing again? Or did the imp have something to do with what was happening to the crown? Gasps rang out as flames engulfed the pumpkin's head, lighting it from within. For a moment, all the attention in the town square focused on the flaming pumpkin king. A spattering of delighted applause started, the crowd assuming this was all part of an overly dramatic Halloween costume.

That is, until their Pumpkin King's head fell off and rolled across the stage.

To Spin a Story

SCREAMS CRESCENDOED THROUGHOUT THE town square as the scarecrow's head thumped and rolled along the stage, coming to rest at the edge and grinning wildly out at the audience. I ignored the screams, watching the pumpkin intently to see if Wizzle the imp would make another move. But the pumpkin stayed still. We'd done it! Or rather, Ignatius had. This whole imp nightmare was behind us. I let out a sigh of relief.

I really should have known better.

Amid the chaos, several other costumed contestants rushed about, adding to the confusion and obscuring Vivienne's view. Each contestant seemed to have their own agenda, either trying to leap from the stage or make one last, valiant effort to claim the title of Pumpkin King. A competitor dressed as a mischievous goblin seized the opportunity, dramatically pointing at the collapsing scarecrow and cackling loudly as he danced a merry jig around the scarecrow. Another contender for the crown, this one dressed as the noble King Arthur of legendary fame, held up his shining replica of Excalibur and silently challenged the taunting goblin to a duel.

The crowd roared with laughter and cheers, their excitement creating a deafening wall of noise that overwhelmed any attempts to regain control. The goblin contestant hammed it up, reveling in the attention as he waggled his fingers by his head and blew a wet raspberry at the fake

King Arthur and then surprised everyone with a back handspring to avoid the dramatic retaliatory blow from the king. Neither one seemed overly concerned with the decapitated pumpkin head as they taunted each other, their japes growing more ostentatious with each escalating cheer from the audience.

Everyone seemed focused on the unexpected battle for the crown, all the audience's camera phones swiveling to keep the entertaining duo in frame. If I hadn't been so worried about what else was happening on stage, I might have been inclined to pull out my phone and start filming as well. However, my eyes were trained on Vivienne Silverthorne as she stared in shock at a slowly collapsing headless scarecrow, no doubt trying to figure out exactly what was going on and how to explain it away to the crowd of excitable onlookers. However, the more dramatic disaster was one only Officer Reggie and I could see.

Isadora had turned her back to the audience and was clutching a flaming crown to her chest. Her breathing came in short, sharp gasps. Rather than screaming in pain from holding on to literal fire, she looked like she was on the verge of a panic attack. Her head snapped up, and she looked around wildly. My breath caught when her eyes met mine. Instead of normal human eyes, Isadora's blazed with a literal, internal magical fire.

In an instant, my mind flashed back to the events of the last few days. My jaw dropped as realization struck me like a lightning bolt. The fires around town had started about the same time Isadora, an elemental mage, had shown up. I'd blamed the fires on the imps, but I'd witnessed how much they hated fire. I remembered seeing Lucas confront Isadora at the fashion show fire. Suddenly, that conversation took on a whole other layered meaning. My breath caught in my throat as the pieces fell into place. And then, there had been one shadow disappearing from the warehouse, not two.

Could it be possible? My heart raced with the implications. Had Isadora been there at the first forest fire, too? Probably. She arrived in town around then, hadn't she? I fell a step back as the full realization hit me. It might have all been circumstantial and probably wouldn't have held up in a court of law, but it was enough to convince me. Snicker and Wizzle were responsible for the pranks and the break-ins, but Isadora was behind the fires. And if I didn't do something soon, there would be another one in a matter of moments.

Behind Isadora, I was vaguely aware of Vivienne snapping her fingers. The scarecrow halted its collapse and slowly rose to its feet. The goblin and King Arthur halted their antics to gape at the rising scarecrow. A tense smile lifted the corners of Vivienne's mouth as she gestured at the now standing, but still headless, scarecrow.

"What a feat of incredible costuming!" she exclaimed, throwing her arms wide. "Please, show us how you managed such an incredible display!"

Isadora caught my eye with her blazing ones. *Help me!* she mouthed, pressing the burning crown to her chest, hiding its blaze from the audience. Her shirt started to smolder, but there was still no pain on her face, only terror.

My heart pounded in my chest, and without a second thought, I rushed forward to help. As I approached, the heat from the burning crown intensified, forcing me to stop a few steps away and flinch backwards, shielding my face with my hands.

Behind her, the scarecrow shifted, raising its hands to unbutton its jacket. I was torn, not knowing where to look as I was caught between the elemental mage at the back of the stage and the drama unfolding at the front. A familiar face in the front row caught my eye. Gabriel Silverthorne stared intently up at the scarecrow standing next to his mother, his mouth moving silently and his fingers weaving through the air.

Whatever illusion Gabriel was weaving convinced the audience that the scarecrow losing its head had all been a clever ploy must've worked, because the crowd erupted in a sudden, deafening cheer. Isadora threw her head back in a silent scream and sparks shot out of her fingertips. Desperation and confusion warred within me. I needed to help Isadora, but how?

The sparks flew through the air, igniting the prepared pyrotechnic effects on either side of the stage. With a whoosh, an enchanting spray of radiant sparks flew into the air, startling both Officer Reggie and me. The policeman stumbled backwards and fell off the stage and onto the grass, landing with a thump somewhere behind me. "Ooh's" and "aaah's" from the crowd met the mesmerizing display of shimmering lights as a large sign reading "Congratulations!" unfurled from the top of the stage's backdrop and two large confetti guns exploded a truly obscene amount of glitter and brightly colored paper over the audience.

If my dad had been here, he would've rolled his eyes. He *hated* glitter and did everything he could to avoid it. To be fair, the shiny stuff didn't really go with his stern Master Sergeant persona. Neither did the unstable elemental mage, who now fell to her knees in front of me, gasping for air and fighting to control her magic. She pressed a hand to the wooden stage, flames flickering along her fingertips. In another moment or two, it wouldn't matter how good Gabriel's illusion magic was, because the entire stage was about to become the start of an epic, unplanned bonfire.

My heart pounded in my chest, and without a second thought, I took a step forward to help. Instinctively, I reached out for Isadora, but the searing heat forced me to pull back again quickly, clenching my fist in frustration and fear. What could I do? Something hard and unexpected dug into my hand. I glanced down in surprise. The glitter of crimson stones met my eyes. I suddenly realized I had the answer, literally in the palm of my hand.

Without another thought, I lurched forward, grabbing Isadora and slipping the lavastone steel and emberite ring onto her finger. The heat from her flames was intense. I nearly yelped and dropped the ring. However, my dad hadn't raised a quitter. I bit back the pain and forced Mason's ring onto Isadora's finger. Immediately, the flames retreated from her eyes and the fiery crown she clutched extinguished.

"What...," she whispered hoarsely, trailing off.

"Let's get you off the stage," I whispered back, helping her to her feet. Between the two of us, we kept the charred remains of the Pumpkin King's crown out of sight as Vivienne and Gabriel distracted the crowd with the incredible costume of the "headless scarecrow."

As soon as we were backstage and out of sight of the crowd, Isadora collapsed to the ground. I wriggled out of my jacket and wrapped it around her, hiding the charred evidence of her loss of control.

"Thanks," she whispered. "Um. Who are you?"

"Harper Sullivan," I said, feeling a little bemused by the social norm in the face of what had just happened.

"Isadora Silverthorne," she replied with a weak smile. "Thanks for your help out there."

I held up my hands, wincing as the movement tugged on a newly formed burns on my hands. "How about you get me that pumpkin from the front of the stage, and we'll call it square."

A genuine smile blossomed on her face. "Deal." She glanced over her shoulder. "What are the chances that you aren't going to tell my mother about this?" she asked.

"Hey, I believe every girl has a right to her secrets, magical or not. But you did just kind of lose control on a stage in front of a crowd of people with camera phones. I don't know how you're going to explain that away."

Isadora shrugged a shoulder. "No one these days believes in magic. We'll spin a story about how I felt faint, and you helped me off stage when you saw I was in distress or something. The audience will buy it. Everything else was just mundane showmanship," she said with a wan smile. Her bravado crumbled, and she added in a trembling whisper, "Please don't tell anyone about this. Especially not my mother."

I hesitated, then decided to push gently. "You might want to tell her about all of the fires," I said, my voice soft but firm. Our eyes locked, and an unspoken understanding passed between us. Isadora's fear was palpable, but so was her guilt. "So she can stop the town-wide hunt for an arsonist before someone innocent is accused," I added, holding her gaze steadily.

Isadora's shoulders slumped, and she nodded in resignation. "You're right. I'll talk to her tonight. The protective spells around Havenwood and a clever cover story can only do so much after all."

"You sound like you've done this before," I observed, waving a hand to indicate the chaos from the previous minutes as I sat down next to her.

"It's not my first rodeo, although I've never seen anything quite like what happened tonight. The pumpkin? Then King Arthur facing off with the goblin? And whatever this thing is that stopped me from burning down the entire stage," she said, holding up the hand with the emberite ring on it and examining it. "Umm, what is it, by the way? More to the point, where did you get it, and can you get me one?"

I smiled, thinking of Mason. The excitement he felt after crafting something to help my unpredictable dragon would no doubt double if I asked him to help the unstable elemental mage.

"I think that can be arranged."

The Hero of the Day

THE NEXT FEW MINUTES passed in a blur. Vivienne appeared with both Gabriel and the magically animated scarecrow in tow. As soon as the scarecrow was out of the audience's sight, Vivienne snapped her fingers and the figure collapsed in a rustle of straw. I never thought I'd be so happy to see straw behave normally. Lucas appeared a moment later, and the Silverthornes swept Isadora away, but not before I reminded her about the favor she'd agreed to. She nodded before whispering urgently to her family.

I waited nervously backstage as Vivienne stepped back in front of the crowd, her presence commanding attention. "Ladies and gentlemen," she began, her voice carrying over the crowd, "I think we can all agree this has been the most exciting Harvest Festival in a long time." A round of polite applause met her words, and she waited until everyone settled before continuing. "I'm pleased to announce that the person responsible for all the pranks and incidents around town has been apprehended. The Havenwood police force and the firefighters should be commended for their brave service in upholding the ideals of peace and unity our town was founded upon. As a new tradition, I am delighted to award the first annual Golden Gourd Award jointly to Sheriff Jackson and Chief Flint!"

A cheer went up from the crowd as Vivienne gestured for the sheriff and fire chief to join her on stage. Both men looked surprised, their eyes widening in confusion as they glanced at each other. Only the people on the stage knew they hadn't actually caught anyone, but Vivienne's proclamation provided a plausible explanation for the assembled tourists while also honoring two of the town's most hardworking citizens. Sheriff Jackson scratched his head, and Chief Flint's brow furrowed as they tried to process the unexpected accolade.

Vivienne, with her radiant smile and unwavering confidence, shook hands with each man warmly, subtly steering the attention away from their bewilderment. "Let's give a big round of applause to the heroes of Havenwood!" she declared, leading another round of enthusiastic applause as the sheriff and fire chief waved at the crowd, still slightly dazed.

As the applause died down, and my attention was drawn away from whatever Vivienne said next as Gabriel descended from the stage, carrying the pumpkin head in his hands. He made his way over to me and handed me the pumpkin with a quizzical look on his face. "Here. My sister insisted I give this to you personally," he said, looking both confused and amused at his sister's strange request. This close, I couldn't help but notice how good-looking he was, especially when he smiled, his dimples prominent on his face.

"Umm, thanks. I have a thing for jack-o'-lanterns," I said lamely as I accepted it from him.

"Really? I thought it might have been the statue inside," Gabriel said, his smile growing as he spoke.

"Oh. Umm..." I trailed off, not sure of what to say that wouldn't get me in trouble with his mother.

"Or, you know, the dragon."

This time I couldn't even manage incoherent mumbling.

Gabriel's smile lit his eyes this time, and he shook his head. "Look, I don't know what's going on between you and my sister, but I know Isa well enough by now to know when she's hiding something. Whatever it is, she's pulled you into it somehow."

"I, um, well—"

He held up a hand, cutting me off. "I don't need to know all the details tonight. I'm just glad Isa found a friend in Havenwood. Things haven't always been easy for her here. I'm glad she has you."

"Yeah. Um. Right. Me too."

"I'm Gabriel by the way. I know we met the other day, but just in case you missed my name. You know, at the candy shop?"

"Harper," I said, trying to juggle the pumpkin in my burned hands so I could do the socially appropriate thing and shake hands even though I really just wanted an icepack and some burn salve.

Gabriel's eyes flicked down to my hands, and his expression shifted to one of concern. "Are you alright?" he asked, his voice taking on a more serious tone.

"Oh, it's nothing," I blurted out, trying to downplay the burns. "Just an accident while helping out, um, a friend."

Gabriel's eyes narrowed slightly, and then widened. A flicker of understanding passed between us. He read between the lines, knowing I was covering for Isadora.

He pressed his right hand to his chest and bowed slightly. "A pleasure to meet you, Harper. I hope to see you again," he said, the intensity in his voice making the moment feel more like a promise than a wish.

He turned to walk away, but I called after him, keeping my voice low. "Umm Gabriel? You should know, the whole prank situation? It's handled. Could you let your mother know and help spread the news? It might ease some more of the tension around town."

His eyes lit up, and he nodded, his smile growing wider. "Of course. I'll make sure she knows. And for whatever part you played in stopping the pranksters, thank you."

Before I could formulate an answer, Vivienne called, "Gabriel? Come see to Isa!"

"Duty calls. Excuse me," Gabriel said before turning towards his family, leaving a wake of confused feelings welling up in me as he walked away. Vivienne shot an appraising look at me that felt like she was reading my very soul in a glance before turning her attention back to her children.

"Harper! Are you okay?" Bella called over the noise of the crowd. I looked up to see her waving at me from the fence.

I headed her way, cradling the pumpkin in my arms. Ignatius stuck his head out of the carved eye socket. "Did good?" the dragon asked.

"So good," I reassured him. "You were the hero of the day."

"What happened to you? Where's your coat?" Bella demanded as I walked up. Alex and Finn stood behind her, looking equally anxious.

I sighed and smiled, suddenly feeling drained. "I'll tell you the whole story on two conditions."

"Name them," Finn said instantly.

"We wrap this imp up in as much plastic as we can, and we find something for burns. Do you think a pharmacy is open at this time of night?"

"We'll find something," Bella assured me as Officer Reggie opened the gate on the metal fence for me.

Finn draped his coat around my shoulders and wrapped an arm around me, holding me tight to his side as the cold evening wind gusted down the street. With as close as it had been, I didn't deserve a treat like great friends and a comforting arm, but I wasn't about to turn them down either.

An Unexpected Invitation

THE NEXT MORNING, I scrolled through the town's social media page while sipping my coffee. A post from Martha Morningstar caught my eye, accompanied by a picture of Vivienne Silverthorne and her family. The caption read, "Thanks to the Silverthornes for catching the magical troublemaker responsible for the pranks!"

I sighed in relief, thankful that the town's panic had been quelled. It seemed the Silverthornes had spun the story to keep the peace. If we were lucky, Havenwood might already be returning to a sense of normalcy. And the magical ointment Honey had given me last night worked wonders on my burned hands, even though the healing skin still was hot to the touch and pulled uncomfortably. Despite that, I held on to my list of suspects, crossing off names as I went. The imps were circled, and lines connected them to various pranks and the break-ins. I noted Isadora for the fires. With the cases all closed, I suddenly wanted nothing more than to celebrate with my friends. I texted Finn and Bella, suggesting a meet-up later to toast to our success.

My phone buzzed almost immediately with replies in the affirmative from both. With a smile, I set my phone aside and looked at my cleared suspect list. It hadn't been easy or straightforward, but with a little—no, make that a LOT—of help from my friends, we'd stopped the pranks and restored peace to Havenwood.

I looked around the shop, somewhat disconcerted by the quiet. Ignatius was staying with Mason while the dwarf crafted his new fire-suppressing bling. Isadora had been whisked away too quickly to return his. Snicker and Wizzle were securely tucked away in Spellbooks' attic under layers of waterproof wrapping next to the wizard until Aunty Agatha returned from her cruise and I could consult with the elderly witch. All in all, it felt like things were finally getting back to normal.

Well, as normal as things ever were in Havenwood.

Luna hopped over with a slim cream envelope in her paws. "Someone slid this under the door last night. It has your name on it, but no postage stamp. Any idea who might be passing you notes?"

"Not a clue," I said honestly as I carefully slid a finger under the flap and tore open the elegantly textured paper. Inside was a card with a location and a time. That was it.

Eight o'clock. Tonight. The corner of Spellbinder Street and Enchanted Lane.

"What's it say?" Luna asked curiously.

I flipped the card over, searching for any sign of who it might be from. The back side of the card was blank. "Not much," I said, showing her the simple message, if it could be called that.

"Radish ruckus, you aren't thinking of going, are you?" Luna said, her ears twitching.

"I only just opened it. I haven't even had time to process the, what would you call this? An invitation?"

"Sure. That's an invitation," Luna said sarcastically. "For your murder. Really, Harper. Have I taught you nothing?"

"Well, no. Not really," I said, perhaps a little too honestly.

Luna sniffed. "That's no reason to be acting like a cotton-minded fluffernutter. Cabbage catastrophe, if your great-granny could see you now."

A light scraping sound behind the counter made me whirl to see a message appearing on the small chalkboard.

She'd be proud.

I laid a hand on the nearest wall, a rush of warmth welling up inside me. "Aw, thanks Spellbooks," I whispered. The gentle vibration under my palm felt like an apology, a silent acknowledgment of the recent misunderstandings. Despite the chaos and the lockout, Spellbooks had always been my partner here in Havenwood.

"Oh, yeah," Luna muttered, hopping away. "Keep talking to the building. That *always* turns out well."

Later that evening, I stood under a streetlamp, flicking the small card with a fingernail. I checked it for the fiftieth time. This was the right spot. I knew it. So why was I here? Or, more appropriately, who was I here to see?

A black BMW with tinted windows purred down the street towards me, nosing into one of the numerous empty parking spots lining the street at this time of night. The driver's door opened, and Isadora Silverthorne got out, waving at me brightly.

A myriad of questions swirled through my mind as she walked over. Why had she been sent away from Havenwood in the first place? Was she going back to wherever she came from? Was the town safe from her fire? Wait, did Vivienne know her daughter couldn't control her powers? And if she did know, why hadn't she said anything? Was Vivienne capitalizing on distractions to cover for Isadora? I considered the possibility that Vivienne knew about the fires all along and was just covering for her daughter, crafting a distraction to blame everything on the pranksters. The mystery of Isadora deepened, leaving me with more questions than answers as the youngest Silverthorne smiled warmly at me.

"Hey! I'm glad you could make it!" Isadora said, beeping the fob on her keys and locking the car.

I couldn't help but feel a twinge of wariness. Isadora had caused quite a bit of chaos with her powers, putting people in harm's way. Was she here to own up to her mistakes, or was there something more going on? Her bright demeanor clashed with the seriousness of the situation, leaving me uncertain of her true intentions. As she approached, I tried to keep my expression neutral, not wanting to give away my mixed feelings. Maybe she was just another victim of her own uncontrollable powers, like Ignatius. I wanted to give her the benefit of the doubt, but I also didn't want more fires breaking out around town.

"Um, hi?" I said lamely. "Did you leave me a note by chance?" I waved the card in the air to emphasize my meaning.

"Yeah, that was me. Sorry about the whole message-under-the-door thing. I didn't get your number which made texting tricky, but I wanted to take you out for a drink or something. You know, to say thank you for helping me out." As she handed me the jacket I'd lent her, she dropped her voice and looked around at the empty street, ensuring we were alone. "And I just wanted to tell you I talked to my mom and told her I was responsible. She promised to work with me to find someone to help me control my powers."

Relief and consternation swept through me at Isadora's admission. I swallowed hard. "That's good. Hey, you didn't, well, you know..." I trailed off, unsure of how to phrase my question.

Isadora's eyes twinkled knowingly. "Tell the dragon lady, who happens to be my mother, about you? No. Believe me, I know how things work here in Havenwood, and most people prefer to stay off her radar. Although if anyone were to confront my mother head on, it would be you. Not many people run toward a fire instead of away, you know."

"It's a character flaw," I said with a self-deprecating grin. "I can't see a fire without the overwhelming urge to sprint towards it taking control of my higher faculties."

She gave a throaty chuckle of surprise at my silly response. "Well, you sound like exactly the type of crazy I need in my life. I make the fires, and you put 'em out."

"If it's all the same to you, I'd rather avoid both activities for a while," I said honestly.

"Deal. How about a drink instead?" she said, tossing her pink tipped hair and jerking a thumb at the building behind her.

I glanced out to see a sedate-looking brick building with a picture on the front facing façade portraying a wellness center offering health and relaxation services. "At a gym?" I asked in surprise.

Isadora chuckled. "You must be new here if you haven't heard of the Veiled Vault. Follow me." Without further explanation, she led me down the narrow alleyway between the brick buildings. Behind the wellness center was a small, enclosed courtyard. In the middle was a gorgeous fountain burbling in the moonlight. The mosaic tiles formed a calming scene that drew me in at once.

Isadora glanced over her shoulder and winked at me before putting her hands on two specific stars and pressing down. To my amazement, there was an audible click and the water in the fountain swept to the side as if an invisible arm was holding it back. With a soft rumble, the floor of the fountain shifted, forming a spiral staircase leading into the darkness below the fountain.

Isadora gestured at the magic staircase proudly. "Welcome to the Vault. The best escape you'll ever find without leaving Havenwood."

She led the way down the stairs. As soon as my head passed beneath the tiles of the fountain, the stairs above me melded seamlessly back into the tiled floor, cutting off the moonlight from above and allowing me to focus solely on the warm glow of the enchanting scene below.

The Vault unfolded before my eyes as a captivating blend of vintage charm and modern allure. Dimmed lights hung in delicate orbs, casting a warm, inviting glow over the eclectic mix of mahogany and polished metal furnishings. The lively chatter of patrons intertwined with the sounds of enchanted games, and the air was infused with the heady aroma of exotic potions and familiar brews. At the bar, magical mixologists crafted spellbound concoctions, while around us, young magic users reveled in laughter, the soft clatter of dice, and the glow of arcade screens, creating a captivating refuge for what appeared to be Havenwood's younger crowd.

Isadora led me to a quiet booth that appeared to be carved directly into a tree trunk nestled in the Vault's corner. I slid onto the bench opposite from her, looking around in amazement.

"This place is incredible!" I exclaimed.

"Thanks," Isadora said, looking around proudly. "My brothers and I made it years ago, but it's really expanded in the past year or so. We were inspired by Peter Pan and his Home Underground. We wanted a place to call our own where Mother couldn't find us. Over the years, it evolved from a hideout into this semi-private club for us and our friends."

I wondered briefly if Bella had ever been here. She hadn't mentioned it, but if it was that private, she might not have been able to. However, there was also the split that she had alluded to more than once between the full-blood magical beings like the Silverthornes and the half-bloods like her. Maybe this was another one of those obvious splits between the haves and the have-nots.

I opened my mouth to ask, but before I could, Isadora said, "It was all Lucas' idea. The spells powering the enchantment surrounding the Vault absorb and retain residual magic from any paranormal who enters or passes by. Not enough that anyone cares or even notices. Just enough to power the charms. Gabriel added in the illusion spells, and I was in charge of the water magic in the fountain at the entrance," she finished, a tinge of pride in her final words.

"Right. Because you're an elemental mage," I said.

"Exactly," Isadora replied. "And because I am an elemental mage, I know how much fire burns can hurt so I thought I'd bring you a little thank you gift. It's a salve the local coven makes, and it works wonders," she said, pulling a small clear jar filled with lavender gel out of her pocket and setting it carefully on the table between us.

"Thanks," I said, opening the jar and catching a whiff of the soothing scent that smelled more of cool pillows and deep sleep than any medicine I'd ever used before. I dipped my fingers into the cool gel and gently applied it to my burns. The instant relief was magical in more ways than one, the pain subsiding as the gel worked its healing properties. "This is incredible!"

Isadora watched me with a mixture of concern and satisfaction. "I'm glad it helps. Should take the sting out pretty quickly."

"It's amazing," I said, flexing my fingers and marveling at the almost immediate comfort. "Thank you."

Isadora nodded, looking relieved. As soon as I tightened the top of the jar of salve and tucked it away, Isadora leaned forward, her voice low and serious. "They pulled me away before I got to say a proper thank you and to return this," she said, her tone tinged with reluctance as she slipped the emberite ring off her finger. "I don't know what this is, but I need one in my life. My control of fire has always been temperamental, but wearing that was, I don't know, like having time to pause and walk away from an argument and then come back the next day when I'm calm. But all in the space of a moment. Does that make any sense?" She held the ring out to me, her eyes pleading.

I took the ring, feeling the weight of her desperation. "Yeah, it does," I said, hoping she wouldn't press further. I really didn't want to either lie to her or tell her the truth about Ignatius.

Luckily, Isadora seemed more interested in something else. "What is the metal anyway? I recognize the emberite gems, but I've never seen a substance that can withstand heat the way it can. Usually, when I lose control, my fire can melt almost any metal, and I've only ever seen emberite used in jewelry or other decorative pieces. What kind of metal can withstand that level of heat?"

I weighed my options. Mason was well known in Havenwood for his abilities with metal, and I could completely avoid any mention of Ignatius if I didn't explain why I needed such an item. I decided the reward of Isadora potentially gaining more control and avoiding setting more fires in Havenwood outweighed the minimal risk to Ignatius' privacy.

"It's lavastone steel. Like I said, Mason Forham made this for a, um, friend of mine. He might be willing to make you one if you ask," I said.

Isadora nodded excitedly. "I think I will. Thanks for the tip. But that's not why I asked you to meet me here. Or, rather, not the only reason."

"What are you talking about?" I asked, intrigued.

Isadora slid an elegant invitation embossed with festive decorations across the table. "It's an invitation to my family's Christmas Eve Ball. It's a tradition my family started years ago, and I'd like you to come. Consider it a vital part of my thank you effort for helping me and for the tip about Mason."

I smiled, touched by the gesture. "That's amazing and so kind!"

"No, that's a thank you, and a small one at that. Say you'll come?"

"Okay, I'll come."

"Great!" Isadora said, a mischievous smile on her face as she pulled out another card and slid that across the table as well.

"What is this?" I asked curiously, tapping a finger on the heavy cream envelope.

"This one is an appointment at a local boutique for dress shopping. My mother likes an extravagant theme, and I insist you have a showstopper of a dress for the ball."

I touched the card but stopped just short of picking it up. Thinking of the limited funds in my bank account, I pushed it back, saying "I really couldn't—"

"Of course you could," she interrupted, nudging the card forward with a fingertip. "In fact, I insist."

"But—"

"Look, if it bothers you that much, consider it a thank you not only for all you did for me personally at the Harvest Festival, but also as an official token of the Silverthorne family's gratitude for protecting our town's secret and keeping Havenwood a refuge for all paranormals. You would be attending the ball as my guest, all expenses paid. Please say yes," she said, leaning forward eagerly.

I opened my mouth to protest. I hadn't just been protecting the town. My reasons had been selfishly motivated as well. However, admitting that to Isadora would mean admitting to not only the imps' existence but also to my role in setting them loose. It was a story I'd rather not recount in a busy club with someone I just met. So, I shut my mouth, biting back the words.

Isadora nodded as if I'd just enthusiastically agreed to her proposal to take me dress shopping. "Good. My brother Gabriel has been pestering me about you. Apparently, you made a lasting impression on more than one Silverthorne," she said with a knowing wink.

My face heated slightly at her words, but before I could dwell on it any further, Isadora leaned across the table and grabbed my hand. "I'm excited to get to know the newest witch in town. Besides, the Christmas Eve Ball is a perfect way to wrap up the year and celebrate new friendships," Isadora said with a grin.

As I left the Vault much later that night, anticipation for the Silverthornes' ball bubbled inside me. With my first Harvest Festival in the books, a new friend in Isadora, and the promise of celebrations with good friends ahead—it seemed my magical journey in Havenwood was only just beginning.

Thank you!

Dear Wonderful Reader,

Thank you for making it this far. I hope you enjoyed the story. Now, I'd like to share another, albeit much shorter one with you, along with a piece of my heart.

Once upon a time, I was a kid with mountains of notebooks, each one bursting with stories and dreams. Writing was my sanctuary, my escape from the world. But as I grew older, reality knocked on my door and whispered, "Writing won't pay the bills." So, I did the "sensible" thing and focused on the real world. For a while, at least.

Then came 2020, a year that turned many of our lives upside down. As an athlete and musician, I suddenly found myself unable to do the things I loved most. In a desperate bid to fight against depression, I turned back to writing. It was like finding a long-lost friend. The stories poured out of me, and I started to feel alive again.

Not that it has been without struggle. Trying to fit writing in around work, kids, and life is like juggling flaming torches while riding a unicycle. But I've kept at it. Since then, I've written and published over 20 books, each one a labor of love and infused with a piece of my heart. I'm not an overnight sensation or a best-selling author, nor do I have a stack of rejection letters from traditional publishers. Instead, I've taken a different path, connecting with incredible readers like you who cherish a good story and a touch of magic. These small victories, and the connections I make with readers like you, are what keep me going.

This is where you come in. Your review is more than just words on a screen—it's a lifeline, a beacon that helps me reach new readers and continue this incredible journey. If you could take just a few minutes to share your thoughts, I would be deeply grateful. I read every single review, and they touch my heart in ways you can't imagine.

So, if my stories have made you smile, laugh, or brought a little magic into your life, please let me know. Your support and feedback mean everything to me, and they help keep this writing dream alive for me.

Thank you for being a part of my story, for believing in my characters, and for sharing this journey with me.

With all my gratitude and a heart full of hope,

Want more Havenwood?

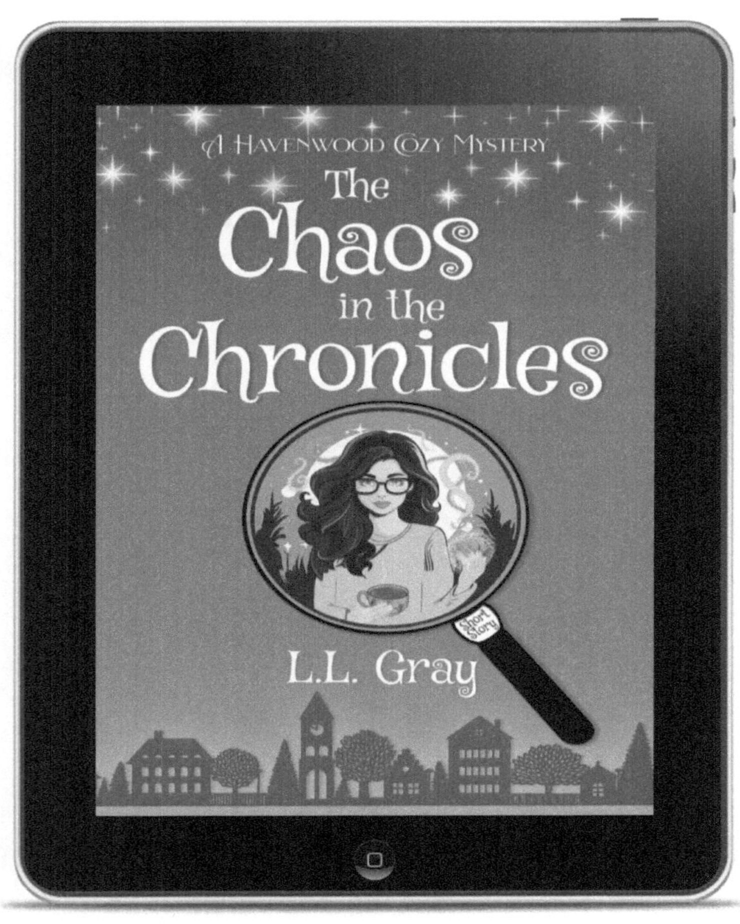

Stay up to date with all the latest Havenwood news!

There's no catch - you do sign-up for my mailing list but you can unsubscribe at any time. I send out 2 emails a month (plus a couple of extra if I'm releasing a new book, just in case you're busy and miss the first one!).
There's also no spam.
Ever.
Sign up here to join!
https://www.subscribepage.io/havenwood

About the Author

L.L. Gray writes fast-paced, captivating fantasy full of wit, warmth, and magic. Her books whisk readers into charming, cozy worlds filled with lovable characters and whimsical adventures. A lifelong enthusiast of fantasy and myths, she weaves humor and heart into her stories, inviting readers to escape into tales that feel like home—cozy, magical, and hard to put down. When she's not writing, you'll find her on magical adventures with her children, battling make-believe elves or outwitting those mischievous gnomes next door.

Psst, it's me—L.L. Gray!

I love connecting with fellow story lovers and adventure seekers. If that sounds like your cup of tea (or coffee, or whatever magical potion you prefer), come say hello! Visit my website www.llgray.com to join my newsletter, where you'll find exclusive goodies, or join us in my Facebook readers group. And if email is more your style, feel free to drop me a line anytime at info@llgray.com.

I hope you stay in touch!

Acknowledgments

To my fabulous ARC and Street teams: you've become like a second family to me, cheering me on through every twist, turn, and chapter. Your unwavering support, encouragement, and excitement fuel my creative fire—I truly couldn't do this without each of you. Thank you for believing in these stories as much as I do.

To you, the reader: thank you for stepping into this world with me. I hope you felt the magic, warmth, and wonder woven into these pages. If you'd like to stay up to date with new releases and special content, head over to my website. And if you're looking to connect with a welcoming, book-loving community, join us on Facebook—there's always room for another story lover.

Lastly, to my wonderful husband: your support is the foundation of every story I write. Thank you for believing in me, for being my rock, and for making all of this possible. I'm endlessly grateful to have you by my side.

Also By

Havenwood Paranormal Cozy Mysteries

The Mystery in the Margins
The Chaos in the Chronicles (exclusive novella)
The Puzzle in the Pumpkin Patch
The Secret of the Silver Serpent
The Riddle at the Revelry
The Heist of the Hidden Heart
The Mayhem in the Masquerade
The Legend of the Leaf

Smoke and Shadows Series

Shadows and Relics
Pixie Pranks (exclusive novella)
Felons and Fangs
Bones and Blades
Tempest and Treason
Daggers and Deception
Sleuths and Scoundrels
Legacy and Lies
Crossroads and Curses

Children's Books

The Secret About Mistakes
Corner of the Sky
To Mom. Love, Me
To Dad. Love, Me
To Grandma. Love, Me
To Grandpa. Love, Me